MAIL ORDER BRIDE SERIES

NO. 1
1871
USA

AL & JOANNA LACY

SECRETS OF THE HEART

Secrets of the Heart

MAIL ORDER 1

AL & JOANNA LACY

Multnomah® Publishers Sisters, Oregon

This is a work of fiction. The characters, incidents, and dialogues are products of the author's imagination and are not to be construed as real. Any resemblance to actual events or persons, living or dead, is entirely coincidental.

SECRETS OF THE HEART
Mail Order Bride Series #1
published by Multnomah Publishers, Inc.

© 1998 by ALJO PRODUCTIONS, INC.
International Standard Book Number: 1-59052-568-X
Previously 1-57673-278-9

Cover illustration by Vittorio Dangelico
Designed by Kirk DouPonce

Scripture quotations are from:
The Holy Bible, King James Version

Multnomah is a trademark of Multnomah Publishers, Inc.,
and is registered in the U.S. Patent and Trademark Office.
The colophon is a trademark of Multnomah Publishers, Inc.

Printed in the United States of America

For information:
MULTNOMAH PUBLISHERS, INC.
601 N. LARCH ST.
SISTERS, OREGON 97759

Library of Congress Cataloging-in-Publication Data:

Lacy, Al.
Secrets of the heart/by Al and JoAnna Lacy.
p. cm.
ISBN 1-59052-568-X
ISBN 1-57673-278-9 (alk. paper)
I. Lacy, JoAnna. II. Title.
PS3562.A256S46 1998
813'.54—dc21   98–19418
                                                  CIP

05 06 07 08 09 — 13 12 11 10 9

This book is dedicated with love to Brenda Jacobson
my friend
my sister in the LORD
and the quiet strength behind her husband's
dreams and accomplishments.
I love you, Bren.
Jo Anna
PROVERBS 17:17

"[God] knoweth the secrets of the heart."
PSALM 44:21

Prologue

THE *ENCYCLOPEDIA BRITANNICA* REPORTS that the mail order business, also called direct mail marketing, "is a method of merchandising in which the seller's offer is made through mass mailing of a circular or catalog, or advertisement placed in a newspaper or magazine, and in which the buyer places his order by mail."

Britannica goes on to say that "mail order operations have been known in the United States in one form or another since Colonial days, but not until the latter half of the nineteenth century did they assume a significant role in domestic trade."

Thus the "mail order" market was known when the big gold rush took place in this country in the 1840s and 1850s. At that time prospectors, merchants, and adventurers raced from the East to the newly discovered goldfields in the West. One of the most famous was the California Gold Rush in 1848–49, when discovery of gold at Sutter's Mill, near Sacramento, brought more than 40,000 men to California. Though few struck it rich, their presence stimulated economic growth, the lure of which brought even more men to the West.

The married men who had come West sent for their wives and children, desiring to stay and make their home in the West. Most of the gold rush men were single and also desired to stay in the West, but they found there were about two hundred men for every single woman. Being familiar with the mail order concept, they began advertising in eastern newspapers for women to come west and marry them. Thus was born the "mail order bride."

Women by the hundreds began answering the ads, wanting to be married and to make the move west. Often when men and their prospective brides corresponded, they agreed to send no photographs. They would accept each other by the spirit of the letters rather than on a physical basis. Others, of course, exchanged photographs.

The mail order bride movement accelerated after the Civil War ended in April 1865, when men went west by the thousands to make their fortune on the frontier. Many of the marriages turned out well, while others were disappointing and ended in desertion by one or the other of the mates, or in divorce.

As we embark on this fiction series, we'll tell stories that will grip the heart of the reader, bring some smiles, and maybe wring out some tears. As always, we will weave in the gospel of Jesus Christ and run threads of Bible truth that apply to our lives today.

1

IT WAS FALL IN ILLINOIS, and each day the winds off Lake Michigan loosened the dry russet leaves and sent them swirling through space until they fell in the yards and streets of Chicago, giving a touch of bright temporary color wherever they settled.

Chicago's 27th District was on the west side of the city, a predominantly Irish settlement. In the two-story house at 139 DeKoven Street, the sunny kitchen was redolent with the aroma of freshly brewed coffee as the Shaemus O'Malley family finished up a hearty breakfast.

Shaemus set his Irish eyes on his wife. "Well, Mama," he said, "we'd best be thinkin' about startin' to commence to begin makin' plans to head for the store."

Maureen O'Malley, who was short and a bit round like her husband, looked somewhat younger than her thirty-nine years. She smiled at Shaemus. "You're right, Papa. We'll have irate customers standin' at the front door of the store a-wantin' in if we don't shake a leg."

Fourteen-year-old Patricia, who was the spitting image of her mother, laughed. "Papa, why do you always say that?"

"Always say *what*, darlin'?"

"You know…'start to commence to begin…' Why do you always say that?"

"Because it always makes you laugh." Shaemus had the mischievous grin of a fabled leprechaun. "And if there's anythin' this ol' Irishman wants, it's to see his children happy and laughin'."

"Well, you've certainly made your son happy today, Papa," said the family's oldest child, Kathleen, who would soon turn eighteen.

"Made me happy?" gusted Donald, who was two years younger than Kathleen. There was a sly grin on his lips. "Why, Kathleen, how can you say that? You know I absolutely *hate* to miss school!"

"Mm-hmm. About the way you *hate* to eat chocolate cake."

"How come us girls can't go with you to get the potatoes, Papa?" Patricia asked.

"'Cause girls aren't strong enough to lift the sacks," Donald said before his father could answer.

"Kathleen and I could handle sacks together," Patricia said, giving Donald a look.

Shaemus chuckled. "Handlin' spuds is for the male species, Patty, and besides, the railroad yard is no place for females. I know you'd like to skip out on school, but life isn't always set up to be what we want it to be."

Patricia shrugged. "Oh, well. Someday I'll grow up and marry a real rich man. Then I can do anything I want, and I can *have* everything I want."

Kathleen shoved her chair back and stood up. "But until then, little sister, you and I still have to do the dishes and clean up the kitchen before school."

The rest of the family rose to their feet.

Donald was already almost a head taller than his father, and he liked to tease him about it. Laying a hand on his dad's shoulder, he said, "Well, Shorty, I guess we'd better get going."

Shaemus chuckled, looked up at Donald, and said, "Shorty, eh? Well, anytime the tall one, here, thinks he c'n handle Shorty, let 'im try it."

"Our son isn't about to do that, Papa," said Maureen, laughter showing in her eyes.

Donald grinned sheepishly. "You're...ah...right about that, Mama."

"Tall isn't everything, Donald," Patricia said.

"No, it isn't, half-pint. But being short isn't either. And you ought to know."

"I'll grow some more," Patricia said.

Donald took his cap off a peg. "You might, but lots of girls already have their height by the time they're fourteen."

"Kathleen didn't. She grew till last year."

"Yeah, but Kathleen was taller than you are when she was your age."

"Not by much. I'll be at least as tall as she is."

Donald looked down at Kathleen and grinned at her. "Which isn't saying much, is it?"

"My feet reach the floor, and that's all that matters," she retorted.

The older O'Malleys and Donald put on their coats before stepping out into the brisk fall air. Kathleen and Patricia hugged their parents good-bye, then turned to Donald, mischievous grins on their faces. It embarrassed Donald—now that he was all of sixteen years—to be hugged by his sisters. He began edging his way toward the kitchen door as Maureen O'Malley said, "You girls do good in school today."

"We will, Mama," Patricia assured her.

"I'll be at the store right after school lets out, Mama," said Kathleen.

"And I'll come home and do some housework," said Patricia.

Donald had his hand on the doorknob. Before he could step outside, Kathleen glided up, smiling from ear to ear, and threw her arms around him, saying, "You have a good time loading and unloading the potatoes, Donnie."

Donald's face turned beet red, and his arms hung at his sides.

As Kathleen stepped back, Patricia moved in to hug him. "Bye, Donnie," she said. "See you later."

He opened the door and allowed his parents to pass through ahead of him, then fell in behind them as they walked toward the barn where the horses were already hitched to the wagon.

Though the air was brisk, the girls stepped outside onto the porch.

"Donnie..." Kathleen called.

The boy paused. "Yes?"

"If you don't hug me back when I hug you, I'll fix you good."

"Oh? And just how will you do that, Miss Smarty?"

"I'll hug you at school in front of your friends."

Donald O'Malley's face paled. "You…you wouldn't do that."

"I'll do it too," Patricia said.

Kathleen laughed. "So if you don't want the supreme embarrassment of having your sisters hug you at school, you'd better hug us back when we're at home."

"All right, all right," he said, turning to catch up with his parents.

"Starting right now!" Kathleen's brilliant sky blue eyes danced with merriment, and a dimple flitted in and out of her right cheek as she set her mouth and fought to control the smile that threatened to break across her lips.

Donald shook his head, muttered something indistinguishable, and returned to the porch. He hugged both sisters then hurried away.

Moments later, the family wagon pulled out of the yard with Shaemus, Maureen, and Donald waving to the girls.

The girls rubbed their arms from the cold and returned to the warmth of the kitchen.

"Aren't brothers fun to pick on?" Patricia said with a giggle.

"If they're all like Donnie, they are."

Shaemus and Maureen O'Malley were hardworking immigrants who had left Ireland in October of 1851 for the shores of America. The Great Potato Famine had struck Ireland in 1845 and lasted until 1850. By 1851, some two million people had died, and the economy was devastated. Shaemus and Maureen, who got married the year after the end of the Famine, decided to emigrate to the United States. There they would build their lives together and start their family.

They dearly loved their new country. Eventually they had put together enough money to open a corner grocery store in Chicago's 27th District, and after three or four years the store was providing a nice living for them. Now it was 1871, and they had been living in Chicago for twenty years. They would not have been considered wealthy, but they were quite comfortable and felt exceptionally blessed.

Their home was a happy one, filled with love. And even though sisters and brother teased each other unmercifully, underneath it all were genuine affection and respect.

While Kathleen washed the dishes, Patricia cleaned the table and cupboards. The younger girl admired her sister very much and hoped that one day she would be as pretty and graceful.

All three of the O'Malley women had the same shade of dark auburn hair. To Patricia, however, Kathleen's hair seemed more beautiful with its shimmer of red-gold highlights.

On that Wednesday morning, October 4, Kathleen had the sides of her hair pulled up and fastened with a bow. The back hung down in rippling waves, almost to her slim waist. Patricia understood why many of the boys at school had eyes for her sister.

"Honey, will you open the door for me?" Kathleen said as she picked up the small tub they used to wash the dishes.

Patricia hurried to open the back door, and Kathleen carried the tub to the far end of the porch and poured the dirty water on the ground. Her peripheral vision caught movement in the yard next door. She turned to look and saw Katie O'Leary carrying a bucket of milk from the barn at the rear of her property.

"Good morning, Kathleen," Katie called.

"And a good morning to *you*, Katie," replied Kathleen, smiling warmly. "Milking the cows again?"

Katie, who was in her midtwenties, paused on her way to the back porch. "I don't mind. Besides, it's just every other day."

"Well, I admire you for doing the milking when Patrick is away."

"Thank you, but I really don't mind. A wife's supposed to help her husband in any way she can, and the milk sales from our cows to

13

your father's store really help with the bills."

Patricia drew up beside her sister. "Good morning, Mrs. O'Leary."

Katie nodded with a smile. "'Bout time for you girls to head for school, isn't it?"

"Sure is," said Patricia. "We best be off."

Katie climbed the steps of her back porch, holding the milk bucket carefully, then disappeared inside the house.

Kathleen glanced at her younger sister. "Patty, I hope I can be half the wife and mother Katie is when I get married and have children."

"When you get *married*? Hah! No man will ever want to marry you, Kathleen O'Malley. You're too ugly!"

Kathleen playfully whacked her sister's posterior and said, "The school bell's going to ring in less than fifteen minutes, Miss Smart Mouth! Let's get going!"

At 1:45 that afternoon, Company Six Fire Chief, Bill Murham, finished his inspection of the station, the fire wagons, the barn, and the horses, in that order. He felt a measure of pride as he returned to the station, where his firemen from both shifts were gathering. Chicago's Chief Fire Marshal, Robert Williams, who was inspecting every station in the city, would arrive at Company Six at approximately two o'clock to talk about the city's present fire hazard.

Company Six—affectionately called the "Little Giant" by the other companies throughout Chicago—was in the heart of the 27th District. Every man in Company Six was Irish and quite proud of it.

A low hum of conversation floated throughout the room as the firemen seated on wooden folding chairs waited for the meeting to begin. As soon as Chief Murham stepped before them, the room went quiet.

"Men, the Little Giant company has done an excellent job. You've cleaned and polished the station house, all three fire wagons, and groomed those six nags in the corral to perfection. I am sure Chief Williams will be pleased. I didn't like to have to ask you men who are off duty to come in, but Chief Williams said that what he had to talk about was of utmost importance, and he wanted all of you here."

"Glad to do it, Chief," said fireman Frank O'Brien. "For sure we need to know what's on Chief Williams's mind."

Murham pulled out his pocket watch. "Well, men, looks like the chief is going to be late. Go ahead and visit if you want. Hopefully he'll get here pretty soon."

Murham entered his office, and the men picked up conversations where they had left off.

Company Six's newest man, Mick Delaney, pricked up his ears when he heard one man say to Patrick O'Leary, "How's the milk business doing?"

"Really good, Murph," O'Leary replied. "It serves us well in providing extra income."

"How's this milk business work, Pat?" Delaney asked.

O'Leary looked at him with mock solemnity and said, "Well, first you have to have at least one cow."

Delaney laughed. "Okay. I think I understand that. So how many cows do you have?"

"Five."

"Jerseys? Guernseys?"

"Holsteins. Their milk isn't quite as rich as Jerseys' and Guernseys', but they give a lot more."

"And how do you market the milk?"

"Do you know where the O'Malley Grocery Store is?"

"Oh, yeah. Corner of Fifth and Bolton. That's where my wife does her grocery shopping. I've been in there a few times since we moved here."

"Then you must know Shaemus and Maureen O'Malley."

"Sure do."

"They're my next-door neighbors. We sell our milk to them."

"I see. So my wife and I have probably bought some of your milk."

"Probably have."

Delaney rubbed his chin. "How do you milk those five cows on the days you're here at the station?"

"I don't. My wife, Katie, milks them."

"Well, whattya know! She milks five cows twice a day?"

"That's right. And does she ever have a grip! If you ever shake hands with Katie O'Leary, brace yourself. She'll give your hand a good squeeze!"

The men sitting around Mick and Pat had a good laugh.

"I don't think my wife could milk cows, Pat, but I might be able to get one of my neighbors to do the milking for me on the days I work," said Delaney. "I'd really like to look into the milk business. Would you care if I come by your house sometime soon and take a look at your setup?"

"Be glad to have you," said O'Leary. "You know where DeKoven Street is?"

"I don't think I've seen it."

"Well, from O'Malley's Grocery, you go one block west on Bolton. That's DeKoven Street. Turn south on DeKoven and go to the second block. Almost in the middle of that second block you'll find 137. That's our house. Come by on any off day. Be glad to have you."

A carriage pulled up in front of the station house and got the attention of the firemen. While Chief Fire Marshal Robert Williams alighted from the carriage, Company Six's chief hurried from his office to meet him.

Chief Murham guided Williams in a tour of the station, starting with the barn, and ten minutes later brought Williams before the firemen and introduced him to those who had never met him. "All right, Chief Williams," he said, "the floor is yours."

Williams, a medium-sized man in his late fifties, looked sharp in his dark blue uniform with badge and small-billed cap. "You men are to be complimented," he said, smiling. "The place looks very good."

A serious look came over his features when he said, "Gentlemen, I am very much concerned about the dry spell we're in. Since the first of July we've barely had two inches of rain. Ordinarily in this same three-month period, we get somewhere between nine and twelve inches. Grass in the vacant lots is tall and dry, and with the leaves falling from the trees and lying in heaps all over the city, we're vulnerable to some real problems if a fire should get out of hand."

"Chief," said one man, lifting his hand.

"Yes, sir?"

"Couldn't something be done about all the leaves in the yards and streets? And couldn't whoever owns the vacant lots at least cut the grass?"

"I'm working on it," said Williams. "I've been trying to get the city fathers to put pressure on the people to clean up the leaves, and to do the same thing about the vacant lots. But even if the city fathers tell the people what to do, most of them pay no attention. The leaves will stay where they are, and the grass will remain tall. It's hard to get the populace to see the potential fire danger."

"He's right," spoke up Chief Murham. "I've worked with the public all my adult life, and it's hard to get them to listen when you warn of potential danger. Somehow they just don't think anything bad can happen to them."

Williams nodded. "Now, let me elaborate to you men some cold, hard facts. Chicago is in a period of rapid growth. Thirty years ago this was a town of some four thousand people. Today there are in excess of three hundred thousand. This growth has demanded the continual construction of homes and places of business, and both kinds of buildings have been put up quickly to accommodate the rising population. Only the very wealthy on the east side of the city are constructing their homes of stone or brick. All other residential buildings are wood, and about two-thirds of the commercial buildings downtown are wood.

"Of course this means that most homes are especially vulnerable to fire. Many of them have woodpiles for the coming winter stacked against their outer walls. If any one of those houses were to catch fire, there would be plenty of fuel to feed it.

"As you men know, all of the 27th District is of wood construction. Some of the homes are little more than shanties. It wouldn't take much to get a major fire going."

Every man was listening intently, and many were nodding their agreement with Williams's assessment of the fire danger.

"To make matters worse," said Williams, "all of the fire-prone structures are tied together by a network of wooden sidewalks and fences, making it easy for fire to spread from one home to another, especially with the kind of winds that whip through this city."

Fireman Mick Delaney raised his hand.

"Yes?" said Williams.

"Chief Williams, I've only lived in Chicago for about a month. I came here as a veteran firefighter from Milwaukee. It appears that these wooden sidewalks and fences have been here for some time. If they are such a hazard, why isn't something being done about getting rid of them?"

"Let me explain…what was your name?"

"Mick Delaney, sir."

"Let me explain, Mr. Delaney, that the wooden sidewalks are very necessary when we do have rain. Without them, the mud is horrendous and would make it impossible to walk in those areas. As for the fences, most people have animals of one kind or another. Fences are necessary. It would be too costly to have all of them replaced by fences of stone or brick."

Delaney nodded. "So the point you are making, sir, is that the fire danger is extreme right now. And this is rare for Chicago, so most everybody would not be interested in making preventive changes."

"That's it."

Another fireman raised his hand.

"Yes?"

"Sir, my name is Thomas MacMahon. I've been here just a little longer than Mick Delaney. Wouldn't it help—since the city has grown so rapidly—if we had a better fire alarm system? I mean, one paid fire watcher in the Courthouse Tower downtown can hardly be sufficient in a city this size. Maybe even as recent as ten years ago the one tower would have been enough. But today—"

"You are correct, Mr. MacMahon," said Williams, "but the city is in no financial position to erect more towers. We're going to have to make do with one tower for now. The main thing I'm trying to say is that when you have a fire, fight it with tenacity and put it out in a hurry. With this lengthy drought on us, the city is a virtual tinderbox. If we get a combination of a fire out of control and high winds, I don't even want to think about what could happen."

Another fireman raised his hand. "Chief Williams…"

"Yes?"

"Have the city fathers talked at all about building more fire stations? Seems to me with this rapid growth, the fire department has to keep up with it."

"It's been mentioned in the meetings, but they all agree there just isn't enough money to buy land and erect firehouses and barns, let alone pay the extra firemen they would have to hire. So it looks like we're going to have to carry the load until—"

William's words were cut off by the clicking of the telegraph key in Chief Murham's office.

Murham dashed to intercept the message from the Courthouse Tower downtown and shouted over his shoulder, "We've got a fire, men! Cal Perkins says it looks to be about five or six blocks east of us and a little south! Let's go!"

Nine of the dozen firemen on duty quickly boarded two fire wagons, set the bells clanging, and raced in the direction of the black smoke billowing toward the clear afternoon sky.

Chief Williams rode in the lead wagon with Chief Murham.

Three men and one wagon were left at the station in case of another emergency.

The fire was indeed some six blocks from the station. A vacant lot was ablaze in the middle of the 700 block on Sampson Street. Tall brown grass and powder-dry weeds and leaves were sending up flames four and five feet high, fed by a stiff breeze.

As the fire wagons drew up, Bill Murham peered through the swirling smoke and said, "Looks like you were a prophet, Chief. This is exactly what you were talking about. And with all the grass, weeds, and leaves in this lot, the fire has plenty of fuel!"

THE LARGE CROWD OF PEOPLE GATHERED near the vacant lot were keeping their distance from the searing heat. They applauded when the men of Company Six pulled up.

Men from the crowd offered to work the water pumps so all the firemen could fight the fire. Other neighborhood people were helping those who lived on both sides of the vacant lot to douse their houses, outbuildings, and yards with water.

The firefighters breathed dry, smoke-scented air as they sprayed the edges of the blazing lot. Sweat poured off their faces in spite of the stiff breeze. The horses that pulled the fire wagons were trained to stand still in the face of heat and smoke, but they fidgeted nervously.

Patrick O'Leary, who was at the front of the line of men holding the hose, sprayed a wide swath of water over the blaze. Periodically the wind blew puffs of hot air into his face, making his eyes smart. Though the grass was quickly blackened, O'Leary could still see a thousand flashing yellow tongues leaping out of the ground, licking at what grass still remained.

Fire Chiefs Bill Murham and Robert Williams moved about, shouting words of encouragement to the men.

Within an hour after their arrival, the "Little Giant" company had the fire under control; some thirty minutes later the blackened lot still smoldered, sending up tiny wisps of smoke, but the danger was over. There was nothing left to burn.

"Good job, men! You handled it well!" Chief Williams said, moving past the firemen as they wound the hoses. He commended each man individually.

The men whose houses and outbuildings had been saved, along with the neighbors who had helped them preserve their property, approached the two fire chiefs.

"Chief Williams…Chief Murham," said a husky Irishman, "you don't know me, but I know you. I'm John Mulligan. I own that house right over there. And this is Cavan Feeny. He lives in the house on the other side of the lot."

"Glad to make your acquaintance, gentlemen," Williams said.

"Likewise," put in Murham. "Did either of you suffer any damage to your property?"

Cavan Feeny shook his head. "No, thanks to our wonderful neighbors and the efficient Little Giant fire company. If not for all of you, we could have been wiped out."

"Well, I'm sure glad you weren't," Williams said.

Mulligan's and Feeny's wives joined them and expressed their appreciation to Chief Murham, and other people from the crowd gathered around to listen.

One man said, "Chief Williams, I'm Dermot Kildare. My family and I live across the street and down the block a ways. These people around us all live close by. We were just talking about the fire hazard Chicago has become because of the dry spell. What cautions are being taken to keep this city safe from such fires as we just had right here?"

"Well, Mr. Kildare, there really aren't any precautions we can take, other than the normal ones. We have the fire stations manned as well as we can, and we've got the man in Courthouse Tower to watch over the city and sound the alarm with his telegraph key anytime a fire breaks out."

"Shouldn't the citizens of Chicago be admonished to be especially careful with everything so dry?"

"They have been, Mr. Kildare," spoke up Chief Murham. "Both of Chicago's newspapers have run articles telling everybody to be extra cautious."

"Oh. Well, I seldom ever read a paper," said Kildare. "And apparently some of these people don't either. None of them mentioned such articles to me as we discussed what might be done to alert the people to the danger."

"How do you suppose this fire got started, Chief Williams?" a woman asked.

"I can only guess, ma'am, but some careless man probably threw a lighted cigar or cigarette butt into the weeds."

"All we can say, folks," said Murham, running his gaze over the crowd, "is that everyone in this city must be very, very careful and stay alert."

"There will be another cautionary article in both papers, I assure you," said Williams.

"Maybe the fire department ought to print up notices of some kind and spread them around," suggested Cavan Feeny. "You know…take them from house to house. Make folks aware of the danger."

"There's no way we can do that," said Williams. "We don't have the manpower."

"Chief Murham," said Patrick O'Leary, threading his way through the crowd, "we're ready to go."

Murham set his gaze on O'Leary's smoke-blackened face and nodded.

As the crowd began to break up, Chief Williams lifted his voice so that everyone could hear. "I suggest that all of you pass the word to everyone you see. Tell them to be careful with fire and to stay alert."

With that, the two fire chiefs followed the tall, slender O'Leary to the fire wagon.

The nine firemen washed up as soon as they returned to the station, while the chiefs told the men who had stayed behind about the successful firefight at the vacant lot.

Shift change came at 4:00 P.M.

"You going to walk with me today, Burgo?" Patrick O'Leary asked his friend, Burgo Murray.

"Planning on it."

"I'm ready if you are."

As the two men left the firehouse, O'Leary said, "I'll have to let you go on when I reach O'Malley's Grocery. Katie gave me a list of things she needs."

"Okay," said the short, stubby man. "Since Katie does the milkin' on your work days, I reckon it's only fair that you carry home the groceries for her."

They walked on for a while without talking, then Burgo said, "Chief Williams seems really scared, doesn't he?"

"Yes. Can't blame him. A good healthy rain would make us all feel better."

"One without lightning, preferably," Murray said with a chuckle.

Teenagers Ross Tralee and Eoin MacNeill were standing on the board sidewalk in front of O'Malley's Grocery on the corner of Fifth Street and Bolton Avenue. Carriages, surreys, and wagons, as well as riders on horseback, moved through the busy intersection while customers came and went from the store.

"What is it, Ross?" said Eoin. "You got the jitters?"

Ross ran the back of his hand across his mouth in a nervous gesture. "Well, I guess you might call it that."

"What are you afraid of?"

"That she'll turn me down."

"A fella can't live like that, my friend," said Eoin, brushing coal black hair off his forehead. "Remember when I first fell for Doreen, and I told you I was going to ask her for a date?"

"Yes."

"And you asked me what if she said no. Remember that?"

"Uh-huh."

"And what did I say?"

Ross looked toward the sky for a moment. "You said, 'Ross, as irresistible as I am, she'll jump at the chance to go out on a date with me.'"

"Right. And did she?"

"Well, I guess! You took her on a date, and now you're her steady beau."

"Yeah! Now listen, Ross, you've got to take a deep breath, walk through that door, get Kathleen into a conversation, then ask her to go to Marybeth Monaghan's party with you. Just tell her that almost everybody in the senior class is going to the party, and how honored you'd be if she would be your date."

Ross wiped sweaty palms on his pants. "But what if she's busy taking care of customers? How will I get up to the counter to talk to her?"

"Honestly, Ross," sighed Eoin, "can't you figure that out?"

"Huh?"

"Be a customer. Buy something."

"Oh. Yeah. Sure. Okay. I'll buy something. Sure. Ah…Eoin…"

"What?"

"What'll I buy?"

"Anything. Just buy…a pencil. That's it. Buy a pencil."

"Okay. I know where the school supplies are."

Eoin gave his friend a gentle shove. "Go on."

Ross took a deep breath and let it out slowly. "Yeah, let's go." He took two steps and stopped. "I can't. I just can't."

People passed by, glancing at the boys' curious behavior.

Exasperated, Eoin said, "Why not?"

"Because…well, Kathleen's so beautiful. I…I'm just plain ol' Ross Tralee."

"Well, I'm just plain ol' Eoin MacNeill, but I landed Doreen, didn't I?"

"Yeah. No offense, ol' pal, but Doreen's not the looker that Kathleen is."

"Hey, that was uncalled for. Now, come on. I'm right here with you…in spite of your insult toward my girl."

"I didn't mean it as an insult," Ross said. "Doreen's a pretty girl. She just doesn't have the looks Kathleen has."

"Well beauty is in the eye of the beholder. Now, let's move. You can't ask her for the date standing out here."

Ross Tralee's knees felt like boiled mush as he walked toward the door with his friend.

An elderly couple came out, and Eoin took hold of the door. He waited for the old folks to pass, then held the door open for Ross.

"Okay, Romeo, your Juliet is waiting."

Inside the store, Maureen and Kathleen O'Malley were behind the counter, checking groceries and adding up totals for customers. Kathleen happened to look up. She smiled when she saw the boys, then went back to her work.

"Did you see that?" Ross whispered. "She smiled at me!"

Ross went to the shelf that held the school supplies and picked up two pencils. Eoin followed him to the line in front of Kathleen's part of the counter. There were five people ahead of them.

Ross fidgeted, first standing on one foot, then the other.

"I think her mother's line is going down faster," Eoin whispered from the side of his mouth.

"If Mrs. O'Malley gets done ahead of Kathleen, I'll just tell her I need to talk to her daughter," Ross said.

"Good boy! Hang right in there, Romeo!"

Ross gave his friend a sick grin.

Soon, a woman with an armload of items drew up and smiled at the boys. "You can move over in front of Mrs. O'Malley," she said. "Her line is shorter, and you've been waiting longer than I have."

"Oh, it's all right, ma'am," Ross said. "You go ahead. We'll wait in this line."

"Such nice young men," said the woman, and moved ahead.

Five more minutes brought the two boys to the counter.

"Hello, Ross," Kathleen said with a smile.

The boy's heart was beating his rib cage unmercifully. "H-hello, Kathleen."

She then flashed a pearly smile at MacNeill. "Hello, Eoin. How's Doreen?"

"She's fine. Just fine."

Kathleen nodded, then looked down at the two pencils Ross laid on the counter. "That's all you need, Ross?" she asked.

"Uh…yes. Just these pencils…as far as what I need to buy. I, uh—"

"That will be five cents," she said, marking it down on her pad.

Ross placed a nickel on the counter. His lungs felt as if they were being crushed. Pulling hard for air, he said, "There's…ah…there's something else, Kathleen, I—"

"Something you couldn't find on the shelves?"

"Oh, ah…no. All I need to buy are the pencils. There's…there's something I would like to ask you."

Kathleen picked up the nickel and dropped it into the cash drawer. "All right."

While Ross labored to find courage, Kathleen put the pencils in a small paper bag and laid it before him. "Yes, Ross?"

"This has nothing to do with the store, here…I…ah—"

"Yes?"

"You know Marybeth Monaghan."

"Of course."

"Well, she's giving a party at her house for all the students in the senior class on Friday night of next week, and…and I'd like to know if you would go with me to the party."

Kathleen tilted her head and said, "Oh, I'm sorry, Ross. I'm dating someone rather steadily right now. I appreciate your offer, but…well, you know how it is."

Ross Tralee did his best to keep his countenance from falling as he said, "Oh, I…I wasn't aware you were dating someone. I haven't seen you with any of the fellas at school, so I naturally assumed—"

"He's not someone from school," she said in a soft tone.

"Oh. I see. Well, you can't blame a fella for trying."

"It was very nice of you, Ross," she said.

Ross nodded silently and headed for the door.

"Bye, Kathleen," Eoin said, lifting his hand in a little wave.

When they were outside the store, Ross wiped the sweat from his brow and said, "Well, this Romeo sure didn't land his Juliet."

"I'm sorry, pal," Eoin said, his eyes trailing down the street. "Hey, here comes Hennie Killanin. Maybe she'd go with you to the party!"

The girl was still out of earshot.

"Oh, sure," said Ross. "That's what I need. Take a religious fanatic to the party. Hennie's a nice girl and all that, but she'd be telling everybody at the party they need to be saved, and she'd be talking about Jesus and all that holy stuff."

Eoin chuckled. "Well, it was just a suggestion."

Ross drove an elbow into his friend's rib cage. "Yeah? Well, that's for making the suggestion."

Hennie Killanin was a pretty girl of seventeen. As she approached the boys, she greeted them with a smile.

"Hi," said Eoin.

"Hi," echoed Ross.

Hennie walked past them to enter the store, then hesitated as she put her hand on the doorknob. She looked back as if she wanted to ask them something, but all she said was, "See you at school tomorrow."

Ross and Eoin nodded.

Kathleen was smiling at her customer and listening to a comment about the woman's grandchildren when she saw Hennie enter the store. As soon as the customer picked up her package and moved away, Kathleen greeted her schoolmate.

"Hi, back," said Hennie, then made her way among the shelves.

For a brief moment, Kathleen watched Hennie's progress through the store. The girl had bright red hair worn in a long braid down her back. Today she had it tied with a large ribbon. Her pert nose and glowing rosy cheeks were covered with a dusting of tiny freckles, and she had a winning smile.

Though Kathleen was a bit on edge in Hennie's presence, she respected her sincere faith and counted her as a good friend. It was just that Kathleen had her own religion and was content with it and with her life.

Hennie often spoke to the young people at school of their need to know Jesus but was never overbearing or obnoxious about it. She had a sweet way about her, and it bothered Kathleen when students at school called Hennie a fanatic behind her back.

Moments later Hennie moved up to the counter, then glanced to her right and said, "Hello, Mrs. O'Malley."

Maureen, who was just thanking her last customer, turned toward the girl. "Hello, Hennie. Everything all right at your house?"

"Sure is, ma'am, thank you."

Kathleen totaled up Hennie's bill. "Comes to five dollars and thirty-six cents."

While Hennie was taking the money from her small purse, Kathleen placed the items into two paper bags, then pulled open the cash drawer and took out some coins. "There you are, Hennie. Your change is sixty-four cents."

Hennie dropped the money into her purse and said, "You're still planning on going to church with us Sunday, aren't you?"

"Yes, I am."

"Both morning and evening?"

"Yes. Mother and Dad said that even though we are of a different faith, it's all right with them if I go this Sunday with you and hear D. L. Moody."

Hennie looked at Kathleen's mother and said, "Thank you for giving Kathleen permission, Mrs. O'Malley."

Maureen smiled. "Kathleen thinks so much of you, dear. Shaemus and I don't mind her going with you for a Sunday. I was reading last Sunday's religious section in the *Chicago Tribune*. It told all about Mr. Moody's engagement at your church, and it mentioned he has a singer coming with him."

"Yes. Ira Sankey. He's a great gospel soloist, ma'am. They just

29

started working together. I'd love for the entire O'Malley family to come and hear both men. Mr. Moody is a wonderful preacher."

"Thank you," Maureen said, "but we won't be coming. However, I am glad Kathleen can spend the day with you and your family."

The door opened and the tiny bell above it jingled.

"Patrick O'Leary!" Maureen said as the tall, slender man entered the store. "What can we do for you?"

"Well, Maureen, I don't believe we'll be needing any milk!" He ran his gaze around the store. "Shaemus here?"

"No, he and Donald have been gone most of the day. They're at the railroad yards, picking up a load of potatoes from our supplier in Idaho Territory."

Patrick pulled the grocery list from his shirt pocket and chuckled. "Too bad you can't get your potatoes from Ireland."

"I'd love to, but I'm afraid the shipping cost across the Atlantic would be a mite prohibitive."

"Just a mite."

Kathleen spoke up. "You were on duty today, weren't you, Mr. O'Leary?"

"Yes."

"At school we heard about the fire over on Sampson Street. Was it bad?"

"Well, at least it was a vacant lot and not someone's home."

"Yes, but did it spread and burn any buildings?"

"No, for which everyone was thankful. We were able to bring it under control before it spread to the homes on either side of it. The neighbors helped soak yards, houses, and outbuildings while we worked at extinguishing the fire in the lot." He looked at the grocery list. "Well, guess I'd better pick up the things Katie wants and get on home."

"Let me see that list, Patrick; we'll help you," Maureen said.

Hennie picked up her groceries. "I'll be going now, Kathleen…Mrs. O'Malley. Nice to see you, Mr. O'Leary."

"You too, Hennie."

As mother and daughter and Patrick took items from the shelves, Patrick said, "You graduate next May, don't you, Kathleen?"

"Yes, sir."

"What are you planning to do after that?"

"Well, I'm really not sure at this point."

"So you haven't made up your mind whether to further your education and be a career girl, or get married and be a homemaker, eh?"

"Truth is, Patrick," spoke up Maureen, "I think Kathleen would like to be a wife and mother rather than take up a career."

"That's right, Mother," Kathleen said. "If I could choose, I would be a wife, mother, and homemaker just like Katie O'Leary. I admire her so much."

Patrick grinned. "Katie's the best, I'll tell you that. And I'm sure it would please her, Kathleen, if she knew how you felt about her."

"You can tell her what I said if you want."

"I'll just do that."

When they had all the grocery items piled on the counter, Maureen started tallying the bill.

Patrick turned to the pretty auburn-haired girl and said, "Is there a young man in your life, Kathleen? You know, some prospective husband?"

"No, sir."

"Well, then, all you have to do to fulfill your dream is meet the right young man. The two of you will fall in love, and before you know it, you'll be at the altar."

"Sounds good, but I might end up an old maid while waiting for the right man to walk into my life."

Patrick chuckled. "Not a chance. Not as pretty and sweet as you are. One of these days the prince of your dreams will show up and whisk you off to his castle of love."

"I sure hope so."

"Here you go, Patrick," said Maureen, who had the groceries all packed in a large box. "Total is ten dollars and forty-one cents."

When Patrick O'Leary was gone, Maureen locked the front door.

"Okay, honey," she said, "let's go home."

They left by the back door and moved down the alley, turned onto the street, and headed toward home.

As they walked, Maureen said, "I'm a little confused, Kathleen."

"About what, Mother?"

"When that Tralee boy asked you to go to Marybeth Monaghan's party, you told him you were dating someone steady right now. Is there some boy your father and I don't know about?"

Kathleen blushed. "No."

"Then why did you tell Ross there was? It isn't like you to lie."

"I had to, Mother."

"Why?"

"Because I don't want to go anywhere with Ross. He's too immature. All the boys I know are too immature. The prince that Mr. O'Leary talked about will be a mature young man, not a boy."

"I understand," said Maureen. "You'll just have to be patient, honey. And one of these days, you'll meet him." She paused, then laid a hand on her daughter's shoulder. "Kathleen…instead of lying, you should have told Ross the truth. I know it would've been harder, but it's always best to be truthful."

"I know, Mother, and I'm sorry."

3

MAIL ORDER BRIDE SERIES
NO. 1
1871
USA
AL & JOANNA LACY

As Patrick O'Leary turned the corner on DeKoven Street, neighbors called to him from their porches and yards, asking about the fire on Sampson Street. He made a quick explanation that there was no damage to personal property, and no one had been hurt.

When he was almost home, he glanced toward his next-door neighbor's house and saw Patricia O'Malley sweeping the front porch of 139.

"Hello, Mr. O'Leary," she said. "Looks like you gave our store some business."

"Sure did. Working hard?"

"Not really; just sweeping the porch. Was the fire on Sampson Street real bad? We heard about it at school."

"All that burned was grass, weeds, and leaves. No buildings. And nobody was hurt."

"Oh. I sure am glad to hear that."

As he stepped inside the front door of his house, he called out, "Daddy's home! Hello!"

There was no response.

"Hello-o-o-o!" He passed the staircase to the second floor and moved down the hall toward the kitchen. "I'm home! Where is everybody?"

He set the box of groceries on the cupboard, then went to the back door and opened it. There were four Holsteins in the corral, and his two horses were standing side by side in a corner, facing opposite directions.

The barn door stood open, swaying slightly in the breeze.

As he headed toward the corral, Patrick told himself Katie and the children had to be in the barn with the missing cow, Dinah.

Sure enough, Katie was on her knees beside the cow. Seven-year-old Ryan and five-year-old Amy stood close by. When Amy saw her father, she squealed "Daddy!" and ran to him, lifting her arms.

Ryan made a beeline for his dad, too, and a worried Katie looked over her shoulder as Patrick took Amy up in one arm and Ryan in the other.

"Dinah's sick, Daddy!" Ryan said.

The cow lay on her side, breathing fast and shallow, her tongue hanging from her mouth.

Patrick looked at Katie. "Honey, when did she get like this?" he said as he stood Amy and Ryan on their feet.

"I actually noticed that she didn't feel well when I milked her this morning, so I didn't use her milk."

Patrick leaned over Dinah and stroked her head. "Her eyes are dull, and I don't like the way she's breathing."

"She didn't start breathing like this till a few minutes ago," Katie said. "I noticed her moping around the corral all morning. I came out to check on her about noon, and she was holding her head low. I put her halter on and led her to the water tank, but I couldn't get her to drink."

Patrick rubbed his chin. "So she hasn't had water all day?"

"No."

He bent down and looked at the cow's tongue. "Dry."

"Yes," Katie said, concern etched on her face. "When I came out to check on her about forty-five minutes ago, she looked real bad, so I brought her into the barn. As soon as she was in here, she went down on her stomach, then laid over on her side. That's when she started breathing in these short little gasps."

Patrick patted the cow's neck. "Dinah, ol' girl, I wish you could talk so you could tell me if there's pain somewhere."

Katie bit her lips. "Oh, Pat, what if she dies? We can't afford to buy another cow."

Patrick put an arm around her shoulder. "Now, honey, she's not going to die."

"She will if we can't give her what she needs. There's no way—"

"I know what it is!" Patrick said.

"You do?"

"Yes. I remember now. When I was a boy in Ireland, one of our family's cows looked like this. Papa determined it was a lack of salt. He gave the cow salt chips and poured water down her throat. In a few days she was back on her feet and felt fine."

"Then we must do it," Katie said, her countenance brightening.

"I'll go to Fitzhugh's Feed and Supply right now."

"But they'll be closed."

"No matter. The Fitzhughs live upstairs above the store."

"May Amy and I go with you, Daddy?" Ryan asked.

Katie stood at the barn door and waved as Patrick and the children drove away in the twilight. She bent over the cow and patted her neck. "I'll be right back, Dinah."

She hurried to the house and crossed the porch. There was a small table just inside the kitchen door where empty milk buckets were stacked inside one another, and a couple of old kerosene lanterns stood beside them. She picked up one of the lanterns and carried it to the cupboard where a newer lantern stood. Striking a match, she lit both of them and went back to the barn with the older one.

Dinah switched her tail and made a grunting sound when Katie returned to the barn and set the lantern on the floor. She knelt beside the cow and petted her as she spoke to her in low tones.

Patrick and the children were back with the bag of salt chips within thirty minutes. Patrick knelt once again beside Katie.

"If I remember right, Papa poured water down the sick cow's throat to moisten it, then put a few salt chips in her mouth and massaged her throat to help her swallow them. He repeated that several times the first day, then did it again for the next couple of days. Pretty soon she was drinking water again, so all we had to do was feed her the salt chips for another two or three days. We'll just do it like Papa did."

When the process was done, Patrick unhitched the horses from the wagon and removed the harness.

"I'll go start supper, Pat, if you're ready to do the milking now," Katie said.

"Sure am. You and Amy go on inside. I imagine Ryan will want to stay here with me, right, Ryan?"

"Yes, Daddy."

After Patrick had milked the four cows, he took the buckets of milk to the house, then told Katie he would milk Dinah and be right in.

"How are you gonna milk her when she's laying down, Daddy?" Ryan asked.

"I'm not, son. I've got to get her on her feet."

"But she's so sick. Couldn't you just wait till she's better to milk her?"

"No. I have to do it now."

"But why?"

"If I don't milk Dinah, her bag will get so full that it'll burst. Then she would die for sure."

"Oh. I didn't know she'd still make more milk when her bag was full."

"Well, you learned something today, didn't you, son?"

"You're always teaching me something new."

"That's at least part of what dads are for, don't you think?"

"Yes, sir." A sudden smile lit Ryan's face, and he said, "They're also for taking us to Lake Michigan so we can play on the beach."

Patrick laughed. "Right. We're goin' to do that on Saturday."

"Yeah, and I'm really looking forward to it!"

On Friday afternoon, the men of Company Six returned to the fire-house after having fought their fourth fire of the day. Thankfully, none of the fires had gotten out of control.

With an hour left before shift change, the tired men poured cups of coffee and sat down. Chief Murham—who worked every day from seven till five—sat down with them.

"So," Murham said, "what're you fellas doing tomorrow?"

Mick Delaney chuckled. "My wife's got a work list for me a mile long. No play time for me."

Burgo Murray nodded. "Mine, too. Women can think up more work for a man than you can shake a stick at. I'd like some time to just lie around and relax."

Everybody laughed, nodding their agreement.

Thomas MacMahon said, "I'm going to start painting my house. It was too hot to do it this summer. Won't be so bad, now that fall's in the air."

"Yard work for me," said another. "Since the newspapers are warning of the fire danger, I'm gonna rake all the leaves out of the yard."

"That'll make you a good example to your neighbors," Murham said.

"Trouble is," put in another fireman, "we rake one day, the wind blows a little, then there's more to rake the next day."

"Well," said Murham, "one of these days the trees will be bare, and that'll take care of the leaf problems."

"For this year, at least."

"Let's hope we get back to normal with rainfall here pretty soon," said Patrick O'Leary. "Then the leaves won't be such a hazard."

"What are you doing tomorrow, Pat?" Chief Murham asked. "Raking leaves, too?"

"Nope. Yard's clean right now. I'm taking Katie and the kids for a wagon ride along the lakeshore. Ryan and Amy love to play at the water's edge. We'll make a picnic of it, too."

The O'Learys were up early the next day in anticipation of their outing to the shore of Lake Michigan. Though it was the first week of October, the temperature was still moderately warm during the daytime.

Patrick and Ryan saw to the cows, which included giving water and salt to Dinah, while Katie prepared breakfast with Amy's "help."

When father and son came in with the milk, Patrick said, "Good news, girls. Dinah was already standing up when we went into the barn."

"Oh, Patrick, that's good!" Katie said. "Looks like your papa's remedy is going to work."

"Sure does. Breakfast ready?"

After they had eaten, father and son went back outside to do some more chores and to hitch up the horses to the wagon.

Mother and daughter did the dishes, then Katie started packing the picnic basket full of goodies.

"Mommy, is someone else going on the picnic with us?" Amy asked as she watched her mother fill the basket.

"No, honey. Why?"

"'Cause you're putting in so much food."

Katie laughed. "I've learned there's something about being out there by the lake, breathing that fresh air, that increases everyone's appetite. I'm just making sure there's enough."

It was a golden day, and when the O'Learys found their favorite spot on the lakeshore, Patrick romped with the children along the water's edge while Katie sat on a patchwork quilt and happily observed the fun.

They ate lunch while squawking seagulls flew overhead and some landed nearby.

"We gonna feed them, Mommy?" Amy asked.

"Not while we're sitting here," said Katie. "If we start that, we'll be in trouble. Some of them will fly to their friends and announce that we've put out a feast. They'd drive us crazy. We'll leave some food on the sand when we go."

"Look, Daddy!" Ryan shouted, pointing due east. "There's a ship coming in!"

The O'Learys watched the graceful, billowing sails until the ship pulled into Chicago's harbor.

As the afternoon sun started to make its downward trek in the sky, they loaded up the wagon and headed westward through the city toward home, tired but happy.

During the drive through Chicago, they saw two different fires being fought. One was a boardinghouse aflame in Company Three's district. Company Five was dousing a burning barn.

They arrived in their neighborhood in time to stop at Fitzhugh's Feed and Supply to buy more salt chips for Dinah.

By now, Dinah was drinking normally again. Patrick hurriedly gave her a dose of salt chips, kissed Katie and Amy and Ryan, and rushed off to make it to the fire station by four o'clock.

Professional fire watcher Cal Perkins greeted his replacement, Nate Canton, at the Courthouse Tower downtown.

"Hello yourself," said Canton as he topped the spiral staircase to the tower. "Busy day, wasn't it? At least I heard a lot of fire wagon bells clanging."

"'Twas pretty busy," said Perkins, leaving the small table that held the telegraph key. "Total of six fires today. Far as I know, nothing that burned more than one building in a single place. It's all yours. Keep a sharp eye, and tell Charlie when he comes in at midnight to stay awake. No napping."

"As if I had to tell him that!" Canton said with a laugh.

"Go ahead, anyhow. I like to see Charlie steam up!"

Nate was still laughing as Cal descended the spiral stairs.

While work shifts were changing in station houses all over the city, and Nate Canton was sitting down at his telegraph table, Chief Fire Marshal Robert Williams was in a meeting with the Chicago Common Council. He stood at the end of a long table where the eighteen men sat, most of them frowning at him.

Williams had been reasoning with the council for over two hours, and now the councilmen were watching the clock, hardly listening, as he told them it was imperative they come up with money from somewhere. He needed more firemen and more equipment, especially in light of the city's present fire danger.

The Chicago Fire Department, Williams pointed out, numbered only 264 men equipped with thirty-three horse-drawn fire wagons. This meager force was supposed to protect the entire city of over three hundred thousand people. Williams had asked for more men and equipment many times in the past. But the council had always insisted that his department was adequately supplied. Today's meeting was no different.

Council chairman Edgar Phelps yawned and said, "Chief Williams, it's getting late. Do you have anything else to say before we close the meeting?"

"Yes, I do. We've had exactly thirty fires break out in this city in the past seven days. So far, we've been able to subdue them before vast damage was done. But gentlemen, if this drought goes on, it's only going to get worse. I asked you three months ago for a fireboat on the Chicago River because of all the warehouses down there. I pointed out that we have twenty-four wooden bridges. But still I can't get you to listen to me. I have no fireboat. If those warehouses ever catch fire, they'll go up in flames without us being able to put a drop of water on them."

"What are you talking about, Williams?" gusted a councilman named Myers. "You have fire wagons. If a warehouse catches fire, bring in your wagons."

Williams's features turned crimson. "Can't do it, Mr. Myers. This council made that impossible when you leased the river street frontage to businesses, making the river inaccessible to fire wagons. Two years ago I begged you not to do it. Now it's unalterable."

"Well, I guess we'll just have to hope no fires get started in the warehouses that line the river," Myers said. "There simply isn't enough money in the city's treasury to buy you a fireboat, Chief."

Chief Williams threw up his hands, turned to the chairman, and said, "I've wasted my time here today, Mr. Phelps." With that, he pivoted and left the room.

"He's an alarmist," Myers said, rising from his chair. "He's got the whole city scared to death. I think we need to look into getting us a new chief fire marshal."

It was almost ten o'clock that night when Nate Canton stood in the Courthouse Tower in downtown Chicago and looked eastward at the moonlight on the churning waters of Lake Michigan. A high wind had come up and was raising whitecaps on the lake's surface.

He turned slowly, letting his gaze roam over the city, and suddenly he saw yellow flames on the west side. He studied the city map by the light of the lantern hanging above his head and pinpointed the blaze in the 27th District.

Immediately he began clicking off a message to Company Six: "Fire just beyond you to the northwest. Looks to be in the vicinity of the Illinois Planing Mill."

At the Little Giant Company Six firehouse, the man assigned to sleep in Chief Bill Murham's office came awake immediately and listened to the clacking key for a moment, then dispatched two of the three fire wagons. Chief Murham lived only a short distance from the station and was alerted by one of the men who stayed behind.

By the time Company Six reached the planing mill, it was consumed in flames and was beyond saving. Not only was the mill burning, but the high wind had spread it to a nearby lumberyard, which was going up in flames. Chief Murham arrived shortly after the wagons and directed them to work at stopping the blaze from spreading further, considering the fierceness of the wind.

A messenger was sent to advise more companies to come help.

By the time a fatigued and discouraged Chief Williams arrived with three additional companies, the high wind was spreading the ravenous fire eastward over a four-block area.

Williams saw at once that his 185 firefighters on the scene could not contain the flames. He enlisted Chief Murham to help him press into service hundreds of men who had gathered to watch the blaze. They set up a bucket brigade from the banks of the Chicago River, but the wind-driven fire continued to gain ground.

The firefighters and citizens fought the stubborn blaze for seven hours before it was finally under control. Both the planing mill and the lumberyard were gone, along with many other businesses and homes in the four-block area. By 5:30 on Sunday morning, 61 firemen and 110 firefighting citizens had been taken to hospitals, suffering from burns or smoke inhalation. A few of the firemen hospitalized were from Company Six.

Chief Murham asked for volunteers to go home and get some rest and come back Sunday afternoon so the Company wouldn't be short of manpower in case of another fire.

Patrick O'Leary was one of the volunteers. He would be back at noon and would stay on duty until Monday afternoon at the regular four o'clock shift change.

In addition to the firemen who had been hospitalized, two horse-drawn fire wagons—one from Company Eight, and one from Company Eleven—were sent to a repair shop. From those same companies, three horses had to be removed from active service because of burns.

Chief Williams estimated fire damage to be in excess of $750,000. He sent a written copy of the estimate by special messenger to Chicago Common Council chairman Edgar Phelps, with a note attached that stated the fire could have been extinguished much sooner if Williams had had the men and equipment for which he had asked.

Sunday morning dawned bright and clear. The high winds had cleared away the smoke from the city and diminished to a mild breeze. It was the beginning of a perfect autumn day.

Kathleen O'Malley awakened as the sunlight peeked through her bedroom window. When she remembered she was going to church with the Killanins, she sat bolt upright in bed and then stretched and enjoyed a big yawn. Leaving the warmth of her feather bed, she headed for the dresser and poured water into a wash basin from a flowered pitcher. When she had washed her face and dried it, she picked up her hairbrush and sat down in front of the mirror, yawning again.

She could hear sounds from other parts of the house, signifying that her parents were up and about.

Kathleen had washed her hair the night before, and it fairly crackled with vibrance as she brushed it. It was a little wild, but she pinned it into place as best she could.

She went to her closet and chose a cobalt blue dress with a large white lace collar and a shiny black satin bow at the neckline. She slipped her feet into her best black lace-up boots and squirmed for a moment. She hadn't worn the boots except for special events and on the rare occasions when her family went to church. She was tempted to wear her everyday boots, since they were so comfortable. But they were a bit worn and scuffed and would not look good at church.

She took one last look in the mirror, decided she had done what she could to tame her wild hair, then patted down her skirt and went downstairs to help her mother prepare breakfast.

Turlough and Evelyn Killanin waited in the family buggy while Hennie dashed to the front door of the O'Malley house and knocked. Moments later, Kathleen and Hennie were sitting in the backseat as the buggy headed toward downtown Chicago.

Butterflies flitted in Kathleen's stomach when she entered the church and walked down the aisle. This was so different from her church. People were actually talking and smiling as they greeted each other. They seemed so happy…like Hennie.

Pastor J. C. Henson taught the auditorium class, and Kathleen enjoyed listening to him because he had a wonderful sense of humor and made her laugh, though most of the lesson on walking with Jesus in the Christian life went over her head.

In the morning preaching service, Ira Sankey led the congregational singing and sang three solos. Before the final solo, Pastor Henson introduced evangelist Dwight L. Moody, who would come to the pulpit and preach immediately after the solo.

Sankey was accompanied by piano and pump organ as he sang the great hymn "O Sacred Head, Now Wounded."

> O sacred Head, now wounded,
> With grief and shame weighed down,
> Now scornfully surrounded
> With thorns, Thine only crown,
> How art Thou pale with anguish,
> With sore abuse and scorn!
> How does that visage languish
> Which once was bright as morn!

Kathleen noted that people around her were wiping away tears. The last two verses gripped Kathleen as the words came from Sankey's deep baritone voice:

> What Thou, my Lord, hast suffered
> Was all for sinners' gain:
> Mine, mine was the transgression,
> But Thine the deadly pain.
> Lo, here I fall, my Saviour!
> 'Tis I deserve Thy place;
> Look on me with Thy favour,
> Vouchsafe to me Thy grace!

> What language shall I borrow
> To thank Thee, dearest Friend,
> For this, Thy dying sorrow,
> Thy pity without end?
> Oh, make me Thine forever!
> And should I fainting be,
> Lord, let me never, never
> Outlive my love for Thee!

Sankey, himself, was weeping as he finished the song and sat down on the platform beside the pastor.

When the stout-bodied D. L. Moody stepped to the pulpit, he opened his Bible and preached from Matthew 27:29–31:

"And when they had platted a crown of thorns, they put it upon his head, and a reed in his right hand: and they bowed the knee before him, and mocked him, saying, Hail, King of the Jews! And they spit upon him, and took the reed and smote him on the head. And after that they had mocked him, they took the robe off from him, and put his own raiment on him, and led him away to crucify him."

Moody's sermon took his hearers from the moment when the crown of thorns was put on the Lord's head until He was nailed to the cross and died for sinners. Moody spoke of the fire that had hit Chicago's west side the night before, using it as an illustration of the reality of a burning hell for those in the audience who were unsaved. But Jesus had come from heaven to earth for the express purpose of making the way for sinners to be saved and forgiven, and to miss hell. Moody wept as he elaborated on the Saviour's suffering to keep sinners from hell. He closed the sermon with an invitation for the lost to come for salvation.

A large number of people responded as the gathering rose to their feet, and Ira Sankey sang an invitation song.

Hennie watched Kathleen from the corner of her eye and noticed that her friend kept her eyes downcast. Hennie felt a constraint to say anything more to her right now. It was up to the Holy Spirit to do His work in Kathleen's heart.

KATHLEEN O'MALLEY WAS UNUSUALLY QUIET as she climbed into the Killanin buggy beside Hennie.

As Turlough Killanin guided the team out of the church parking lot, he said over his shoulder, "So what did you think of the services, Kathleen?"

Evelyn adjusted herself on the front seat so she could easily turn and look at the girl.

"Your services are quite different than those at our church, Mr. Killanin. I...I have never heard preaching like Mr. Moody's."

"How is it different from the preaching in your own church, dear?" Evelyn asked.

Kathleen blinked rapidly and smoothed the skirt of her dress. "We are never warned of ending up in a burning hell if we don't repent and receive Jesus Christ into our hearts. We are simply told that if we follow our religion and do the best we can, we will go to heaven when we die. But Mr. Moody's sermon was different. He seemed to have it in for religion."

"Well," Turlough said, "the devil has come up with religion as a substitute for salvation. With religion, the emphasis is on what people can do to get themselves into heaven with the help of religious leaders and by following certain ordinances and the like. The true salvation God has provided is in the Lord Jesus Christ, Himself, and His finished work at Calvary. You heard Mr. Moody point out from Scripture that we are all guilty sinners in need of forgiveness, and in need of salvation. We cannot do something to save ourselves, and there is nothing some religious leader can do to help save us. Jesus does all the saving when we're willing to repent of our sin and put our faith in Him and Him alone to save us."

Kathleen nodded, but a small frown wrinkled her brow.

"You see, dear," put in Evelyn, "if religious leaders had some power to remove our sins, and we could please God by our own so-called good deeds, Jesus would not have gone to the cross. He wouldn't have suffered as He did, nor shed His blood."

Kathleen nodded again, and the words from Ira Sankey's last solo and what Dwight Moody had preached repeated over and over in her mind.

"Do you understand, Kathleen?" Evelyn said.

Kathleen thought on her reply for a few seconds, then said, "I need to think about it, Mrs. Killanin. It's…it's just so different than what I'm used to."

Hennie took Kathleen's hand. "Will you still come home with us, spend the afternoon, and go to church with us tonight?"

Kathleen nodded in jerky little movements and said, "Yes, Hennie, I will."

As the buggy moved through Chicago's residential areas toward the west side, Kathleen O'Malley's insides churned. She struggled to suppress her fear of another hellfire and brimstone sermon that evening.

At the O'Leary home, Katie fed her family an early lunch so Patrick could make it to the firehouse by noon.

When the meal was over, Patrick hugged his children, then took Katie in his arms. "Sorry to leave the milking to you four times in a row, honey."

"That's all right," she said, rising up on tiptoe to kiss him. "You needed your sleep when you got home this morning. I'm glad to do my part."

Patrick hugged her tight, then said, "I appreciate your attitude, sweetheart. Dinah's looking better, and I hate to ask you to do it, but it's best that she be given salt for another three or four days for good measure. I'll be home to do some of the salt-giving, at least."

"Darling, it's not a problem. Now, you go on and do *your* duty for the Chicago Fire Department."

As Patrick O'Leary walked down the street, he looked toward the sky. *Not a cloud in sight.* He shook his head in despair, thinking of the worsening fire hazard in the city as each rainless day came and went. Last night was bad enough. He hated to think of a fire more widespread and destructive than that one.

When evening came, Katie O'Leary milked the cows and, as usual, threw Dinah's milk away, though she hated the loss of funds it represented.

After feeding Ryan and Amy a nourishing supper, Katie did the dishes with their help, then heated water for their baths. Amy bathed first, while Ryan straightened up his room. Little sister's hair was still damp, and her face glowing from a good scrub, when Katie put her in a fresh, clean flannel nightgown.

When Ryan's bath was over and he was in his nightshirt, Katie said, "Let's get out your paper and pencils, and you two can sit here at the table and draw pictures while I go give Dinah her last salt chips for the day."

She lit the old lantern by the back door and carried it to the barn.

The ailing cow was kept in a special stall. When Katie opened the gate and moved inside, she said, "Okay, sweet bovine, it's time for your medicine."

As she spoke, she reached for the cloth sack hanging on a nail and remembered that it was nearly empty. She had meant to fill it up earlier in the day.

"Sorry, honey," Katie said to Dinah, "I have to go back to the house and get some more salt."

She set the lantern in a corner on fresh straw she'd placed there that morning. "Be right back, Dinah."

The cow chewed her cud placidly as she gave Katie a slight glance and swished her tail.

Katie walked slowly through the darkness toward the glowing windows of the house. As she stepped up on the porch, she heard her children laughing and shouting at each other. What greeted her when she entered the kitchen immediately ignited her anger.

Ryan and Amy had the flour bin open and were throwing handfuls of it at each other.

"Ryan! Amy! Stop it!"

At the sound of their mother's voice, the children's laughter stopped abruptly, and they stared at her wide-eyed.

"Look at this!" Katie said, tossing the salt sack on the table and stomping to where the sobered children stood. "You've got flour all over yourselves and all over the floor!"

"Ryan started it," Amy said. "I was drawing a picture at the table, and he snuck up and dropped flour on my head."

"I was only playing a little trick on her, Mama. I didn't mean—"

"You both know better than to act like this," Katie said.

Both children were spanked, cleaned up, and sent to their room.

"I'll come up to check on you in a few minutes," Katie said, then began mopping the floor. Next she took the sack of salt from the pantry and poured about half of it into the smaller sack. She left the sack on the small table beside the back door and mounted the stairs. As she walked down the hall, she could hear the wind beating against the sides of the house. There had been only a breeze when she'd come to the house for salt.

The lantern in the children's room was turned down to a low flame, and both Ryan and Amy were in their beds, sniffling quietly.

"Well, how about it?" Katie said, standing between the two beds. "Did you two do wrong?"

"I'm sorry, Mama," Ryan said. "I shouldn't have put the flour on Amy's head. And I shouldn't have gotten it all over the kitchen. Please forgive me."

Katie nodded, then set her piercing gaze on the five-year-old.

Amy sniffled and said, "I'm sorry, too, Mama. I was bad. Please forgive me."

Katie immediately told them they were forgiven, and tucked them in with hugs and kisses. While the wind slapped at the bedroom window, she talked about avoiding spankings by thinking about the things they were tempted to do before they actually did them. When they knew that what they were tempted to do was wrong, they should make the proper decision and not do it.

Soon their bright eyes were drooping, heavy with sleep. Katie kissed them again and settled the colorful quilts up close under their chins.

Ryan and Amy were asleep almost instantly. Katie looked down at their sweet faces, so innocent in slumber. She blew out the lantern, then paused at the door to look back at them. She moved her lips silently, saying, *I love you,* then released a small satisfied sigh and headed down the hall.

As Katie descended the stairs, she noticed an orange glow through the windows on both sides of the house. When she reached the first floor, she pulled the curtains back and saw that the back side of the O'Malleys' house was aglow, as were both yards.

She dashed through the kitchen and out onto the back porch, sucking in a sharp breath as she saw that her barn was engulfed in a massive ball of wind-fanned flames.

A scream wrenched itself from her lips, and she turned toward the O'Malley house. There were no lights in the windows.

Katie screamed as she ran toward the neighbor's house on the other side. The back door opened, and Brian Joyce stepped out, his eyes fixed on the blazing barn.

"Help me, Brian!" Katie cried. "My house will catch fire if we don't soak it down!"

Brian Joyce turned to his teenage son, who was on the porch with Mrs. Joyce. "Jonathan! Run and get the other neighbors! Quick!"

The wind caught sparks from burning hay and timber, hurling them in three directions.

In no more than a minute, neighbors were swarming all over the yard, many with buckets. There were shouts and cries as they began dipping water from neighbors' stock tanks and throwing it on the back of the O'Leary house.

Some began dousing the Joyces' house and the O'Malleys'.

Ryan and Amy had been awakened by the commotion and stood at their upstairs window, trying to see what was on fire.

Amy began to cry.

In the Courthouse Tower downtown, Nate Canton had spotted the flames on the west side and was alerting Company Six with his telegraph key.

At the Little Giant firehouse, the horses were being hitched to the wagons when one of Patrick O'Leary's neighbors came running in, saying breathlessly, "Pat! The fire is at your place! It's your barn!"

O'Leary's face lost color. "My *barn!* How about the house?"

"Bunch of the neighbors are dousing it right now."

"How about Katie and the kids?"

"Katie's the one who spotted the fire. Just as I took off to run over here I saw her dash back into the house."

When Katie topped the stairs, her children were standing at the door of their room. Ryan had his arm around his little sister, trying to comfort her.

Brian Joyce was on Katie's heels. "Don't be afraid, Ryan…Amy," he said.

"What's on fire, Mama?"

"It's our barn, honey. Mr. Joyce has come to help me take you outside."

"Is our house going to burn down, Mama?" Amy asked, sniffling.

"The neighbors are soaking it with water," Katie said. "That should keep it from catching fire. But just in case, we need to go outside."

Joyce hefted Ryan into his arms, and Katie took Amy. They hurried down the stairs and out into the smoke-filled night. Joyce planted Ryan next to his mother and ran back to join in the bucket brigade. Katie pulled her children close and fervently thanked God for their safety.

Other women drew up to Katie, offering encouragement. The O'Learys' other four cows and their horses had been taken to a corral and barn down the block. Dinah, by now, had perished in the flames.

Seconds later, the Company Six wagons arrived and began pumping water on the barn. Patrick was overjoyed to see that his wife and children were all right. He spent a couple of minutes consoling his family, then dashed back to join in the firefight.

Soon the heat became so intense that those who stood in the backyards adjoining the O'Leary property had to move away.

Someone shouted that the Joyce barn was on fire. The wind had carried sparks to its roof, and the shingles were aflame. Wind-driven flames leaped and danced across it, and smoke rose toward the night sky.

At the Courthouse Tower, Nate Canton saw more firelight in the sky and decided Company Six needed help. Having received no confirmation on the exact spot of the fire, he misjudged it and sent two of Company Seven's fire wagons to the corner of Halsted and Canalport, nearly a mile from the actual blaze.

That left Company Six alone to fight the blaze, and soon the O'Leary house burst into flame while another nearby barn caught fire, and paint on the O'Malley house began to peel from the heat.

Katie O'Leary stood weeping as she held her children close. With a sickening sense of horror she remembered the lantern she'd set down in a corner of Dinah's stall. The ailing cow had no doubt knocked it over. This whole thing was her fault.

In spite of the water brigade, the O'Malley house began to burn.

As the fire leaped to new fuel, the gathering crowd moved farther down the block. Children began to wail, and frightened mothers tried to console them. If the fire was not contained soon, the entire block was going to go up in flames.

The Company Seven wagons finally arrived, having followed the glare in the sky.

Moments later, Shaemus and Maureen O'Malley, along with Donald and Patricia, were coming home from Chicago's south side. They had spent the afternoon and early evening with friends.

As the O'Malley buggy swung onto the main avenue leading to the west side, Maureen pointed to the sky. "Shaemus, there's a fire in our part of town."

A cold dread touched Shaemus's heart as he viewed the orange glow, and he put the horses to a gallop.

The wind became a deafening roar overhead as Shaemus drove the buggy toward their neighborhood, pressing the horses to go faster.

"Papa!" Patricia gasped. "It's our neighborhood!"

A tiny whimper escaped Maureen's lips. "Oh! I think it's our block!"

Shaemus snapped the reins and shouted at the horses, trying to get more speed out of them. Moments later they rounded the corner on DeKoven street, four blocks from their house, and it was quite evident the fire was in the center of the block.

"Shaemus!" cried Maureen as they drew near and saw all the people gathered. "Our house!"

Shaemus uttered a string of profane words and said, "It's burning on the back side! We'll go in through the front door and get everything out that we can!"

"But Papa!" Patricia wailed, "isn't it dangerous for us to go in there?"

"Not if we get in and out in a hurry. We've got to get our money!"

"Oh, Shaemus!" Maureen said, clutching at his arm. "How many times have I tried to get you to put our money in a bank?"

"And how many times have I told you I don't trust banks?" he countered. "We'll get the money and as many other valuables as possible. The four of us can carry a lot if we work together!"

People gawked as the four O'Malleys darted across the street, Maureen and Patricia holding their skirts ankle-high. One elderly man, who was not able to help fight the fire, called out from the crowd, "Don't go in there, Shaemus! It's too dangerous!"

"Have to!" Shaemus shouted back. "We've got valuables to save!"

The smoke was thick inside the house, and the fire had spread almost as far as the staircase to the second floor.

"Papa!" Donald said, coughing. "We need to get out!"

"It won't take long to save the most important things if we work together!" Shaemus coughed as he spoke, but doggedly led his family to the stairs. "I'll get the money. The three of you get what clothing you can carry."

"We should grab some of Kathleen's clothes, too!" Maureen said as they reached the top of the stairs.

One of the upstairs bedrooms had been used as an office. Shaemus dashed inside and opened the safe, which stood in the closet. He grabbed a shirt from a hanger and swiftly wrapped the family's entire fortune in it, then rolled it into a ball and tied it with the sleeves.

When he reached the master bedroom, Maureen was coughing nonstop as she pulled clothes out of her closet.

"Don't take too much, Maureen!" Shaemus said as he reached for his own clothing. "I've got our money here. We can buy new clothes. If you can stuff some of the family pictures amongst the clothes, go ahead."

A few minutes later, the family met in the smoke-filled hall.

Maureen, who had her arms filled with dresses, looked back up the stairs. "Did anybody get any of Kathleen's clothes?"

"It'll only take a minute to grab some, Mama," Donald said. "I'll get them."

"We'll all help you," said Shaemus. "Come on!"

Arms already loaded, the four of them crowded into Kathleen's room and divided eight dresses among them.

"Oh-h-h!" Maureen wailed. "My house! My house! My house is going to be destroyed!"

"We'll build a new one!" Shaemus shouted, leading them back to the hall.

As they hurried toward the staircase, they could hardly see for the smoke. They heard glass shatter somewhere, and there was a sudden gust of wind inside the house. The intense heat had broken a window, and the hot wind, like a blast from a furnace, blew stinging glass particles into their faces.

When they reached the stair landing, the entire staircase was on fire, and flames were being driven upward by the howling wind.

"Papa-a-a-a!" Patricia cried. "We can't get out! We're trapped!"

Katie O'Leary let out a wild scream and the crowd gasped as the O'Leary house collapsed in on itself, sending up a huge ball of flame with a deafening roar.

Chiefs Williams and Murham led their firefighters toward the street. The fire was spreading through two square blocks, and the fire wagons needed to be repositioned.

In the midst of the chaos, a woman ran up to Chief Murham and cried, "The O'Malleys are inside their house!"

The chief stopped in his tracks. "They're *what?* My men said the house wasn't occupied!"

"It wasn't, but the O'Malleys came home a while ago and went in there! We warned them not to, but they did it anyhow!"

Murham and Williams turned to look at the O'Malley house, which was covered with flames on both sides and the front.

"Look up there!" shouted a man in the crowd.

There was movement at a window in a front bedroom. Someone was trying to pull up the sash.

"No way we can get a ladder up there," Williams said. "The wall's on fire."

Bill Murham moved as close to the O'Malley house as he could and lifted an arm to ward off some of the heat. "Break the window!" he shouted at the top of his lungs. "Can you hear me? Break the window and jump!"

The figure in the bedroom moved away, and a few seconds later the glass shattered, sending a shower of splintered glass into the yard. Wooden chair legs stuck out through the broken window for an instant, then were gone. The figure appeared briefly at the window with smoke billowing around him. Then a thunderous roar was heard as the floor of the second story collapsed. A few seconds later the roof caved in, and like the O'Leary house, it went down in a heap. Flames leaped forty feet in the air, and the wind carried away the spark-filled billowing smoke.

Cries and moans raced through the crowd as they realized the O'Malleys had perished in the flames.

More fire companies began to arrive, bells clanging, horses snorting.

Katie O'Leary stood in shock, still clutching her children close. The O'Malleys were dead because she had left the lantern in the stall with Dinah.

By the time the chiefs got together to assess the situation, the fire had spread to four other places, including houses and barns. The occupants had loaded their wagons and buggies as best they could and were moving to the far edge of the crowd.

While the firemen and many of the citizens were fighting the spreading blaze, a man dashed up to Patrick O'Leary and said, "Let me take the hose, Pat! Katie has fainted, and your children are terrified. They need you!"

O'Leary ran to the spot where he knew his wife and children had been standing. Two women were kneeling beside an unconscious

Katie. Patrick quickly scooped up Ryan and Amy and stood over the neighbor women who were ministering to his wife. One woman rubbed Katie's hands briskly, trying to revive her, while the other used her apron to fan Katie's face.

Amy's and Ryan's tears began to subside as they clung to their dad.

Patrick turned his attention to one of the women. "What happened, Martha?"

"Don't know," said Martha Mulligan. "She was standing here with Ryan and Amy and just started crying. Pretty soon she collapsed."

Still keeping a grip on his children, Patrick knelt down and looked into Katie's pale face. "I think that seeing our house go up in flames was too much for her."

Even as he spoke, Katie moaned, and her eyelids fluttered. She looked up at Patrick, trying to focus on his face.

"Honey, are you all right?" Patrick said.

Katie's mind cleared, and she began to weep anew. "Oh, Pat, this is all my fault! It's all my fault!"

5

DWIGHT L. MOODY HAD PREACHED HARD to sinners in the Sunday evening service, but Kathleen O'Malley had endured the invitation without making a move. She felt relieved to walk up the aisle toward the vestibule when the service was over.

Suddenly a man who had exited the front doors a moment before came dashing back in, shouting, "There's a big fire on the west side!"

People poured outside—Kathleen and the Killanins included—to see a saffron glow in the sky to the west. The stiff wind blew the pungent scent of smoke all the way across the city.

Soon the Killanin buggy was racing along with others toward the west side. As they drew near their own neighborhood, which was on the southeast side of the 27th District, Turlough let out a pent-up breath. "Looks like our house is safe for the time being. Let's get to Kathleen's neighborhood."

Soon it was apparent that Kathleen's neighborhood was close to the heart of the fire. People were bunched up on street corners and in yards, watching the flames that were shooting thirty and forty feet into the air.

As they turned onto DeKoven Street, Turlough slowed the buggy because of the crowd, and Kathleen jumped out while it was still in motion, crying, "My house! My house is gone!" She lifted her skirts and ran toward the spot where her family's house had been.

Turlough pulled the reins, and Hennie slipped groundward, running after Kathleen. Her mother shouted something, but it was lost in the hubbub.

As Kathleen pushed and elbowed her way through the crowd,

59

trying to get close to the flaming ruins of her house, a neighbor lady grabbed her arm and said, "Kathleen! Kathleen! Oh, thank God, you're alive!"

Kathleen ran her gaze over the woman's face and then looked at others in the crowd. "Mrs. Carbery! Where's my family? Have you seen my family? Our house is gone!"

Hennie Killanin drew up behind Kathleen as Della Carbery gripped Kathleen's hands as if to keep her there. "Honey, I thought you were in the house when it went down! Oh, I'm so glad you weren't!"

"She was with me, ma'am," Hennie said. "We were in church."

Kathleen seemed to be unaware of Hennie's presence. "Mrs. Carbery," she said, looking a bit dazed, "haven't you seen my family?"

"Kathleen, honey, you...you have to understand that your parents, and Donald, a-and Patricia...well, they were in the house when it was burning. They got trapped in there, and it...it collapsed with them inside."

Kathleen shook her head. "No, no! They're here somewhere, Mrs. Carbery. I've got to find them!" Her voice trailed off as she pulled her hands from the woman's grasp and shoved her way through the crowd.

Hennie hurried to catch up to her. "Kathleen!" she called. "Wait!"

Others who knew Kathleen tried to stop her as she threaded her way through the crowd, calling to her parents and siblings. They repeated what Mrs. Carbery had said, but their words went unheeded.

Hennie squeezed her way ahead of Kathleen through the crowd and turned to stand in her path. "Kathleen, listen to me!" she said, taking her friend by the shoulders. "Your family is not here. I want you to come home with my parents and me."

The dazed girl looked at Hennie as if she were seeing her for the first time. Blinking, she said, "I have to find them. They're here somewhere."

Hennie gripped her even tighter. "Kathleen! Your parents, and

Donald and Patricia, are not here. Please. Come with me."

Patrick O'Leary, who was passing close by, heard Kathleen scream at Hennie, "Let go of me! I have to find my family! Our house burned down! Don't you understand? I have to find them!"

Someone hollered that two more houses were on fire as O'Leary stopped beside the two girls and said to Hennie, "Has no one told her about her family?"

"Yes, but she's not comprehending. I'm trying to get her to come with my parents and me."

"I can't do that, Hennie!" cried Kathleen. "Mama, Papa, Donnie, and Patricia are here somewhere! I can't leave them! We don't have a house anymore!"

The frantic girl freed herself from Hennie's grasp and attempted to continue her search, but the crowd was pressed too tightly around her. She waved her arms and attempted to push past them, screaming, "Get out of my way! Out of my way!"

Hennie's parents squeezed their way through the press and reached Kathleen just as Patrick grabbed her around the waist and stopped her frenzied movements.

"Listen to me, Kathleen!" he said. "I wish it wasn't so, but your family went into the house after it had caught fire. They were trying to save some valuables, I'm sure. But they didn't make it out. They died in the fire. Do you understand what I'm telling you?"

Kathleen clenched her teeth, shaking her head. "Patrick, don't hold on to me! I have to find my parents! I have to find Donnie and Patricia!"

"Listen to me!" he said, gripping her upper arms. "Do what Hennie is asking. Go home with her. Your family is dead!"

Suddenly her head bobbed in utter defeat. Then an expression of horror etched itself on her face, and she began to stammer with an incredulous stare, "P-Papa and Mama...are dead? And Donnie and Patricia? In—in the fire?"

"Yes."

Kathleen's knees gave way, and Patrick kept her from falling. As he held her up, her tear-filled eyes found Hennie, and she said with quavering voice, "Hennie, my family is dead. They burned to death in this awful fire. Why, Hennie? If God is so loving as you say, why did He let it happen?"

Hennie touched her friend's shoulder and said, "Kathleen, we need to take you home with us."

"Now?"

"Yes, now."

Patrick loosened his grip on Kathleen as her gaze went to the spot where the O'Malley house had stood. She stared at the ruins for a long time, then said, "All right, Hennie. I'll go with you."

Hennie's parents closed in around the girls.

"Follow me," Turlough said gently. "I'll get us through the crowd."

Hennie and Evelyn walked arm in arm with Kathleen. They had taken only a few steps when Kathleen stopped and looked back at the blackened spot where the house had been, as if she expected to see her family somehow rise from the ashes.

As the Killanins drove home, Kathleen sobbed and wailed, calling out the names of her family, begging them to come back. Hennie and Evelyn tried to comfort her, but she was inconsolable.

When they arrived home, Turlough stood on the front porch and looked back at the spreading fire while Hennie and Evelyn took a sobbing Kathleen to the spare bedroom and helped her to lie down on the bed.

While Hennie stayed with her, Evelyn went to the kitchen and returned with a glass of warm milk. When Kathleen had stopped crying long enough to drain the glass, Evelyn said, "Honey, I'm heating some water so you can take a bath. There's soot on your face and clothing, and in your hair. Hennie and I will wash your clothing. It'll be dry by morning."

"You can wear one of my nightgowns," Hennie said.

Turlough appeared at the bedroom door. "How's she doing?"

"Not too good, yet," said Evelyn. "She's going to take a bath.

She'll feel a little better then, I think. What about the fire?"

"The wind keeps changing directions. Right now, from what I can tell, it's going north, and of all things, southeast of us."

The fire raged on as Hennie stayed with Kathleen and helped her into the tub. The grieving girl continued to weep, sometimes mumbling things Hennie couldn't understand.

When the bath was over and Kathleen was clad in a borrowed nightgown, she curled up in an overstuffed chair in a corner of the bedroom and wept anew. Evelyn and Hennie stood over her, looking at each other helplessly, wishing there was something they could do to ease the girl's anguish.

Throughout the long night of October 8, 1871, the sky over Chicago was alight with an orange glow. By the time the fire was brought under control the next day, a total of 2,124 acres in the city were charred and still smoking. Eighteen thousand houses had burned to the ground, leaving ninety thousand people homeless. Many commercial buildings were also in smoldering ruins. Approximately one-third of the city had been destroyed.

The *Chicago Tribune*'s evening edition estimated that some three hundred people had lost their lives in the fire. Some of the deaths were from drowning. With the fire raging on both sides of the Chicago River, many people found themselves trapped on the wooden bridges. Caught in a pushing, frightened mob, some fell into the river and drowned.

On Monday night, a merciful rain fell for three hours, helping to quench the small fires that were still burning.

On Tuesday morning, October 10, trainloads of food, medical supplies, clothing, tools, and building materials began to arrive from other cities.

Chicagoans doggedly went to work, clearing debris in preparation to rebuild.

During the next few days, stories of Katie O'Leary's cow kicking

the lantern over spread far and wide, but the O'Learys were not casti-
gated by the people of Chicago, helped in part by an article on the
front page of the *Chicago Tribune* that quoted Chief Fire Marshal
Robert Williams. He boldly laid the blame on the Chicago
Common Council, who had shown no desire to provide more firemen and firefighting equipment, though he had pleaded with them
for many months. Williams stated that had there been more men
and wagons in the 27th District, the fire in the O'Leary barn could
have been extinguished. He closed the article by saying that had Mrs.
O'Leary's cow not kicked over the lantern, a similar destructive fire
would probably have taken place because of the city's dry condition.

Even though Chief Williams's article helped Katie O'Leary's emotional and mental state, she would be a long time getting over her
part in the fire.

On Thursday, October 12, a gaunt and pale Kathleen O'Malley
attended the memorial service held for all who had died in the fire.
Because the fire had destroyed so many of the church buildings, the
service was held in the city's largest church, which was in the heart of
downtown Chicago.

The coffins were already at the cemetery and would be waiting
for separate burial services to be conducted by the individual pastors
when the memorial service was concluded. For some of the dead
there were no coffins, for their bodies had been annihilated in the
fire. Kathleen had been notified by her minister that the bodies of
her family were identifiable and would be in separate coffins at the
cemetery. The coffins had been paid for by people who had done
business with the O'Malleys and knew Kathleen's situation.

As she sat in the funeral service the girl's usually sparkling eyes
were dull and red-rimmed from her unceasing tears.

While Scripture was read and ministers of different denomina-
tions made their comments about the fire and its wake of destruc-
tion, Hennie and her mother sat on each side of Kathleen, offering

their strength and comfort, but Kathleen was barely responsive to their efforts. Though she was there physically, her heart and mind seemed closed to what was going on around her. Hennie's tight squeeze on her hand finally caused her mind to clear, just as the service was coming to a close.

"Kathleen, are you all right?" Hennie asked.

"Yes. I'm all right."

"Do you want to go to the cemetery, honey?" Evelyn asked. "We'll be glad to take you if you want to go, but if you're not up to it, we'll take you home to our house right now."

Kathleen was still shivering as she said softly, "I…I want to go to the cemetery. I must tell my loved ones good-bye."

A cold wind whipped across the cemetery as Kathleen's minister spoke a few solemn words over the coffins of her family. When the minister was finished, he stepped toward Kathleen and told her she would be all right because she was in God's hands; then he left.

A small group of people had come along to pay their last respects to the O'Malleys, who had sold them groceries for many years.

The Killanins, who remained standing close beside Kathleen every step of the way, left her side to allow the others to speak with her. While words of comfort were being offered to the grieving girl, the Killanins spoke in quiet tones among themselves, agreeing that they would offer to let Kathleen live with them permanently. The poor girl had nothing. The grocery store had burned to the ground, and Kathleen had mentioned that the family savings had gone up in smoke because her father did not trust banks.

When the last person had left the gravesite, the Killanins returned to Kathleen's side.

"We'll stay here just as long as you want," Turlough said. "You tell us when you're ready to go."

Kathleen nodded and walked to the four coffins, which stood side by side on carts next to the first of four graves dug in a row. As she tenderly touched the first coffin, tears spattered its wooden surface. "Good-bye, Papa. I love you. I will miss you terribly. I…I hope someday we will meet again."

The Killanins looked on with heavy hearts as Kathleen moved to each coffin, speaking her final words to her mother, brother, and sister. When she had said good-bye to Patricia, she turned and took hold of Hennie's hand and said, "I'm ready to go now."

During the ride to the Killanin home, Evelyn turned on the front seat and looked back at the weary girl for a moment, then said, "Kathleen, we want you to live with us. The room is yours, and we'll just sort of adopt you."

Kathleen's heart fluttered, and her mouth went dry. She did not want to live in the Killanin house. She was uncomfortable with the Bible being read every morning at the breakfast table and the Killanins talking so much about Jesus and so many things related to their Christian life.

She cleared her throat nervously and said, "That is awfully nice of you, Mrs. Killanin, but…but I will have a place to go to within a few days."

"Oh, really?" said Evelyn, surprised.

"Where will you go?" Hennie asked.

"With some friends of my parents. You remember when those people gathered around me there at the cemetery?"

"Mm-hmm."

"Well, one of those families offered me a place in their home, and I told them I would come. I…I didn't know you were going to make this offer, but I can hardly back out on them now. You understand."

"Of course we understand," Evelyn said. "But we'll leave the door open just in case the other place might not work out."

"Thank you," Kathleen said. "I'll need to stay with you just a few more days until they can fix up my room. Will that be all right?"

"Of course," Evelyn said.

The next day, Kathleen walked downtown alone. She needed some money to rent a room somewhere. And she would have to drop out of school and get a job. She also needed to buy some shoes. The dress lace-up boots were hurting her feet. That is, the right one was. On the night of the fire, when she was frantically trying to find her family, she'd caught her right foot in the wooden sidewalk and torn the sole loose. It wasn't flapping yet but it soon would be, and the way she had to turn her foot when she walked made it hurt.

At the Chicago Land Office, Kathleen was met at the front desk by a man named Ralph Martin. She introduced herself and explained about the death of her family and that she was the rightful heir to the lot where the house had stood at 139 DeKoven Street. What would she have to do to sell it?

"I might be interested in the lot, myself, Miss O'Malley, but first you would need to bring some witnesses to this office who will swear that you are who you say you are."

"That would be no problem, Mr. Martin. Would tomorrow be all right?"

"Yes…fine."

"How much do you think the property will bring, sir?"

"If you're the rightful heir, I'll give you $250."

Kathleen figured the lot was probably worth twice that amount, but with a buyer standing right in front of her, she told him she would take it.

Martin instructed her to bring in three people who would swear before a justice of the peace that she was indeed Kathleen O'Malley. Then he gave her twenty dollars earnest money until the transaction could be completed and had her sign a receipt.

The next day, Kathleen and three women who had been faithful customers at the store went with Ralph Martin to a justice of the peace.

Afterwards, Martin explained to Kathleen that it would take a week or so to get the paperwork done, but when it was all set up legally, he would pay her the rest of the money. She should come back to the Land Office the next Saturday.

Kathleen decided to rent a room near Chicago's east side, where the rich people lived. That side of the city was untouched by the fire. Her plan was to approach the wealthy people along the lakeshore and seek employment doing cleaning jobs and housework.

After renting a room in a boardinghouse for six dollars a month, which included meals, she walked downtown to a secondhand clothing store and bought two dresses to work in, a shabby black overcoat, and a pair of used shoes. She discarded the lace-up boots in a trash receptacle on the way home.

By the time she reached the boardinghouse, the shoes she had bought were hurting her feet. They were apparently too small, though they had felt all right when she tried them on at the second-hand store.

In spite of the uncomfortable shoes, Kathleen walked to the Killanin home and told Evelyn her room was ready at the house where she would be living, so she would be moving in today. When Evelyn asked where that would be, Kathleen was evasive and managed to get away without giving an address.

On her way back to her new neighborhood, Kathleen stopped at a grocery store and bought a few food items, though her main meals would be eaten in the dining room at the boardinghouse.

The next day, Sunday, Kathleen rested her tired feet. Monday morning would come soon enough when she would have to do a lot of walking and a lot of knocking on doors.

On Monday morning, Kathleen winced as she slipped into her secondhand shoes, but she had no choice but to lace them up and wear them. She was down to only a few dollars. New shoes would have to wait until Ralph Martin paid her for the lot.

She ate a hearty breakfast and left the boardinghouse to see what the day's search might bring in the way of a job.

The sky was cloud covered, and as she made her way down the street, a wind as raw and cold as her heart assaulted her. Life was a vacuum of emptiness for her now, but she also felt a strong sense of self-preservation as she mentally prepared to do whatever it took to survive. This was what her parents would have expected of her.

Soon Kathleen was walking down a street in the wealthy section of Chicago. The huge houses on either side stood boldly in massive, tree-filled yards with wrought-iron fences and fancy driveways.

She stopped in front of the first house. The trees were nearly bare, and what few leaves were left trembled in the wind, some of them letting go of the branches even as she watched.

A sign made of iron hung on a wooden post and had bold letters engraved on it: *GEORGE W. WILKINSON.* Kathleen recalled that there was a banking family in Chicago by the name of Wilkinson. No doubt, this was that family.

She pulled her coat collar tightly around her throat and warily headed for the sweeping front porch. Barely moving her lips, she said, "Papa...Mama...help me. I'm a little scared."

She lifted the heavy door knocker and let it fall, the sound echoing inside the house. Her pulse quickened when she heard heavy footsteps and the rattle of the inside latch. Then the door swung open. A gray-haired man dressed in a swallow-tailed coat with vest and bow tie looked her up and down and said, "Yes, mum."

Kathleen had heard about butlers and had seen drawings of them, but she had never seen a real one. "Sir, my name is Kathleen O'Malley. My family died in the fire a week ago Sunday night. Our house was destroyed. I...I am looking for work. I can do cleaning jobs of all kinds, and...and I can do housekeeping chores. Would the Wilkinsons be interested in my services?"

The butler shook his head. "No, mum. We have a live-in housekeeper. She does all that is needed."

"Oh, I see. Well, thank you, sir."

"Yes, mum," said the butler, closing the door before she had even turned to leave.

Kathleen held her head high and walked down the long driveway toward the next house.

As she moved between properties, she was surprised that her mind ran to the soul-shaking experience at the Killanins' church, and the words Dwight Moody had spoken. Moving her lips without sound, Kathleen said, "But if Jesus loved me enough to suffer and die on the cross for me, why didn't He love me enough to keep my family from dying?"

The sign at the next gate announced that the Alfred Morleys lived there.

The pain of losing her family was sharp in Kathleen's heart as she stepped up on the huge porch and lifted the knocker. When there was no response after several seconds, she lifted the knocker again. This time there were light footsteps. When the door opened, a middle-aged woman, dressed in an expensive dress and wearing flashy jewelry, looked at Kathleen with disdain and said, "What is it?"

"Are…are you Mrs. Morley?"

"Yes. And we don't give handouts."

Kathleen glanced down at her shabby coat, then back at the woman. "Oh, I'm not asking for a handout, Mrs. Morley, I'm looking for work. You see, my entire family died in the fire a week ago yesterday, and I'm all alone. I can do cleaning jobs and household chores. I'm willing to—"

The door slammed in her face.

Kathleen headed for the next house. Her shoes were hurting her feet, but it didn't come close to the pain in her heart.

By early afternoon, Kathleen had knocked on thirty-one doors. A few people were kind when they turned her down, but most were curt, as if her presence on their doorstep was an offense to them.

Before starting on another street, Kathleen sat down on a tree stump and took off her shoes. The raw wind bit through her stockings as she rubbed her aching feet. "Papa, Mama…" she said, her voice breaking, "I need you."

She wept for a few minutes, then slipped her shoes back on. As she was tying the laces, a fancy carriage drove by. A young man with sandy hair was at the reins, and riding alone. He smiled at her, tipped his hat, and drove on.

Kathleen finished tying her shoes, wiped her tears, and said, "Well, at least a few people in this neighborhood are friendly. All right, Miss O'Malley, let's see what you can find in this block."

6

KATHLEEN COVERED FOUR MORE BLOCKS on one side of the street, and after rejections at every house she leaned against a large oak tree and wept. Her feet were hurting too much to go on. She would find a place to sit down, rub her feet good, then head home.

Through her tears, Kathleen looked up the street and saw the fancy carriage that had passed by earlier, the one with the handsome young man at the reins. The carriage was pulling out of the driveway of a large, beautiful brick house a block away. It turned her direction as the driver put the horse to a trot.

Kathleen quickly dried the tears from her cheeks.

The same young man was driving the carriage, and he was alone. He pulled rein when he saw Kathleen. When the carriage had come to a complete stop, he smiled down at her and said, "I saw you earlier today, didn't I?"

"Yes. I was several blocks over that way."

"Are you looking for some particular address I could help you find?"

Kathleen looked down at her worn and faded clothing and felt unworthy to be greeted by such a well-dressed and obviously wealthy man. "Ah…no sir, thank you. I…ah…I'm just enjoying a nice walk."

"Oh. All right. Well, I hope you enjoy it."

Kathleen managed a half-smile.

The handsome young man tipped his hat, clucked to the horse, and drove away.

Kathleen sighed deeply and headed back toward her part of town and her drab little room. She would come back here tomorrow and take up where she'd left off. She walked to the tree stump she'd sat on earlier and removed her shoes. A big red blister had formed on her left heel and it burned like fire.

She rubbed both feet to soothe them, put the shoes back on, and limped westward. The cold wind off the lake nipped at her ears and knifed through the secondhand coat.

By the time Kathleen reached downtown the sun was setting, and at the rate she was walking, it was still another thirty minutes to the boardinghouse. She had eaten nothing since early morning, and her empty stomach growled in protest.

While limping across Kedzie Avenue, Kathleen spotted a small café. She forced her cold, weary body up the two steps to the door. As she moved inside, warm air greeted her, along with the fragrant, tantalizing smells of homemade bread and roasting beef. She looked around timidly and spotted an unoccupied table next to a front window. The place was cozy with glowing lanterns and a roaring fire in the brick fireplace.

Kathleen removed her coat, draped it over a chair, and sat down. There were eating utensils on the table, wrapped in napkins, and a pair of tin cups. Behind salt and pepper shakers, menus leaned against the windowsill.

A pert young waitress stepped to Kathleen's table. "Hello," she said, smiling. "Cold outside, isn't it?"

"That it is," Kathleen said, picking up a menu and placing it on the table in front of her.

"How about some hot coffee to warm you up?"

"That sounds good," said the weary redhead, pushing a cup toward the waitress.

"Maybelle!" came a male voice from the kitchen. "Order for table five!"

The girl poured the steaming black liquid into Kathleen's cup and said, "I'll deliver that order and be right back."

Kathleen picked up the menu and studied it for a moment. The coffee was five cents a cup. The least expensive food item on the menu was a bowl of vegetable beef soup with two slices of home-made bread. The soup and bread order was sixty cents. Kathleen let her eyes rove around the room. A man at a nearby table was slurping soup from a bowl and chomping on a slice of bread. It looked good.

"Okay, Maybelle's back," the waitress said in a cheerful tone. "What would you like, honey?"

"Would it…would it be possible to order a half-bowl of the vegetable soup and one slice of bread?"

Maybelle's brow furrowed. "A *half-bowl* of soup?"

"Yes, please."

The waitress bent down close to Kathleen's face. "Honey, is this because you're not very hungry, or because you're a little short on funds?"

Kathleen swallowed hard. "Well, it's, ah…it's—"

"Tell you what. I'll bring you a *full* bowl of vegetable beef soup and two slices of bread, and you will only pay half price. How's that?"

"Oh, I couldn't—"

"Yes, you could. And the second cup of coffee will be on the house."

"I don't know what to say, I—"

"Just say, 'Hurry up with the bread and soup, Maybelle; I'm hungry.'"

Kathleen laughed for the first time since her family had died in the fire. "It's very nice of you to do this, Maybelle. Are you sure you won't get in trouble with your boss?"

"Nah-h-h. The boss is that fella back there in the kitchen. He's my dad. I won't get in trouble."

Kathleen nodded. "Thank you."

As the girl hurried away, Kathleen put the menu back against the windowsill and picked up the tin cup. She studied the other customers in the café as she sipped hot coffee. People were talking and laughing, enjoying each other's company. The only other person in the place alone was the man eating the soup.

74

Her loneliness felt like a cold hand squeezing her heart. Life would never be the same without her parents…without Donnie and Patricia. What would become of her? Would she find a job or starve to death?

"No, Kathleen," she said under her breath. "You're not going to starve to death. You *will* find a job. Someone in that fancy side of town will hire you. Just keep knocking on doors. There's bound to be someone who could use your services. Like the parents of that nice young man in the carriage. He—"

Kathleen shook her head and continued to mutter to herself. "You really messed up, Kathleen. You should've told him the truth. He seemed to like you. Maybe he could have talked his rich parents into— Wait a minute. Why not start at his house tomorrow? Who knows, maybe his parents are as nice as he is. First on the agenda will be 1402 Mockingbird Lane."

When Maybelle arrived with her order, Kathleen's eyes bulged at the size of the soup bowl, which actually looked like a large gravy bowl. The bread plate had four slices of bread and four chunks of butter.

"There you go, honey," Maybelle said. "Eat up. If that doesn't fill your tummy, there's more in the kitchen."

Kathleen smiled. "I…I don't know how to thank you."

Maybelle chuckled. "You can thank me by eating till you're full."

"I'll do my best."

Kathleen hadn't realized how hungry she was until she looked at the thick vegetable beef soup and the hot bread on the plate. She picked up her spoon with gusto and suddenly thought of Hennie Killanin and her family. They always prayed before they ate and thanked the Lord for their food. Kathleen was very appreciative of what had just been set before her, but she was not about to bow her head and pray in front of people. She dug in. After a few minutes, Maybelle came back and poured her another cup of coffee.

Kathleen didn't put her spoon down, except to butter the bread, until she had eaten all the soup and all four slices of bread. When it was all gone she sat back with a sigh, and for a moment she stared out the window and watched people passing by under the street lanterns. Then she rose to her feet and put on her shabby coat, buttoned it up tight around her throat, and went to the counter. Maybelle met her there, took her money, and said, "You come back again, won't you, honey?"

"I will. And thank you. Thank you very much."

Maybelle showed her big smile again. "You are so welcome. Bye now."

The sky was overcast when Kathleen stepped into the cold and headed for home.

When she entered the boardinghouse, her landlady was in the hall about to enter her own room. Hattie Murphy was a short, stout, jolly widow of sixty.

"Kathleen! There you are. I recall you said you wouldn't be here for lunch, but I expected you for supper. Come on down to the dining hall. I have some leftovers I can heat up, and—"

"I already ate supper, Mrs. Murphy," Kathleen said politely, "but thank you."

Hattie cocked her head to one side. "So did you find work, honey?"

"Not yet. But I'll try again tomorrow. See you at breakfast." As Kathleen spoke, she headed down the hall.

"Honey, why are you limping?"

"Oh, I've just got a blister on my left heel. I bought these shoes in a secondhand store, and they're a bit small for my feet. I'll have to go the price and buy a new pair."

"Come in, child, and let me look at that blister."

Kathleen entered her room feeling more cheered than when she'd first returned to the boardinghouse. She had a small container of salve in her hand and a bandage on her blister. There was also money to buy a new pair of shoes, which she would do as soon as she could.

Her landlady had told her not to worry about paying back the money until she sold her land.

Each room in the boardinghouse had its own potbellied stove. Kathleen kept her coat on while she built a fire, and soon the room was warm. She set a pail of water on the stove to heat up, then sat down and removed her shoes. The blister felt much better after Hattie's doctoring.

She washed up, brushed her hair, then put on the only flannel nightgown she had—a used one she'd purchased at the secondhand store. She snuffed the flame in the room's only lantern, padded across the floor, and slipped between the cold sheets.

As Kathleen thought of her family, the tears began to flow. She forced herself to put her mind on what she would do in the morning. The first door she knocked on would be at 1402 Mockingbird Lane. If she got turned down there, she would keep on knocking on doors until she found work. She came very close to asking God to let her get a job at the house where the nice young man lived. Instead, she nestled her head deeper into the pillow. Her body was fatigued from all the walking she had done, and soon her eyelids drooped, ushering her into a dreamless sleep.

There wasn't a cloud in the sky the next morning as Kathleen turned onto Mockingbird Lane. The blister had not hurt so much when she first left the boardinghouse, but after walking all the way to the wealthy section of town again, it was giving her some pain. No matter what happened today, she would make it downtown before closing time to buy shoes that fit.

The sun gave off little heat, and the wind off the lake seemed colder than yesterday. Kathleen tugged at her coat collar as she drew up in front of the posh mansion. Her mouth dropped open when she read the name on the metal plate attached to an iron post: *JOHN M. STALLWORTH.*

Everybody in Chicago knew that name. John Michael Stallworth owned the Great Lakes Railroad Company. He was one of the wealthiest men in the city.

Kathleen took a deep breath and limped onto the porch. She stared at the ornate knocker for a moment, then lifted it and let it fall. She expected a butler to answer, but the footsteps she heard were definitely that of a woman. *Probably the maid,* she told herself.

The door swung open to reveal a stately woman in her midfifties. Her dark hair was streaked with gray and pulled back in a lovely upsweep. "What can I do for you, young lady?" she said.

Kathleen's stomach churned. "Are you Mrs. Stallworth, ma'am?"

"Yes. I am Maria Stallworth."

"My name is Kathleen O'Malley, Mrs. Stallworth, and I just need to talk to you for a moment."

Maria Stallworth took a step back, swung the door wider, and said, "Please come in out of the cold, dear."

This was the first time Kathleen had been invited inside a house since she started canvassing the neighborhood. "Oh. Why, thank you, ma'am," she said, moving inside.

"Come," Maria said, "let's sit down in the parlor."

The dignified woman led Kathleen into a beautiful room where a fire was crackling in the fireplace.

Kathleen was directed to sit on a love seat, and Mrs. Stallworth sat down opposite her on an overstuffed chair. "Now, Kathleen O'Malley," she said, "what did you need to talk to me about?"

"I don't want to take up a lot of your time, Mrs. Stallworth, so I'll be brief. My entire family died in that awful fire a week ago last Sunday. I am the only one left. Our house was destroyed."

"Oh, you poor thing. Are you needing a donation to help meet your necessities?"

"I am not looking for a donation, ma'am. I'm looking for work. I can do all kinds of cleaning jobs, and any kind of housework. I've been knocking on doors here in your part of the city, but so far no one has needed my services."

Maria squinted, tilted her head, and said, "Shouldn't you be in school?"

"I am a senior this year, ma'am, but I can't stay in school because I have to earn a living now."

"I see. And you are willing to do any kind of cleaning? You know, bathrooms, kitchen, hardwood floors, windows?"

"Yes, ma'am." Kathleen's pulse quickened.

"You said your house was destroyed in the fire?"

"Yes, ma'am. My—my parents, brother, and sister were trapped in the house when it went up in flames."

"I'm so sorry, dear. What I am wanting to know is, where are you living now?"

"I have a room in a boardinghouse just west of downtown."

"And if you find work here in our area, you will walk every workday from there?"

"Yes, ma'am."

"Well, honey, no one can say you're a lazy person, that's for sure."

Kathleen pressed a smile on her lips. Butterflies flitted in her stomach. Was she about to be offered a job?

"Tell you what, Kathleen, we had a live-in maid and cook, but quite recently we had to let her go. John—that's my husband—and I have agreed that I would do the cooking, and we'd simply find a cleaning lady and have her come three days a week. The live-in situation just didn't work. We've never had a butler because we're such private people."

Kathleen nodded, waiting hopefully.

"I can handle the cooking with no problem," Maria went on. "There are only three of us in the house…John, our son Peter, and me. You do know who we are, don't you, dear?"

"Yes. You're the railroad people."

"That's right. The Great Lakes Railroad Company. Well, Kathleen, if you'd like the job, it's yours. You would come Tuesdays, Thursdays, and Saturdays to do the cleaning. We'll pay you a dollar a day, and we'll buy you a couple of uniforms. We'd like you to wear a uniform when you're working here, so that when we have guests, they will be pleased at the way our cleaning lady dresses."

A warm feeling washed over Kathleen. Smiling broadly, she said, "I'll take the job, Mrs. Stallworth. Thank you!"

"And we'll be happy to have you, dear. Now, before you go, let me take some measurements. One of my husband's employees has a wife who makes dresses, and she also makes uniforms."

When the measurements had been noted, Maria walked her new cleaning lady toward the door. "Can you start Thursday?"

"Certainly."

"All right. Your workdays here will start at eight o'clock in the morning, and you will finish at four. I'll see that you have some lunch each day. Your uniforms will probably not be ready till Saturday, so we'll get by on Thursday with whatever dress you wear."

"Fine, ma'am," said Kathleen. "What I'll try to do now is find a cleaning job on the alternate days."

Maria's hand went to her cheek. "Wait a minute! I think I can get you that very job."

"Really?"

"Yes. We have some close friends who live just a couple of blocks from here on Sunset Drive. Are you acquainted with Massey's department store downtown?"

Kathleen knew Massey's was where rich people bought their clothes and other expensive items. "I've seen it, but I've never been inside."

"Well, the Ralph Massey family owns it, and they're looking for a cleaning lady. At least they were up till two days ago. If they haven't hired one yet, I know you'll get the job."

As she spoke, Maria went to a small desk on one side of the large vestibule and opened a drawer. "Tell you what, Kathleen," she said, taking out a sheet of paper, "I'll write LuAnn a note and tell her I just hired you, and that if she hasn't already filled the position, she should hire you."

Kathleen could hardly believe how well things were going today.

Maria dipped a pen in the inkwell on the desk and scratched a hasty note. She blotted it, stuffed it into an envelope, and handed it to Kathleen. "Here you are, dear. Just ask for Mrs. Massey when you knock on the door. They have a butler and a cook, but their cleaning lady got married about ten days ago and quit her job."

As she ushered Kathleen toward the door, Maria said, "I hope you aren't getting married anytime soon."

"No, ma'am. I don't even have a beau."

"Pretty as you are? That's hard to believe. All right, Miss Kathleen O'Malley, I'll see you on Thursday morning at eight o'clock."

"You sure will, Mrs. Stallworth. Thank you for giving me the job...and thank you for recommending me to Mrs. Massey."

"You are very welcome, dear."

Kathleen tried not to limp as she walked toward the street, but she knew it was still obvious if Mrs. Stallworth was watching her. When she passed through the open gate, she looked back and saw Maria standing at the door in spite of the cold air. The woman waved, and Kathleen waved back.

When Kathleen limped away from 1440 Sunset Drive, a great burden was lifted from her shoulders. LuAnn Massey had hired her on the spot after reading Maria Stallworth's note. Kathleen would work Monday, Wednesday, and Friday each week at the Massey home. This would give her Sunday to rest up.

Mrs. Massey said she would pay $1.10 a day since the Stallworths were furnishing Kathleen her uniforms.

This was a source of even greater encouragement to Kathleen. The use of the uniforms would save her having to buy as many clothes, and the extra ten cents a day over what the Stallworths were paying would help pay the rent for her room.

Kathleen entered the mercantile store in downtown Chicago where her parents had often gone to buy clothing and shoes. After trying on several pairs of shoes, she remembered that winter was near, and that meant there would be long walks on snow and ice. She decided on a pair of soft leather boots that buttoned up the side in a row of small buttons.

She left the secondhand shoes for the salesman to throw away and departed the store, wearing her new boots. They were wonderfully comfortable.

By the time Kathleen arrived at the boardinghouse lunch was over, and Hattie Murphy was washing dishes in the kitchen off the dining room.

The older woman looked up to see Kathleen limp into the kitchen and broke into a smile. "Hey!" she said. "You got some new boots!"

"Thanks to you."

"You're back earlier than yesterday," said Hattie, as she stacked plates on the cupboard next to a tray of clean cups.

Hattie was small, silver-haired, and about sixty, but Kathleen figured she could outwork the average woman half her age. The older woman wiped her hands on her apron and turned around to look at Kathleen. "Does your early return mean you had success?"

"Oh, did I ever!"

"Wonderful, darlin'!" Hattie said, her Irish brogue quite evident in her excitement. "Tell me!"

Kathleen waggled her head in mock pride, "Well, Mrs. Murphy, you are now looking at the cleaning lady at the mansions of John Michael Stallworth and Ralph Massey!"

"No-o-o!"

"Yes! I'm doing the Stallworth house on Tuesdays, Thursdays, and Saturdays. And I'm doing the Massey house on Mondays, Wednesdays, and Fridays! I get Sundays off…and guess what!"

"What?"

"The Stallworths are providing uniforms for me to wear while I'm working both places!"

Hattie clapped her chubby hands, "Oh, honey, that's wonderful! This calls for a celebration!"

"What do you mean?"

"I have a couple of women here in the boardinghouse who fill in for me, cooking the meals, when I go visit my son and his family in Indianapolis. I'll have them cook supper for the boarders tonight, and I'll fix us up a special meal to celebrate your new jobs. A nice big meal! How's that?"

"It's great, Hattie, but I don't want you to go to all that trouble."

"*Trouble!* Honey, it's no trouble. I *want* to do it. Now, you've probably not had any lunch, have you?"

"No, but if you're going to prepare a big meal for tonight, I'll pass. I need to get me a good bath and maybe rest these feet for a while."

"Tell you what. My apartment has a nice big bathroom, and a big bathtub. You go get your clean clothes and I'll meet you upstairs."

Kathleen felt a special tenderness toward Hattie Murphy, who was filling an empty spot left by her mother. She gazed fondly at the little round woman whose snow white hair was always worn in a perfect bun on top of her head. Her cheeks never lost their rose red color, and her bright blue eyes always had a twinkle.

"Mrs. Murphy," said Kathleen, "you're so good to me. I can never tell you how very much I appreciate you."

Hattie's features flushed. "Go on, now, honey. I've got hot water right here. I'll bring a couple buckets up to my room."

"I'll come back down and help you carry it."

"No, you won't. I'll have it up there before you get to my door. Go on, now. Get your clean clothes."

In the privacy of Hattie's bathroom, Kathleen sank down into the fragrant hot water and felt the tension of the past several days gradually seep out of her body. Hattie had slipped some kind of perfume into the water, and the sweet aroma filled the room.

She gave herself a good scrub, then soaped and rinsed her hair. She stayed in the tub to soak, enjoying the knowledge that she had two good jobs and could make herself a decent living. When the water began to cool, Kathleen reluctantly left the tub, dried off, and wrapped the towel around her wet, dripping hair.

Once she was in her clean undergarments and the robe Hattie had supplied, she stuck her head out and saw the little woman sitting by the fireplace in a rocking chair.

"Come on out, honey," Hattie said with a smile. "Dry your hair by the fire."

Knowing how long it took to dry her luxuriant head of hair, Kathleen gladly accepted the invitation.

A half hour later her auburn hair shone beautifully, and she returned to the bathroom to put on her clean dress.

That afternoon Kathleen took her much-needed rest. At suppertime, she returned to Hattie's apartment. The little widow was humming an Irish tune when she came to the door to let Kathleen in, and after greeting her, hummed the tune some more.

Kathleen's mother used to hum the same tune, but Kathleen couldn't remember the name of it. The familiar melody shot a keen sense of longing through her.

"Okay, honey," said Hattie as they moved into the kitchen, "it's just about ready."

The kitchen was warm and cheery, and the sweet aroma of Irish stew and soda bread smelled wonderful. Hattie had laid out dinner on a snowy white tablecloth that sufficiently covered the round table.

"I wish you had let me come down earlier to help you," Kathleen said.

"You needed the rest, honey. Those boots doing your feet better than those ol' shoes?"

"They sure are. My left heel feels better already."

Kathleen talked about her new jobs, and Hattie rejoiced with her. When they had eaten sufficient amounts of stew, the two women topped off the meal with hot tea and gingerbread.

After cleaning up the dishes, they sat by the fireplace and talked for a while. Soon Kathleen's head began to nod.

"Okay, darlin'," said the widow Murphy, "it's time for little girl leprechauns to go to bed."

Hattie walked Kathleen to her room, kissed her cheek, and told her good-night.

A short time later, Kathleen slid between the crisp, clean sheets and sighed. Things were so much better tonight than they had been the night before. Tomorrow she would begin her job with the Masseys, and on Thursday she would start her job with the Stallworths.

Though no one was there to see it, a small dimpled smile played on the Irish girl's face.

7

MAIL ORDER BRIDE SERIES

NO. 1
1871
USA

AL & JOANNA LACY

PETER STALLWORTH WAS ONE of the Great Lakes Railroad Company's three junior vice presidents, and the youngest at twenty-one. Behind his desk was a large window overlooking Chicago's downtown area, with a far-off view of Lake Michigan to the east.

In front of his desk stood the other two junior vice presidents, twenty-eight-year-old Derek Walton, and Jack Ballard, who would turn thirty on his next birthday.

Peter looked up at them and said, "Really, fellas, you don't have to say it just because I'm the boss's son."

"We're not, Peter," Ballard said. "We're saying it because it's the best idea."

"Right," Walton agreed. "Look, Peter, haven't we already been over this 'I have to walk on eggs because I'm the boss's son' thing? If my dad owned this company, I'd want to build my career right here, just like you are. Your dad has already proven to all of us that you get no favors because you're Peter Michael Stallworth. You have to pull your own weight and do your own thinking, just like the rest of us."

"And you've most certainly done your own thinking on the accounts receivable problem," said Ballard. "My idea doesn't come near yours."

Walton nodded. "Neither does mine. And for that matter, the other ideas don't appeal to me like yours does. I think what you've come up with will solve the problem of collecting from those customers who've been dragging their feet when it comes to paying us for hauling their freight all over the eastern United States. You're sure going to get my vote."

"And mine," said Ballard. "And from what I've heard the other guys say, your idea is getting their votes, too."

The handsome man with the sandy hair and cool blue eyes smiled. "You guys sure make it easier on me, I'll tell you that."

"Hey, we know it's tough enough working for John Stallworth when you eat and sleep under his roof and wear his last name," said Walton. "Why should we make things tougher for you here? You're doing a good job, Peter."

"Yeah, especially being the youngest officer in the company, and with no help from your dad," put in Ballard.

"I don't want him to help me. If he were to change his approach and decide to help me work up through the ranks just so one day his son could take over his position as chief executive officer, I wouldn't want the position. I only want what I earn."

"Everybody in this company knows that," said Walton. "That's why you've got so much respect around here."

"I appreciate your kind words, guys," Peter said, rising from his desk and picking up a folder. "I'll see you in the meeting. Right now I've got some papers to deliver to Dan Clayton."

Peter's colleagues returned to their offices, and he headed down the hall. When he approached the door marked "Daniel Clayton, Senior Vice President," he tapped on the door and waited for permission to enter.

Instead, Clayton opened the door. "Hey, Peter! Come in!"

"I have the papers ready on the Fleming Steel account, Dan. If you want to wait till after the meeting to go over them, I can come back then."

"Let's do that," Clayton said, who at sixty-one was four years older than Peter's father. "But if you've got a minute, I'd like to talk to you."

"Sure." Peter stepped inside.

Dan closed the door and laid the folder on his desk. He turned to face the younger man and said, "I like your solution on the accounts receivable delinquents. You pick that up at C.I.B., or is that your own masterpiece?"

Peter had graduated from the Chicago Institute of Business a year early at the head of his class. His father had given him the junior vice president position upon graduation five months ago.

Peter chuckled. "No, sir, they don't teach you those kinds of things at C.I.B."

"Well, I mean what I say, son, it's a masterpiece."

"Thanks, Dan. You and Derek and Jack have been very encouraging."

"Just wanted you to know how I felt, and to tell you your idea will get my vote."

"That's good to know. Well, I'll head on back to my office and get ready for the meeting. Afterward we'll come back here and go over those Fleming papers."

John Stallworth stood at the large window in the conference room with his hands clasped behind his back as he looked down at State Street five floors below. Like his only son, he was an inch under six feet and had cool blue eyes and sandy hair, now showing a great deal of gray.

When his officers began filing through the door, Stallworth pivoted and greeted them with a smile. "Good afternoon, gentlemen," he said, moving toward the long conference table.

They greeted him in return, and others came in behind them.

When Peter entered, sided by Derek Walton and Jack Ballard, John eyed his son furtively, feeling a great swell of pride. Peter's idea was a colossal one.

As soon as all the officers had gathered and taken their seats, Stallworth sat down at the head of the table and said, "All right, gentlemen. Two weeks ago today I presented you with the nagging problem the Great Lakes Railroad Company has experienced in making collections on delinquent accounts receivable. I asked each of you to come up with a solution that would not harm our image nor send our customers to Illinois Central or one of the other railroad companies.

"As I told you then, the solution would take some ingenuity on your part. All of you have turned in your ideas to me, and in turn I have had them copied and placed in all of your hands so you could study them. The best thing to do here is take a vote. If we have a tie, or anywhere near it, we'll discuss the ideas we like the best."

Dan Clayton raised his hand.

"Yes, Mr. Clayton," Stallworth said.

Clayton rose to his feet. "Sir, every man here has taken the time to come and share his thoughts with me. I think we can conserve some time if I simply ask one question."

"All right, Mr. Clayton, ask these gentlemen your question."

Clayton looked around at his colleagues with a smile on his face. "Will everybody in favor of adopting Peter Stallworth's collection plan raise your hand?"

The vote was unanimous.

Peter's face reddened at the applause, and he glanced quickly at his father, relieved to see the pleasure on his face.

The chief executive officer and owner of the Great Lakes Railroad Company said, "Mr. Stallworth, you are to be congratulated. Every man in this room has discussed your plan with me, and we all feel it is the most sensible and by far the most acceptable of all. It meets every criterion I laid down when I asked each of these officers to come up with his own solution. Well done."

"May I speak, sir?"

"Please do."

Peter stood up. "Maybe all of you should hold off your congratulations until we see if my plan works!"

There was laughter all around, then Dan Clayton spoke up. "Peter, you've covered every possible loophole. Believe me, it will work. Go ahead and take your bow!"

There was more laughter and then a twenty-minute discussion on the induction of Peter's plan into the bookkeeping system. When the assignment went to the comptroller to work it out, the meeting was dismissed.

On their way out, many of the officers took time to personally congratulate Peter.

Peter walked with Dan Clayton to the latter's office, and they proceeded with their work on the Fleming Steel Company account.

At five o'clock, the officers and employees of the Great Lakes Railroad Company were starting to leave the building. Inside John Stallworth's office, Peter looked on as his father shrugged into his overcoat and put on his hat.

"Son," Stallworth said, "I couldn't say this in the meeting, but I'm so proud of you for your good thinking that I'm about to pop my buttons."

Peter grinned sheepishly. "Aw, Dad, it wasn't that big of a thing."

"It sure was. It's going to save this company a lot of money, and part of it is going into your paycheck. As of right now, you're getting a two-hundred-dollar-a-month raise in salary."

Peter grinned wider. "Thanks, Dad. The extra will come in handy for whenever I get married."

As they left the office and headed for the stairs, John said, "Speaking of getting married…how are things between you and Harriet?"

At that moment, two employees came out of the accounting office and greeted both men, then followed on their heels.

Peter leaned over and whispered, "I'll fill you in on Harriet when we're in the carriage."

John Stallworth let his son handle the reins as they headed east toward home. Peter seemed a bit preoccupied, so John waited patiently for him to speak.

The Stallworths were hoping to hear soon that wedding bells were in the offing. Harriet was the daughter of Chicago shipping magnate Clarence Scott. The Scotts lived just a few doors down from the Stallworths, and having Harriet as their daughter-in-law wouldn't hurt their social standing at all. Plus she was a pretty girl, vivacious, intelligent…and rich. It was only natural that John and Maria would want their son to look her way.

Peter said nothing for the first ten minutes of the drive, then he glanced at his father and said, "I've been trying to think of a way to let you down easy, Dad, but I can't. So I'll just tell you how it is with Harriet. I'm not in love with her, and she's not in love with me. We had a good talk about it on our last date two nights ago."

"It was that cut and dried?" said John.

"Mm-hmm. We agreed that we don't share the same interests. Our goals are different. She dearly loves opera, it bores me to death. She doesn't want any children, I do. And I think you and Mom want grandchildren."

"Well…ah…yes. We sure do."

"And besides, Dad, Harriet has one big problem."

"And that is?"

"I won't deny that she's good-looking, but she thinks she's the most beautiful female that God ever made. You know…God's gift to men. She's a real flirt, and I just don't cotton to a woman who ignores the man she's supposed to be with in order to catch the eyes of all the other men. So it's all off with Harriet."

"Well, I'm sorry to hear it, son. Your mother and I were really looking forward to being in-laws with the Scotts. We weren't aware, of course, of some of the things you just brought up."

Peter remained silent.

"Son, before you started getting serious with Harriet, you were dating other girls from our part of town. What about Lucinda Weatherby?"

"She's engaged to some guy from New York."

"Oh. Well, what about Margaret Laughlin?"

"She's getting married in Philadelphia next month."

"Okay. Lavonne Parker?"

"Don't know for sure if she's got a steady beau right now. I'll find out."

"And Muriel Kincaid?"

"Might be a possibility there, too. I'll have to look into it."

"Good. Lavonne or Muriel, either one would make us a good

daughter-in-law. And if they don't work out, there are other young ladies in our part of town."

"Sure, Dad. I promise. I won't be a bachelor too long."

When the Stallworths sat down to the dinner table, Peter said, "Sure smells and looks good, Mom."

"It'll get better by Saturday," Maria said, passing her son the meat plate.

Peter eyed her questioningly.

"Well," she said with a sigh, "I said I wouldn't do it, but I hired a cook about twenty minutes ago."

John nodded his approval. "Honey, I'm glad. As long as she's not live-in."

"No. She was Cliff and Pat Bowen's cook. Cliff doesn't need a cook anymore since he's traveling so much. He knew we didn't have a cook, so he came by with her and asked if we'd be interested in hiring her. She's twenty-six and married, but childless. She and her husband live near downtown on the east side."

"What's her name, Mom?" Peter asked.

"Carlene Simms. Sweet girl."

"I'll miss your cooking, Mom, but it's good that you won't have to slave in the kitchen anymore."

Maria waved him off. "It's not slavery, Peter. I enjoy it, but it is time consuming."

"Hey!" said John. "Something to tell you about Peter!"

Maria lifted a palm toward him. "Maybe I should tell you about someone else I hired today, too. Then you can tell me about our boy."

John smiled. "You hired a cleaning lady!"

"Sure did."

"Not live-in. We agreed not to—"

"She's not live-in."

"Good. Tell me more."

"Her name is Kathleen O'Malley."

"Married?"

"No. Single."

"So she's for sure got Irish blood," Peter said.

"Mm-hmm. And she looks it, too. Beautiful deep red hair…lovely complexion."

"So how'd this happen?" John asked.

"She knocked on the door and said she was looking for a cleaning job or general housework, or both. Her family died in the fire. Lived over on the west side. She's all alone. Had to drop out of school and find work to survive."

"Drop out of school," Peter echoed. "How old is she?"

"Almost eighteen. She lives in a boardinghouse near downtown."

John shifted his position on the chair. "Should you have hired a girl so young, honey?"

"I really don't think her youth will be a problem. The girl impressed me. I have no doubt Kathleen will do a good job. She's going to work Tuesdays, Thursdays, and Saturdays. We're paying both young ladies a dollar a day, but of course Carlene will work seven days a week. *And* I sent Kathleen to the Masseys. LuAnn hired her for Mondays, Wednesdays, and Fridays. She came over this afternoon and thanked me for sending Kathleen to her. She really likes the girl, too."

"Sounds like your mother's had a busy day hiring help, Peter," John said with a chuckle.

Maria noted that both her men's coffee cups were empty. When she shoved back her chair, Peter jumped up.

"Stay put, Mom. I'll get the coffeepot." He hurried to the kitchen, took the coffeepot from the stove, and when he returned to the dining room, his father was telling his mother all about their son's solution to the delinquent accounts problem, and that he had garnered himself a raise in salary because of it.

Maria smiled as Peter poured coffee all around. "I'm proud of you, Peter. If your father doesn't look out, he's liable to lose his job to you!"

Peter snickered. "Sure, Mom. Dad'll lose his job to me when elephants climb trees."

When Peter sat down again, Maria said, "You must tell Harriet about this accomplishment, and about your raise. She'll be excited, I'm sure."

Peter flicked a glance at his father, and John looked at Maria.

"Did I say something wrong?"

"No, Mom. It's just that…well, Harriet isn't interested in what goes on in my life."

Maria's head bobbed. Eyes wide, she said, "What do you mean?"

"When Harriet and I went to the opera the other night…we had a long discussion and agreed that we're not for each other."

"Oh. I…I'm sorry to hear that. From the look you two just exchanged, I assume you've already told your father about it."

"Yes. On the way home. He asked how things were going between Harriet and me, so I told him it was all off."

"I was so hoping it would work out," Maria said.

"We don't have a lot in common," Peter said. "She just isn't the girl for me."

Maria perked up. "Well, I'm sure when the right one comes along, you'll know it's her, and your father and I will know it, too. Main thing is that she's suitable for your station."

"Sure, Mom," Peter said, chuckling. "Would I dare bring home a girl from the—pardon the railroader's pun—wrong side of the tracks?"

The October afternoon was bright, dry, and a bit cool as Storey County Commissioner Dale Horne mounted his horse and rode west out of Virginia City, Nevada.

Horne had lived in Virginia City since it was incorporated in 1859 and had watched it boom shortly thereafter as a result of the silver found in the hills to the west. People had come from all over the country to stake their claims. The most famous and best-producing mine was the Comstock Lode at nearby Mount Davidson, where the commissioner was headed.

Dale Horne loved Nevada. Especially Virginia City. As he trotted his mount westward, he glanced to the southeast and drank in the beauty of the rolling desert hills painted varying hues of deep violet, pale orange, and sand brown by their Creator. Ahead of him, beyond Mount Davidson, was the majestic Sierra Nevada mountain range, streaked with ever-changing sinuous shadows as the sun ran its brilliant arc across the azure sky. He enjoyed the sweetness of the fragrant desert wind upon his face.

The ride to Mount Davidson was brief, and soon Horne was reining in at the log cabin that served as office for the Comstock Lode. As he dismounted he glanced toward the mouth of the main mine, which faced east, and saw men and mules moving full carts of silver ore out of the bowels of the mountain on narrow gauge tracks.

As he looped the reins over a hitching post, two miners came out of the office. One of them said, "Howdy, Mr. Horne. I understand Mr. Comstock is gonna give you the 'cook's tour' this afternoon."

"Yes, and I'm looking forward to it," replied the commissioner, smiling amiably.

The door opened again, and Henry T. P. Comstock stepped out. He was a man in his late fifties, tall, slender, with a full beard. He had become wealthy over the years since staking his claim.

"Welcome, Mr. Horne," said Comstock. "Ready for your tour of the mine?"

"Sure am. But right off I want to thank you for the generous gift you gave Storey County to help build the new courthouse."

"My pleasure. We can't have a courthouse that's coming apart at the seams now, can we?"

Horne laughed. "It'd be a shame, wouldn't it?"

"A little embarrassing, too, since this place is known for its affluence. Well, let's get started."

As the two men headed toward the mouth of the mine, Horne said, "How many men do you employ, sir?"

"Exactly sixty at the moment. And they're all staying busy."

"Good!"

A tall, rawboned young miner had just come out of the mine and was squinting because of the brilliant sunlight. When he caught sight of Mr. Comstock and his guest, he headed toward them.

"Pardon me, Mr. Comstock," he said. "I know you're about to give Mr. Horne his promised tour, but it might be best if you wait a few minutes. And hello, Mr. Horne."

The commissioner had seen the young man's face around town but had never met him. "Hello," said Horne, extending his hand.

The miner gripped his hand firmly. "I'm Tom Harned, sir."

"Glad to meet you, Harned. Is there a problem?"

"Only a slight one, sir." Then to Comstock: "An axle broke on one of the carts, and we're having to transfer a full load of ore from that cart to another one. It's right where you gentlemen will walk, and at the moment there's a lot of dust in the air. Should be taken care of in about twenty to twenty-five minutes."

"Fine," said Comstock. "I hope that broken axle is on one of the old carts."

"Yes, sir."

Comstock snapped his fingers. "Say, Tom, didn't your little boy have a birthday recently?"

Tom's face beamed at the mention of his son. "Yes, sir. Caleb was one year old on September 30."

Comstock pulled out his wallet from an inside coat pocket, slipped out a twenty-dollar bill, and stuffed it in Tom's hand. "I've been meaning to give Caleb a little birthday present. Buy him something he needs."

Tom's blue eyes sparkled. "Why, thank you, Mr. Comstock! Thank you very much! I'm sure Loretta will put the money to good use for Caleb."

"Mothers have a way of doing that."

"I'll get back to my job now, gentlemen," said Harned. "If you want to go sit down in the office, I'll come and let you know when the tour can start."

"Thanks for thinking of our lungs, Tom," said the commissioner.

"Actually, sir, it was our foreman who asked me to come and

advise Mr. Comstock of the problem."

"Well, thank him for us."

"Will do." Tom gave the men a nod and headed back for the mine.

"Tom Harned seems like a sharp young man."

"He is," agreed Comstock. "He's foreman material, but he's only twenty-two, so he'll have to get a few more years on him before I can put him in a position of authority. That is, if he sticks around that long."

"What do you mean?"

"Well, like some of the other men here, Tom has a hankering to go out on his own and stake a claim. He's talked to me about it. But he wants to go for gold. Only thing that's holding him back is the kind of money it takes to do it. If he ever gets his hands on a sufficient amount, he'll be gone."

"Can't blame him for that."

"Sure can't. But he's a hard worker. I'd hate to lose him."

The sun was lowering over the jagged peaks of the Sierras as the miners emerged from the mountain and headed for their homes in Virginia City.

Tom Harned, Hank Mitchell, Ed Carstairs, Harold Sheetz, and Nick Tobias usually walked into town together at the close of each workday. As the five of them walked along the side of the road, Nick Tobias said, "So, Tom, have you got an idea when you might strike out on your own and stake a gold claim?"

"Sure don't. Loretta and I try to put a little money aside every payday, but sometimes it just isn't possible. At the rate we're going, all the gold in Nevada and California will be dug up before we have enough money to stake a claim."

"Well, at least you and your family have a roof over your heads and food on the table," said Ed Carstairs. "Gotta be thankful for that."

"We are. *Very* thankful. But we're not satisfied. Loretta and I were talking about it last night. Mr. Comstock hit it good here at Mount Davidson on a claim that cost him comparatively little. If he can do it, we figure we can, too. Only, as I've told you guys before, we're going to shoot for a gold claim when our day comes."

"Might as well," said Hank Mitchell. "Doesn't take any more work to dig gold out of 'them thar hills' than it does silver."

"That's the way I look at it, Hank," Tom said. "But until then, I plan to keep on working for Mr. Comstock. He pays us better than a lot of silver mine owners pay their men."

"Yes, he does," spoke up Harold Sheetz. "He's been plenty fair with me."

"We can all say that," said Hank.

The quintet reached the edge of town, and Carstairs, Sheetz, and Tobias veered off and headed toward their humble shanties. Soon the two friends were on Main Street on their way to the other side of town. As they drew near the Silver Plume Hotel they noticed a crowd gathered in front of the newspaper office next door.

Chuck Ramsey, the editor of the *Virginia City Sentinel,* was standing on the boardwalk, talking to the crowd, as his assistant sold papers.

Two of Comstock's miners were in the crowd. They each purchased a copy of the day's edition and headed up the street toward Harned and Mitchell.

"Hey, guys," Hank called, "what's all the excitement about?"

"Big fire in Chicago," one of the men replied, holding up his folded newspaper. "Chuck was just telling us that a third of the city has been destroyed. About three hundred people burned to death. Bad. Real bad."

Moving on, Tom said, "Guess I'd better buy a paper, Hank. Loretta's got two cousins who live in Chicago. She'll want to know about this."

MAIL ORDER BRIDE SERIES
NO. 1
1871
USA
AL & JOANNA LACY

8

LORETTA HARNED WAS AT HER KITCHEN cupboard preparing supper when she looked out the window and saw Tom and his friend Hank Mitchell. They were walking down the alley from the main street, their usual route to and from the mine.

The two men paused to finish their conversation when they reached Tom's place, then Hank moved on and Tom angled across the backyard toward the porch.

Loretta smiled to herself as she peered out the kitchen window with the white starched curtain and watched Tom's approach.

The small shanty where she and Tom lived with their little son was typical of other miners' shacks. Loretta kept it spotlessly clean, but it was drafty, with ill-fitting doors and windows.

There was a rough-hewn table and two chairs in the tiny kitchen area, and a handmade high chair that Hank Mitchell had made for Caleb when the boy was about nine months old. Loretta had put a cloth with embroidered blue flowers on the table and matching blue cushions on both chairs.

In the parlor there were two old rocking chairs in front of the fireplace and a rag rug of many colors on the uneven floor. Loretta had made a cozy home for her family, though she had very little to work with.

Behind a curtained doorway off the parlor was a double bed in the corner, covered with a calico quilt. A large trunk sat at the foot. Caleb's crib was on Loretta's side of the bed piled high with a mound of small blankets to keep Caleb warm on cold nights at the 4,600-foot altitude.

Loretta glanced into the parlor where her little son was playing on the rug and said, "Caleb, Daddy's home."

The one-year-old, with golden blond hair like his mother's, looked up and smiled. His blue eyes glinted with excitement.

Caleb had been walking only a short time, and it took him a few seconds to get on his feet. In the meantime, Loretta opened the door at the same moment Tom stepped up on the back porch. "Well, who's this man with the dust all over his face?" she said. "He sort of resembles my husband!"

Tom folded her in his arms. "Do I get a kiss before I wash off the dust, or do I have to wait?"

When they heard the pitter-patter of feet on the kitchen floor and a tiny voice cry, "Da-Da! Da-Da!" Loretta laughed.

"Go ahead and pick up your son, Da-Da, and I'll kiss you in a minute!"

Tom laid the newspaper on the table and grabbed the baby, who was lifting up his arms. Tom hugged Caleb, then nibbled on his ear, saying, "Mm-mm-mm, Mommy! Caleb's ears sure are good! Mm-mm-mm!"

While the fun was going on, Loretta opened the folded newspaper and read the headlines. "Oh, how awful!" she gasped.

Tom shifted Caleb to one arm and put his other arm around Loretta's waist. "Can you imagine, honey? A third of Chicago burned to the ground, and three hundred people dead!"

"Oh, Tom! I hope Marianne and Samantha and their families are all right!"

"I read just a little of it. Seems the fire started in a barn on the west side. A cow kicked over a lantern. Since your cousins live on the north side, maybe their homes weren't burned."

"I'll write to them tomorrow and hope for the best."

Tom nodded. "Now can I have that kiss?"

Loretta turned within the crook of his arm and raised up on tiptoe, kissing him soundly.

"Thank you," Tom said, gazing into her eyes.

"You're entirely welcome," she replied softly. "Now you get washed up."

Tom set Caleb on his feet and the little boy followed his father to the washbasin and watched carefully while Tom washed the dust from his face, neck, and hands.

When Tom had finished and Loretta was still working at the stove and cupboard, he sat down at the table and lifted Caleb to his lap, then read the entire story of the Chicago fire aloud while Loretta finished preparing supper.

When she was ready to sit down for the meal, Tom put Caleb in his high chair and kept him close at hand. Their food wasn't fancy, but it was filling and plentiful.

Tom fed Caleb bites from his own plate, and Caleb smacked his lips with relish. He would say "Da-Da" when he wanted more food, and both parents found themselves laughing at the little boy's antics. When Caleb caught on that what he did was making them laugh, he did it all the more.

Finally Tom gave Caleb a piece of bread to gnaw on and said, "Honey, I don't know how we're going to do it, but one of these days we'll put together enough money to stake our gold claim, and things will get better for us."

"I'm not complaining, darling. We're happy with things as they are. Sure, I'd like to have more money so we could live in a real house, and we could have more clothes and more variety in our meals, but as long as I have you and Caleb, I'll get along fine."

Tom reached across the table and squeezed her hand. "You're the best, Loretta May Harned. You're the absolute very best. A man couldn't ask for a wife any better than you."

Loretta's face tinted. "I'm glad you feel that way about me."

"Caleb feels the same way. He's been telling me what a fortunate boy he is to have such a wonderful mother."

Loretta laughed softly and looked at her little son, who had bread crumbs stuck to his face with butter. Light from the lantern above the table glowed on his golden hair.

When supper was over, Tom played with Caleb on the rug in front of the fire while Loretta cleaned up the kitchen. Caleb squealed with delight as Tom tickled him on his tummy and under his arms.

After a while, Loretta stood over father and son and said, "Okay, boys. Play time is over. Time for Caleb's bath."

As she spoke, Loretta gathered the boy into her arms and took him to the kitchen table, where she had laid a large towel and a basin of warm water.

Tom rose to his feet. "Are you going to bathe me next, Mommy?"

Loretta giggled. "Nope. Big boys have to bathe themselves."

"Oh, all right. Then I guess I'll read the book I started last night."

While Tom picked up a book from the small table by his rocking chair and started reading, Loretta removed Caleb's soiled clothes and tenderly washed his little body. He squirmed and fretted a little, but all in all he was a good boy. Once he was clean and dry and in his sleepwear, she carried him to her rocking chair next to Tom's and sat down.

Caleb immediately snuggled close and popped his thumb into his mouth. Smiling around the wet thumb, he reached up with his free hand and patted his mother's cheek. This was Caleb's routine, and as always when he did it, Loretta's heart swelled with love. She rocked the chair slowly and began crooning a soft lullaby.

Tom looked up from his book and smiled.

Soon Caleb's eyelids began to droop, and his sturdy little body relaxed in sleep.

While Loretta carried their son to his crib, Tom made the house ready for the night by throwing more logs on the fire and stirring the flames. Moments later, Loretta appeared in her flannel nightgown, carrying a hairbrush. Husband and wife also had their routine.

Loretta sat down on the floor in front of Tom's rocking chair, facing the roaring fire, and handed him the hairbrush. Tom laid aside his book and began taking the pins from her hair. When the last pin was removed, her golden hair cascaded down her back, and Tom took up the brush. Her long blond hair crackled with electricity as Tom drew the brush through the entire length.

"Loretta, I really am serious about staking our own gold claim."

"I know that, sweetheart," she said, bending her head against his gentle strokes. "We've been putting a few dollars in the cookie jar almost every payday."

"Yes, but there's got to be a way to come up with more money faster. All the gold will be dug out of the hills before I can get started."

Loretta reached back and patted his hand. "Don't you fret, darling. It'll be all right. Our day will come."

When Kathleen O'Malley pillowed her head on Wednesday night, October 11, she was tired but happy. Her first day at the Ralph Massey home had been a good one. Mrs. Massey welcomed her with a smile and was quite helpful to her all day long as she broke in on the job. Mr. Massey had come home only minutes before Kathleen's workday was done, and he had treated her kindly.

She was a bit nervous about tomorrow. Mrs. Stallworth certainly had treated her well when hiring her, but she was nervous about meeting Peter Stallworth. She thought of the day when he'd stopped the carriage. She hoped he wouldn't hold the lie against her.

Then a roseate thought slid into her mind. *Maybe...maybe he won't even remember me. Maybe he won't know I'm the same girl he spoke to on the street.*

Kathleen spent a rather restless night and was up at dawn. She prepared herself for meeting Peter Stallworth by arranging her hair differently than she had worn it the day he'd seen her on the street.

She was at the dining room table ahead of the other boarders, and Hattie Murphy made sure she had a hearty breakfast of creamy oatmeal with brown sugar, biscuits with strawberry jam, and plenty of hot coffee.

The cold wind off Lake Michigan put high color in Kathleen's cheeks. As she approached the Stallworth house, she thought the Stallworth men had probably already headed for downtown to the Great Lakes Railroad Company building. No doubt she would have to face Peter at the end of the day unless for some reason he got home too late. If that happened, she would just have to face their first meeting on Saturday.

As she passed through the open gate she felt butterflies in her stomach, and for a brief instant she thought of her dead family, their faces flashing on the screen of her mind. She pushed the painful memory aside and walked past the front entrance. She had learned at the Massey home that it was considered proper for employees to enter the house at the back door. She hurried alongside the huge house, turned the corner, and stepped up onto the back porch.

Kathleen turned the small handle beside the door and heard the bell ring inside. Her mind went to her family again, but she would not allow her grief to show. When she heard footsteps she squared her shoulders, lifted her delicate chin, put a smile on her rosy lips, and waited for the door to open.

When the latch rattled, Kathleen's lovely blue eyes glistened with anticipation and a touch of nervousness.

"Good morning, Kathleen!" Maria Stallworth said. "You're right on time! Just as I expected. LuAnn Massey was over last night. She said you did a marvelous job on their house."

"I'm glad she was pleased, ma'am," said Kathleen, pulling off her coat. "I'll do my best to please you the same way."

"I have no doubts about that. Let's start by taking a tour of the house; then you'll know what you're dealing with. I'll explain some things as we go along."

As Maria Stallworth guided her through the mansion, Kathleen saw that it was a bit larger than the Massey house and somewhat fancier. She knew she would have to keep moving at a good pace to get everything done according to Mrs. Stallworth's instructions and wishes.

When the tour was over, Kathleen was given her two uniforms. They were black with white collars and cuffs, and white, stiffly starched aprons that covered the dresses from collar to hem. To complete the uniform she was given two soft white mobcaps, each with a small ruffle encircling it.

Maria Stallworth showed Kathleen to a room where she could change. When she appeared in one of the uniforms—which fit perfectly—Maria said, "You look fine, Kathleen!"

"Thank you, Mrs. Stallworth."

Kathleen worked hard all morning, and Maria found her at noon in the master bedroom upstairs, polishing the dark wood of the huge bedstead. She took her downstairs to the kitchen, where she had prepared lunch for the two of them. While they ate, Maria told her of hiring Carlene Simms to cook, explaining that Carlene would start her job on Saturday but would not be living in.

The conversation then led to the Stallworths' railroad company, and Maria explained that their son Peter—who had graduated from the Chicago Institute of Business in May—had been given a position of junior vice president upon graduation.

Kathleen went back to work and was just finishing up her last job for the day in the big pantry off the kitchen when she heard male voices. They were coming down the hall from the front of the house toward the kitchen. Her heart began to race.

"Kathleen!" came Maria's voice. "My men are home. I want them to meet you!"

Kathleen swallowed hard and stepped into the kitchen.

"Kathleen, this is Mr. Stallworth…and this is our son, Peter."

Kathleen smiled at John, watching Peter from the corner of her eye. She did a curtsy and said, "I'm very glad to meet you, Mr. Stallworth."

Peter stared at her.

"And I'm glad to meet you, Kathleen," said John.

When her eyes met Peter's he said, "I know you, young lady!" He took a step closer. "We talked on the street the other day, remember?

You were leaning against a tree up the street, and—"

"Yes, I remember."

Peter had been stricken with Kathleen's beauty and sweet personality when they met on Tuesday. He was trying to recall what she had told him she was doing in the neighborhood, but it wouldn't come to mind.

Kathleen curtsied and said, "You were very kind to me the other day, Mr. Stallworth. I am glad to know who you are."

Peter chuckled. "Tell you what, Kathleen. Mr. Stallworth is my father. You can call me Peter."

Kathleen smiled and nodded.

As the sun dropped close to the western horizon, Kathleen made her way home. It had been a hard day but a good one. A tiny smile pulled at the corners of her mouth as she thought of how exceptionally handsome Peter was, and the way he had looked at her.

Then she shook her head and said aloud, "Don't be ridiculous, girl! He was only being nice and trying to put you at ease. Nothing more."

Upon arriving at the boardinghouse, Kathleen ate supper with Hattie and the other boarders. At bedtime she crawled into bed, picturing Peter Stallworth's warm eyes in her mind, and soon fell asleep.

At eight o'clock on Saturday morning, Kathleen rang the bell at the back door of the Stallworth mansion and was greeted by Maria, who took her into the kitchen and introduced her to Carlene Simms. Carlene was rather plain, with light brown hair and brown eyes, and was of a sweet disposition. The two young women liked each other immediately.

Upstairs, Kathleen encountered Mr. Stallworth in the hallway while sweeping. He was cordial and stopped to talk to her for a moment before vanishing down the winding staircase. While Kathleen was changing the sheets and pillowcases in the master bedroom, she heard Peter come out of his room and hasten to the staircase.

The morning went by quickly as she cleaned the master bedroom then changed the bedding in Peter's room and cleaned it thoroughly. She dusted and swept in the other bedrooms, then carried the bedding downstairs to the laundry room. She was doing the wash when Carlene came in and said, "It's our lunchtime, Kathleen. I've already fed the Stallworths."

"Oh. All right. What time is it?"

"Twelve-forty-five."

Kathleen left her washing and followed Carlene. She had baked several small loaves of bread, and the aroma filled the kitchen. They had bread and cheese together, along with hot tea.

After lunch Kathleen returned to the laundry room and finished the washing. Her next task—as directed by Maria—was to clean and dust the library on the ground floor at the rear of the mansion.

A small cart had been provided on each floor to transport cleaning equipment. As she pushed the cart down the hall toward the library, the door of the sitting room opened, and Maria appeared.

"How's it going, dear?" asked the dignified woman.

"Fine, ma'am. I'm finished with today's work upstairs, and the washing is done. The wash is hanging up to dry. I'm about to clean the library next."

"Good. Sounds like you're right on schedule. You did have lunch with Carlene, didn't you?"

"Yes, ma'am. Carlene makes good bread."

"We found that out," said Maria. "I won't detain you any longer, dear."

With that, Maria went back into the sitting room, and Kathleen pushed the cart to the rear of the house and opened the library door. She jumped when she saw Peter sitting at the desk. He shoved the chair back and rose to his feet.

"I didn't know you were here, sir!" she said.

Peter took a couple of steps toward her. "Please don't feel you have to apologize, Kathleen," he said in a gentle tone. "It's your job to clean the house. You can't be worrying about who's in what room."

"Well, sir, I knocked on your bedroom door before I entered it, but I didn't think about knocking at this door. I…I'm so embarrassed."

Peter took another step. "Please, Kathleen. Don't be. It's all right."

She released a slight smile. "Thank you, Mr. Stallworth."

Moving back to the desk, Peter said, "You go right ahead and do your work. You won't bother me."

"You're sure? I can come back later."

"No. Mom's got you on a work schedule, and far be it from me to interfere. You go ahead."

As she took her feather duster from the cart, Peter said, "And, Kathleen…"

"Yes, sir?"

"Remember, Mr. Stallworth is my father. I am Peter. I want you to call me Peter."

"Yes, sir."

"And you don't have to call me *sir*. Just Peter. Okay?"

She nodded. "Yes…Peter."

He smiled broadly. "That's better."

While Kathleen dusted expensive paintings, washed mirrors, swept rugs, mopped the hardwood floor, and polished furniture, Peter told her all about his father's company and his job as junior vice president.

As the one-sided conversation continued, Maria came out of the sitting room and moved down the hall. She stuck her head in the open library door and cut Peter off midsentence.

"Peter, you've been talking incessantly since this poor girl came in here to clean. I could hear you all the way from the sitting room. You need to stop the chatter and let her work."

"But, Mom," Peter said, "my talk hasn't slowed her one bit. She *is* getting her work done."

Maria glanced at Kathleen, who was polishing the mantel over the fireplace. "Well, honey, it looks like you're able to work in spite of my son's chatter."

"Yes, ma'am," said Kathleen with a smile. "I'm enjoying Peter's chatter. He's telling me all about his job and the company."

Maria grinned, shook her head, and walked away.

During the following week, Peter Stallworth could hardly get his mind off Kathleen O'Malley. She had captured his imagination and was close to capturing his heart. He couldn't wait till Saturday when he would see her again.

Kathleen, too, thought of Peter often. She admired him as a gentleman and found herself wishing he was from her part of town so they could be friends. At other times, Kathleen found portions of Dwight Moody's sermons going through her mind, especially when he used the words from the song Ira Sankey had sung:

> What Thou, My Lord, hath suffered
> Was all for sinners' gain:
> Mine, mine was the transgression,
> But Thine the deadly pain.

When Saturday came, Peter made sure he was in the kitchen with Carlene at eight o'clock. When the doorbell rang, Peter hurried to the back door and surprised Kathleen by being the one to let her in. Peter's mother happened into the kitchen at that very moment and saw her son fall all over himself as he ushered the Irish girl inside.

An expression of displeasure crossed Maria Stallworth's face.

Carlene, who had quietly observed it, ducked her head when the mistress looked her way.

During the morning, Kathleen was surprised when Peter appeared in different places in the mansion where she was working. He even offered to help her a couple of times, and she kindly told him it was her job and she would do it.

Early that afternoon, Maria hunted through the house for Peter and found him in the large parlor, where he was scooting the long, heavy couch back into place. He looked up and said, "Oh, hi, Mom. I was helping Kathleen. You know, so she didn't have to move the couch to clean underneath it and behind it."

"Your son is such a gentleman, Mrs. Stallworth," Kathleen said.

"Well, we've raised him to be that," Maria said, smiling at the girl. Then to her son: "Peter, your father is busy with some business papers in the library. I need you to drive me downtown. I have to do some shopping."

While mother and son rode in one of the Stallworth carriages toward downtown Chicago, Maria said, "I want to talk to you, Peter."

"About what, Mom?"

"About Kathleen."

"Yes?"

"You mustn't be so friendly to her, Peter. It doesn't look good."

"To whom?"

"Well, anyone who would see it. You mustn't show so much interest in a girl who cleans for us. You understand."

Peter was quiet for a moment as the carriage moved along State Street. Then he said, "Well, Mom, I guess I might as well be honest with you about it. I'm quite attracted to Kathleen. I've never met a girl with so much natural beauty and such a pleasant and warm personality."

Maria's eyes widened and her face went dead white. The lines around her mouth hardened as she said in a tight voice, "Peter, I'm not going to have this. You stay clear of Kathleen or I will terminate her job. Do you understand me?"

"All right, Mom. I'll not spend so much time around her on Saturdays. But you'd have a hard time finding a girl who does the quality of work she does."

Maria set her jaw. "Peter, you will not spend *any* time with

Kathleen. I mean what I say. If I see you giving her any more than a passing word, she goes. Am I making myself clear?"

Peter stared straight ahead. "Yes. You're making yourself clear."

That night, Peter was in his room getting ready for bed when he heard a tap on his door.

"Yes?"

"It's Dad. Can I come in?"

Peter opened the door. "Sure, Dad. Come in."

John stepped inside and closed the door. "Son, your mother talked to me about the attention you've been showing Kathleen."

"Mm-hmm."

"She said she's given you an ultimatum."

"Mm-hmm."

"You *do* understand that if you should get interested in Kathleen and let yourself fall in love with her, we would have a big problem on our hands. We can't have our son wanting to marry our cleaning lady."

John leaned close and looked Peter square in the eye. "You *do* understand that we couldn't let this happen, don't you, son?"

"Yes, sir."

"So?"

"All right, Dad. I won't pay any more attention to Kathleen."

John smiled, laid a hand on Peter's shoulder, and said, "That's my boy. I knew you'd see it our way."

9

WHEN KATHLEEN WASN'T THINKING of anything in particular, she often found her thoughts returning to Dwight Moody's sermons. On this Sunday, as she washed windows in her room that overlooked the street, it happened again. Immediately she forced her thoughts to the contemplation of handsome Peter Stallworth. *If only we were on the same social level...*

As she dried the window, movement on the street below caught her attention. A carriage was pulling up in front of the boarding-house—a very familiar carriage.

She set aside her cloth and pail and dashed out the door and down the stairs.

Hattie Murphy, who had seen the carriage arrive, moved toward the front door and what she thought was a prospective roomer.

"I'll take care of it, Hattie," Kathleen said, rushing past her. "He's a friend of mine."

"A mighty good-lookin' friend, I might say!" Hattie said with a wink.

Kathleen opened the door and looked up breathlessly at young Stallworth.

"Hello, Peter. I...I was upstairs in my room washing my windows when I saw you drive up."

Peter tipped his hat, smiled broadly, and said, "It's nice to see you, too, Kathleen."

"I suppose you happened to be in the neighborhood and decided to drop by?"

"Ah…no. As a matter of fact, I'm here because I need to talk to you."

"Oh? Mrs. Murphy has a rule that no men are allowed upstairs unless they're boarders. But we could go to the parlor and talk."

"All right," Peter said.

When they entered the parlor, Peter stopped short as his gaze took in the gathering. Some of the boarders were sitting together and chatting, while others were reading, and still others were occupied playing checkers or chess.

He looked around. "It's…a bit crowded in here, Kathleen. Could you and I take a walk?"

"All right. I'll just run upstairs and get my coat."

Peter's heart skipped a beat as he watched the beautiful Irish maiden descending the stairs wearing her coat and bonnet. He held open the door for her and guided her down the porch steps. His horse nickered as they walked past the carriage and along the boardwalk.

Kathleen looked up at Peter expectantly.

"I've run into a problem," he said.

"Is it something I can help you with?"

He looked at her with a slanted grin. "Well, not exactly. It's just something I need to tell you, and I'm hoping you will understand."

"I'll try."

Peter hesitated for a long moment, then said, "Kathleen, I like you very much, and as you've probably figured out, I find ways to be with you when I'm home. The problem is…well, my parents have noticed, and they're afraid I'm getting interested in you. People with the kind of money my parents have always want their children to keep their friendships within the circle of people who are on the same level financially."

Kathleen felt a cold flutter in her stomach.

"My parents have told me if I don't stay away from you, they'll find another cleaning lady."

She slowed her pace and came to a stop. "Peter, I'm sorry to be a problem to you and your family. When I come to work Tuesday, I'll tell your mother I'm quitting."

"No, no! Please don't do that. I have another solution."

The afternoon breeze toyed with Kathleen's long hair as she watched his face with sober eyes.

"I really do like you a lot," Peter said. "And…and I think you like me, don't you?"

"Very much."

Peter smiled. "I'm glad! Then my solution will allow you to keep your job *and* allow us to see each other."

"Are you sure your parents want to keep me on?"

"Oh, yes. They like your work, and they like you."

"So it's just my social status that concerns them."

"That's it. I don't like this different social level stuff, but it exists, and I have to live with it, at least for the present."

"I understand, Peter. And I appreciate your attitude about it. So what is your solution?"

"Simply this: When I'm home on Saturdays—or any other time you're in the house—I'll stay away from you. But I'll come by your boardinghouse often to see you. We can take walks together, and I can take you for rides in my carriage. That way we can be together without causing any problems for either of us with my parents."

Kathleen thought on it a moment. "But if your parents find out, I'll still end up getting fired, and you'll be in deep trouble with them."

"How would they find out? They certainly don't know anybody in this part of town."

Kathleen shrugged.

"So can I come see you often?"

"All right," she said softly.

"Wonderful!" Peter said, grabbing her hand in his enthusiasm. "Most of the time it will have to be Sunday afternoons, but I'll try to come by at other times, too."

"Peter," Kathleen said, her heart thumping wildly, "you are always welcome."

He gazed deeply into her sky blue eyes. "I'm glad to hear that. Could we walk a little longer before I take you back to the boarding-house?"

"Why, yes. Of course."

Peter tucked her arm through his and they proceeded to stroll down the street, enjoying the crisp fall day.

An hour later he watched her climb the stairs to the second floor of the boardinghouse. When she entered her room, she dashed to the window and looked down on the street from behind the curtains. Peter was just climbing into the carriage. As he pulled away, a smile played across Kathleen's lips, and she let out a deep sigh.

"Oh, Peter," she said in a half whisper, "I wish things were different. I wish we could meet on equal terms."

As the days turned into weeks, Peter visited Kathleen every Sunday and sometimes showed up late evenings. On those occasions, they sat in the parlor and just enjoyed being in each other's presence.

Whenever Peter was in the Stallworth mansion on Kathleen's workdays, they only spoke casually in passing.

John and Maria were pleased, assured by Peter's conduct that he had lost interest in the girl.

In her heart, Kathleen's secret meetings with Peter made her feel disloyal to the Stallworths. They had given her a job when she was almost at the end of her rope, and they had treated her well.

At times she chastised herself and even felt that if her parents knew about it they would disapprove of her conduct. But Kathleen O'Malley was falling in love with Peter Stallworth, and try as she might, she could not stop seeing him.

The new year came, and on a January Sunday in 1872, Kathleen waited at her window, knowing that Peter would arrive around one o'clock. The ground was covered with a foot of snow. When he pulled up in front of the boardinghouse, she slipped into her coat, put a wool scarf over her head, then pulled on wool gloves and hurried down the stairs.

Peter was in the front hall, greeting Hattie Murphy.

"I'm ready for our ride," Kathleen said, rushing down the last couple of stairs.

Peter's face lit up when he saw her. "I've heated stones and put them in the carriage for your feet."

"What a gentleman!" Hattie said. "Kathleen, you'd better hang on to him."

"Well, I plan to!"

When Peter helped Kathleen into the carriage, his breath came out in small clouds as he said, "Did you really mean that?"

"Mean what?" She eased onto the seat and reached for the lap robe.

"That you plan to keep me?"

"Of course."

"I'm sure glad about that." He rounded the carriage and pulled himself onto the seat beside her.

"Good friends should never throw each other away," she said while watching him adjust the blanket over their legs to keep in the heat from the stones.

He took up the reins and set the carriage in motion. "And people who are *more* than good friends shouldn't either, young lady."

"Young lady, eh? Well, I'm not as young as I was yesterday."

The carriage rocked as it went over a pile of snow in the street.

"So you're another day older," Peter said, smiling wryly. "So am I."

"I didn't mean another *day*, silly. I meant another *year*. Today's my birthday. I'm eighteen now."

"Oh, Kathleen, I wish I'd known. I would have brought you a birthday present."

"That's not necessary," she said, looking toward a group of boys who were sledding down a hill. "It's birthday present enough just to be with you today."

On Monday Kathleen worked at the Massey mansion. She finished the day's assignments late in the afternoon and told LuAnn Massey good-bye.

The outside air was bitterly cold, and as Kathleen tramped through the snow, she pulled her collar tight around her neck and turned her face from the wind. She soon reached the edge of the wealthy section, crossed the street, and headed for downtown.

Moments later, as she walked briskly along the boardwalk, a carriage pulled alongside her.

"Hello, pretty lady," Peter said. "May I offer you a ride?"

As he helped her into the carriage she said, "Aren't you off work a little early?"

"Just a bit. Dad's staying at the office for a special meeting with his attorneys. One of them lives close to us, so he'll deliver Dad home. I just had to see you right now."

Kathleen's pulse quickened as she waited for Peter to circle the carriage and climb in beside her. He reached behind the seat and brought out a small gift-wrapped package.

"Happy birthday one day late."

"Oh, Peter, you shouldn't have!"

"Yes, I should. Go ahead. Open it."

Kathleen took off her gloves to untie the ribbon on the black velvet jewelry box. Her heart leaped when she lifted the lid and set her eyes on the expensive onyx brooch.

"Oh, Peter, it's beautiful! I will treasure it always."

Peter took Kathleen's hand and said, "You're the sweetest, most beautiful girl I have ever met. I...I think I'm falling in love with you."

When he saw fear shadow her features he said, "I'm sorry, Kathleen. I didn't mean to—"

"No, don't be sorry, Peter. I must admit I have very strong feelings toward *you*, but we dare not let this go any further."

"Why?"

"Because it would turn your parents against you. I can't allow myself to become a wedge between you."

He looked at her for a long moment, then said, "I've tried to keep my feelings for you a secret, but...well, it just had to come out.

117

I can't help it, Kathleen. You're on my mind day and night. I've never known a girl like you."

"Peter," she said with quavering voice, "you're on my mind day and night, too. But we can never be more than good friends. I'm not from your world. If we were to let our feelings take their natural course, it would ruin things between you and your parents. Why, your parents might even disinherit you. I've heard of things like that happening. I just can't be the cause of it, Peter."

"See what I mean? You are the sweetest, most beautiful girl I've ever met."

Kathleen looked down at the brooch. "This means more to me than I could ever tell you, Peter. We must let it be the symbol of a beautiful friendship." She raised her eyes to his and revealed the tears welling up.

Peter sighed, his breath making tiny puffs on the cold air. "I wish things were different, Kathleen."

"Me, too. But they're not."

"I can still come and see you on Sunday afternoons, can't I? And sometimes in between, as I've been doing?"

Kathleen shook her head. "It's best that we not see each other that much. Maybe just once in a while."

"But I need to be with you. The only time I feel really alive is when we're together. Please, Kathleen—"

"Oh, Peter, I need to be with you, too. But we dare not—"

"At least on Sundays?"

Kathleen pressed shaky fingers to her temples. "I just—"

"Please?"

She set her soft gaze on him and let a tiny smile tug at the corners of her mouth. "All right. Sundays."

As the weeks passed, Peter managed to be away from home on Tuesdays and Thursdays when Kathleen worked at the Stallworth mansion. On Saturdays, he would pass by her and speak cordially, but that was all.

Sundays were a different matter. Spring came, and one Sunday afternoon in April, Peter and Kathleen were strolling through a park not far from her boardinghouse. Trees were budding and the grass was turning green. Birds flitted through the trees, chirping noisily. As they drew near an unoccupied park bench, Peter said, "Could we sit down here for a few minutes? I need to talk to you about something."

He removed his hat and turned to face her. "I can't stand this 'friendship' situation any longer. I love you, Kathleen. Just being friends is not enough. I want you to be my wife. I'm asking you here and now to marry me."

A tremor rocked through Kathleen O'Malley. "I—"

"You *are* in love with me, aren't you?"

Tears surfaced in her eyes as she said, "Yes, Peter, yes! I am just as in love with you! But—"

"Will you marry me?"

She bit her lips. "I want to be your wife more than anything in this world. But it can never be. Think about your parents. If you tell them you're going to marry me, they'll disown you."

Peter moved closer and took her in his arms. For a brief moment she held herself stiff, but as he looked deeply into her tear-filled eyes, she gave in to his embrace…and to his lips. The kiss was sweet and tender, and when he released her, he held her close and spoke in a half whisper.

"Darling, will you marry me?"

"Oh, Peter, I want to say yes so badly, but I can't allow you to—"

"I'm willing to let the chips fall where they may, darling. If Dad fires me, I'll get another job. More than anything in this world I want you for my wife. Will you marry me?"

Kathleen brushed tears from her cheeks. "I love you, Peter. I really do want to be your wife. But I don't think I can stand it if I come between you and your parents."

"Maybe I can change their minds. Will you let me handle it?"

She swallowed with difficulty. "All right."

Peter put the horse and carriage in the barn and headed for the back door of the Stallworth mansion. Upon entering the kitchen he found Carlene Simms at the stove and asked if she knew where his parents were. Carlene told him they were in the parlor.

John and Maria broke off their conversation when Peter found them and said he needed to talk to them.

He sat down and faced them with a sober expression on his face. "Mom…Dad…I'm your only child, and I know you want what is best for me now and in the future."

"Of course we do, Peter," his father said. "And we were just talking about your social life. We haven't heard anything about any young women you've been seeing, yet you're out quite often."

All at once Peter blurted out, "I've been less than honest with you these past few months. I haven't cut off my friendship with Kathleen. I've been seeing her every Sunday afternoon and sometimes during the week. I'm in love with her, and she's in love with me. I want to marry her."

John's face went crimson, and Maria looked as if she might faint.

John was the first to speak. "You're not serious!"

"I *am* serious, Dad."

Maria's ashen features turned rigid. "That girl's got plenty of nerve! Coming in here acting so sweet and innocent, and all the time she was seeing you behind our backs!"

"Don't blame Kathleen, Mom. It's my doing. I'm the one who talked her into seeing me and keeping it from you. She balked at first, not wanting to do it without you knowing about it."

"At *first?* Well, she did go along with it, didn't she!"

"Mom, Kathleen is the most wonderful girl in all the world. She's the perfect girl for me. The fact that she comes from the other side of town doesn't change a thing."

"Well, it does as far as we're concerned!" John said. "You've got to come to your senses!"

"Peter, if you were to marry this peasant girl, you'd bring shame on our family!" Maria said, her hands trembling. "Our friends and neighbors…what would they think?"

"Tell us you'll reconsider," John said. "Take some time and think it over."

Peter shook his head in frustration. "But doesn't my happiness mean anything? What about the love I have in my heart for this precious girl? Doesn't that matter?"

"Your happiness matters to us tremendously, son," Maria said.

Peter's father nodded. "We want nothing but the best for you. We want you to marry a girl who will make you happy, but it has to be the *right* girl."

Peter looked at the floor for several moments, then said, "I love you both, and I want things to be right between us. For now, all I'm asking is that you try to understand my feelings."

"We don't want to hurt you, son," John said. "We just want what's best for you."

"All right, I'm glad of that. I apologize for seeing Kathleen behind your backs. I should have been honest with you. So I'll be honest with you right now. I'm still going to spend time with her. And I will not act like she's invisible when she and I are in the house at the same time. I'm being up-front with you, okay?"

A look passed between John and Maria, and he gave her a slight nod.

"All right, son," John said.

On Tuesday, Kathleen rang the bell at the back door of the Stallworth mansion and was greeted by Carlene. She immediately headed through the house for the winding staircase, for on Tuesdays she always started her work on the second floor.

She mounted the stairs and went to the closet where her cart and cleaning equipment were stored, and reached for the doorknob.

"Kathleen! Just leave the cart in the closet!"

Kathleen backed away from the door, waiting for Maria to reach her. "Is there a change in plans today, ma'am?"

"There sure is. You're not cleaning one more day in this house. You're fired! Get out!"

"Wh-what do you mean?"

"Peter confessed that he's been seeing you on the sly! Shame on you, Kathleen! I brought you in here and gave you a job because I trusted you. I thought you were a nice girl. Well, I found out Sunday night that you've been seeing my son behind my back when you knew how I felt about it. Peter told his father and me that he's through with you. He doesn't want anything to do with you anymore. Now get out!"

Kathleen felt the strength drain from her body. Her voice sounded faint as she said, "I...I'll bring the uniforms back to you, Mrs. Stallworth."

"Forget the uniforms! I just want you out of my sight and out of my house, *right now!*"

As Kathleen walked toward the spiral staircase, Maria shouted, "Sneak! Seeing my son behind my back! How much lower can you get? I'm going over to LuAnn's house right now and tell her all about you! She'll fire you, too!"

A wave of nausea washed over Kathleen as she moved down the hall. When she entered the kitchen, Carlene gave her a sorrowful look, "I'm sorry," she whispered.

Kathleen nodded without speaking and picked up her coat. As she walked away from the Stallworths' neighborhood her shoulders drooped, and tears coursed down her cheeks. There was no use in even going to the Massey house tomorrow. Maria Stallworth would have already persuaded Mrs. Massey to fire her.

People stared at the girl who walked with her head bowed, tears dripping from her chin. She didn't even notice them, so great was her sorrow. She had lost her family in the fire, and now she had lost her livelihood and...Peter.

That evening, Hattie Murphy happened to be near the front door of the boardinghouse when she saw Peter Stallworth come in.

"Hello, Hattie!" Peter said, smiling. "How are you?"

Hattie's cheeks were flushed, and her eyes were aflame with indignation. "I was fine till I saw you!"

"What do you mean? Hattie...what's the matter?"

"What's the matter? How do you expect me to feel after the way you broke that poor girl's heart?"

Peter frowned. "What are you talking about?"

"Kathleen didn't come down to supper tonight. I went up to her room to see if she was all right, and she was crying her eyes out. Your mother fired her this morning and told her you said you were through with her. You didn't want anything to do with her anymore. And your mother told her she'd get Mrs. Massey to fire her, too."

Peter was stunned. "Mrs. Murphy, what my mother told Kathleen about me was a lie! I never said any such thing. I love Kathleen with all of my heart, and I want to marry her!"

Hattie cocked her head and looked him straight in the eye. "Do you really mean that, Peter?"

"I sure do!"

"Then I'm giving you permission to go up there and tell it to Kathleen in the privacy of her room. Come with me. She probably won't open the door if you knock and tell her it's you."

Kathleen lay sprawled across the bed. She had cried until there seemed to be no more tears left. The only good thing that had happened to her all day was that Hattie had told her she could stay in the room and eat her meals without cost until she was able to find work.

When the tap came at the door, she sat up and called out, "Who is it?"

"It's Mrs. Murphy, honey."

Kathleen's eyes were swollen and her hair was somewhat unkempt as she opened the door. "Yes, Mrs. Murphy?"

"Honey, there's somebody here who wants to talk to you."

When Peter stepped into view, Kathleen was speechless.

"My mother lied to you this morning," he said. "I did *not* say I was through with you, and I did *not* say I wanted nothing more to do with you. I love you, Kathleen. I want you to be my wife."

"That's why he's up here with my permission, honey," Hattie said. "I want you two to have a good talk."

"May I come in?" Peter asked.

When Kathleen threw her arms around him, Hattie's eyes filled with tears. Sniffing, she said, "I'll see you two later."

It took only a few moments for Peter to apologize for his mother's cruelty. After a tender kiss, he held Kathleen in his arms and said, "Sweetheart, you don't have to worry about finding more jobs."

"I know, Peter. Your mother's not going to hire me back, and Mrs. Massey won't either—"

"That's not what I meant. What I mean is, we're going to get married right away. I will provide for you. You won't have to work."

"But your father—"

"If he fires me I'll get another job. This is a big city. I have a good education in business. We'll be fine. Will you marry me?"

"Oh, yes, my darling! I'll marry you!"

They sealed it with a kiss.

On Saturday, April 27, 1872, Peter had been gone from the Stallworth mansion since early morning. When he returned late in the afternoon, Carlene Simms was mopping the kitchen floor. Most of the cleaning work had fallen on her until Maria could find someone to take Kathleen's place.

As he passed through the kitchen, he saw his mother in the hallway near the dining room.

"Well, there's my wandering boy," she said. "Where have you been all day?"

"That's what I want to talk to you and Dad about. Where is he?"

"In the library. Is there something wrong?"

"Very."

Maria felt a tightening in her stomach as she led the way.

"John," she said, pushing open the library door, "Peter wants to talk to us. He says it's about something very serious."

John's desk was spread with papers. "I'm pretty busy right now," he said, looking at Peter. "Couldn't this wait till after dinner tonight?"

"I won't be here after dinner tonight, Dad," Peter said softly.

"What do you mean?" Deep lines formed across John Stallworth's brow.

Peter pulled a chair up beside his father and seated his mother in it, then eased onto a chair facing them and said, "Mom, Dad...I love you both with all my heart. I hope you know that."

They nodded, studying his face.

"We love you the same, son," said John.

"Enough to wish me happiness in my marriage?"

10

"Y-YOUR WHAT?" STAMMERED Peter's mother.

"Kathleen and I were married about two hours ago. A preacher performed the ceremony in his office."

A look of horror flashed over his parents' faces.

Before either could speak, Peter said, "We rented a house in an upper-middle-class neighborhood on Thursday evening. Kathleen is there now. I told her that once you knew we were married, I believed you would accept her as your daughter-in-law. She's pacing the floor, waiting for me to return and tell her that you will."

Maria seemed in the grip of a mighty paralysis, but there was a cold flame in John Stallworth's eyes as he jumped to his feet and roared, "We will *not* accept that peasant as our daughter-in-law! And what's more, you're fired! And you're disinherited!"

Peter took a deep breath. "Social position means more to you than your love for me…is that it, Dad?"

Maria finally found her voice. "Peter, I tried to save you from that girl."

"I know, Mom, and you lied to do it. You're my mother, and I love you more than words can ever describe, but you were wrong to tell Kathleen that I said I was through with her."

"I was only trying to spare you a miserable and unhappy life with her!"

"No, you were trying to spare yourself some embarrassment by keeping your son from marrying a girl you think is beneath you. That's it, isn't it, Mom?"

Maria stared at him silently, her lips pressed into a thin line.

Peter sighed as he rose to his feet. "I'd better get back to my bride. I'd hug you, but I guess you don't want that from me anymore. I'll come to the office and clean out my desk on Monday, Dad. I'll take my clothes and personal items here in the house with me now."

He turned and headed for the library door.

John and Maria exchanged pain-filled glances.

"Wait a minute, son," John said as Peter reached for the doorknob.

Peter looked over his shoulder and waited for his father to speak.

"I can't do what I said. I was angry, son. You can keep your job if you want it."

"Of course I want it, Dad. I love working for you and for the company."

Relief showed on the senior Stallworth's face. He glanced at his wife, then looked back at Peter. "And you can forget what I said about disinheriting you."

Maria moved up beside her husband. "I'm glad you're going to stay with the company, Peter. And I'm in agreement with Dad. I don't want you disinherited. But—"

"But what, Mom?"

"Neither of us want anything to do with Kathleen. You can come here whenever you want, but we don't want that girl in our home."

Peter felt a surge of anger and his jaw hardened, but he bit his tongue. "I'm sorry you feel this way about Kathleen…but I'll still come by the house often. And Dad, I'll see you at the office on Monday."

He opened the library door.

"Wait a minute, Peter." Maria rushed up and put her arms around him.

He hugged her in return and said, "I love you, Mom."

"I love you, too," she said on a sob.

Peter noted the anguish on his father's face, then went upstairs to get his belongings.

Kathleen was brokenhearted when Peter came home and told her how it went with his parents, but she agreed that he'd made the right decision to keep his job.

Their love for each other deepened and grew daily as the weeks passed. Kathleen kept their home lovely and inviting, and Peter learned that she was an excellent cook as well as a loving, devoted wife.

The wall between Kathleen and the Stallworths was a heavy burden on her heart, but she was finding happiness in spite of it with the man she loved.

They had a few friends in the neighborhood, but no one they were especially close to. They seemed happiest when they were alone together.

Spring faded into summer, and summer was soon giving way to autumn. Nothing changed in how the Stallworths felt about their daughter-in-law.

Kathleen had sent personal birthday gifts to both John and Maria, trying to show them she cared about them. Both times Peter returned home with the rejected gifts.

Soon the leaves fell from the trees, the grass turned tawny, and cold weather returned to Chicago.

In early November, there were a few days in a row when Kathleen felt light-headed and seemed to run out of energy. She kept it to herself, not wanting to worry Peter.

Then came a Monday morning when she sent Peter off to work and started washing the breakfast dishes. The smell of bacon grease was suddenly repulsive, and Kathleen had to run to the "necessary," where she lost her breakfast.

When she returned to the kitchen her head began to swim, and the room seemed to whirl around her. Perspiration coated her brow, and she used the wall to brace herself as she edged toward the bedroom.

Gingerly she eased onto the bed and closed her eyes to make the room stop swirling.

Suddenly a tiny smile crept across her pale face, and she patted her midsection. *Could it really be?*

She rested for a few minutes, then went back to the kitchen. Four weeks ago she had suspected she might be pregnant. Now she decided it was indeed quite possible. However, she'd wait a few more days before saying anything to Peter.

Morning sickness prevailed for four more mornings, each time after Peter had already gone to work. By Friday morning, Kathleen was sure there was new life growing within her. It was time to share this heaven-sent news with her husband.

When Peter came home from work that evening, he was surprised to see candles on the dining room table and the lanterns in the dining room turned low. Looking a bit puzzled, he took his wife of seven months into his arms and said, "Hey, darling, what's this? Supper in the dining room…and by candlelight?"

Kathleen giggled and kissed him. "Mm-hmm."

"What's the occasion?"

"Oh, it's a very special one."

Peter noticed a glow about his wife that he'd never seen before, and there was a hint of mischief in her beautiful Irish eyes. "All right, Mrs. Stallworth," he said, laying his hands on her shoulders, "what's this all about?"

"Darling, I was going to make you wait all through the meal and then tell you, but I can't put it off any longer. We…we—"

"Well, come on. Out with it! We *what?*"

"We're going to have a baby!" she exclaimed, throwing herself into his arms.

"What? A baby! Really?"

"Yes!"

"Are you sure?"

"Yes!"

"Me…a father! Wow!"

Kathleen giggled again. "I knew you'd be happy about it."

"Happy! Sweetheart, I'm *ecstatic!* When?"

"If all goes as I've calculated, it'll be in early June."

Peter kissed her, then held her close and whispered words of love and endearment. This was the greatest moment since the day of his marriage.

The next day Peter drove to his parents' home, sat them down, and told them about the baby. They had a hard time knowing how to act. They wanted Peter to know they were happy they would soon be grandparents, but they couldn't forget who their grandchild's mother was.

When Peter was gone, John said, "Honey…our only child. He's the only one who can give us grandchildren. I don't want that child growing up without knowing us."

Maria shook her head slowly. "Yes, we might have to change our approach here. Let's think on it some more."

On June 9, 1873, Kathleen Stallworth gave birth to a beautiful baby girl they named Megan Kathleen and called "Meggie." Peter was the typical proud father and wanted desperately for his parents to know her. When he informed them they had a new granddaughter, they asked him to bring her to the house.

Peter said the only way Meggie could come was if Kathleen came too. The Stallworths readily agreed, saying they had been discussing it. Kathleen could come to their home.

Peter was elated and rushed home to tell Kathleen. An hour later, the proud parents were on the doorstep of the Stallworth mansion. John and Maria were cool toward Kathleen, but they were instantly captured by little Meggie, who had a head of thick black hair and big blue eyes the same shade as Kathleen's.

After that, Peter and Kathleen brought Meggie to the Stallworth mansion twice a week. With each visit it was obvious that John and Maria only tolerated Kathleen, but they adored Meggie and showered her with gifts. The more the Stallworths saw of their grand-daughter the more they doted on her. Though it hurt Kathleen to be treated coldly by her in-laws, for Peter and Meggie's sake, she endured it.

Four years passed. It was a warm afternoon in May 1877, in Virginia City, Nevada, when a very pregnant Loretta Harned sat holding a glass of lemonade and watched Hilda Jensen dust the furniture in the parlor.

Tom and Loretta now lived in a real house instead of a miner's shack. It was small compared to some of the houses in town, but quite comfortable. The Comstock Lode was still producing silver, and though Tom's wages had increased somewhat over the years, they still had only a small amount put aside for Tom to stake his own claim on a gold mine.

Loretta had suffered two miscarriages since giving birth to Caleb, losing both babies in the last stages of pregnancy. The first miscarriage had taken place nearly three years ago, and the second a little over a year and a half ago.

Hilda Jensen's husband, a silver miner, had died five years previously in a mine accident. When Tom learned that Loretta was expecting another child, he hired Hilda to do the housecleaning. It was enough that Loretta insisted on cooking the meals, but Tom would not hear of her doing the washing or the housework. This new baby must live.

The old clock on the mantel began chiming almost as soon as Hilda touched it with the dust cloth. When it chimed the third time, Loretta worked her way out of the overstuffed chair, picked up the half-full glass of lemonade, and said, "Well, Hilda, it's almost time for my boy to get home from school."

Hilda smiled as she watched Loretta make her laborious way to the front porch. Then she picked up her broom and dustpan and moved from the parlor to the bedroom down a short hallway.

Loretta eased herself into an old rocking chair on the porch and sipped at the lemonade as she kept her eyes on the road. A few minutes later, she saw some children coming her way, and among them was her six-year-old son.

She set loving eyes on the boy who ran toward the porch. The afternoon sunshine gleamed on his golden hair. To Loretta it looked like a halo.

"Mommy!" he called, bounding up on the porch and into her arms.

Loretta squeezed him tight. "I love you, Caleb!" She kissed the top of his head and said, "You're Mommy's little angel boy!"

Caleb giggled as he looked into her eyes. "You've called me that before, Mommy. Why do you say I'm your little angel boy?"

Loretta kissed him on the cheek this time and said, "It's the sunshine on your hair. Some people say heaven's angels have a light around their heads. The light is called a halo. That's what your blond hair looks like when the sun shines on it."

Caleb wrapped his arms around her neck and kissed her cheek, saying, "I love you, Mommy. You're the best mommy in all the world, an' I love you with all my heart!"

They held on to each other, then Loretta said, "Mommy's got to go to the kitchen and peel some onions, potatoes, and carrots for supper."

As she stood up, Caleb looked at her swollen middle. "How long is it till my baby brother is gonna be born?"

Loretta winced as a sharp pain ran across her back. "Just about four weeks, honey. But Caleb…"

"Yes, ma'am?"

"I've told you many times that it could be a little sister. I know you want a little brother to play with, but you can play with a little sister, too."

"But not cowboys an' In'ians. Only boys play cowboys an' In'ians."

"But you would love the baby if it turned out to be a girl, wouldn't you?"

"Uh-huh. Only I know it's a boy."

Loretta smiled to herself. "Are you going to stay outside or are you going in the house with me?"

"Could I help you fix supper?"

"I'm sure I can find something for you to do."

"Okay. That's what I'll do."

Caleb took his mother's hand as if to help her through the door. Just as they stepped inside, Hilda said, "I'm all through for the day, Loretta. I'll be going now. Hello, Caleb."

"Hello, Mrs. Jensen," the boy said politely.

"Thank you, Hilda. You sure do a wonderful job. Has your arthritis been bothering you today?"

"Quite a bit, honey," said the gray-haired woman, rubbing her right arm and shoulder. "I sure hope you'll be able to take over the household duties shortly after the baby is born. I'm not going to be able to do it much longer."

"There's no reason I can't," said Loretta. "Once the baby's born, I'm sure I can handle it."

"I'll help her, too," put in Caleb. "I'll take care of my little brother so Mommy can do the housework an' the washin' an' stuff."

Hilda glanced at Loretta, who shook her head and looked at the ceiling.

"I know you'll be a great help to your mother, Caleb," Hilda said, patting the top of his head.

"I sure will! I'm gonna teach my brother how to play cowboys an' In'ians, too!"

Hilda did a quick calculation and realized that Loretta was now better than a month past the time in her pregnancy when she'd lost the other two babies. "I'm glad you're doing so well, honey," she said. "Looks like you'll go full term on this one."

"I'm very encouraged," Loretta said, smiling. "Everything's going to be all right this time."

Tom Harned arrived home at suppertime and was greeted with a big hug by Caleb, and a hug and kiss by his wife.

During supper the Harneds talked about the new baby and Hilda's worsening arthritis. Loretta assured him she could handle the housework once the baby was born.

When the meal was over, Tom helped Loretta do the dishes and clean up the kitchen. He was just drying the last dish when there was a knock at the front door.

"I'll get it, honey," he said.

A man and woman in their midthirties stood on the front porch. "Mr. Harned?" the man said.

"Yes."

"My name is Bruce Humbert, sir, and this is my wife, Laurie. I have just become pastor of the church here in town. Laurie and I are visiting everyone in Virginia City to get to know them."

Tom reached out and shook hands with both of them. "Please, come in," he said. "My good friend Hank Mitchell and his wife, Donna, are members of the church. Hank told me a new pastor was coming."

As Tom closed the door behind the Humberts, the preacher said, "The Mitchells told us about you and your family. They were especially wanting us to visit you."

Loretta came into the parlor with Caleb, and Tom introduced them to the Humberts.

The preacher smiled and ruffled the boy's hair. "I like the name *Caleb*. It's a Bible name."

"We named him after one of Loretta's uncles," Tom said.

Everyone sat down, and Laurie turned to Loretta. "When's your baby due, Mrs. Harned?"

"In just about four weeks."

"I'd be very happy to help you in any way I can when the baby comes."

Loretta smiled. "I just might take you up on it."

"Please do. I really mean it."

Tom looked at Humbert appraisingly and said, "Loretta and I know that Virginia City has been tough on preachers. From what Hank and Donna have told us, the last two got so discouraged they just gave up and left town. Do you think you can take the rough treatment the miners will put on you, Pastor Humbert?"

Humbert grinned. "I'm willing to try. I'll preach the gospel of Jesus Christ and do everything I can to get the people of this town saved. Death comes to all, and eternity's beyond that. I want to keep as many people from going to hell, and take as many with me to heaven, as I can."

Neither Tom nor Loretta commented.

Humbert went on. "Hank and Donna told us they've talked to both of you about salvation."

"Yes, they have," said Tom, "but we don't look at it like the Mitchells do."

"How's that?"

"Well, Hank and Donna say we have no chance to go to heaven when we die unless we repent of our sin and open our hearts to Jesus Christ."

"And how do you look at it?" Humbert asked.

"Loretta and I believe that we'll go to heaven when we die because we're good, honest people, and we live moral lives."

"Are you sinners?"

"Well...yes. We don't always do everything right."

"What about your sins? Is God going to let you into heaven with your sins on your record?"

"Well...I...uh..."

The preacher pulled a small Bible from the inside pocket of his suit coat and said, "Mind if I read to you what God says about it?"

Tom glanced at Loretta, then turned back to the preacher. "No, go ahead."

Humbert read several Scripture passages describing mankind's sinful condition. Then he said, "Mr. and Mrs. Harned, the apostle Paul tells us in the book of Romans that the gospel of Christ is the power of God unto salvation to everyone who believes it. And in 1 Corinthians Paul gives us God's definition of the gospel, when he writes that 'Christ died for our sins according to the scriptures; and that he was buried, and that he rose again the third day according to the scriptures.'

"Jesus literally died and was buried. But a dead Christ could save no one. He broke the bands of death and came out of the tomb. He's alive to save all who will believe and repent of their sin and put their faith in Him alone to save them. In the gospel there's not one mention of our good works or religious deeds such as baptism, communion, church membership, and the like. The most righteous deeds we can perform are filthy rags before God. There's no way we're going to live good enough to get ourselves to heaven. Salvation is open to everyone who will put their faith in Jesus and Him alone to save them."

"Pastor," Tom said, "the Mitchells have shown us this before, and we understand it, but Loretta and I will tell you, as we've told Hank and Donna, you have your way of believing about God, and we have ours."

Bruce Humbert's heart was heavy. "But our way of believing is based on the Word of God, Mr. Harned. What's yours based on?"

Tom blinked and looked around for a moment, then settled his gaze on Loretta as he said, "Just how we feel, sir. The 'gospel trail' simply isn't our cup of tea. But I'll tell you what I've told Hank over and over again. I appreciate your caring enough about us to give us your point of view."

Pastor Humbert returned his Bible to his coat pocket and said, "All I can do is ask you to think on what I've shown you from the Bible and invite you to come to church and listen to me preach. Will you do that?"

"We'll think on it, Pastor," Tom said. "And who knows? Maybe one of these days we'll pop in and surprise you at church."

Humbert rose to his feet. "You folks have been very kind to listen, and I thank you."

Laurie moved to Loretta's side and said, "Mrs. Harned, please let me help you if there's anything at all I can do after the baby comes."

Loretta struggled to her feet and smiled at Laurie.

"I'll do that, Mrs. Humbert. And thank you."

11

SUNRISE STREAKED ACROSS LAKE MICHIGAN in sheets of vivid colors under a buttermilk sky, tinting the city of Chicago a reddish gold.

Peter Stallworth opened his eyes as the brilliant colors streamed through the bedroom windows. Kathleen was stirring next to him, making little sounds that indicated she was coming awake.

Peter rolled out of bed and padded to the closest window. He stood in awe at the glory of the sunrise and turned to see his wife blinking her eyes as she tried to focus on him.

"Kathleen," he said, a lilt in his voice. "Come here and look at this!"

The beautiful redhead covered a yawn, threw back the covers, and picked up her robe. Just as she reached the window, Peter took her by the hand and put an arm around her waist. "Set your peepers on that sunrise, honey!" he said.

Its graphic beauty put Kathleen in awe. "Oh, Peter! Isn't it marvelous!"

"I've seen a lot of sunrises in my time," he said, "but this one tops them all."

"I won't disagree, but do you *really* want to see something beautiful?" She took his hand. "Come with me."

Together they moved into the hall and paused at the open door of the adjoining room. Four-year-old Meggie Stallworth lay in her bed fast asleep. Her long, jet black hair was spread in sharp contrast over the white pillowcase, and her perfect ivory complexion and long eyelashes capped off the picture of elegance and grace.

Kathleen laid her head against Peter's shoulder and whispered, "Now *that's* beauty!"

"She's a living doll—the epitome of beauty, just like her mother."

Kathleen smiled and raised up on tiptoe to kiss his prickly cheek. "I'll get breakfast started while you shave," she whispered.

She remained at Meggie's door as Peter disappeared into their room. She gazed for a long moment at her daughter and thought of how much Meggie's grandparents loved her, though they still barely tolerated the daughter-in-law who had brought Meggie into the world. Kathleen had learned to live with the situation, and she would continue to bear it for Peter and Meggie's sake.

The kitchen was a cheery place as the morning sunshine streamed through the sparkling windows. Kathleen hummed a lively Irish tune as she put breakfast on the table: buttermilk pancakes with lots of butter and maple syrup—one of Meggie's favorite meals.

Earlier, while the fire was heating up the stove, Kathleen had gone back to Meggie's room and found Peter holding her in his arms. Father and daughter adored each other, and Kathleen was thrilled to see the love that had developed between them.

Mother and daughter had a special relationship also, and it seemed their hearts were knitted closer with each day.

While she poured coffee for Peter and herself and milk for Meggie, Kathleen thought of how happy the three of them were; she was grateful there was only one small cloud hovering over her world. Well, make that *two* small clouds. One was the Stallworths' continued sour attitude toward her. The other was that she had not been able to conceive again. She dearly wanted to give Peter another child.

She heard familiar footsteps in the hall and put aside the troublesome thoughts.

While they ate breakfast, Peter said, "Honey, I've been meaning to tell you, I think there might be a crack in the wall my parents have put up against you."

"Really? In what way?"

"Dad has said things at the office about private conversations he and Mom have had. They agree you've handled the burden they put on you quite well, and a wee bit of admiration has crept into their attitude toward you."

"Oh, Peter, that's good to hear," she said, her eyes moistening with tears.

"I'm thinking that maybe one day soon they'll actually accept you as their daughter-in-law."

As Kathleen used a napkin to sponge away her tears, Meggie said, "Daddy, why don't Grandma and Grandpa ever hug Mommy?"

Kathleen flicked a warning glance at Peter.

"Well, sweetheart," he replied, "Grandma and Grandpa have some funny ideas. They think that since Mommy didn't come from the part of town where they live, she doesn't really fit into the family, so they have been slow to accept her."

The lovely child's brow furrowed. She cocked her head to one side and said, "We don't live where Grandma and Grandpa live, but they hug you and me, Daddy. Mommy lives here too, so why don't they hug her?"

"Meggie," Kathleen said, "do you remember that today, while Daddy is at work, you and I are going shopping together?"

The child's big blue eyes brightened. "Oh, yes! You said you would buy me something, Mommy! What are you going to buy me?"

Kathleen left her chair, bent over and hugged her daughter, then kissed her soft, smooth cheek. "If you'll be real good, I'll buy you something very, very special."

"What?"

"Right now it's a secret, but like I said, if you'll be very, very good, you'll know what the secret is when we get to a certain store downtown."

Peter finished his coffee, and said, "Kathleen, you do remember that Derek Walton and Jack Ballard and I have to work late tonight?"

"Yes, darling. You'll remember to eat some supper, won't you?"

"Sure. It won't be like your cooking, but we'll grab some supper at one of the cafés near the office."

"Did you say you'll be home about ten-thirty or eleven?"

"That's right. So you kiss my baby daughter good-night for me just before she goes to sleep, and I'll sneak into her room and kiss her when I get home."

"Daddy!" gusted Meggie, "I'm not a baby anymore! I'm a big girl. I'm four years old!"

Peter reached over, gently pinched her round little cheek, and said, "Sweetheart, no matter how old you get, you'll still be Daddy's baby girl!"

Kathleen and Meggie hugged and kissed Peter, waving at him as he drove away in the carriage.

"All right, Miss Meggie," Kathleen said, "let's get this kitchen cleaned up so we can go shopping."

They arrived downtown at a little after ten o'clock that morning. Their first stop was at DeLand's Department Store, Meggie's favorite.

"Mommy, is this the store where you're gonna buy me my special s'prise? I've been good. I helped you clean the kitchen."

"Well...this *could* be the store where it is. Do you remember seeing anything in this store that you really, really wanted?"

Meggie thought on it for a moment, then her eyes lit up. "A baby doll! The one with red hair like yours, and the yellow ribbon in her hair! Oh, Mommy, do I really get it?"

Kathleen smiled and playfully touched the tip of Meggie's nose. "Yes, you do. Can you remember where it is?"

The child recalled the exact spot in the toy department where she had seen the doll, and she hurried through the store, leading her mother by the hand.

Five minutes later, Kathleen and Meggie left the toy department with the baby doll in Meggie's arms. Her face beamed as she cradled the doll and said, "What's her name, Mommy?"

"She doesn't have one yet, honey. It's up to you to give her a name."

"Awright. Her name's Kathleen, like yours."

Kathleen stopped and looked down at her daughter. "Honey, are you sure you want to give her my name?"

"Uh-huh."

"Why?"

Meggie looked up into her mother's eyes and smiled. "'Cause you're my favorite lady person in all the world. Daddy's my favorite man person in all the world, an' if my baby doll was a boy, I would call him Peter. But she's a girl, so I want to call her Kathleen."

The young mother bent over, hugged Meggie, and kissed her cheek. "You're my favorite little girl person, and that's why I bought you Kathleen."

"No, Mommy, I'm not a little girl no more, remember? I'm four years old."

"Oh, yes, I forgot. You're my favorite *big* girl person!"

"Thank you for buying Kathleen for me, Mommy. Thank you very much."

"You're very welcome, honey."

Suddenly a voice from behind her called out, "Kathleen!"

She turned to see Hennie Killanin rushing toward her, carrying a baby boy about a year old in her arms, and pulling a little girl by the hand who would be about Meggie's age.

"Hennie! It's so good to see you!"

The reunion between Hennie and Kathleen was sweet, and the mothers proudly showed off their children.

Hennie had married Seth O'Banion, whom Kathleen remembered meeting at Hennie's church when she'd heard Dwight Moody preach. At the time, however, Hennie and Seth had not been courting.

"And what is your married name, Kathleen?"

Hennie was shocked to learn that Kathleen had married into the wealthy Stallworth family, especially when Kathleen told her she had been the Stallworths' cleaning lady.

Kathleen spared Hennie the sordid details of the Stallworths' disapproval of her as a daughter-in-law and simply said, "Peter and I are deeply in love, Hennie, and our beautiful Meggie makes our love perfect."

"Well, Kathleen, I'm meeting some friends in a few minutes, so I need to go. It sure has been good to see you and know that you're doing so well. I hated losing touch with you after the fire…"

"I know, Hennie, but that's all behind us now. That's not to say that I've forgotten my family… Oh, how I miss them, Hennie! Sometimes I wish—"

"Sometimes you wish what, Kathleen?"

"Oh, nothing. What's done is done."

Hennie's brow furrowed. "Kathleen, I need to know one thing…"

"Yes?"

"Did you ever become a Christian?"

"I've certainly thought a lot about it. I mean, some of the words Mr. Moody preached keep coming back to me, and lines of the song Mr. Sankey sang often echo through my mind."

"But you've never opened your heart to Jesus?"

"Well…no."

"Honey, the greatest need you have is to be saved. Nobody knows when they've seen their last sunrise, but we'll all have our last day on earth, and many people die young."

Kathleen nodded in little jerky movements. "I know. I know. Well, I really shouldn't detain you, Hennie. You need to meet up with your friends. It sure was nice to see you again. I…I hope we run into each other again sometime. Come on, Meggie, let's go."

Hennie felt burdened for Kathleen as she watched her hurry away, tugging at Meggie's hand.

When they had reached another department in the store, Kathleen said, "There are some things I need to get right here, Meggie."

"Okay," said the little girl, cuddling her doll.

While Kathleen was picking out new linens, Meggie said, "Mommy, what's bein' saved? What's a Christian?"

"Oh, look here Meggie!" Kathleen said. "Here's a new quilt that will just fit your bed! Would you like to have it?"

The quilt was of soft pastel colors and trimmed with a white eyelet ruffle. "Oh, yes!" said Meggie. "It's real pretty, Mommy!"

It was almost ten o'clock that night when junior vice presidents Peter Stallworth, Derek Walton, and Jack Ballard finished the project they had been working on in the offices of the Great Lakes Railroad Company.

While the other two men closed up their briefcases, Peter said, "You guys go on. I've got some papers in my office I have to put in the safe. I'll see you in the morning."

Ten minutes later, Peter emerged from the building and headed down the deserted street toward the stables where his horse and carriage were kept. Street lamps flickered along the way, pulsing with tentative light like dim ghostly beacons.

Peter was just passing the dark alley between the office building and the stable when he heard the kick of a small rock from somewhere in the deep blackness and heavy footsteps on the boardwalk.

He wanted to look over his shoulder but thought it would look foolish to whoever had moved out of the alley. He was halfway to the stables already and could see the lantern light in the small office.

Suddenly a male voice directly behind him said, "Hold it right there, mister!"

Peter looked back and saw a short, stout man holding a revolver pointed at his chest.

"Gimme your wallet!" the man said, stepping up close.

Peter's initial panic turned swiftly to determination. His fist shot out, connecting with the man's jaw and making the gun fly out of the man's hand.

Before Peter could do anything else, a dark form came out of the shadows and swung a heavy club. The blow to the back of Peter's head was a glancing one, and he went down stunned but still conscious.

The man Peter had knocked down was shaking his head to clear it as he said, "I'll get his wallet. If he makes a move, hit 'im again!"

When the robber reached inside Peter's coat for the wallet, Peter grasped him by the hair and slammed his face against the boardwalk. The other man swore, and before Peter could avoid the club, it struck his head again.

Kathleen glanced at the clock on the mantel for the hundredth time. Twelve midnight, and Peter wasn't home yet. She was still in the dress she'd put on that morning. Every few minutes she went to one of the front windows and peered out into the night, looking for the carriage that would bring her husband home to her.

It wasn't like him to be late.

Kathleen had a passing thought of wishing Hennie was there to pray for Peter. She resumed pacing the floor, then heard footsteps on the porch, followed by a knock on the door.

Kathleen's heart lurched. She could see that whoever it was had a lantern, and she could make out two shadows against the curtains as she turned the knob and opened the door a crack. Peering out, she saw a pair of men in blue uniforms with badges on their chests.

"Chicago police, ma'am. Are you Mrs. Peter Stallworth?"

"Y-yes," she stuttered, opening the door wider.

"I'm Officer Jason Wells, ma'am, and this is Officer Beaudry Compton. May we come in and talk to you?"

Kathleen's knees turned watery. "Something's happened to Peter, hasn't it?"

"We will explain, ma'am, but we'd like to come in and have you sit down."

Kathleen drew a shuddering breath. "What's happened? Tell me!"

Wells took her by the arm and guided her to the nearest chair while Compton stepped inside and closed the door.

"Mrs. Stallworth," Wells said in a low, level tone, "your husband was struck down by robbers on the street in front of the Great Lakes Railroad Company building. They took his money and threw the wallet on the ground beside him. The identification in the wallet told us who he was."

"You're telling me that Peter was unconscious when you found him? Where is he now? Is he all right?"

"Mrs. Stallworth—" the officer began. "Ma'am…we rushed your husband to Central Hospital, and—"

"And what?" Kathleen's heart was pounding.

"Well, ma'am, apparently your husband resisted the robbers. They beat him severely. He…died…about twenty minutes ago."

Kathleen's breathing grew labored as the reality of Peter's death came over her. She could no longer see for the tears flooding her eyes, and the cry trying to escape her throat remained there. The delay was only momentary. Suddenly she wailed and broke down, sobbing her anguish.

After some time her shuddering sobs began to diminish, and Officer Beaudry Compton hurried to get her a cup of water.

"Here, ma'am," he said. "This should help."

Kathleen raised the cup to her lips, drinking deeply.

"Do you want some more water, ma'am?" Compton asked as she handed him the empty cup.

She shook her head.

"Mrs. Stallworth," Officer Jason Wells said, "we've already sent officers to the John Stallworth home to advise them their son has been killed. Would you like us to take you to your in-laws' home?"

Kathleen felt numb in mind and body. She wondered if the Stallworths would want her there, but right now she needed to be with somebody. Peter's parents would have to do.

She wiped at her tears and said, "My…my four-year-old daughter is asleep in her room, sir. I'll get her up, then you can take us to Peter's parents."

Wells helped Kathleen to her feet. "Is there anything we can do to help with your daughter, ma'am?"

"No, thank you. I'll only be a few minutes. Please, sit down."

As Kathleen slowly made her way to Meggie's room, she felt a wave of dizziness wash over her. She reached out to steady herself against the wall for a few seconds until the feeling passed, then entered the room and lit the lantern on the small table next to Meggie's bed. Her precious girl was curled on her side, tightly clasping the new baby doll.

How will I ever explain this to Meggie? How can I make her understand when I don't understand it myself?

Kathleen leaned over and gently caressed Meggie's cheek. The little girl stirred.

"Sweetheart, Mommy needs you to wake up."

It took Meggie a moment to come awake. She rubbed her sleepy eyes and set them on her mother and instantly knew something was wrong.

Kathleen pulled back the covers and took Meggie onto her lap.

"Mommy, you're crying. What's the matter?"

"Honey…" Kathleen stopped abruptly and made a great effort to control her trembling voice. "There are some policemen in the parlor. They came to tell us that…that Daddy has gone to heaven. He won't be coming home."

Meggie's lower lip began to quiver. "Daddy won't be coming home…ever?"

"No, honey. When people go to heaven, they don't come back to earth anymore."

Meggie broke into tears, repeating over and over that she wanted her daddy to come home. Kathleen held her close and tried to comfort her, but all she could do was clasp the child close and rock her.

After several minutes, Kathleen took a deep breath and said, "Meggie, the policemen are going to take us to Grandma and Grandpa's house. We need to get you dressed."

Meggie looked up at Kathleen and said, "Will Daddy be at Grandma's house?"

"No, honey. He won't be there. But Grandma and Grandpa need us right now, and we need them. Come on. Let's get you dressed."

As the police wagon made its way eastward through the dark streets of Chicago, Kathleen sat in the back, holding a sniffling Meggie on her lap.

Kathleen's thoughts ran back to the beginning of the day when Peter had stood at the window, marveling at the beautiful sunrise. Then, like a cold wind striking her face, she recalled Hennie's words: *"Nobody knows when they've seen their last sunrise, but everybody has their last day on earth...and many people die young."*

Kathleen forced her thoughts back to Peter, gazing through the window at the sunrise, not knowing it was his last day on earth. A flame of anger toward God leaped in her heart.

First God had allowed her family to die in that horrible fire, and now her husband had been taken from her. As of this night, she was a widow with a child to raise. Dwight Moody called Him a loving God, but why would a loving God do this to her?

Kathleen's mind went in circles as she frantically tried to make sense of it all.

She would have to get a job and find someone to look after Meggie while she worked. The weight of this sudden tragedy, and the total responsibility of providing for Meggie seemed to crush her.

Why, God? Why?

They arrived at the Stallworth mansion to find two police officers in the huge parlor, and John and Maria trying to comfort each other. When they saw Kathleen and a sleepy-eyed Meggie, they rushed toward them, and Maria took Meggie from Kathleen, hugging her close as she began weeping anew. John stayed close to Maria, patting her shoulder.

Maria, still holding Meggie in her arms, turned to Kathleen and said, "This has to be very hard on you, Kathleen. I'm sorry."

"Yes, Kathleen," John said. "I know Peter was a good husband to you, and he loved you very much."

Still they made no move to physically include Kathleen in their grief.

The officers informed the Stallworths and Kathleen that a manhunt was on, and the Chicago police department would do all they could to find and punish the men who had robbed and killed Peter.

When the police had gone, Meggie's grandparents poured their love on her, trying to comfort her with the words that her daddy had gone to heaven.

The more Meggie squirmed, the tighter Maria held on to her. Finally, the child broke loose and dashed to Kathleen, who folded her in her arms.

As the Stallworths and Kathleen and Meggie sat in the parlor, the older couple spoke to each other in low whispers, saying nothing to their daughter-in-law.

When Meggie's eyes began to droop and she fell asleep in her mother's arms, John rose from his chair and said, "Meggie needs to get some rest, Kathleen. Let's take her up to Peter's room. I'll carry her."

Meggie stirred as she was transferred to her grandfather's arms but did not awaken.

Maria walked alongside him as he carried her up the stairs, and Kathleen stayed a couple of steps behind.

When they reached Peter's old room, Kathleen hurried ahead of them and turned down the covers on the bed. John laid Meggie down and pulled the covers around her, patting her little cheek, then turned to Kathleen. "If she needs anything, you know where our room is."

Kathleen nodded.

"Good night, darling," Maria said, bending low over the little girl. "Grandma will see you in the morning."

The Stallworths left the room without another word.

Kathleen made sure Meggie was covered snugly, then sat down in a soft chair that faced the room's large window. She curled her legs underneath her and stared out at the blackness that reflected her sore and aching heart.

As the long hours of the night passed, Kathleen O'Malley Stallworth reached deep within herself for strength. She was a strong and determined young woman, and before dawn she came to grips with the situation and resolved to make a good life for Meggie, somehow, some way.

12

JOHN AND MARIA STALLWORTH SAT in their bedroom, talking occasionally, but mostly just contemplating the future without their only son.

John sat hunched over in his grief and looked at the floor. After a while, he sat up straight and said, "Maria, we've got to take Meggie away from Kathleen."

Maria turned her gaze from the blackness beyond the window. "I was thinking the same thing. But how could we do it?"

"We can have Kathleen declared an unfit mother. I'll talk to our attorneys. Kathleen's not going to be able to make enough money as a cleaning lady to support herself and Meggie. She sure won't be able to afford that house she and Peter are renting. She'll have to move somewhere cheaper."

John and Maria knew that Peter had used the excess funds left over from his salary each month to purchase additional stock in the company. They also knew that Peter had meant to set up a will to provide for Kathleen, but he hadn't done it yet. Now he never would.

"Kathleen knows about Peter's stock in the company, John. Certainly when the shock of his death wears off, she's going to think of it and ask for her money. We can't have her declared unfit to provide for Meggie if she has that."

John waved her off. "Don't fret, Maria. I've already figured a way to take over Peter's stock and put it in our names. Nobody will ever know. If Kathleen makes trouble over it, she'll never be able to prove a thing."

"I don't doubt you can do that, John, but this whole thing will have to go to court. And even though Kathleen will be dirt poor, there aren't too many judges who will take that little girl from her mother because of it."

"I know. But let me tell you something else. There aren't too many judges who have much money. If we can't get Meggie legally because of Kathleen's poverty, there's another way. One way or another, very soon our granddaughter is going to live in this house with us, where she belongs, and her mother is going to be out in the cold."

At breakfast the next morning, Carlene Simms waited on the grieving Stallworth family, her heart heavy for them. Kathleen had no appetite but ate a small portion to keep up her strength. Meggie sat next to her at the table.

Kathleen waited until they were almost through eating before saying, "Mr. Stallworth, would you have time this morning to take me to the hospital? I would like to see the body. And then I'll need you to take me to a mortuary to make funeral arrangements."

John wiped his mouth with a napkin, shook his head, and said, "No need for you to worry about the funeral arrangements, Kathleen. I'll take care of it. You certainly don't have the money to give Peter the kind of burial he deserves. And as for seeing the body, it would only upset you worse."

"But I—"

"Don't argue, Kathleen. You just stay here with Maria and Meggie. Leave everything to me."

"Then would you do this for Meggie and me, Mr. Stallworth…would you take us home on your way downtown?"

"You don't want to stay here?" Maria said hollowly.

"It's best that Meggie and I go home, Mrs. Stallworth."

Maria's eyebrows arched. "Oh. Well, all right. John will drop you off at your house."

John delivered Kathleen and Meggie to their house, then headed downtown. His first stop was at the hospital to view the body, then he drove to Chicago's finest mortuary to make funeral arrangements. From there he drove to the office of his attorneys.

That evening, on his way home from the office, John stopped by Kathleen's house and told her what mortuary was handling the funeral and informed her that the services and burial would be on the following Monday. He offered to come by and pick her and Meggie up so they could sit together, both at the funeral home and at the graveside service.

The next evening, Kathleen persuaded a neighbor family to drive her to the mortuary so she could view Peter's body. She left Meggie with them and entered the mortuary alone, identifying herself as the widow of Peter Stallworth, and was given private time before the open coffin. The undertaker had informed her that John Stallworth had decided the coffin would remain closed for the services.

Kathleen's small frame shook as she stood over the body. Peter's head was severely damaged, and the morticians could hardly disguise it.

He had been a wonderful husband, and she loved him with all her heart. She couldn't imagine life without him, but seeing his body made the fact of his death more real. He was gone, and she would have to raise Meggie alone.

As she looked down through a wall of tears at the cold, ashen face, she lovingly clasped his folded hands then leaned over the coffin, her tears falling on his still features, and kissed his cheek. Her constricted throat permitted only a whisper as she said, "Oh, my darling…Good-bye, Peter. I love you."

Seth O'Banion pulled the family buggy up in front of the Peter Stallworth house just as Kathleen and Meggie were getting out of the neighbors' vehicle after returning from the mortuary.

Hennie slid from the buggy, telling her husband she wouldn't stay long.

When Kathleen recognized her friend, she began to cry. Hennie explained that her husband would wait in the buggy while she came in for a few minutes. But as Kathleen clung to her, Hennie excused herself and ran out to Seth, telling him to come back in an hour.

"Hennie," Kathleen said brokenly, "how did you know?"

"I read about Peter's death in the *Tribune* and came as soon as I could."

Hennie held Meggie on her lap as the two women sat down at the kitchen table. Kathleen's nerves settled some as they shared an aromatic pot of tea.

With kindness and compassion Hennie once more brought up the subject of salvation but found that her friend was too angry at God to accept His love.

Kathleen did allow Hennie to pray for her and Meggie, and when the hour was up, Hennie told her she would be at the funeral to pay her respects.

There was a large gathering at Peter Stallworth's funeral. His parents were well known and respected by the upper class of Chicago, and Peter's character had attracted many friends.

During the service, Kathleen and Meggie sat with John and Maria Stallworth. Meggie pressed close to her mother's side and kept looking up at her face beneath the black veil she wore. The child was unsure of what was happening and a bit puzzled about what she was supposed to feel and do.

While the solemn service progressed, Kathleen was quite aware of her daughter's glances, and she kept her expression as stoic as possible. Occasionally she looked down at the small, serious face and gave her a wan smile.

Finally the long service came to a close. Kathleen caught a glimpse of Hennie in the crowd as she and Meggie went with the Stallworths to the carriage that would follow the hearse to the cemetery.

Meggie stuck to her mother like a second skin and was holding her hand with all her might as the funeral procession moved slowly down Chicago's narrow streets to the cemetery at the north edge of town.

Upon arriving at the cemetery, the family was guided to wooden folding chairs placed under a canopy near the grave. The minister approached Kathleen and told her that since she was the widow, she would be the one to drop the first handful of dirt on the coffin after he had said, "Ashes to ashes, and dust to dust." John and Maria would follow and do the same thing.

The graveside service was brief, and Kathleen was soon tossing the dirt on the lid of the coffin as Meggie stood by her side. Her veil obscured the tears flowing down her set features as Peter's parents tossed their handfuls of dirt on the coffin. When the minister closed in prayer, people immediately began gathering around John and Maria, expressing their condolences.

Kathleen took hold of Meggie's tiny shoulders, turned her around, and led her down the gentle slope toward the waiting carriage.

Hennie O'Banion emerged from the crowd and rushed up to them. "I love you, honey," she said to Kathleen as she embraced her, then Meggie. "Is there anything I can do for you?"

Kathleen wiped tears from her cheeks. "No, Hennie, but thank you. We'll be fine."

Hennie pressed a small slip of paper in Kathleen's hand. "This is my address," she said. "If you need me, please let me know."

They embraced again and Hennie walked away.

Kathleen and Meggie climbed into the carriage and waited for the Stallworths.

Kathleen had been informed that John and Maria's closest friends and associates from the company would be coming to their home for refreshments, and of course, Kathleen was expected to be there.

"Kathleen, I've hired a neighbor girl to look after Meggie during the time our guests are here. She's seventeen and quite responsible. Her name is Alta Washburn. Alta will see that Meggie is fed and will keep her upstairs in Peter's room."

Kathleen nodded.

Maria took Meggie in her arms, kissed her cheek, and said, "Grandma loves her little Meggie doll."

"I love you, too, Grandma," Meggie said, putting her arms around Maria's neck.

Maria turned cool eyes on Kathleen. "Go on into the parlor and sit down; I'll take Meggie upstairs to Alta."

John left Kathleen alone and went outside to stand on the front steps, waiting for the carriages and buggies pulling into the drive.

When the guests had gathered and refreshments were passed out, Kathleen tried to mingle with the friends and associates of her late husband and his parents, but she was snubbed by most of them, and the rest were only slightly cordial. She couldn't ask John to take her home before the guests were gone, so she found herself a corner chair in the parlor and sat down to wait.

After an hour or so, when the first guests departed, Kathleen left her chair and stepped up to John, who was in conversation with two men in the hallway outside the parlor. When he paused to give her his attention, she said, "Mr. Stallworth, I really am very tired. Would you mind taking Meggie and me home now?"

John smiled and said, "Pretty soon, dear. Could you give me a few more minutes?"

"All right. I'll go upstairs and see how Meggie's doing. We'll come down in a little while."

John nodded, and Kathleen headed for the sweeping spiral staircase. When she reached Peter's room, the door was ajar. She could hear Alta Washburn's voice.

She tapped on the door lightly. "Hello…it's Meggie's mother."

"Come in, Mrs. Stallworth."

Kathleen pushed the door open and saw Alta sitting in a chair next to a window, with Meggie on her lap, holding a book.

"Mommie!" Meggie cried, sliding off Alta's lap and dashing to her mother's side. She wrapped her arms around her mother's legs and squeezed hard. "Are you all right, Mommy?"

"I'm fine, honey," Kathleen assured her. She loosened Meggie's grip, bent down, and took her in her arms. "Are *you* all right?"

"Uh-huh. Alta's been reading me some stories from a book."

"That's nice, honey." Kathleen rose to her feet and smiled at the girl. "Hello, Alta. I really appreciate your looking after Meggie."

"It's been my privilege, ma'am. She's such a sweet little thing."

"Can't argue with that," Kathleen said, patting her daughter's head.

"Are you leaving now?"

"Yes. Meggie's grandpa is going to drive us home."

Alta hugged the child and told her good-bye.

Maria was waiting at the bottom of the staircase when they descended. She greedily lifted her granddaughter in her arms and said to Kathleen, "John told me you wanted to go home."

"Yes. I'm very tired."

She set Meggie on her feet again and said, "All right. I'll get him. Most of the guests are gone now."

After a few minutes, John returned and indicated he was ready to take them home. He hesitated at the door and looked over his shoulder at Maria. She gave him a tight smile and nodded. Then he ushered Kathleen and Meggie out the door.

Only a few words were spoken between John and Kathleen during the ride to Kathleen's neighborhood. When they rounded the corner onto her street, Kathleen's jaw slacked at sight of a Chicago police wagon parked in front of the house.

"I wonder why they're here," she remarked.

John remained silent and pulled up behind the police wagon.

Two officers waited on the porch, watching as Kathleen stepped out of the carriage and lifted Meggie out.

Kathleen turned to say something to John about staying until she learned what the policemen wanted, but he snapped the reins and drove away. She looked after the hastening carriage for a few seconds, then turned to see the officers coming down the porch steps.

"Mommy, why are the policemen at our house?" Meggie asked.

"I don't know, sweetie, but it looks like they're about to tell us."

One of the officers was short and stout. The other was tall and slender.

"Mrs. Stallworth?" the shorter officer said.

"Yes?"

"I'm officer Bud Fox, ma'am, and this is officer Kale Warneke." He pulled a white envelope out of his coat pocket. "We have a court order to deliver to you, ma'am."

Kathleen opened the envelope and took out the official-looking paper. It declared that Megan Kathleen Stallworth was to be removed from the custody of her mother, Kathleen Stallworth, and placed with her grandparents, John and Maria Stallworth.

The reason given was that Kathleen Stallworth was financially unable to provide for her daughter, and because the John Stallworths were more than able to do this, the court's decision was to place the child in their care until such time as Kathleen could produce evidence that she was financially able to provide for her daughter. It was signed by Cook County Judge Clarence Waymore.

Kathleen felt a mixture of anger and fear. For a moment she stood there breathless, a stitch knifing at her side. Her hands trembled as she held the paper toward the officers and said, "I can't believe this! How could these people do this to Meggie and me? How could they stoop so low?"

"What do you mean, ma'am?" Officer Warneke asked. "The grandparents are just concerned that this little girl be taken care of properly."

Meggie ran her gaze between her mother and the policemen, confusion showing on her face.

"No, they're not!" Kathleen said. "If that was their concern, all they'd have to do is give me the money it would take to stay in this house. They're filthy rich! No, that's not their concern. What they want is to take Meggie away from me! They never wanted me as their daughter-in-law, and they still don't! Well, I'm telling you right now, I'll fight them! They have no right to take Meggie!"

The little girl's voice quavered as she said, "Mommy, aren't we going to live together anymore?"

Kathleen leaned over and hugged her. "Don't cry, sweetheart. Mommy won't let them take you away from me."

"Ma'am," said Fox, "we have orders from the judge to take the little girl to your in-laws' home as soon as we've placed the court order in your hands."

"This whole thing is illegal, officer. Don't I have to be proven unfit to care for my child before the law can take her from me?"

"I can't comment on that, ma'am. We simply have orders from the judge. If you want to fight this court order, it'll have to be in court. We must take the child now."

"Wait a minute! Why won't you comment on it? I see a badge on your chest! Aren't you supposed to be the law? Tell me I'm wrong when I say this is illegal!"

"We aren't here to interpret the law, Mrs. Stallworth," Kale Warneke said. "Our job is simply to do what we're told. We must take the child. Would you like to pack some clothes for her?"

Fury coursed through Kathleen and made her chest heave. "No!" she cried. "You're not taking Meggie from me!"

Meggie grasped her mother around the legs and sobbed, "Don't let them take me, Mommy!"

"Look," Kathleen said, her breath coming in short gasps, "I want to talk to this Judge Waymore. Do I at least have the right to do that before you take my daughter away from me?"

Fox scratched his head. "Well…"

"Let's take her to the judge," said Warneke.

Judge Clarence Waymore had finished his last case for the day at the county courthouse and was taking off his robe in his chambers when there was a knock at his door.

He laid the robe on the back of his desk chair and waddled to the door. He was a short, rotund, bald man who wore half-moon glasses low on his nose. He opened the door to find officers Bud Fox and Kale Warneke standing there with a young mother and her little girl.

"Your honor," said Fox, "this is Kathleen Stallworth and her daughter, Megan Kathleen."

"Yes?" A look of irritation passed over the judge's face.

"Mrs. Stallworth asked to talk to you, sir. She does have that right, doesn't she, since you signed the court order?"

Waymore glanced at the wall clock behind his desk. "It's almost five o'clock. I don't have time to see her now."

"But we're supposed to take the child to John Stallworth's home, sir. And this mother has asked to see you."

"Oh, all right…come in."

Waymore did not offer Kathleen a seat. Fixing her with penetrating gray eyes, he said, "What is it, Mrs. Stallworth?"

"I want to know how you can legally take my child from me and place her with my in-laws when the law has not proven me to be an unfit mother."

"It is a matter of finances, ma'am. You're not capable of providing your daughter proper food, housing, and other necessities."

"How do you know what I'm capable of? Have you seen my bank account? Have you looked into my holdings?"

"Mr. Stallworth told me that you have a very small bank account, and I have taken his word for it. Tell me, how much money do you have in the bank?"

Kathleen swallowed hard. "Well, only about three hundred dollars. But Peter has stock in the company. I don't know exactly what it's worth, but I'm sure it would be seven or eight thousand dollars. All I have to do is sell the stock."

Waymore was shaking his head. "This can't be true, ma'am. I asked John Stallworth if Peter had stock in the company. He told me he didn't and that all you have is what's in that bank account."

Kathleen felt as if she'd been struck in the face. "John Stallworth is lying, your honor, but there's no way I can prove it. I asked you a moment ago if you could legally take Meggie from me and place her with my in-laws without proving I'm an unfit mother. You didn't answer my question. All you said was that it's a matter of finances. Well, I've worked jobs before, and I can work jobs again. I'll find a way to see that Meggie is well cared for. I'm taking her with me now, and we're going home. If you want to investigate me in a month, fine. In the meantime, I'll prove that I can provide for Meggie and myself."

She took the child's hand and started toward the door.

"Wait a minute!" Waymore growled. "These officers are taking this child to her grandparents right now. You can peacefully allow it or go to jail. The choice is yours."

Kathleen's voice thickened with anger. "I know what this is! John Stallworth slipped you a bribe under the table, and you took it! You don't care about the law! All you care about is getting your palms greased with money!"

The judge's eyes bulged in fury, and he motioned to the officers who had brought Kathleen to see him. "Officer Fox! Officer Warneke! Arrest this woman! Put her in jail for contempt of court!"

John and Maria Stallworth stood outside Kathleen's jail cell, looking at her through the bars while a guard stood nearby. Meggie leaned against her grandfather, weeping.

"You have no right to do this to me!" Kathleen said. "Just because I'm not from your snooty, uppity level of society, you've never approved of me nor accepted me into the family! You've no doubt plotted to take Meggie from me from the moment you learned Peter was dead! Well, Meggie is one-half Kathleen, as sure is as she is one-half

Peter! Why would you want her under your roof? I'm going to fight you! I know you bribed that fat judge, and I'm going to—"

"Kathleen!" John cut across her words. "Shut up and listen to me! I can have you released with a word to the police chief. Now, if you'll cool down and keep a civil tongue in your mouth, I'll do just that. You can walk out of here in a few minutes. But if you continue this tirade, Maria and I will let you rot in this place. We're taking Meggie with us, but you can go on with your life *outside* this jail if you stop this foolishness."

"Kathleen," Maria said, "you know we love this sweet child with everything that is in us. And you know we have plenty of money. Meggie will get the best of care and grow up in the lap of luxury. She will have everything she wants and needs. I have even hired a nanny to watch over her twenty-four hours a day."

Kathleen took a deep, shuddering breath, set her eyes on her in-laws, and said, "How often can I see her?"

John's mouth turned down. "Maria and I talked about it. We've fixed it with the judge that you do not have visiting rights. It would only keep Meggie upset."

Kathleen fought down her wrath, looked past her in-laws to the guard, and said, "May I have a few minutes alone with my daughter before these people take her?"

The guard took a forward step. "I think that is reasonable," he said. "Would you like her in the cell with you?"

"Yes, please."

To the Stallworths the guard said, "You folks can wait in the office. I'll bring the child to you in ten minutes."

John and Maria left the cell block reluctantly as the guard opened the barred door to Kathleen's cell. He closed it behind Meggie and said, "I'll be back in ten minutes, ma'am."

Kathleen sat down on the cell cot and pulled Meggie onto her lap. The little girl clung to her mother, confused and afraid.

"Honey, listen to Mommy," Kathleen said in a soft, steady voice.

Meggie pulled back and looked into her mother's eyes.

"Meggie, I want you to go home with Grandma and Grandpa for now. They love you and they will take care of you. I will come for you as soon as I can. Do you understand?"

Meggie nodded.

When the time was up, the guard came and opened the cell door. "I'll take her to the grandparents now, ma'am. And I have instructions to release you within half an hour."

Meggie was trying not to cry as she looked over the guard's shoulder at her mother. Kathleen waved and said, "I love you, sweetheart. Mommy will see you as soon as I can."

As promised, Kathleen was released half an hour after the Stallworths had left with Meggie. As she walked home, a boiling hatred churned within her. She vowed that somehow, someday, she would lay her hands on enough money to hire a lawyer and get her daughter back.

13

MAIL ORDER BRIDE SERIES
NO. 1
1871
USA
AL & JOANNA LACY

"YOU STILL DON'T HAVE IT QUITE RIGHT, Stan. Put more shoulder into it when you swing. Gerald, you seem to have gotten the knack of it. Take another swing and let Stan watch."

It was midafternoon as Tom Harned instructed two new men on how to use pickaxes to cut into the walls of the Comstock Lode. They were deep inside the dark bowels of Mount Davidson. The only light came from overhead lanterns hanging from thick wooden beams.

"Tom!" came the familiar voice of Hank Mitchell.

"Over here, Hank!"

There was the sound of rapid footfalls, then Hank came into view. "Tom! Hilda Jensen is outside, all upset. She wants to see you. She's got Caleb with her."

"Is something wrong with Loretta?" Tom asked.

"I don't know. Hilda only said she needed to see you in a hurry."

Tom turned to the new men. "You guys go ahead. Practice your swing, Stan. You help him, Gerald. I'll be back when I can."

When Tom emerged from the mouth of the mine, Caleb ran toward him, crying, "Daddy, Mommy's real sick!"

Tom gathered his son up in his arms and looked at Hilda's pallid face.

"It's the baby, Mr. Harned," she said. "The baby's comin'! Loretta's in labor, but she's losing blood."

A cold dread seized Tom. "Is the doctor at the house?"

"Yes, sir. He's got his nurse with him."

Tom set Caleb on the ground. "Son, Hilda will take you home."

With that, he bolted toward town.

Tom bounded onto his front porch, puffing from exertion, and rushed through the door.

Dr. Frank Nelson's nurse, Edna Roberts, had heard him coming, and was waiting for him at the bedroom door. The look on her face terrified him.

"Mr. Harned," she said, taking a step toward him, "Dr. Nelson is doing everything he can, but—"

Tom rushed past her into the bedroom.

The doctor glanced up as Tom drew near the bed. "I'm doing what I can, Tom," he said, the seriousness of the situation evident on his face.

Loretta's face had a gray pallor, and deep lines of pain were etched on her lovely features. Her hair was matted to her forehead with sweat. Suddenly she gasped for breath, her eyes pinching shut. The labor pains were coming so close together that she had no time to rest between contractions.

Tom took her hand in his and tried to loosen her grip on the bedsheet. "Honey, I'm here."

Loretta opened her pain-dulled eyes and gave him a weak, shaky smile.

"It's going to be all right, honey," Tom said, pushing a lock of hair off her damp forehead. He leaned over and kissed her cheek.

Loretta jerked and moaned as another spasm of pain hit her and more blood flowed.

Dr. Nelson shook his head and glanced at his nurse.

Footsteps thumped on the parlor floor, and they heard Hilda's voice telling Caleb he couldn't go into the bedroom.

Tom leaned close to Loretta's ear and said, "I'll be right back."

He was back in just a few moments and said to Loretta, "I sent Hilda to get Pastor Humbert. I want him to pray for you."

Loretta nodded as her body jerked under the pain of another contraction.

Less than twenty minutes had passed when Hilda appeared at the bedroom door and said, "Pastor and Mrs. Humbert are here."

Tom hurried to the parlor and was met by Caleb, who flung himself at his father and clung to him. As he gripped his little boy's hand in his own, Tom looked at the pastor and said, "Thank you for coming, Pastor…Laurie."

"How is she doing?" Humbert asked.

Tom explained Loretta's condition as best he could, telling them she had lost two previous children in miscarriage. "Please pray for her, Pastor," Tom pleaded, his face pinched with anxiety. "I've got to get back to her."

Tom returned to Loretta's bedside and held her hand. She was exhausted, both from the constant hard contractions and the blood loss.

"The baby's coming," said Dr. Nelson. "Push, Loretta! Push!"

Loretta summoned every ounce of strength she could muster and gave one final push.

The doctor handed the tiny, limp form to Edna without a word, then glanced at Tom as she hurried away with the baby.

"I don't hear the baby crying," Loretta said weakly.

Dr. Nelson remained silent as he worked to stop the hemorrhaging.

Tom gazed into his wife's pain-darkened eyes and could barely say the words. "Honey, the baby's…the baby's dead."

The exhausted mother closed her eyes and ejected a heartrending cry.

Before Tom could say anything more, she reached up a shaky hand and caressed his cheek, saying in a cracked whisper, "I…love…you." Then her hand fell limply to the bed, and she stopped breathing.

"No!" Tom lifted her in his arms. "No! No! No, God! No! Don't take her from me! Please don't take her from me!" Tom held Loretta's lifeless body and sobbed.

The Humberts stood at the bedroom door while Hilda kept Caleb in the parlor.

Dr. Nelson let Tom stay with Loretta a few minutes, then laid a hand on his shoulder. "Come, Tom. Pastor Humbert will take you to Caleb."

The pastor put an arm around Tom's shoulders and guided him to the parlor. Tom sat numbly on the sofa with Caleb in his arms, and the two of them wept together.

Nurse Roberts had washed the baby and placed it in a soft pink blanket. She then cleaned up Loretta and placed a clean sheet over her body, leaving the face exposed. She waited until Tom and Caleb's weeping had subsided, then called to Tom from the bedroom door. "Mr. Harned, would you come here a moment?"

When Tom entered the bedroom, the doctor was putting his instruments into his medical bag, and Edna was holding the bundle. She showed it to Tom, saying softly, "It's a girl, Mr. Harned. She's perfect in every way, but she never drew a breath."

"I don't want to look at her," Tom said, closing his eyes.

Dr. Nelson paused in his work and said, "Mr. Harned, I know from many years of experience in handling miscarriages at this stage that you'll regret it one day if you don't look at your baby."

Tom slowly reached trembling hands to gather the precious bundle into his arms. He looked at his baby daughter through a mist of tears and studied her for a long moment, then placed her beside Loretta and kissed them both, saying, "She looks like you, darlin'."

Dr. Nelson was now washing his hands in a basin at the dresser. "I'm sorry, Tom," he said. "I did everything I could."

"I know that, Doc."

On returning to the parlor, Tom looked at the preacher and said, "Pastor Humbert, I don't understand. You prayed, but God still took my wife and baby daughter. Why did He do this? I need Loretta, and so does Caleb."

"Tom," Humbert said, his voice compassionate, "I know you may be tempted to be angry at God, but—"

"Well, I am angry at God!" Tom blurted out, breaking into tears once again. "He could have spared Loretta and my little girl, but He didn't! I don't want anything to do with Him!"

Bruce Humbert laid a hand on the grieving man's shoulder and said, "Tom, I'll do anything I can for you. And when your emotions have settled down, we can talk some more about it."

Tom reached for Caleb, then looked up at the preacher. "I appreciate you and Laurie coming when I sent for you. Would you conduct the funeral for me?"

"Of course. I will be honored to do so."

Two days later, Loretta and the baby were buried in the same coffin, with Loretta's little girl folded in her arms.

Most of the miners and other people of the town were at the graveside to pay their respects. Hank and Donna Mitchell stood with Tom and Caleb, along with Laurie Humbert.

After the service Henry Comstock was first to reach Tom and offer his condolences. "I want you to take a week off with full pay," he said.

Tom thanked him, saying he would only take a couple of days.

When everyone had passed by Tom and Caleb, expressing their sympathy, Bruce and Laurie Humbert and Hank and Donna Mitchell asked if there was anything they could do for them.

Tom shook his head. "Thank you, all of you, but Caleb and I will be fine." His eyes belied his words.

"Tom," Pastor Humbert said, "could I come by the house sometime soon and talk to you?"

"You're always welcome, Pastor, but preaching to me isn't going to do any good."

Humbert smiled. "I won't preach to you. I just want to help you adjust to your loss if I can."

Tom nodded. "Thank you for caring, Pastor."

The next day while Caleb was in school, Tom went to Hilda Jensen's house and asked if she could keep Caleb in the afternoons, and all day Saturdays. He would pay her well.

"Oh, Tom, I wish I could do it, but I'm feeling poorly these days.

I don't have the energy I used to. In fact, I hate to tell you at a time like this, but I don't think I can even clean for you and do the washing. I'm so sorry, Tom."

Tom kindly told her he understood and thanked her that she had worked for him so faithfully till Loretta's death.

He let himself out Hilda's front door and stood on the porch a minute, a feeling of panic washing over him. He knew he wasn't much of a cook, but he figured he could learn with practice, and he and Caleb would get by. But the thought of taking care of the house and doing the laundry, along with everything else it took to care for a home, seemed overwhelming. And who could he get to watch over Caleb when he was working at the mine six days a week? He mentally straightened his shoulders and vowed to be the best father *and mother* to Caleb that he could be.

Tom found it heart-wrenching to watch Caleb's grief. The boy often sat and just stared into space, and he had told Tom that he dreamed about his mother at night and heard her calling him her little angel boy. He was trying hard to accept the loss of his mother and to be brave about it, but tears often coursed down his cheeks.

Tom waited outside the school that afternoon when the teacher rang the bell and the children poured out the door. Caleb ran into his father's arms and clung to him.

That evening, father and son were washing and drying dishes after supper when they heard footsteps on the front porch and a knock at the door.

Still carrying a dish towel, Tom opened the door to see Hank and Donna Mitchell.

"Hello, Hank…Donna," he said. "Come in."

They hugged Caleb, then Hank said, "We just came by to see how you two are doing. Is there anything we can do for you?"

"Don't think so," Tom said. "We're plugging along. I've got to find someone to take care of Caleb after school in the afternoons, and all day on Saturdays. I thought Hilda Jensen might be able to do it, but her health is getting pretty bad."

"I wish there was something *I* could do, Tom," Donna said, "but my job makes it impossible."

"I understand," Tom said. "I know you'd help if you could. I'm going to talk to some people around town tomorrow and see if I can find somebody who'll take care of him."

"How about we just pray about it right now, Tom?" Hank said.

"Well, uh…sure, that's fine."

Hank led in prayer, asking the Lord to provide someone to watch over Caleb when his dad was at work. He also weaved the gospel into his prayer.

When Hank had spoken the amen, Tom grinned at his friend and said, "You're a persistent cuss, Hank. Preach to me while you pray, eh?"

"I'm just concerned for you, Tom. You already know that."

"Mm-hmm. Well, I'm doing fine, Hank."

"You'd do a lot better if you'd open your heart to Jesus. Knowing Him and having Him in control of your life is the most wonderful thing in this world."

Tom quickly asked how things had gone at the mine that day, and soon the Mitchells told Tom and Caleb good-night.

The next day, Tom went around town trying to find someone who could take care of Caleb, but to no avail. In the afternoon, as he headed toward the school to meet the boy, he told himself the only thing he could do was have Caleb come to the mine after school and sit there till the workday was over. Surely Mr. Comstock would understand.

That evening, father and son had finished cleaning up the kitchen after supper and were about to sit down in the parlor when Pastor and Mrs. Humbert knocked on the door.

"Hello, Tom," said the preacher. "Laurie and I have had you and Caleb on our hearts, so we thought we'd come by and see how you're doing."

Tom welcomed them in and invited them to sit down.

When Laurie turned to greet the blond little boy, she saw tears in his eyes. "Caleb, you're crying."

Tom laid a hand on top of his head. "What is it, son?"

The child's lips quivered as he said, "When I saw Mrs. Humbert I thought of my mommy."

Laurie left the overstuffed chair and took the boy in her arms. "Come over here and sit with me, Caleb," she said softly.

Tom and the pastor quietly watched as Laurie held the boy, speaking soothing words to him. Caleb clung to her, sniffling, and laid his head against her shoulder. Soon Laurie stopped talking and just held Caleb close.

"Tom," the preacher said, "we came by to offer any help we might be able to give, and to make a special offer where we *know* we can help."

"I know," Tom said, nodding. "You can help me get saved."

"Yes, we could if you'd let us. But I promised you I wouldn't preach to you when we came by the last time, and I'll keep my promise."

Tom looked relieved.

"Tom," Humbert said kindly, "the most important thing in your life is to be ready for eternity. But I will not attempt to shove salvation down your throat. However, Laurie has something she wants to say to you."

"I was talking to Hilda Jensen today, Tom," Laurie said, keeping her arms wrapped around Caleb. "She told me you were needing someone to take care of Caleb after school and on Saturdays. And of course when school lets out you'll need someone to take care of him six days a week."

Tom nodded. "Yes, ma'am. I've asked people all over town for help, and there just isn't anybody who can do it. So I figure till school's out, I'll have him come to the mine and stay in the office. I have to ask Mr. Comstock, but I think he'll go for it. Saturdays will be something else. I might just have to ask Mr. Comstock to give me Saturdays off."

"How about letting *me* take care of Caleb?" Laurie asked.

"You mean it?"

"Yes. I…ah…"

"Is there a problem?" Tom said. "I'll be glad to pay you."

"Oh, no! I won't accept money for doing it!"

"Laurie hesitates because we just found out she's going to have a baby," said Humbert. "She would only be able to watch over Caleb until…when, honey?"

"I could take care of Caleb beginning tomorrow, Tom, and at least through the summer. You would have to find someone else by September."

Relief washed over the young widower, and it was his turn to vent his emotions through tears. After a few moments he wiped his cheeks and said, "This would give me some time to make other arrangements. Thank you so much. I appreciate this more than I can say!" Then to Caleb, "Son, would you like to stay with Mrs. Humbert after school and on Saturdays—and all day, six days a week, when school's out?"

Caleb smiled broadly for the first time since his mother had died. "Oh, yes, Daddy! I sure would!"

"Then it's a deal!" Laurie said, hugging Caleb tight. "We'll start tomorrow!"

"I'd feel better if you'd let me pay you," Tom said.

"Absolutely not," Laurie replied, shaking her head.

"I wish I could tell you how much this means to me."

"I believe I know," Laurie said with a smile.

"Daddy!" Caleb said. "God answered Uncle Hank's prayer, didn't he?"

Tom's face tinted. "Why…uh…yes, He did, son. He sure did." Tom explained to the Humberts that Hank and Donna had come by the house the night before, and Hank had prayed for someone to take care of Caleb.

"Isn't God good?" Laurie said.

Tom smiled weakly.

"Tom, how are you coping with your loss?" the preacher asked.

"I'm just numb, Pastor. I'm still puzzled as to why God took Loretta and the baby."

As he heard the trace of bitterness in Tom's voice, Bruce Humbert silently asked the Lord to show him the best way to win this man to Jesus.

Kathleen O'Malley moved out of the house in the upper-middle-class district and rented a cheap apartment near downtown. She had wanted to take a room again at Hattie Murphy's boardinghouse, but all the rooms were occupied.

Kathleen's apartment was on the bottom floor at the back of the apartment building. There was a small backyard containing an old shed next to the alley. The apartment consisted of two dreary rooms—a parlor and bedroom combined, and a small kitchen. There was only one window, and it was covered with grime and a faded limp curtain.

Kathleen had taken a few pieces of furniture from the house, and in order to have a little more money she had sold the rest of it to a secondhand store. She was so discouraged she didn't care where she lived or how it looked.

Her first effort to find work was in the neighborhood where her in-laws lived, but the Stallworths had blackballed her, and she could find no work.

Since people in the lower-class neighborhoods did their own housecleaning, she decided to take in washing and ironing and do sewing.

She talked to her landlord and was given permission to use the old shed out back as a laundry room but was told she would have to supply her own coal for heating water on an old stove in the shack.

Kathleen trudged from house to house in the neighborhood where she and Peter had lived, and in neighborhoods not quite as nice. For three days she returned to her drab apartment with no jobs. On the fourth day, she was given washing and ironing jobs by two people, and by the time she had knocked on doors for a week, she was able to pick up enough work to produce a meager income.

The young widow did not touch the three hundred dollars she had in the bank. She hoped to somehow add to it until she had enough money to hire a lawyer and get Meggie back.

Every night Kathleen cried herself to sleep, missing her little daughter and mourning for Peter. A deep bitterness toward John and Maria Stallworth filled her heart. This bitterness spilled over into her attitude toward God and life in general. She felt that God had picked her out to torment her. The one thing that kept Kathleen going was her vow to one day take the Stallworths to court over Meggie, and she hoped to find a way to make them pay for their wicked deeds.

When two weeks had passed since losing Meggie to the Stallworths, Kathleen took a walk into the wealthy neighborhood and peeked through the Stallworths' back fence. After waiting for over an hour, she caught a glimpse of Meggie when the nanny brought her outside for a few minutes. All too soon the nanny took Meggie back inside the mansion, and Kathleen began to cry. It hurt to see Meggie when she couldn't take her in her arms and hold her, but it hurt worse *not* to see her.

As time passed, Kathleen was able to pick up more washing and ironing jobs—referrals from her steady customers—in addition to some sewing jobs. She laid aside almost every penny in her "Meggie fund."

As often as she could, Kathleen made her way to the back fence of the Stallworth yard, hoping to see Meggie. Sometimes the journey paid off, but most times her long walk was in vain.

She purchased a small handcart to pick up and deliver her laundry and sewing. Before long her hands became red and chapped, and sometimes the cracks broke open and bled, but she drove herself to keep working. She didn't even mind when her clothes became faded and worn. All that mattered was getting Meggie back and ultimately hurting the Stallworths as much as possible.

Kathleen worked long hours every day and became a virtual hermit, going out only to collect and deliver the washed and ironed clothes and to make frequent trips to peek through the Stallworths' back fence.

As her stockpile of dollars slowly grew, Kathleen began to lose weight for lack of nourishing food. Late in the afternoon on a windy spring day, under heavy clouds, Kathleen hurriedly pushed her cart to get home before it started to rain. Suddenly her head went light and she broke out in a cold sweat.

By the time she reached her dismal apartment, she was shaking with a cold that came from within. Doggedly, she took the dirty laundry into the shed, built a fire, heated water, and put the clothes in the tub to soak. When she returned to the apartment she was so weak and cold she could hardly move. Her head was throbbing with pain.

Kathleen forced herself to build a fire in the cookstove to heat up a small bit of leftover soup and make a pot of strong tea. She huddled close to the stove as she ate. Every muscle in her body ached. She poured steaming, fragrant tea into a cup and added a hoarded spoonful of honey. She sipped it slowly, soothing the rawness in her throat.

When she had finished eating and had drunk all the tea, she went back to the shed, finished the wash, and hung it up to dry. *I should do some sewing before I go to bed,* she thought, but realized she was too sick to do it. Her headache was almost unbearable, and she was still shivering.

Back inside the small apartment, Kathleen washed her face and slipped into a warm flannel nightgown, then blew out the lantern and wearily crawled into bed, welcoming the warmth that slowly seeped into her body and stilled the shivering.

As she lay in the darkness, Kathleen looked up toward heaven and said, "God, it's been a long time since I asked You for help. Please don't let me get any worse. I have to do my work tomorrow. I have to earn every dollar I can so I can get Meggie back. Please help me."

Several times during the night, Kathleen awakened in a cold sweat but was able to go right back to sleep. Always up before daybreak, she was shocked the next time she woke and the sun was trying to shine through the grime on her window.

She sat up with a start, and a groan escaped her pale lips as she grabbed her head with both hands. "Oh, please, God," she whispered.

"Help me. I can't afford to get sick."

With effort, Kathleen left the bed to start her day. She cooked herself some oatmeal. Though her head was still a bit light and the chill was still inside her, the soreness had left her throat.

By the time she had eaten all the oatmeal she could hold, along with downing three cups of hot tea, her chills were lessening. She was actually feeling somewhat better. She whispered a thank-you to the Lord, and while she washed the dishes, her mind ran to Dwight Moody's sermons and the one song that kept coming back to her. Were these memories always going to haunt her?

She went to work on the sewing, and when it was done, she did the ironing. As she finished the last piece in early afternoon, she smiled to herself, dreaming of the day when she and her precious little daughter would be together again. She ate a nourishing lunch, then loaded the cart.

By the time she was ready to leave, she was feeling even better. Another word of thanks went to the Lord. Maybe He was going to stop tormenting her now.

Kathleen made her deliveries and picked up more laundry and sewing to take home. Since she was near downtown and needed to purchase some lye soap, along with a few groceries, she pushed the cart to her favorite store.

It was late afternoon when she came out of the store and headed down the crowded street. Children were laughing and playing along the way, and people were bustling about. Kathleen was almost to the intersection where she would turn in the direction of her apartment when she heard a small voice shout, "Mommy! Mommy!"

Some child's lost her mother, thought Kathleen.

"Mommy!" came the call again.

The voice was closer this time, and Kathleen stopped the cart and turned to find her little daughter running toward her. The nanny was hurrying to catch up.

Tears flooded Kathleen's eyes. "Meggie! Oh, Meggie!"

"MOMMY, I'VE MISSED YOU!" Mother and daughter came together as Meggie leaped into Kathleen's arms. "I want to go home with you! I don't want to live with Grandpa and Grandma anymore. Please! Take me home with you."

The nanny drew up, agitated and puffing from exertion. She watched mother and daughter for a moment, sympathy for their depth of feeling springing up within her. "Mrs. Stallworth, I'm Alice Downing…Meggie's nanny."

Kathleen brushed at her tears as she turned to look at Alice, thinking of the times she had seen Meggie and this small middle-aged woman in the backyard of the Stallworth mansion.

"Meggie, honey, we have to go," Alice said, laying a tender hand on the little girl. Then to Kathleen: "I'm sorry, ma'am. I…I know this must be very hard for you. But Meggie and I have to meet her grandmother at a certain store in just a few minutes. If we're late, it will go bad for me."

Kathleen had an impulse to turn and run away with Meggie, but she knew the police would find them, and she would go to jail. "Meggie," Kathleen said, her voice choking, "Mommy loves you. I want you to come home with me, but it can't be, not right now. You have to stay with Grandpa and Grandma."

"Come, Meggie," said Alice, her face showing anxiety. "We have to hurry, honey, or Grandma will be very angry."

Kathleen felt as if her heart would shatter as she kissed her daughter and said, "You have to go now, honey. Please try to understand that there's nothing Mommy can do about how things are

177

right now." As she spoke, she handed Meggie to Alice.

"Thank you, ma'am," the nanny said, hurrying away.

Through a wall of tears, Kathleen watched them go. Meggie was reaching back toward her, wailing, "Mommy-y-y!"

The child continued to call for Kathleen until Alice carried her into the crowd and lost sight of Kathleen.

Meggie was sobbing by the time they reached the store where they were to meet up with Maria Stallworth.

"Meggie, please don't cry," Alice begged. "We don't want to upset Grandma, do we?"

"I want my mommy!"

Alice stopped at the door. *Maybe I can get Meggie to stop crying before Mrs. Stallworth—*

"You're late, Alice! Where have you been?" Maria pushed through the door and set stern eyes on Alice and the child.

"Well, Mrs. Stallworth, I—"

"Meggie, what are you crying about?"

"I just saw my mommy," Meggie said, sniffling. "She said she wants me to come home with her. Please, Grandma! I want to go live with Mommy!"

Maria's mouth tightened and her eyes darkened with anger.

Several people passing by looked on curiously as Maria snapped the words, "What's the matter with you, Alice? You should never have let Meggie so much as talk to Kathleen!"

Alice's face flamed with embarrassment, and she dipped her chin. "I'm sorry, Mrs. Stallworth, but Meggie saw Kathleen before I did and ran to her before I could stop her. You…you really can't blame her. She loves her mother, and—"

"Her mother is a bad woman!" cut in Maria. "Meggie doesn't understand that yet. But Kathleen is not fit to be a mother!"

Meggie's little body stiffened. "My mommy is *not* bad, Grandma! She is *not* bad!"

"Come on, Alice," Maria said, her body rigid with anger. "Let's go home."

As the days passed, Alice Downing was disturbed to see little Meggie so unhappy, but she realized there was nothing she could do about it. Her first loyalty was to the Stallworths, who paid her well. She was a widow and needed the money. She would do everything she could to comfort the child and show her love and kindness. But she would also keep Meggie as busy as possible so she had little time to think about how much she missed her mother.

One warm, sunny day, Kathleen was concealed from view of the Stallworths' backyard, watching Meggie as Alice taught her how to play croquet. Meggie seemed to enjoy it, and a thrill of happiness went through Kathleen to see her little girl having fun and giggling. *Alice must truly love Meggie,* she thought. The separation would have been unbearable if Meggie's nanny had been a coldhearted grouch.

When a half hour had passed, Alice took Meggie inside the mansion. Kathleen turned away, unmindful of the tears that flowed down her cheeks. She remembered how it felt to hold Meggie close that day they had met on the street. Mingled with a mother's longing for her child was a bitterness that made her renew her vow to get Meggie back.

The days continued to come and go.

Kathleen worked hard to please her clients, and some nights she was so weary and burdened down with the cares of life that she almost despaired. But memories of Peter and Meggie and the special family warmth they had shared would come to mind, and her hope and determination to have Meggie back grew strong again.

Though Kathleen's clothes were faded and worn, she kept herself squeaky clean and neat as a pin. Often when she pushed the cart along her route—heaped high with freshly laundered items—people turned to look at her. Some even stopped her and became new customers. She continued to take on new clients until she realized that if she was going to have any time to eat and sleep, she would have to turn down any new offers for work.

Though Kathleen had gone to the store downtown for groceries and supplies since starting her business, her pattern changed in late May, when a small neighborhood market opened up half a block from the apartment building. It reminded her of the store her parents had owned, and she became friends with the owners, Isaac and Ruth Goldberg. The Goldbergs had five lively children, and when Kathleen was in the store with them, she was taken back to her own happy childhood.

Every Saturday after her deliveries were made, the young widow went to Goldberg's Market and purchased enough groceries and supplies to last her the coming week. Somehow the Saturday ritual brought comfort to her as she visited with the Goldbergs, who knew a little of her circumstances. Without Kathleen's knowledge, at times Isaac and Ruth charged her somewhat less than the posted prices.

One Saturday evening in late June, Kathleen returned to her little home, put her meager stores away, and prepared supper. Before she sat down to eat, she put a large kettle of water on the stove to heat and let herself enjoy the memory of Meggie that afternoon, happily playing hide-and-seek with Alice in the Stallworths' backyard.

Once the dishes were washed and dried, Kathleen took an old galvanized tub off the back porch wall, placed it on the kitchen floor, and poured the hot, steaming water into it. She tested the temperature and added enough cold water to cool it a bit, then set a bucket of water next to the tub to use for rinsing her hair.

When she was ready to climb into the tub, she cautiously poked a toe in, then slowly lowered her tired body into the soothing water. How wonderful it felt as her tense muscles began to relax. She lathered herself, then soaped her long, luxuriant hair. Using a cup, she poured the rinse water over her head to remove the suds. Then she sank down as far as she could in the small, cramped tub and soaked.

When the water turned tepid she stepped out of the tub, briskly dried herself off, and towel dried her hair. Moments later, dressed in a cotton nightgown, she sat in her one comfortable chair close to the woodstove and took up a hairbrush to work the tangles out of her hair.

Soon the heat from the stove had dried her hair enough to brush it, and the light from a nearby lantern cast golden highlights throughout her dark auburn locks. Before her hair was completely dry, Kathleen went to the cupboard to take out a small ornate wooden box, then sat back down in her chair and spilled the box's contents in her lap—a wad of paper bills and a large number of coins.

She counted out every dollar and every single cent. Her savings was growing slowly but surely, and each week she felt more encouraged. She had looked in newspapers about investments, but every company seemed to want an initial investment of more money than she had yet collected. She still possessed the three hundred dollars in her bank account, but that combined with her saved income was still not enough to open an investment account. Kathleen would just keep adding to her funds until she could find a sure thing that would make money fast.

As she placed the money back in the box, she thought of her daughter. It seemed that every time she saw Meggie through the Stallworths' back fence, the little girl had grown and changed. Her heart broke anew as she realized precious days were slipping away that could never be recaptured.

When Kathleen's hair was finally dry she banked the fire in the stove, blew out the lantern, and snuggled down in her small, hard bed. Blessed sleep quickly claimed her.

As July came to Nevada, Tom Harned had exhausted his search to find a caretaker for Caleb. Laurie Humbert's baby was due in September. At best, Tom had eight or nine weeks to come up with a solution.

Caleb had grown to love Laurie, and their relationship was a close one. It comforted Tom to know that his young son was well cared for when he was at work in the mine.

In addition, Laurie went to the Harned house once a week and gave it a good cleaning. Tom had offered to pay her, but Laurie wouldn't accept any money. Sometimes she invited Tom and Caleb to have supper with her and Bruce.

On those occasions, Pastor Bruce refrained from preaching to Tom, but he slipped Scripture into their conversations and silently prayed that the Lord would drive the Word deep into Tom's heart.

The weather in that part of Nevada was hot and dry, and as Laurie approached her eighth month of pregnancy, her steps were slowed by her girth and her swollen ankles. Caleb was a great help, saving her as many steps as he could.

Every afternoon, Monday through Saturday, Laurie and Caleb sat on the shaded front porch of the parsonage, enjoying a cold glass of tea or lemonade. Laurie had gained Tom's permission to read Bible stories to Caleb, and with every story Laurie told the boy of Jesus and His love.

On a hot midweek day, Tom left the mine and walked into town. His route to the parsonage always took him through the business district. As he drew near the office of the Butterfield Stagelines, he saw miner Jess Sherman watching the stagecoach that was rolling into town ahead of a cloud of dust.

Tom was almost abreast of the Butterfield office when the stage came to a halt and Jess stepped up to open the coach door. A lovely young woman emerged. Jess helped her down and they embraced. Tom was a bit surprised, for he knew Jess was a bachelor.

As other passengers alighted from the stagecoach the crew began handing down the luggage. Jess reached for the young woman's luggage and noticed Tom coming along the boardwalk.

"Howdy, Tom!" he said. "Hold up a minute. I want you to meet someone."

The young lady turned her gaze on Tom, and Jess said, "Tom Harned, I want you to meet Betty Thompson. She's my mail order bride."

"I'm very happy to meet you, Miss Thompson," he said, touching his hat brim. Then to Jess: "Mail order bride, eh? All the times you and I have worked together, and you never told me about this!"

Jess laughed. "Betty's been my little secret, but in a few days she'll be Mrs. Jess Sherman."

Smiling broadly, Tom said, "Well, congratulations to both of you! Especially *you*, Jess. She's beautiful! And…ah…Miss Thompson, if there's anything about Jess you want to know…"

"You keep out of this!" Jess said with a laugh. "Betty will learn enough without your help!"

Tom congratulated the couple again and moved on down the street. He had known about mail order brides, but the possibility of advertising for a bride himself had never crossed his mind.

He rolled the idea around, telling himself it might be the only option left to find someone to care for his six-year-old boy.

Chuck Ramsey, editor and owner of the *Virginia City Sentinel,* was at his desk as the sun slanted through the side windows of the building. He looked up as someone opened the front door.

"Well, howdy, Tom! To what do I owe this pleasure?"

Tom smiled a greeting and moved up to stand in front of Ramsey's desk. "I'm here because of a real need in my home, Chuck."

"Oh?" Ramsey laid down the pencil in his hand. "You don't take my paper?"

Tom laughed. "Oh, I most certainly do. What I need is your help in knowing how to place advertisements in some of the large eastern newspapers."

"I can help you with that. What exactly do you want to advertise?"

"First I have to ask you to keep it confidential."

Ramsey raised his right hand. "I promise."

"All right. Do you have time right now?"

"Sure. And I'm all ears."

On a hot, sticky day in Chicago, Kathleen O'Malley Stallworth wheeled her cart up to the home of Harold and Claudia Stuart, who were regular customers. When she knocked on the door, silver-haired Claudia opened it with a ready smile. "Hello, Kathleen. I'll help you carry in the laundry."

"Oh, no, I'll do it."

"There's no reason I can't help you, dear," Claudia reasoned.

While both women carried ironed clothes and clean linens into the house, Claudia said, "I have to tell you, Kathleen, that we've sold our house, and we'll be moving to Indianapolis before the week is out."

"I…I wasn't aware you had the house up for sale."

"We didn't. But our next-door neighbors knew that Harold was about to retire, and we had planned that when he did, we would move to where our children and grandchildren live. The neighbors have relatives who are moving to Chicago, so they brought them over a couple of days ago and they made us an offer on the house."

Claudia saw Kathleen's countenance fall and said, "Harold and I know this means you'll miss the income from us until you find someone to take our place. We talked about it last night, and we don't want you to come up short."

"Oh, I'll be all right," Kathleen assured her.

Claudia moved toward her purse, which lay on a cupboard nearby. "Kathleen, you have worked hard to please us and have always done a good job with our washing and ironing." She dipped a hand inside the purse and came up with a wad of currency. "We want to give you some money as our way of saying a special thank-you."

Kathleen's eyes widened. "Oh, Claudia, I couldn't—"

"You're going to, dear," said the older woman as she pressed the money into Kathleen's hand.

"But I haven't earned it. I—"

"Yes, you have." Claudia closed Kathleen's hand over the money. "Let's just call it a little bonus for your hard work."

Kathleen blinked against the tears that welled up in her eyes and wrapped her arms around Claudia. They embraced for a long moment, then took a few minutes to bid each other good-bye. Kathleen pushed her cart on down the street. When she reached the corner and started down the next street, she paused to count the money. Two hundred dollars! Added to the three hundred she had in the bank, and the $69.38 she had stashed in her little box, there was almost enough money to open an investment account!

The next day, Kathleen came home to her run-down apartment building with a load of clothing and linens to wash and iron. She had enjoyed making the acquaintance of her next-door neighbor, Sandie Patton, who was also a widow. Sandie's husband and two children had died in the Chicago fire. Sandie worked as a clerk in a clothing store downtown.

As Kathleen wheeled her cart into the hallway of the building, she saw Sandie bidding good-bye to a middle-aged woman who lived in the apartments. She had a newspaper in her hand.

When Sandie saw Kathleen, she lifted the paper and said, "Have you seen this morning's edition of the *Tribune?*"

"No. Something special in it?"

"There sure is. Something of interest to both of us since we lost loved ones in the big fire." She turned to page three and folded the paper, displaying the page so Kathleen could see it. Bold headlines read: CITY COUNCIL APPROVES NEW FIRE ALARM SYSTEM.

"The city council has finally listened to the fire marshal. They're providing the money to install fire alarms on street corners all over Chicago!"

"Well, it's about time," Kathleen said.

"I'll say. The writer of the article says that if the city had installed this alarm system back when Chief Williams first asked for it, the loss of lives and property in the fire of '71 would've been minimal. Our families might still be alive, Kathleen."

To Kathleen those words were like the prodding of an old wound that would never be completely healed. "I'd like to read the entire article when you're through with the paper, Sandie," she said. "Could I borrow it?"

"Here you go. I've read all of it I'm going to read. You can throw it away when you're through with it."

"All right. Thank you."

Kathleen entered her apartment, tossed the folded newspaper on a small table in the bedroom-parlor, and went to the kitchen. She put her supper on to cook, then wheeled the cart of dirty laundry out to the shed. She built a fire in the stove, heated the water, and put the laundry in the tub to soak.

The apartment was stifling. Kathleen left the outside door ajar and opened her one small window, hoping an errant breeze would find its way in.

After eating supper and doing the dishes, she went back to the shed and used a broken broom handle to stir the tub of hot soapy water. After rinsing the clothes and linens, she hung them on the clothesline in the small backyard, then checked to make sure the fire was out in the stove. She looked up at the darkening sky and the first twinkling stars. *Oh, for a good cooling rain!* she thought.

She ambled back to her apartment and reluctantly closed and locked the door, wishing she could leave the door open all night.

Still thinking of the longed-for rain, she poured cool water into the wash basin and removed her soiled clothes. The cool water on her skin helped to revive her. She dried herself and pulled on a faded cotton gown and put on her slippers.

As she eased into her overstuffed chair, she picked up the newspaper from the side table and began reading about the new fire alarm system. Her thoughts returned to the events of the night of the big fire and all the horror of that terrible disaster. If only they had installed the fire alarms when Chief Williams pressed the city council for them.

Kathleen pushed the painful thoughts from her mind and idly flipped through the paper, glancing at articles that captured her interest.

When she came to the classified advertisement section, her eyes fell on a special segment titled: WANTED: MAIL ORDER BRIDES.

A small article within the segment told how businessmen, miners, farmers, ranchers, and fur trappers were finding women quite scarce in the West and were advertising for eastern women to come out and marry them.

Kathleen found ads from men in each of the categories listed and smiled to herself. "Ridiculous," she said aloud. "A woman traveling all the way out there to marry a man she's never met!"

At that instant, her eyes fell on an ad placed by a man in his late twenties named Thomas Harned, who lived in Virginia City, Nevada. Harned was in silver mining and had plans to mine for gold. He was a widower and had a son named Caleb who would soon turn seven. Harned needed a wife, and the boy needed a mother. Any woman who was interested should send a recent photograph of herself, along with a letter, giving facts about herself. He wanted to know her time and place of birth, her family history, her likes and dislikes, and such.

Kathleen shook her head and chuckled. "Only a fool of a woman would do such a thing!"

She laid the paper on the small table and padded to the kitchen for a cup of water. Sudden weariness from her long workday set in, and before the end of her first yawn she headed for the welcoming bed.

Late the next afternoon, Kathleen wheeled her laundry cart up to the front of the apartment building and saw Sandie Patton coming along the boardwalk toward her.

"Hi, Kathleen."

"Hi, yourself," said the redhead.

"You get a chance to read the article about the fire alarms?"

"Sure did. I'm glad to see things improving in this town."

Kathleen wheeled the cart into her apartment and out the back door to the wash shed. She built a fire in the stove and put a tub of water on to heat up.

When she returned to the apartment, her eyes fell on the *Chicago Tribune*. She sat down in the overstuffed chair and picked up the paper, flipping pages. She thought of the ad placed by the man in Virginia City, Nevada. What was his name? *Thomas…mmm…oh, yes. Thomas Harned.* She turned to the Mail Order Bride section and read Harned's ad again.

Kathleen had heard about the Comstock Lode in Virginia City, and that other mines were being discovered near there. Some men had struck it rich. Suddenly her heart quickened pace.

Kathleen went to the shed and put the laundry in the tub to soak. As she walked back to the apartment, she said aloud, "Kathleen, maybe a woman wouldn't be such a fool, after all. Maybe this is the break I need to get my Meggie back!"

Kathleen sat down at the kitchen table and wrote a letter to Tom Harned. She told him the things he wanted to know about her date and place of birth, the tragic loss of her family in the famous Chicago fire, and that her husband had been killed by robbers on a dark Chicago street.

She didn't mention her daughter. And she didn't mention her married name. If Tom Harned knew about her entanglement with the wealthy and powerful Stallworths, it might scare him off. She'd keep Meggie her secret for now.

Some three weeks after the Chicago fire, Kathleen had been interviewed by the *Chicago Tribune*. Her photo had accompanied the interview.

Kathleen had kept the paper amongst her personal items. She cut the picture out and placed it in the letter, stating the year it was taken, but that it was the only photograph she had of herself. She told Thomas Harned that her hair was a dark shade of auburn and her eyes were dark blue.

She hesitated for a moment and then quickly sealed the envelope, sighing as she said, "Well, Meggie darling, this may be our big chance!"

15

DURING THE LAST WEEK OF AUGUST, Laurie Humbert's sister, Mardy Richton, arrived in Virginia City from her home in Akron, Ohio. Her arrival was a surprise to the Humberts, but a welcome one. Mardy was two years younger than Laurie, and unmarried. She had come to help Bruce and Laurie prior to the birth of their child and was planning to stay a couple of months afterward to do the housework and cooking.

Upon her arrival, Mardy learned that Laurie was taking care of Caleb Harned, and she quickly made known to Tom that she would take over in Laurie's place.

Laurie gave birth to a healthy baby girl on Saturday, September 1, 1877.

On the next Saturday afternoon, Tom Harned stopped by the post office on his way to the parsonage from work and picked up his mail. He hurried on to the Humbert home and found Caleb in the parlor with the new baby. Young Caleb watched the infant with fascination.

"Dad," he said as they left the house and headed home, "I hope someday when you get married again, we can have a baby in our house."

"Oh, really? And do you want a brother or sister?"

"I wouldn't really care. I'd like to have a brother, but if we could have a cute little girl like Pastor and Mrs. Humbert's, that would be fine."

Tom patted Caleb's blond head. "Well, I'm glad you're open to either, 'cause when babies come, we don't get a choice as to whether they're a boy or a girl."

When father and son turned into their yard, three boys from down the street came running up, asking if Caleb could play with them.

"Just be home by sundown, Caleb," Tom said as he watched his boy run down the street with his friends.

The sun was dropping behind the distant mountain peaks when Caleb came home, puffing from a hard run. Tom was sitting at the kitchen table holding a newspaper photograph in his hand.

"Hi, Dad!" Caleb called.

Tom glanced up. "Hello, son. Have a good time?"

"Sure did. Uh…Dad?"

"Yes?"

"I don't smell anything cookin'. Are we gonna go to one of the cafés for supper?"

"Yes, we are."

Caleb jumped up and down. "Whoopee!"

"Something wrong with my cooking?" Tom said with a frown.

Caleb looked at the photograph in his father's hand and the letter and envelope lying on the table. "Is that another letter from one of those ladies back east, Dad?"

Tom had already received nine letters but had not replied to any of them. None of the women who had responded to his mail order bride ads appealed to him.

But this letter held him fascinated, as did the photograph. Angling the picture so Caleb could see it, he said, "What do you think of this pretty Irish lady, son?"

Caleb's eyes widened. "Wow, Dad! She's really pretty! Are you gonna marry her?"

"Well, maybe. Would you like to have her for your new mother?"

Caleb's face twisted and his lower lip quivered.

Tom took him onto his lap and held him. "I'm sorry, Caleb. I didn't mean to make you cry."

"It's all right, Dad."

"Caleb, I know you miss Mommy. I miss her, too. Something awful. But we can't have her back. You…you need a mother more than anything. I just don't know how to do that job."

Caleb nodded and brushed at a tear rolling down his cheek. "You try, Dad," he said.

"Yes, but a father just doesn't have the know-how and the tenderness of a mother."

Caleb nodded once again, thought on it for a moment, then said, "It would be real good to have a new mother, but I won't call her *Mommy.*"

"I understand, son."

Father and son ate supper at a café in town, then spent the evening together at home, playing games.

Later that night, when Caleb was in bed asleep, Tom sat down at the kitchen table and wrote a letter to Kathleen O'Malley.

On Monday, September 17, Kathleen O'Malley came home with her laundry cart loaded. While she was pushing it down the hall toward her apartment door, her landlord came out of his apartment with an envelope in his hand. "Letter came for you today, Kathleen. I wasn't aware you knew anyone in Nevada."

Kathleen's heart fluttered as she plucked the envelope from his fingers and said, "Oh, life does have its little surprises, doesn't it? Thank you, Mr. Jones."

She pushed the cart inside her apartment and opened the letter with trembling hands. A recent photograph of Tom and Caleb was enclosed. Kathleen was struck by Tom's good looks and Caleb's golden hair and big eyes. She held the photograph in one hand while she read the letter:

September 8, 1877

Mrs. Kathleen O'Malley
148 Orchard Street Apt. 3
Chicago, Illinois

Dear Kathleen,

I received your letter today, and by the newspaper photograph, I can see that you are a beautiful young lady. There is something in your eyes that tells me you are just as beautiful on the inside.

I am sorry you had to experience the loss of your husband. Especially in such a violent way. My wife Loretta was a wonderful wife and mother. She died giving birth to our baby girl, and the baby also died. Caleb was very close to Loretta and misses her very much, but I have no doubt he will have plenty of love for a new mother.

Let me explain that I am an employee of Mr. Henry Comstock of the famous Comstock Silver Lode. However, I have been saving as much money as possible in order to stake my own claim on a gold mine here in the Virginia City area. I am still somewhat short of funds (about $500), but I will have that much saved up in a year or so, then I will have my own claim. I am confident I will do well, as other men have done in this area, and will become a wealthy man.

I am asking you to come to Virginia City and become my bride. I do not expect you to marry me upon arriving. We can get to know each other, and I will let you pick the time. I will provide you a separate place to live until we marry, but you will need to take care of Caleb at your place when he comes home from school, and all day on Saturdays.

I have a nice six-room house and will provide well for you if you will come to Virginia City, marry me, and be a mother to Caleb.

I will eagerly await your reply. If the answer is affirmative, I will send you the money to cover your railroad fare by return mail.

Yours hopefully and sincerely,

Tom Harned

Kathleen felt a touch of disappointment upon reading that Tom was simply an employee in the silver mining business, but something about the letter touched her, and she read it over two more times, looked at the photograph, then read the letter again.

After doing her washing and eating supper, Kathleen sat down and wrote a reply to Tom Harned. She labored over the letter, making sure each word she chose was exactly the right one. She told Tom that she had a little over five hundred dollars saved up, and if they married, she would invest it to help him stake his claim on a gold mine. All she asked was that they divide the profits evenly when they struck it big, because she had a personal need for a large sum of money. If Tom agreed to her terms, she would come to Virginia City, marry him after a proper amount of time, and be a good mother to Caleb.

Fourteen days after Kathleen sent her letter to Tom, a letter came from him containing a check for more than enough to cover her railroad ticket to Reno, Nevada—the nearest railroad town to Virginia City.

Tom's letter stated that he deeply appreciated her willingness to invest her savings in his proposed mining business, and he agreed to her terms of dividing the profits. As he closed the letter off, he told her how happy and excited he was that she had agreed to come, and that Caleb—in his boyish way—was looking forward to having her for his new mother.

The next morning, Kathleen went to the Chicago railroad station and purchased her ticket. She wrote Tom a brief letter, telling him she would leave a week from that day and arrive in Reno on the Central Pacific train at 1:30 P.M. on Friday, October 12.

On the day before she was to leave for Nevada, Kathleen delivered her final batch of laundry in early afternoon. Knowing that Alice Downing usually took Meggie into the Stallworths' backyard to play around 3:30, she made one last trip to see her little girl. It was about 3:15 when Kathleen drew up to the fence behind the Stallworth mansion.

The air was chilly on that October afternoon. When Meggie emerged from the mansion she was clad in an expensive fur-trimmed coat and bonnet and wore a nice pair of mittens. Kathleen breathed a prayer of thanks that Alice's routine had not been interrupted that day.

Kathleen drank in the sight of Meggie as Alice pushed the child in a swing that hung from a tree limb. There was no way of knowing when she would set eyes on Meggie again.

It was almost five o'clock when Alice told Meggie it was time to go inside. Kathleen blew Meggie a kiss, saying in a low whisper, "Mommy loves you, sweetheart. I'll be back to take you away from those evil people as soon as I can."

She waited until the little girl had disappeared through the door, then turned and walked away, tears streaming down her cheeks.

Friday, October 12, was a warm and sunny day in Nevada as Tom Harned and his son drove up to the railroad station in Reno.

Tom was dressed in suit and tie, and wore a white shirt he had ironed himself. His black boots were polished, and he wore his best Stetson.

Caleb had been scrubbed by Mardy Richton until his cheeks were rosy. In the sun's light his blond hair was a shining halo around his head.

The blue eyes of father and son—so much alike—shone with a mixture of excitement and apprehension. This momentous occasion would alter their lives completely, and each was more than a little scared for his own reasons.

It was 1:10 P.M. when Tom and Caleb stepped onto the platform where a small crowd had gathered.

"Dad…"

"Mm-hmm?" Tom cast a glance toward the east where the train would appear, but there was no sign of it yet.

"Should I call my new mother Ma? Or would Mom be better? I can't call her Mommy, because that's what I called my real mother."

"Tell you what, son," said Tom, "why don't you wait until you two get to know each other? Then you can ask her what she'd like you to call her."

"Okay. But until then, I gotta call her somep'n. What should I call her?"

"Just call her ma'am. That's a polite way to address her."

Kathleen was experiencing her own anxiety as the train thundered westward. She stood before the mirror in the washroom of her coach and freshened up as best she could. It had been a long and tiring trip, traveling day and night, with many stops. Dust and soot had a way of blowing into the coaches and covering everything with a gritty film.

Kathleen dipped a handkerchief into the basin of cool water and dabbed the grime from her face and hands. She removed her new hat, smoothed back her hair with wet fingers and pinned it securely, then replaced her hat. She gave her pale cheeks a pinch and tried in vain to brush the wrinkles out of her dress, which—along with the hat—she had bought new just before leaving Chicago. She took one last look at herself in the wavy mirror and knew she was as ready as she would ever be. She drew a deep breath and returned to her seat to wait out the few minutes until they pulled into the station.

The conductor set Kathleen's heart to pounding like a trip-hammer when he came in the front door of the coach and called above the clack of the wheels, "Reno...five minutes!"

First Tom and Caleb saw the billowing smoke, then caught sight of the train chugging down the track. A moment later the whistle blew.

"I'm scared, Dad," Caleb said.

Tom looked down and laid a hand on his son's shoulder. "Of what?"

"Well, what if my new mother doesn't like me? What if she won't marry you because she doesn't want to be my new mother?"

The engine bell was clanging now, and the train was slowing to enter the station. "Don't you worry about that, Caleb. You're a good boy, and she's going to like you."

Caleb swallowed hard and set his gaze on the train.

Soon people appeared on the platforms of each passenger coach and began to step down from the train. Tom let his gaze sweep along all four cars, wondering which one Kathleen was in. As the agonizing minutes passed, his eyes darted from platform to platform, searching for the face he had memorized from the newspaper photograph.

There she was, descending from the rear platform of car number three, carrying a small satchel. Tom's heart thumped his rib cage and his mouth went dry. "Caleb," he said shakily.

"I see her, Dad."

Kathleen scanned the small crowd as she started down the steps of the car's rear platform. It took only seconds for her to recognize the man and boy from the photograph. When her feet touched the wooden depot platform, she stepped aside, then stood still as if frozen in time. Her eyes were fixed on the father and son who remained immobile.

Tom felt Caleb tugging on his pant leg. "Dad, shouldn't we go to her?"

As soon as Tom and Caleb began moving toward her, Kathleen took a step toward them, too.

When they drew up to each other, Caleb was still clutching his father's pant leg.

Kathleen smiled at Tom with a touch of apprehension in her eyes, her stomach churning.

"Kathleen," Tom said, his heart pounding, "I…I'm not sure what to do."

Trembling slightly, Kathleen let her smile broaden and said, "Well, maybe a gentlemanly hug would be appropriate." She set down her satchel as she spoke.

Tom embraced her gently as if she might break and said, "I'm so happy you've come."

"And I'm so happy you wanted me to come."

Caleb watched them with wide eyes.

When Tom and Kathleen let go of each other, she turned to the boy and said, "Hello, Caleb. My, you're quite the young man. How about a hug from you?"

Caleb dipped his chin in silence.

The smile on Tom's face faded as he said, "Caleb, aren't you going to give the nice lady a hug?"

Caleb brought his eyes up to meet Kathleen's, took one faltering step toward her, then stiffened as she bent over and put her arms around him. Kathleen said nothing as she let go of Caleb and took a step back, but Tom caught the flash of disappointment on her face.

"Kathleen," he said falteringly, "I'm sorry. I don't understand this. Caleb has been looking forward to your coming."

Kathleen smiled softly at Caleb. "I understand," she said. "He doesn't know me yet. We'll get acquainted as time goes by."

"Well!" Tom said. "I'm sure glad you're here!" His eyes dropped to the one lonely satchel at her feet. "Do you have more luggage in the baggage car?"

"No." Kathleen dipped her head in embarrassment.

"Okay, let's go!"

Soon they were headed south toward Virginia City, sitting three abreast on the buggy seat.

Having the child seated next to her made Kathleen think of Meggie, and her heart ached for her little daughter. *All of this is for you, precious Meggie.*

Kathleen pointed out to Caleb different landmarks as the buggy rolled south. She chattered to him about the rock formations, the streams and hills, and the small wild animals. Soon the boy had warmed up some.

When Kathleen grew quiet, Tom asked about her parents, her childhood, and about Peter.

Kathleen gladly told him about her formative years and talked about her close-knit family. When she started to talk about the day they died in the fire, she choked up a little and said how very much she still missed them. She talked briefly about her marriage to Peter—avoiding any mention of his last name—but said nothing about Meggie.

Kathleen then asked Tom about his past and his marriage to Loretta. When the conversation edged close to Loretta's death, Kathleen felt Caleb tense up, and she steered the conversation to questions about his school, his teacher, and his friends.

When Virginia City came into view as they topped a hill, Tom said, "Guess I'd better tell you what arrangements I've made for your place to stay until…until we have the wedding."

"All right," she said, smiling.

"I've put you in the Silver Plume Hotel. It's only three years old, so it's in good condition, and the rooms are really nice. You'll have maid service daily. There's a very good restaurant connected to the hotel, and you can eat your meals there and charge them to the room. Of course, Caleb and I will take you other places for meals, too."

It felt good to Kathleen to have a man looking after her. Tom was a warm person and a gentleman, and he made her feel wanted.

Kathleen smiled with pleasure when she saw the hotel. The ornate designs of the doors and windows, and even the sign, showed excellent taste in architecture. This was something she had not expected in the "wild" West.

Tom guided her inside the hotel, and Kathleen was even more pleased at the interior. The lobby was lavishly decorated with attractive tapestries, curtains, drapes, carpet, and furniture.

The lady behind the desk saw them coming and smiled warmly at Kathleen, then greeted Caleb. "Her photograph didn't do her justice, Tom," the woman said.

"My sentiments exactly. Kathleen, I want you to meet Donna Mitchell. Her husband, Hank, works with me at the mine. Hank and Donna are dear friends."

Kathleen smiled sweetly. "I'm very happy to meet you, Mrs. Mitchell."

Donna threw up her palms in protest. "Oh, honey, Mrs. Mitchell is Hank's mother. You can call me Donna."

"All right. Donna it is. And I'm Kathleen."

"I'm just so happy for you and Tom, Kathleen, and for this precious little boy. Tom didn't tell any of us about you coming until just a few days ago. We were surprised, and very pleased to learn he was going to have some happiness again."

"I'm glad," Kathleen said. "We can both use some of that."

"Hello, Tom," came a familiar voice from behind him.

Tom turned to see the Humberts.

"Laurie and I noticed your horse and buggy parked in front of the hotel. Is this your bride-to-be?"

Tom put a hand under Kathleen's elbow and drew her gently toward the couple.

She felt warmed by their smiles, but a touch of discomfort coursed through her as soon as Tom introduced them as Pastor Bruce Humbert and Laurie. As Tom explained that Laurie had taken care of Caleb after Loretta died, Kathleen wondered if Tom attended Pastor Humbert's church. He had said nothing about church in his letters. She thought of her friend Hennie and remembered the sermons she had heard from D. L. Moody. She remained pleasant toward the Humberts but was eager to leave their presence.

Moments later, as she and Tom and Caleb topped the stairs and moved down the hall, Kathleen pictured God's Son dying for her on Calvary's cross. She tried to force it from her mind as Tom stopped in front of a door and said, "Here's your room, Kathleen."

AFTER SETTLING KATHLEEN IN HER HOTEL ROOM, Tom drove her to Mount Davidson to see the Comstock Lode where he worked, then to the house where she would live when they were married.

Caleb rode in silence, except when Tom or Kathleen addressed him.

"Here it is, Kathleen," Tom said, as he pulled up in front of a one-level white frame house. He had painted it shortly before Loretta died and had kept the yard looking good.

"It's nice," Kathleen said as Tom hopped out of the buggy and Caleb jumped out behind him.

Tom hurried around the rear of the buggy and offered Kathleen his hand. Smiling, he said, "May I help you down, m'lady?"

"Yes, you may, kind sir," she replied in a light tone, noting the look on Caleb's face as he waited where the lawn met the street.

She placed her gloved hand in Tom's, and as he helped her down, she felt a warmth flow through her. She'd wondered if men in the Wild West were as gentlemanly as those in the East. Certainly Tom Harned was, for which she was thankful.

When Kathleen's feet touched ground, their eyes met for a long moment. Feeling a bit off balance, she covered her feeling of awkwardness by saying, "Let's begin the tour."

"I made some changes inside the house after I received your letter saying you would come, Kathleen. I didn't want you to feel uncomfortable if you wanted to redecorate it, and it was still the way Loretta had left it."

Kathleen nodded. As Tom took her into each room, Kathleen

could tell that the most recent decorating—if she could call it that—had been done by a male.

When they stood at the front door of the parlor once again, Tom said, "What do you think?"

"It's a lovely house, Tom. With…ah…your permission, I would like to give it the feminine touch."

Tom chuckled. "So you can tell where I made some changes?"

"Ah…yes," she said with a grin. "That shouldn't be a surprise, should it? I mean, after all, God made males and females different, didn't He. Males weren't meant to be housekeepers."

Tom looked around at the parlor and said, "That's for sure!"

They laughed together as Caleb stood quietly looking on.

"It's just about suppertime, Kathleen. Are you getting hungry?"

"I am," spoke up Caleb. "You're not gonna cook, are you, Dad?"

Kathleen's eyes widened. "Don't you like your father's cooking, Caleb?"

"Well-l-l-l…"

She laughed again and laid a hand on the boy's shoulder. "When your father and I get married, I'll cook your favorite things, and I think you'll like my cooking."

Caleb smiled for the first time since Kathleen had arrived.

"What I was going to suggest," Tom said, "was that Caleb and I take you to the restaurant at the hotel."

"Sounds good to me," said Kathleen.

The six-year-old nodded his enthusiastic agreement.

The dining room at the Silver Plume Restaurant was filled with the wonderful aromas of savory food, and the place was fairly crowded.

Tom spotted a table in a far corner and took Kathleen by the elbow as he held Caleb's hand and steered them toward the table covered with a snowy white linen tablecloth. A small vase stood in the center with the last of the fall flowers. A candle burned next to the vase, casting a soft glow over the table.

Tom seated Kathleen while Caleb settled his small frame on the chair of his choice.

"Thank you," she said, looking up at Tom and smiling warmly.

"My pleasure, ma'am."

A waitress bearing menus and a steaming pot of coffee drew up to the table just as Tom was sitting down. "Good evening, Mr. Harned," she said. "Hello, Caleb."

"Good evening to you, Lydia. I would like you to meet Kathleen O'Malley."

The young woman, who was no more than twenty-one, said, "Welcome to Virginia City, Miss O'Malley. Mr. Harned told me that you were coming."

"Thank you. I'm pleased to be here."

"Lydia's husband works at a silver mine about ten miles southwest of town," Tom said.

Kathleen smiled at the waitress. "I see."

When Lydia had poured coffee and left them to decide what they wanted from the menu, Kathleen said, "Apparently you and Caleb eat here quite often."

"We have since Loretta—"

"We didn't come here much when Mommy was with us," Caleb said. "But Dad likes this food better than the kind he cooks at home. And I do, too."

Tom cleared his throat and gave his son a *children are to be seen and not heard* look. Kathleen made a mental note that the boy called Lorreta *Mommy*.

While Tom and Kathleen looked the menu over, discussing the many selections, Tom said, "Just about a year ago, they brought a chef in here from one of San Francisco's big hotels. Whatever you choose will be tasty."

When the waitress returned with more coffee, Tom gave her the food orders.

He and Kathleen made small talk while waiting for their meal. But when she tried to draw Caleb into the conversation, he pulled back and only replied with a yes or a no.

Kathleen had felt she was making some headway with the boy, but there was still something bothering him. She hoped it was only difficulty in accepting a prospective stepmother and not something he disliked about her.

Tom's thoughts were taking a similar turn. Kathleen was such a sweet person, and she was making every effort to win Caleb's favor. He couldn't imagine there might be something Caleb didn't like about her, but the boy was certainly acting funny.

When Lydia arrived with their food and began placing it on the table, Kathleen hesitantly removed her white cotton gloves. She had been putting salve on her work-worn hands during the journey from Chicago, and they looked better, but they were still red and rough to the touch.

They began to eat but soon found they weren't as hungry as they'd thought. The food looked and smelled good, but their stomachs were too filled with butterflies to do justice to the meal.

When Lydia came by with coffee, she said, "Is something wrong with the food, Mr. Harned?"

"Ah...no, Lydia, there's nothing wrong. It's just that we've had quite a bit of excitement today with Kathleen arriving and all. I guess it has affected our appetites."

Lydia smiled. "I can understand that. How about more coffee?"

Back at the hotel, Tom and Caleb walked Kathleen up the stairs to her room.

When Kathleen took the skeleton key from her purse, Tom reached for it. "Here. Let me do it for you."

He inserted the key, turned the knob, and gave the door a slight shove. "You get some rest," he said softly, placing the key in her gloved hand. "I know you've got to be tuckered out."

"That I am," Kathleen admitted with a sigh.

"Tomorrow you just relax, and I'll get in touch with you sometime during the day. If you need to go shopping, I'll take you. Or if you'd like to walk to the stores alone, I'll give you some money to get whatever you want or need."

"You really don't need to give me any money," Kathleen said sweetly. "I'm not your responsibility yet."

"As far as I'm concerned, you are."

Kathleen smiled. "You're a good man, Thomas Harned. You come by any time you can tomorrow. I'll be here."

"All right." Tom looked at his son. "Caleb, you can hug her good-night first."

Caleb wrapped his arms gently around Kathleen's neck when she bent down to hug him.

"Good night, Caleb," she said.

"Good night, ma'am," came his soft reply.

Tom gave her another gentlemanly embrace and said, "You get some rest now. I'll see you tomorrow."

Caleb was in bed, waiting for his father, when suddenly he thought of how much he missed having his mother tuck him in and kiss him good-night. Bedtime was always a special time. Loretta would take a few minutes to read to him from the few books they had in the house. Often he knew the stories by heart, but it made no difference. He loved the sweet sound of her voice as she sat on the bed beside him and read. His lower lip started to quiver. When he heard his father steps coming down the hall, he stifled the tears welling up inside him.

"I think we need to talk, son," Tom said as he entered the room.

Caleb did not reply.

Tom sat down on the edge of the bed. "All right, Caleb. What is it?"

"Hmm?" The boy looked up at him and frowned.

"You know what I'm talking about. When I told you Kathleen was coming from Chicago to be my wife and your new mother, you seemed happy and excited about it. Why the sudden coldness toward her?"

Fat tears hovered in Caleb's eyes and silently slipped down his little face.

"Caleb, I asked you a question. Why did you barely talk to Kathleen, and why were your hugs so weak?"

Caleb brushed the tears from his cheeks. A lump clogged his throat.

"Caleb...I'm waiting."

The boy sniffed, blinked more tears onto his cheeks, and said, "Mommy wouldn't want me to love another mother."

"You mean you think that if you give love and affection to Kathleen, you're being unfaithful to your mommy?"

The towheaded boy bit his lower lip and nodded. "Yes, sir."

"Come here," Tom said, opening his arms.

Caleb left the covers and let his father's strong arms encircle him.

As Tom held him close, he said, "Son, I know all that's happened—losing your mommy, and having to stay with other people while I work—has been awfully hard for you. I'm sure it's been confusing. And now I bring in a new mother for you and wife for me. That has to be very difficult for a boy your age to accept. But listen to me."

Caleb pulled back so he could look into his father's eyes.

"Son, your mommy was a very sweet and loving person, wasn't she?"

Caleb nodded.

"Then she wouldn't feel that you were being unfaithful to her if you showed love to Kathleen. Your mother would want you to love Kathleen and make her feel welcome and let her know that you need her. Does that make sense?"

"I think so."

"Kathleen has come a long, long way to be with us, not only to be my wife but to be your mother. I think you hurt her feelings today."

Surprise showed in the boy's big eyes. "Really?"

"Really. I saw it on her face. Don't you think she deserves to be loved and appreciated?"

"Yes, sir."

"Then how about from here on, you let her know how much you appreciate that she's come to be your mommy."

Caleb swallowed hard. "Dad, I…I couldn't call her *Mommy.* I just couldn't."

"All right. When the two of you get to know each other better, you can ask her whether she wants you to call her Mom or Ma. Okay?"

"Uh-huh."

Tom hugged Caleb close. "That's my boy. Now, you need to get to sleep. I know we're going to be a happy family, Caleb. And please understand that this doesn't mean you ever have to forget your birth mother. She will always be a part of your life. But you now have a second mother to take care of you…and me."

Caleb left his father's arms and slid back down under the covers. Tom kissed his forehead, pulled the covers up tight under his chin, and said, "I love you, son."

"I love you, too, Dad," came the small voice.

Tom blew out the lamp and started toward the door.

"Dad?"

"Mm-hmm?"

"Would…would you tell my new mother that I'm sorry I hurt her feelings, and explain in big people's talk why I acted like I did? And then when I see her, I'll tell her I'm sorry."

"I'll do that for you, Caleb. And I'm proud of you. I know the three of us are going to be very happy together. Good night, son."

"Good night, Dad. Dad?"

Tom paused. "Yes?"

"My new mother is really pretty, isn't she?"

"That she is, son."

The little boy's face seemed brighter. "Dad…"

"Yes?"

"Thanks for talking to me."

Tom walked back to the bed and stroked the boy's soft blond hair. "You go to sleep now. I'm staying right here with you until you do."

Caleb gave him a sleepy smile and nestled close to the man who was his hero. Within seconds, his big blue eyes closed with the smile still in place.

Kathleen decided to order hot water up to her room and take a good, soothing bath. When the bath was over and she had slid between the clean sheets on the luxurious feather bed, she gave a big sigh. Tom was all she had expected and more—a gentleman supreme—and she knew he was an honest, hardworking, intelligent man who could provide a good living. He had certainly shown her he was happy she had come, and there was no hesitation on his part concerning the marriage proposal he'd made by mail.

But Caleb. What if he decided not to accept her as his stepmother? Was she going to fail with him?

Kathleen lay with her eyes closed in the dark room. Suddenly the distance between her new home and Meggie seemed overwhelming. Hot tears pressed against her eyelids as she thought of the enormity of the whole thing. Getting Meggie back depended on making a good marriage with Tom...and Tom's success in the gold mining business.

Aloud, she said, "I'm working on it, sweetheart. You hold on. Mommy's going to come and get you one day soon."

With those words like a prayer on her lips, Kathleen slept more peacefully than any time since Peter had been murdered and Meggie had been taken from her.

When Kathleen arose from her bed the next morning, she noticed a slip of paper on the floor under the door. She picked it up, unfolded it, and read:

Good morning, sweet Kathleen! I hope you slept well. Have yourself a nice breakfast in the hotel restaurant, then meet me there for lunch at noon. I will be looking forward to it!

Tom

Kathleen decided to skip breakfast and work at making herself especially presentable for Tom.

Yesterday she had looked travel-worn, but today—after a good night's rest—she felt better, and when she looked at herself in the mirror there was an optimistic gleam in her eyes. There was also some color in her cheeks. She washed her face in cool water, dried off, then sat down with a hairbrush and went to work on her hair.

She brushed her wavy, gold-streaked auburn hair vigorously, then pinned it in a loose chignon at the nape of her graceful neck. No matter how hard she tried to tame it, small tendrils came down and curled around her face and neck.

She had bought two dresses before leaving Chicago, one to travel in, and the other for the first time she would see Tom after arriving in Virginia City. She put on her high-button shoes, then slipped into the dress. It was made of soft sunshine yellow dimity with a thin white stripe. There was a delicate ruffle around the high neck, and the sleeves were long. The dress hugged her tiny waist and fell in soft folds to the tips of her shiny shoes.

Suddenly she couldn't wait to see Tom again, and it showed in the deepening flush of her cheeks.

Tom left the bowels of the mine and washed up at the office before heading for town. He arrived at the Silver Plume Hotel just before noon and went to the door of the restaurant, which was just off the lobby. He scanned the room to see if Kathleen had already arrived and found a table, but she was nowhere to be seen.

Several people were standing in the lobby, chatting, when Tom glanced up at the top of the stairs and then couldn't take his eyes off what he saw.

As Kathleen paused on the stair landing with her hand on the banister, her stunning beauty took Tom's breath away. He moved forward, and she smiled at him, then started down the stairs.

There was a look of expectancy on both their faces as she reached the last step and he offered his hand. He guided her into the restaurant to a table on the far side and was amazed to see she was unaware that men and women in the dining room were admiring her.

He waited until their food was on the table, then said, "Kathleen, someone has asked me to explain something to you."

She raised her eyebrows. "Oh? Who and what?"

"The *who* is my six-year-old son. The *what* is that he and I had a little talk last night about his coolness toward you." He took a sip of coffee, then said, "You did notice it, didn't you?"

"Well, yes. But I know this whole thing has to be difficult for him. I'm hoping that in time he and I will become very close."

Tom grinned. "Bless your heart. Since we had our talk, I think the 'getting close' process is well on its way."

"Oh, I hope so. Tell me about it."

While they ate, Tom explained Caleb's sudden fear that he would betray his mother if he showed affection to Kathleen. Now he wanted to apologize for hurting her feelings.

"That's very sweet of him, Tom," she said. "But he really doesn't have to apologize."

"He *wants* to. Let him. It will be good for him. You know, part of the growing up process."

She nodded. "Well, whenever you want me to start taking care of Caleb after school and on Saturdays, I'm ready."

A broad smile captured the handsome man's features. "You don't know how good that sounds. How about tomorrow?"

"Tomorrow is fine."

"Okay. Can you meet Caleb at the house at 3:15 and bring him to the hotel?"

"Sure."

"On Saturdays I'll bring him to the hotel on my way to work."

"It's a deal," Kathleen said. "And speaking of deals, Tom, I have the five hundred dollars I told you I would give to help stake your claim to a gold mine. I'll give it to you when we marry."

"Fine. And let me assure you, Kathleen, I won't push you. You can choose the time when we get married."

"Thank you, Tom. I do feel good about our upcoming marriage, but I think we should wait a while on it. We need to get to know each other better, and we should allow time to find out if either of us wants to back out. Also, and utmost in my thinking, waiting will give Caleb time to adjust."

A smile curved Tom's lips. "I agree. I can't believe there would ever be a reason I'd want to back out, but I want you to feel absolutely comfortable."

Kathleen's eyes sparkled as she said, "I'm really excited about spending afternoons and Saturdays with Caleb. In fact, I've already been thinking of some things he and I can do together. He's a precious child, Tom. And even though I got a bit of the cool treatment yesterday, he's already found a place in my heart."

Tom Harned pondered the situation with Kathleen as he walked toward the mine. He was glad to hear that Caleb had found a place in her heart. Next he hoped to hear that *he* had found a place there, too. She had already made it clear that she liked him.

If he knew his own heart like he thought he did, it wasn't going to take him long to fall in love with this beautiful woman who was just as beautiful on the inside. She would make a wonderful wife for him, and he could already tell that she would be a good mother to Caleb.

The only question was why she needed so much money. Whatever it was must be quite important to her, since she was willing to give up her five-hundred-dollar nest egg to help him stake his claim. But she hadn't volunteered the reason. Well, he could live with a little mystery for a while.

That evening, Kathleen answered the knock at her hotel room door and found Tom and Caleb standing in the hall.

"Well, hello," she said with a smile. "It isn't every lady who has *two* handsome men come to take her to supper."

Tom grinned and looked down at Caleb. "Did you hear that, son? She thinks we're both handsome."

"Yeah, but I'm handsomer than you, Dad!"

Kathleen winked at Tom and said to the boy, "You're just a smidgen handsomer than your father."

Caleb laughed. "See there, Dad? I told you!" He turned back to Kathleen. "Ma'am?"

"Yes, Caleb?"

"What's a smidgen?"

"A smidgen is a little bit."

"Kathleen," Tom said, "before we go to supper, there's a young man here who would like to talk to you in private…at his request."

Kathleen looked down at the fair-haired boy and said, "Come in, Caleb, and we'll talk."

"I'll wait down in the lobby," Tom said, turning to leave.

Kathleen gestured toward one of two overstuffed chairs. "Would you like to sit down, Caleb?"

"I would rather stand, ma'am, but I would like for you to sit down."

"All right," she said, easing into the chair. She looked him in the eye and smiled. "What did you want to talk to me about?"

"I owe you an apology, ma'am. I wasn't very nice to you yesterday, and I'm sorry. I asked Dad to explain it to you, and I hope you understand about…about how I felt Mommy might feel if I showed love to you."

"I understand completely, Caleb. I know you loved your mommy very much, and that's what a boy *should* do. Please understand that I will never try to take her place in your heart. But if I could have my own place in your heart, it would make me very happy."

Caleb nodded. "Ma'am, do you forgive me for not being nice to you yesterday?"

"Yes, I forgive you."

A sunny smile broke across the little boy's face. "Thank you, ma'am."

"You're a very good boy, Caleb. It took courage for you to talk to me like this—to say you were wrong and to ask forgiveness."

His blue eyes watched her face closely as he said, "Ma'am?"

"Yes?"

"I didn't hug you very good yesterday. Could I hug you good right now?"

Kathleen's heart seemed to swell, and tears surfaced. "You sure can."

This time Caleb hugged her with feeling. When they let go of each other, a shy but serious look settled in the child's deep blue eyes. "Ma'am, you do have your very own place in my heart. I love you."

Kathleen barely managed to speak past the lump in her throat. "Thank you, Caleb. Thank you! And you know what? You have a very special place in my heart, and I love you, too."

When they embraced again, Kathleen thought of her little Meggie and how very much she missed her.

Tom took Kathleen to Maude's Café for supper. It wasn't a fancy place, but the food was excellent.

While they waited for their food, Kathleen said, "Tell me about mining, Tom. I know virtually nothing about it."

It took about ten minutes for Tom to explain the functioning of a silver mine, which was quite similar to mining for gold, he pointed out.

When he had finished with the mechanics of it all she said, "How deep are you working in the mountain?"

"Oh…about three hundred feet."

"Isn't that dangerous?"

"Well, I can't say there isn't an element of danger, but it's nothing for you to worry about. Mr. Comstock insists on a careful setup of the wooden beams that support the tunnels. Besides, when you and I get married, I'm going to start looking for a spot to stake a gold claim. Maybe when I work my own mine, I won't have to work so deep in the ground."

Kathleen thought of Peter and how quickly his life had been snuffed out. Becoming a widow the second time would be more than she could stand.

It was a glorious autumn day, with the sun slanting against the high Sierras to the west as Kathleen left the hotel and walked toward the Harned house on the east side of town.

This was her first day to meet Caleb at the house after school, and she was excited. Not only had their talk the evening before removed the wall between them, but she knew she had this little boy's love, and she would try her best not to disappoint him.

She basked in the golden sunshine beneath a clear and brilliant cobalt blue sky. The deep green of pine trees accentuated the yellow of the shimmering aspen and the red and russet of the maple and poplar trees. Scrub oak on the surrounding hillsides were yet a different shade of red-orange, and even the soft green of the sagebrush blended into the eye-catching palette of color.

Kathleen had left the hotel plenty early and took her time enjoying the beauty of her new hometown and its surroundings. The only mar on the landscape were the mines dug deep into the sides of the hills.

It was almost 3:05 when she arrived at the Harned house and stepped onto the porch. Tom had told her he never locked the house, and she was welcome to go inside and wait for Caleb. Though the air was crisp, it was invigorating. She decided to wait on the porch. She was also a little hesitant about going inside the house when Tom and Caleb weren't there, though she knew when the cold weather came, she would have to do so. Of course, maybe they would be married by then.

There were two rocking chairs on the porch. Kathleen sat down in the one closest to the porch steps and let her eyes roam up and down the street. It was a nice neighborhood, and very quiet.

Movement caught her eye. Across the street and down the block a funeral coach pulled up in front of a house, and a man dressed in black slid from the driver's seat. He hurried around the coach as people started coming out of the house. There were three women and two men. The women were weeping and dabbing at their eyes beneath black veils.

When the coach pulled away, Kathleen wondered who had died. The thought of death took her mind to Dwight Moody's sermons. She recalled vividly how the evangelist had wept as he'd pleaded with lost people to come to Christ and be saved. She tried to shake the

Scriptures from her mind that Moody had used, but they seemed to be indelibly written on her memory. And then there were those haunting words from that unforgettable song, "What Thou my Lord hath suffered was all for sinner's gain...."

Kathleen pressed fingertips to her temples and shook her head as if to dislodge the words, but they remained fixed in place. She had done her best to live a decent life. Why wasn't that enough? Why did Moody and people like the Killanins have such a fixation for this business about Calvary and the crucifixion of Christ?

Caleb Harned was eager to get home today. As he walked with his school chums, they laughed and skipped along the street, taking their time. Usually Caleb was satisfied to be part of it, but today was the first day his new mother would meet him at the house.

One by one, the boys and girls peeled off when they reached their houses or had to turn a corner and head down another street. Two blocks from home, Caleb said to his remaining pals that he would see them tomorrow, then broke into a run.

When he reached the corner of his block, he looked up the street and saw someone sitting in the rocking chair. For a brief instant, Caleb envisioned his real mother there. She had always sat in that same chair while waiting for him to come home from school.

His heart skipped a beat, and he blinked against the glare of the afternoon sun, then got a clear view of Kathleen and started running again.

When Caleb stopped at the corner and peered at her, Kathleen instinctively knew what must be going on in his mind, and she left the chair.

As he bounded up the steps, she opened her arms and said in a quiet voice, "Hello, Caleb." She held him close for a long moment, then looked down into his bright eyes and said, "How was school today?"

"Uh...fine, ma'am."

"Do I detect that something didn't go so well at school?"

"I…uh…I have some problems with remembering the alphabet. And…uh…my teacher says I don't write very good."

"You mean your penmanship needs improving?"

"That's exactly what Miss Wilson said. I'm supposed to work on it."

"How about if I help you with both your problems?"

Caleb's eyes brightened. "Would you? Would you really, ma'am?"

"I sure will. Put your lunch pail in the house, and we'll go to the hotel. I'll wait here for you."

As they walked toward the business district, Kathleen matched her steps to the boy's shorter ones.

A cold, brisk wind came down off the surrounding hills, and Caleb said, "It's starting to feel like winter."

Kathleen reached over and rolled up his coat collar around his ears. "Do you like winter, Caleb?"

"Oh, yes, ma'am! I really like the snow! Dad made me a sled last year. I had lots of fun with it, and I can't wait to go sledding again!"

When they reached the hotel, Kathleen said, "I know you're probably hungry. Did your mother let you have an afterschool snack?"

"Uh-huh."

"They've got some cookies in the restaurant, and milk. Would you like some?"

"I'd really like that, ma'am!"

After the snack, when they had gone up to Kathleen's room, she took out pen and paper and asked Caleb to write something for her. As she observed him, his main problem was apparent. He tended to hurry when he wrote. When she got him to slow down, his penmanship improved.

Next they worked on the alphabet. Kathleen made a game of it and told him some fun ways to remember the letters and their order.

When his lessons were finished, Kathleen taught him some new games he had never heard of. They had fun laughing together as he caught on.

Time passed swiftly, and when Kathleen glanced at the clock for the first time since they had entered the room, she started. "Oh! Caleb, it's almost time for us to go down and meet your father for supper. Hurry! Let's get washed up."

A scrubbed-up Tom Harned stood in the hotel lobby, watching the stairs. A smile broke across his angular face when he saw Caleb and Kathleen appear at the top of the carpeted staircase. They were holding hands.

As they slowly descended the stairs, Caleb waved to his dad but returned to chatting with Kathleen, and she smiled at his youthful exuberance.

Thrilled to see them together like this, Tom said under his breath, "Loretta, I've done my best to find a good mother for your boy, and I have no doubt I've been successful."

When Tom met them at the bottom of the stairs, Caleb said, "Dad! She helped me with my writing, and with the alphabet, and I'm gonna do better now!"

"Thank you," Tom said to Kathleen, an expression of deep gratitude in his eyes.

"My pleasure, Tom. Caleb's a bright boy. He just needs some guidance in his schoolwork above what the teacher is giving him. It's hard to give much individual attention when you've got lots of boys and girls to teach. Caleb and I will continue to spend time on his lessons."

"I appreciate it more than I can tell you," Tom said.

"I'm happy to do it," she replied softly.

The trio enjoyed a hearty supper, and the mood was light and carefree. After dessert, Tom and Kathleen lingered over coffee.

"I saw you two holding hands as you came down the stairs," Tom said. "Does this mean I'm out, and this kid is in?"

Kathleen laughed. "It just might!"

Tom rolled his eyes and looked at his son. "So that's it, eh, Caleb? Are you going to marry this lady and take her away from me?"

"Dad, you know I'm too young to get married!"

"Whew!" Tom said, wiping a hand over his brow. "I'm sure glad. Or I'd sure enough lose her to you."

A peaceful bond of happiness settled around them.

As the days came and went, and the bond between Caleb and Kathleen grew stronger and closer, Tom realized it was time for him and Kathleen to spend more time alone together. He was able to get Hank and Donna Mitchell to take Caleb for supper two or three evenings a week.

Since the nights were cold, it became Tom and Kathleen's custom to stay in the hotel lobby after supper and sit by the fire. Tom knew he was falling in love, though he didn't voice it.

On one particular evening, they were the only ones enjoying the fire's warmth. They had been talking about their childhoods, laughing and having a good time. When the laughter faded, Tom's face took on a serious mien. He took hold of Kathleen's hand and looked into her eyes, and she let her hand relax in his.

"Kathleen—"

"Yes?"

"I've got to come out with it. I'm falling in love with you."

Her heart pounded. "Something's happening within me, too."

"It's what we were hoping for, isn't it?"

"Yes, Tom, and thank you for allowing me time with this, and not pushing me into marriage."

"I only want what's right for both of us, and for Caleb," he said with feeling. "I'm willing to wait till you're ready to say, 'Tom, I'm in love with you.'"

"You're a wonderful man, Tom. There's everything about you to love."

Tom raised her hand to his lips and kissed it tenderly. "Goes double for you."

—⁓—   —⁓—   —⁓—

Kathleen lay in her bed that night, looking up at the ceiling and the soft illumination from the street lamps below.

"Peter," she whispered, "I know you want Meggie and me to be together, and I know you want us to be happy. We were so violently torn apart, and there's nothing you or I can do to change it. I don't like keeping Meggie's existence a secret from Tom, but once I get her back, I'm sure he'll love her and be a good father to her.

"I'm doing the best I can for Meggie, Peter. I know you would like Tom if you met him. He'll never take your place in my heart, but it seems a new place is being created for him. If I could hear you speak, I have no doubt you would say, 'Kathleen, I want you to be happy. Find that happiness with Tom if you can.'"

A similar monologue was going on at the Harned household. As Tom lay sleepless, he began to voice his thoughts aloud to the only person he needed to tell them to.

"Loretta, you know I've missed you something terrible. It's like a great jagged hole was torn in my heart the day you went away. Please understand that I'll never forget you. How could I? I see you every time I look at our son. Kathleen is a wonderful woman, Loretta, and she's so good for Caleb, as well as for me.

"I'm so lonely, and it's so difficult to be both mother and father to Caleb. I can't cook nutritious meals for us. I've kept the house neat and in order, but it needs more than that to be a home. Our clothes are clean, but my ironing skills leave a lot to be desired. At the end of a hard day at the mine, I'm just too tired to give much attention to cooking, cleaning, or even to Caleb.

"I'll always love you, my sweet Loretta, but I know you understand not only my need, but Caleb's as well."

When Tom had finished his quiet talk with Loretta, a peace stole over him as though she had given him her blessing to marry Kathleen and to have a happy and full life without her.

Over the next several days, Tom carefully observed Caleb with Kathleen. The boy seemed perfectly at ease in her presence. She had been a tremendous help to him with his schoolwork, for which Tom was grateful.

Sometimes when Tom and Caleb spent time with Kathleen in her hotel room, he would watch the two play games, or listen as she read stories to Caleb from books she had bought. Most of the time Kathleen and Caleb just chatted about the events at school that day.

Tom could see a genuine love shining in Kathleen's eyes for his son, and Caleb, needing a mother's touch and care, responded warmly to her.

One day in late October, Kathleen could stand it no longer. She took the chance that a return letter sent to the hotel would only be seen by the desk clerk, and wrote to Hennie. In the letter, she simply asked that Hennie go by the Stallworth mansion and try to see Meggie when she came outside with her nanny. Kathleen needed to know if Meggie was all right.

On a cold night a few days later, after spending the evening alone together, Tom and Kathleen were sitting in the hotel lobby by the fireplace. Tom held her hand as they talked about Caleb for a while. When a small silence settled between them, Tom said in a low tone, "Kathleen, with every passing day I fall more in love with you."

She smiled. "It's the same with me."

"You mean that?"

"Yes. I'm in love with you, Tom, and I want to become your wife."

"Whoopee!"

The night clerk and two hotel guests at the front desk stared at the couple sitting by the fireplace.

Tom glanced around as if searching for someone to share the good news. When he saw their startled faces, he said, "Hey, folks! I just got engaged! I'm going to marry the most wonderful and beautiful woman in the world!"

The guests smiled and nodded, and the clerk said, "Congratulations, Mr. Harned! And you, too, Miss O'Malley!"

Before Tom left the lobby, he and Kathleen had set the date for their wedding. They would marry on December 6.

When Kathleen asked Tom if he wanted Pastor Humbert to perform the ceremony, Tom said it might be best if they simply went to the town's justice of the peace. If they had Humbert do the ceremony, he might put pressure on them to attend church services. Tom didn't want any "preacher pressure."

Tom and Kathleen had not discussed religion at all. She was relieved to know that he felt the same way she did.

Later that evening, Tom was helping Caleb get ready for bed. The boy talked nonstop about what he and Kathleen had done that day after school.

"Son," Tom said, interrupting Caleb's chatter, "can we have a man-to-man talk?"

"Sure, Dad. About what?"

Tom dropped to one knee to be on Caleb's eye level. "You're my son, Caleb, and I love you with all my heart. I need you to be honest with me."

"Sure, Dad." Caleb looked at his father steadily, his eyes big and round with curiosity.

"Son, are you ready to let Kathleen become your new mother?"

Tom felt a tiny tremble go through the boy.

"You mean am I ready for you to marry her and she will come and live here with us?"

"Yes."

Caleb's chin dipped for a moment. Then he drew in a deep breath, raised his head to look into his father's eyes, and said, "My own mommy was the very best, Dad. But…but since she can't ever come back, the pretty lady who loves me so much is next best."

Tom smiled. "Well, tonight Kathleen and I set a date for our wedding. It's not that far away—December 6 to be exact."

"December 6! She'll almost be our Christmas present, won't she?"

Tom chuckled. "Yes, my boy. Almost."

Caleb jumped into bed, and Tom tucked him in, telling him he loved him, then blew out the lantern.

When Tom's hand touched the doorknob, Caleb said, "Dad…"

"Yes, son?"

"I suppose I should ask her now whether she wants me to call her Mom or Ma."

"I'd say that would be a good idea."

There was snow on the ground the next day, and the air was quite cold. Kathleen waited inside Tom's house for Caleb to arrive home from school. She had built a fire in the parlor fireplace and had it toasty warm. When Caleb came inside, Kathleen was waiting for him.

"Well, how'd it go at school today, Mr. Harned?"

"It went real good, ma'am," he said, smiling. "Since you started helping me, I'm doing a whole lot better!"

"That's good. Ah…did your father tell you about what happened last night?" Kathleen slipped the stocking cap from his head and smoothed his blond hair.

"Uh-huh. And I'm real glad."

Kathleen knelt down to look him in the eye. "Really?"

"Really! I'm glad you're gonna be my *real* new mother."

Kathleen hugged him. "I'm glad too, Caleb. We're going to be a very happy family."

"Yes, ma'am," he said, his eyes sparkling. "Uh…ma'am?"

"Yes, honey?"

"I…well, since you're gonna be my real new mother soon, I

would like to call you Mom or Ma—whichever you like best."

"Well, I like Mom the best of the two."

Caleb wrapped his arms around her neck and said, "I love you, Mom."

"I love you, too, Caleb."

18

HENNIE O'BANION'S LETTER ARRIVED at the Silver Plume Hotel on December 5. It was delivered to Kathleen's room by Donna Mitchell. As soon as Donna left, Kathleen tore open the envelope and quickly read the letter.

Hennie explained that she had gone to the Stallworth mansion often, but it had taken her this long to send word because the nanny wasn't taking Meggie outside while the weather remained so cold. However, when it warmed up some, Hennie had caught a glimpse of the child with the nanny, playing in the snow. Meggie was just fine, and she looked good.

Kathleen immediately sat down and wrote Hennie again, thanking her, and explaining that she would be getting married the next day. She hoped to see Hennie when she came to Chicago to get Meggie sometime soon.

That evening, as Kathleen and the Harneds ate supper at the Silver Plume Restaurant, Caleb gobbled his meal, noting that the adults were just picking at their food.

"How come you aren't eating?" he asked.

Tom and Kathleen exchanged glances, then Tom said, "It isn't every day that we get married. Tomorrow is our wedding day, and we're both a little nervous."

"Oh. Well, I'm not nervous, and I'm about to become a real new son to Mom."

"I'm glad you're not nervous, Caleb," said Kathleen. "It's good to see you enjoying your food."

When supper was over, Tom and Caleb walked Kathleen to her room.

"Okay, son," Tom said, "you get to hug her first."

Caleb squeezed Kathleen's neck as they embraced. "I love you, Mom," he said, "and I'm really glad you're gonna be my real new mom tomorrow."

Kathleen kissed his cheek. "I am too, honey."

"Tell you what, son," Tom said, "how about you go down and wait for me by the fireplace?"

Caleb grinned. "How come?"

"Never mind how come," Tom said, giving him a mock scowl. "Just get your little self down there."

Caleb's smile took on an impish look as he said, "I know why you don't want me here, Dad. 'Cause you're gonna kiss her good-night on the mouth, and you don't want me to watch."

Tom chuckled. "Smart little dude, aren't you? Now git!"

Caleb skipped along the hall to the top of the stairs, then looked back. Both adults were watching him.

"Git!" Tom said again.

Caleb laughed and disappeared down the stairs.

Tom folded Kathleen in his arms, kissing her soundly. When he lifted his mouth from hers, he said, "I love you."

"And I love you," she responded in a whisper.

"I'm excited about tomorrow."

"Me, too."

"Since I'm taking the day off, I'll be here to check you out of the hotel at noon, and carry your things down to the buggy. We'll take them to the house and I'll go pick Caleb up at school. We'll need to leave the house at 3:45 to be at Judge Olson's house on time."

"Sounds good to me," Kathleen said.

"I assume the new dress we bought fits you all right."

"Perfectly."

"Good. See you tomorrow."

Tom kissed her tenderly, then moved down the hall. When he reached the top of the stairs, he turned and waved.

She blew him a kiss.

Kathleen stepped inside the room, closed the door and locked it, and pressed her back against it. She took a deep breath and said, "Tom, you told Caleb we didn't eat much because we're a *little* nervous. Well, I'm a *bundle* of nerves!"

As Tom and Caleb headed down the street toward home the boy said, "You did it, didn't you, Dad?"

"What's that?"

"Kissed her good-night on the mouth."

Tom's breath plumed out before him as he chuckled and said, "None of your business, pal!"

Caleb giggled but said no more.

The night was cold, and a bright moon cast its silver shadows on the snow. Father and son walked together in silence, each lost in his own thoughts.

After bathing in fragrant rose-scented water, Kathleen put on a warm robe and slippers and sat before the mirror at the dresser, brushing her hair to a glossy sheen. It was still slightly damp on the ends that cascaded down her back to meet her waist.

Can this really be happening? She walked to the window and gazed out at the sparkling, star-studded sky.

Aloud she said, "Peter, I feel guilty about keeping Meggie a secret from Tom. Am I doing the right thing?"

Her attention was drawn to a carriage that pulled up in front of the hotel. She watched the man and woman alight then disappear.

"I know I've fallen in love with Tom. And…and I'll be a good wife to him. And a good mother to Caleb."

Tears started down her cheeks. "Meggie, sweetheart," she said in a whisper, "Mommy will be coming for you as soon as I can. Don't forget me."

—⁓—   —⁓—   —⁓—

At midafternoon the next day, the snow still lay white and pristine under a brilliant azure sky. The sun had been shining all day, but the temperature had not risen above twenty degrees.

The wedding took place in the parlor of justice of the peace John Olson, whose wife and twenty-two-year-old son stood as witnesses.

Tom looked handsome in his one and only suit. Caleb wore a white shirt with string tie and dark corduroy pants. Both father and son looked spit and polished.

Kathleen was beautiful in her new dark green wool dress trimmed with a soft collar of creamy lace that was almost the color of her glowing, translucent skin.

Tom and Kathleen made a striking couple as they stood before Judge Olson.

A cozy fire popped and crackled in the fireplace, throwing a rosy glow on the faces of both bride and groom. Caleb stood in front of them, facing Olson. He was trying to stand still but kept shifting from one foot to the other while looking up over his shoulder at his father and Kathleen.

A serene smile graced Kathleen's lips as she looked down at the boy and gently put a hand on his shoulder.

Kathleen thought that the only thing to mar her day was the small twinge of guilt she carried for keeping Meggie the secret of her heart. But she refused to let it dampen the happiness of the moment. She was about to become Mrs. Thomas Harned, and it was a wonderful feeling.

After the wedding, Tom, Kathleen, and Caleb rode in the family buggy toward the Silver Plume Hotel, where they would celebrate the occasion at the restaurant.

While the buggy rolled along the snow-covered streets, Caleb sat between the bride and groom, covered with the same blanket they had over their laps. He took hold of Kathleen's hand, looked up at her with big blue eyes, and said, "Now you're my *real* new mom!"

Kathleen squeezed his small hand and smiled. "Yes, and now you're my *real* new son!"

"I'm glad you two are happy with the arrangement," Tom said, chuckling, "because I sure am!"

At the restaurant, they ordered roast turkey with all the trimmings. Tom and Kathleen ate little while Caleb chattered away and devoured his food.

The newlyweds gazed into each other's eyes, barely hearing anything around them.

At the house, Tom helped Caleb take a bath before going to bed. Though Loretta had helped bathe him, Caleb was a bit embarrassed for Kathleen to do it.

While he was getting his bath in the kitchen, Kathleen moved through the house, going from room to room. She thought of how Tom had carefully made room for her belongings. He'd told her that the night before he had put all of Loretta's personal articles in a trunk to save them for Caleb if he should want them someday.

As she went throughout the house, she took mental notes of changes she would like to make right away.

When she returned to the parlor, Kathleen found father and son sitting by the fireplace, enjoying its cheery warmth. Caleb was in his flannel nightshirt and looking sleepy.

Kathleen stood over them. "I think we have a very tired little boy here, Dad. Caleb, could I have the privilege of tucking you in bed?"

"I'd like that, ma'am—I mean, Mom."

Tom's heart warmed as he watched Caleb and Kathleen leave the parlor, holding hands.

Ten minutes later, Kathleen came back. She had been crying.

"What's wrong?" he asked.

"Nothing's wrong. It's so right! Caleb gave me an extra big hug, kissed my cheek twice, and told me he loves me. He's such a precious child, Tom."

"Yes, he is."

"Would you like me to make some coffee so we can sit by the fire for a while?"

A broad smile captured Tom's handsome features and he nodded yes.

When Kathleen came back into the parlor, she carried a tray with two cups, a steaming coffeepot, and a white envelope. She placed the tray on a small table near the fireplace, handed Tom the envelope, and said, "Here's the five hundred dollars I promised to help stake your claim on a gold mine."

"Oh, Kathleen. I wish I didn't have to take your money."

"I'm happy to do it. I have all the confidence in the world that you'll strike a rich vein and we'll both enjoy the benefits."

Kathleen poured the coffee, handed Tom his cup, and sat down with her own cup in the identical chair next to his.

"Won't be long now," Tom said, "before I begin my search for a gold claim. I have several choices of where to start. All are either government or privately owned. Some of the areas are only a few miles from here, and others are as far as thirty miles away. I'll camp out while searching, and I won't come home till I've made my strike."

"Would you explain to me how staking a claim works?"

"Sure, if I can have a kiss first."

After they had kissed, Tom told her that some prospectors searched on remote land nobody cared about. Others did their searching like he was going to do—on government-owned land, or land that was privately owned. The land in the remote areas was usually not as productive.

When a prospector felt he'd found a rich vein, he paid either the government or the private individual whatever price they had set. The price depended on the size of the plot the prospector wanted. If it turned out to be a rich vein, the prospector was then a miner.

The miners also had to pay the owner of the land royalties—on a percentage basis—on all the gold they extracted from their claim. They also had to pay rent for the space their tent or shanty stood on while working the claim. The other main expense was for tools and the equipment it took to get the gold out of the ground, such as sluices, wheelbarrows, and the like.

When a rich vein was found, gold seekers flocked to it. Since staking a claim was rather expensive, most prospectors could only afford a small plot in which to dig. Hence, a rich discovery would bring a crowd, and a mining camp would spring up almost overnight.

Each mining camp would elect officers from among themselves and appoint a committee to draw up rules about encroachment on a man's claim. Anyone caught stealing another man's gold would be hanged on the spot.

Tom left his chair to throw more logs on the fire. Before he sat down again he said, "Come here, my sweet bride, and sit on my lap."

Kathleen slid her arms around his neck and kissed him sweetly.

Weary from their emotional day, the bride and groom cuddled together in front of the fire and made plans for their future.

The following Monday, Tom Harned loaded the used wagon he had bought and hitched up the pair of mules that came with it. The wagon contained mining supplies, a tent, and groceries. He drove it from the small barn and corral behind the house and drew up at the front porch to say good-bye to Kathleen and Caleb, who waited for him just inside the door.

"I'll be back when I've staked the claim, sweetheart," Tom said as he took Kathleen in his arms.

"We'll be waiting." She rose up on her tiptoes to kiss him.

Caleb and Kathleen watched Tom until the wagon and team were out of sight. Then Kathleen looked down at her new son and said, "I'd better get your lunch packed. Soon it'll be time for you to go to school."

Less than an hour later, Kathleen draped a shawl over her shoulders and stepped out onto the porch to watch a bundled-up Caleb bound off the porch to catch up with his school chums who were coming along the street.

"See you this afternoon, Mom," he called.

"I'll be here, honey."

Such a precious boy, Kathleen thought as she watched him moving down the street with his friends. Her heart yearned for Meggie, but she was thankful she had Caleb.

The small group of children was almost out of sight when Kathleen saw Caleb stop and say something to his friends, then wheel about and run toward the house as fast as he could.

He looked terrified as he ran into the yard and made a beeline for the porch and into her outstretched arms. "Honey, what's the matter?"

"Mom, you said you would be here when I come home..."

"That's right."

"Do you promise?"

"Of course I promise, Caleb. Why do you ask?"

The boy swallowed hard, and in a tiny squeak of a whisper, said, "Please! Please don't go away like Mommy did! Please, Mom! Don't ever go away from me!"

A lump formed in Kathleen's throat, and she held him close. "I won't leave you, Caleb. I promise."

He clung to her for a moment, then looked up into her eyes. "Thank you, Mom."

He bounded off the porch again, then paused to wave before running back to his friends, who had waited for him.

Inside it was toasty warm. Kathleen tossed the shawl on a chair and went to the kitchen. She filled the dishpan with hot water and soap and plunged her cold hands into the sudsy warmth.

Once the kitchen chores were finished, she went through the house, going over the changes she wanted to make. Tom had told her two or three times to make any changes she wanted to.

She ran a critical eye over the parlor and decided that some of the pictures on the walls needed rearranging, as did some of the furniture.

The curtains needed cleaning, and their bedroom could stand some sprucing up.

Mostly what was needed in the house was a good cleaning, even as Tom had said. She set about doing just that.

Kathleen knew that money was scarce, so she determined to make do with what was there. She also wanted to be careful that she didn't upset Caleb with too much rearranging, especially in his bedroom. And some things she would leave as Loretta had placed them.

As the day wore on, she altered a few things in the kitchen and rearranged some light pieces of furniture throughout the house, as well as pictures on the walls. Tom had left no photographs of Loretta in sight but had placed them in the trunk with her other things.

She washed blankets, sheets, quilts, and rag rugs, including the large multicolored one in the parlor. She also washed and ironed curtains and gave the floors a good scrubbing.

By the time Caleb came home from school, the house was sparkling, and the yeasty aroma of baking bread greeted him as he opened the door.

Kathleen heard him come into the kitchen, and she turned from the stove to give him a hug. He took off his wet mittens, coat, and stocking cap, and she sat him down at the kitchen table on the side closest to the heat from the stove.

"How about some oatmeal cookies and milk?" she asked him.

"Oh, boy! Yes, thank you!"

As he ate his snack, Caleb's eyes roamed around the kitchen, taking in the changes she had made.

Kathleen watched him closely to see if she could detect any sign of disapproval.

He spoke around a mouthful of cookie. "The house looks nice and smells good like it used to when Mommy—before Mommy went away."

Kathleen smiled happily. She hoped Tom would approve of the changes when he came home. She so much wanted to please her two men.

As the days passed, with Tom gone in search of a gold strike, Kathleen often thought of her precious Meggie. Every time Kathleen and Caleb played games together, or went to the store together, she couldn't help wishing she were also doing those things with Meggie.

When she was alone, she often cried over the burden and heartache of missing her daughter. It was especially hard because she couldn't share her pain with anyone.

The same doubts taunted her over and over. When Tom found out about Meggie, would he understand why she had kept her existence from him? Would he stand beside her and help her win her daughter back? And what would Caleb think when he found out he had a sister his mom had not told him about? Would he want to share his family with another child?

Even so, Kathleen steeled herself and determined to find the strength to keep Meggie a secret until the appropriate time, and to believe that Tom loved her enough to understand and help her when the truth came out.

Kathleen and Caleb were happy to see Tom come home temporarily on Christmas Eve, bearing presents. Mom and son had also purchased presents, expecting that what they bought for Tom would simply be given to him whenever he came home.

Kathleen was pleased when Tom told her he liked all the rearranging she'd done in the house.

He'd found some attractive sites for staking a claim but wasn't ready to settle on one yet. He thought there might be better ground elsewhere.

They had a wonderful Christmas together, and on the next day, Tom was gone again.

In the aftermath of having Tom home, Kathleen found herself plagued with fears once more. This time she was afraid Tom might spend the money she had given him to stake a claim, and the claim wouldn't produce as expected.

She tried not to dwell on the possibility of failure, and she fought her doubts with all her might. Tom was a resourceful and intelligent man. He was determined to strike it big, and he would just do it, that's all. And he would give her the money to hire the best lawyers in Chicago to beat the Stallworths at their own game.

As a couple more weeks passed, Kathleen made friends with some of her neighbors, most of them miners and their families.

On Thursday, January 17, she and Caleb had finished supper and were about to play a game in the parlor when they heard a knock at the door.

"I'll get it, Mom, if you want me to," said Caleb.

"Let's go to the door together."

When she opened the door, Caleb said, "Oh, boy! It's Pastor and Mrs. Humbert!"

Kathleen smiled at the couple and welcomed them inside.

She took their coats and hats and said, "Come into the parlor. I've got a good fire going."

Laurie set her soft eyes on Caleb and said, "I've sure missed you around our house, Caleb, and so has Mardy."

"I've missed you, too. Is your baby at home with Miss Mardy?"

"Yes. Mardy's going back home next month. Our house is going to seem empty without her."

"I miss those Bible stories you used to read to me, too," Caleb said.

Pastor Humbert twisted one end of his handlebar mustache, and with a twinkle in his eye, said, "I'm glad you liked those Bible stories, Caleb." Then to Kathleen: "We just wanted to stop by and see if there's anything we can do for you while Tom is out of town."

"That's very nice of you, Pastor. I appreciate it, but Caleb and I are doing fine." She turned to Laurie. "Mrs. Humbert, I want you to know that I very much appreciate the way you took care of Caleb after Loretta died. Tom speaks often of your kindness."

"Believe me, it was a pleasure. Caleb is a well-behaved, polite boy. I enjoyed his presence every minute he was in the house."

The preacher adjusted his position on the love seat and said,

"Mrs. Harned, I had hoped you and Tom would come and visit us at church."

Kathleen grinned sheepishly. "Well...maybe when Tom gets back. I'll have to see if he wants to. If he does, we'll come. I promise."

19

THE CHICAGO POLICEMAN STOOD in the lavishly decorated parlor of the Stallworth mansion, watching John and Maria as they sat distraught on one of the love seats. Alice Downing, her face deathly pale, sat across from them.

John put his arm around his wife. "We can't give up hope, Maria," he said, his voice strained. "They've got every available man on the force looking for Meggie right now. It won't be dark for another two hours."

"Daylight isn't going to make any difference if Kathleen has come back and kidnapped her!" Maria said.

John could hear a note of hysteria in her voice. His wife was on the verge of collapse. "Now, dear, how could Kathleen have come into this house and taken Meggie? You know the doors are always locked. And we know we locked them before we left the house this afternoon. It's as Alice said: Meggie let herself out while Alice was upstairs taking her bath."

Sergeant Harrington adjusted his gun belt. "That's what it has to be, Mrs. Stallworth. I checked the latch on the front door, and there's no question in my mind that a four-year-old child could turn the dead bolt, flip the latch, and go outside. The little tyke must have decided to take a walk."

Maria's chin quivered as she looked up at the officer. "But Meggie couldn't even get her fur-collared coat off the rack in her closet. She's too short. You heard Alice; the coat's missing. What else could have happened but that Kathleen somehow sneaked in here and took her away?"

"Well, if she did," John said, "I'll see that she rots in prison!"

The brass knocker at the front door rattled.

The sergeant headed for the door. "I'll get it. It may be they've found her."

Seconds later, two other uniformed men appeared with the sergeant, who was carrying Meggie.

"Oh, thank God!" Maria said.

John helped her to her feet. "Oh, Meggie, where have you been?" Maria continued. "Your grandpa and I have been worried sick, and so has Miss Alice! Where have you been?"

Meggie began to cry. "I was looking for my mommy."

One of the other officers said, "Meggie was downtown at the intersection of Madison and Western, Mr. and Mrs. Stallworth. A clerk at one of the department stores was on his way home and found her crying. She told the man she was looking for her mommy, so he brought her to the station."

"Madison and Western!" Alice said. "Mrs. Stallworth, that's the intersection where Meggie saw Kathleen the day we met you at the store! Meggie and I have passed there dozens of times since, and she always looks at all the people."

John turned to his granddaughter. "Meggie, how did you get downtown from here?"

"I walked, Grandpa."

"But how could you possibly have found your way?"

"I know the streets to walk. Miss Alice and me have walked downtown lots of times."

"That's right, honey," Alice said. "You know the way as well as I do."

Meggie's face pinched as she said to Maria, "I couldn't find Mommy, Grandma. Please take me to where my mommy lives. I want to be with her."

"Meggie, how did you get your coat off the rack in your closet?" John said.

The little girl blinked. "I dragged a chair into my room from across the hall. I got up on the chair, took my coat down, then dragged the chair back across the hall."

"Take her to her room and wash her face, Alice," Maria commanded, suddenly feeling the need to sit down.

The policemen excused themselves.

When the Stallworths were alone, John said, "Maria, I don't know how you could even *think* that Kathleen would come back here and try to kidnap Meggie."

Her head came up and her eyes flashed anger. "I wouldn't put anything past her, John. Something deep inside tells me she's plotting and planning a way to get Meggie away from us."

On Wednesday, January 30, Kathleen was sewing a new dress at the kitchen table when she heard the rattle of a wagon beside the house. She opened the back door and saw Tom pulling rein at the small barn out back. She grabbed up her shawl and dashed out to meet him.

"Hello, beautiful!" he called. "Want to hear some good news?"

Kathleen stepped off the porch as he climbed down from the wagon seat. She watched him reach into a coat pocket and hold up something that glittered in the sun.

"Tom! You made a strike!"

"Sure did, sweetheart! A big one!"

She ran to his open arms, and after they had kissed several times, he said, "Let's go inside where it's warm. I'll unhitch the mules in a little while."

At the kitchen table, Tom took both her hands and said, "Kathleen, I struck gold in a rich vein in the Virginia Mountains about twenty miles north of here. Took me a while, but I found a good one! And only being twenty miles away, I can come home every night!"

"Oh, darling," she said, her eyes brimming with happy tears, "I'm so glad! So you staked your claim?"

"Sure did. Took care of it at the government office in Reno. I'll be going back to start digging hard in a couple of days. I want to take you and Caleb with me so you can see it."

Kathleen wasn't even aware of her words when she cried, "Thank God, Tom! Thank God!"

As the warm days of spring came to Nevada, the Harned Lode proved to be even richer than Tom had anticipated. In late February he started hiring a crew, and by the end of March his crew totaled a dozen men. The mine was doing so well he needed a foreman to oversee it. He offered the job to his good friend Hank Mitchell.

Hank could foresee the demonetization of silver because of rich gold veins being found all over the West, and he knew his job with Henry Comstock would be gone before long. Though Tom could not yet pay him what Comstock was paying him, Hank accepted the offer.

One warm afternoon in early April, Kathleen was setting a potted plant on the front porch of the house when she saw Caleb leave his school chums and run toward the house.

"Hi, Mom!" he said as he ran up the steps.

"Hi yourself, honey." She gathered him close in a big hug and kissed the top of his head. "Caleb, you know what I saw a moment ago when you came into the yard?"

"Huh-uh."

"The sun on your hair made it look like an angel's halo." She kissed the top of his head again. "You're Mom's little angel boy!"

Caleb looked up at her, stunned. "Mom…?"

"Yes, sweetheart?"

"Did Dad tell you that's what Mommy called me?"

Kathleen's face went blank. "No. He never told me anything like that."

"You didn't know anything about it?"

"No. Of course not."

"Well...Mommy told me about my hair looking like a halo in the sunshine, and she kissed my head and called me her little angel boy."

"Oh, honey, I'm sorry. I had no idea. I didn't mean to take your mother's place. Really, I didn't. I'm sorry."

Caleb shook his head, smiling. "Oh, no! Don't be sorry." He hugged her, then looked up into her eyes. "I *want* you to call me your little angel boy, 'cause—"

"'Cause why?" Kathleen said, running her fingers through his golden locks.

"'Cause that means I can call you *Mommy.*"

Kathleen stared at him in astonishment, unable to say a word.

"Can I call you Mommy?"

"Oh, Caleb," she said, taking him into her arms. "You've made me so happy! I still wouldn't ever try to take your real mommy's place, but it means more to me than I can ever tell you that you want to call me your mommy!"

For the rest of the day, Kathleen rejoiced in her heart that she had gained Caleb's full trust and love. The knowledge made her miss Meggie even more.

That evening after Kathleen had tucked Caleb into bed and kissed him good-night, she joined Tom at the kitchen table where he was going over his mine records with pencil in hand.

"Darling," she said, "we've never really talked about how much we've made since you opened the mine."

"We've done quite well, considering all the expenses. You know, the payroll, the continual need to buy new equipment, royalties to the government...that sort of thing."

"So how much have we profited after paying for all those things?"

"Up to now, we've netted about twenty thousand. I've been putting most of it in the bank. The way it's going, we'll do a whole lot better than that in the days to come."

Kathleen nodded. "So how soon would I be able to have my share of the profits?"

Tom laid down his pencil. "Kathleen," he said in a loving tone, "isn't it about time you told your husband what it is you need this money for, and how much it has to be?"

She felt a tingle at the back of her neck and licked her lips nervously. "I can't tell you yet what it's for, but it has to be at least $30,000."

Tom's eyebrows arched. "Thirty thousand? Well, that *is* substantial. But I don't understand. I'm your husband. We shouldn't have secrets from each other. Why can't you tell me what this is all about?"

Kathleen flushed. "I…I just can't."

There was a slight edge to Tom's voice when he said, "Who do you owe, Kathleen? And for what? I'm your husband, and I have a right to know!"

"I don't owe *anybody,* Tom! Why can't you trust me? You agreed at the very beginning that if I gave you my five-hundred-dollar nest egg to help stake the claim, I would get my share if the mine paid off. You just said that since we opened the mine we've netted $20,000. Shouldn't $10,000 of that be mine? And you just said we would do better in the days to come. So it shouldn't be too awfully long till I could have an additional $20,000."

"Kathleen, it's not the *amount* of money I'm concerned about, it's *why* you need it!"

"I can't tell you! Don't you understand? I—"

"Mommy, what's the matter?" came a small voice at the kitchen door. "Dad, why are you arguing with Mommy?"

"And why aren't you asleep, son?"

"I was. But I heard you and Mommy arguing. Please don't argue. I want you to love each other."

Kathleen went to the boy and wrapped her arms around him. "I'm sorry, Caleb. The argument was my fault."

Tom came over and laid his hand on Caleb's shoulder. "No, son, it wasn't her fault. It was mine. I let my temper get the best of me."

"But what are you arguing about, Dad? Don't you love each other anymore?"

"Just some things about money, and we shouldn't have argued about them. And yes, we still love each other. Your mom and I—wait a minute! Did I hear you call her Mommy?"

"Uh-huh. That's what I call her now, 'cause she called me her little angel boy."

Tom looked at Kathleen, who still held the boy close. "You called him your little angel boy?"

"Yes. I had no idea Loretta called him that. I saw the sun make a halo on his head today, and I called him my little angel boy. That was when he said he wanted to call me Mommy."

When Caleb was back in bed, and Tom and Kathleen were back in the kitchen, he took her in his arms and said, "I'm sorry, sweetheart."

"I'm sorry, too," she said, caressing his cheek. "I love you, darling. I…I just have to ask you to trust me about this money thing right now. Someday—and I hope it's soon—when I have the amount I need, I can tell you all about it. Then you'll understand."

Tom nodded. "All right. I'll trust you on it."

Kathleen raised up on tiptoe and kissed him. "Thank you."

As time passed the Harned Lode continued to produce more gold, and the personal finances of the mine's owners increased. Kathleen watched the bank accounts grow, and she knew the day was coming closer when she could return to Chicago.

She thought about Meggie constantly and found it unbearable not to know how she was doing. Finally, one day when Tom was at the mine and Caleb was at school, she decided to write to Hennie again and ask her to look in on Meggie. She had not written to Hennie since she'd married Tom for fear he would see the return letter.

She'd just have to chance it now.

On a Thursday night in early May, Tom, Kathleen, and Caleb were playing one of Kathleen's Irish games at the kitchen table.

"You know, Tom, I just remembered something," Kathleen said. "A couple of weeks ago, when you were out of town, the pastor and his wife came by again and said they wished we'd come visit their church some Sunday."

"I'm not surprised. They've been trying to get me to come ever since I met them."

"I don't much care to go, but maybe we should, just once...you know, so they won't keep asking us."

"Tell you what, Kathleen, let's do it this Sunday and get it over with. Maybe that'll get the preacher off our backs."

On Sunday after the morning service, the Harneds walked home in silence, both Kathleen and Tom lost in their own thoughts.

Pastor Humbert had preached salvation plain and clear, giving the gospel of Jesus Christ with power. He warned sinners of the danger of dying in their sins and spending eternity in hell. A few people had responded to the altar call.

Caleb had listened intently to the fiery preaching and walked along in the same silence that hovered around his parents.

The next day at noon, Kathleen answered a knock at her door and looked into Donna Mitchell's smiling face.

"Hello," Kathleen said, opening the door wide. "Come in, Donna."

"I'm on my lunchtime," Donna said, "so I can only stay a minute. I just wanted to tell you how good it was to see you and your family in church yesterday."

"Thank you."

"Will you be coming back again?"

"Oh, I expect we'll be back sometime."

"We'd sure love to see you come on a regular basis."

243

Kathleen hunched her shoulders. "Maybe, someday."

"Hank sure loves working for Tom. They get along so well."

"And Tom thinks the world of Hank. He's a hard worker, and Tom appreciates it."

"I'm a little concerned with them working so deep in the mountain now. I imagine you are, too."

Kathleen frowned. *"How* deep?"

"Hank says they're about two hundred and fifty feet in."

Kathleen smiled weakly. "Tom knows I was worried about that when he was employed by Mr. Comstock. He's probably not said anything about it because of that."

"No doubt. Hank assures me they've taken every precaution to make it cave-in safe. Well, I must get back to the hotel. Just wanted to tell you how glad Hank and I were to see you in church yesterday."

That evening at the supper table, Caleb sat quietly while Kathleen talked to Tom about safety measures at the mine. Tom assured her that his mine tunnels were braced with heavy timbers, just like Henry Comstock's. There was always a possibility that something could go wrong, but it was unlikely.

When that discussion ended, Tom eyed his preoccupied son and said, "Caleb, you're not talking, which is very unusual for you. Is something bothering you?"

The boy looked up timidly and said, "What's hell?"

Tom and Kathleen looked at each other, nonplussed.

"Where did you hear that word?" Tom said.

"At church, yesterday morning. Pastor Humbert said if people didn't get saved they'd go to hell, and there's fire there."

"Has this been bothering you, Caleb?" Kathleen asked.

"Yes, Mommy." The boy paused. "What does it mean to be saved?"

Kathleen looked to Tom, who said, "Caleb, hell is where real bad people go when they die. You don't have to worry about that."

The child cocked his head to one side. "But Pastor Humbert read from the Bible that everybody is a sinner, and that Jesus died on the cross so sinners could be saved from hell if they would ask Him to come into their heart and save them."

Tom's felt a prick of irritation. "Did Mrs. Humbert read you those kinds of things from the Bible when you stayed with her?"

"No, sir. She talked a lot about Jesus, but she didn't say anything about hell. She read me stories about God making the world, and about King David killing that big giant, and about Noah in the ark, and Jesus dying on the cross, and things like that."

Tom changed the subject abruptly and talked about going on a family picnic the next Sunday.

At bedtime, Caleb brought up the subject again when Kathleen was tucking him in. Kathleen told him everything was all right. He didn't need to worry about hell, but he did need to get to sleep.

The next day, Kathleen went to the post office as usual about one o'clock in the afternoon. There was a letter from Hennie O'Banion. She ripped it open as soon as she was on the boardwalk.

Hennie had been able to peer through the fence and get a good look at Meggie. The child was fine but looked a bit unhappy. Hennie felt sure it was because Meggie missed her mother.

Kathleen wept when she read those words. Drying her tears, she finished reading the letter, which closed off:

> I miss seeing you. I pray often that one day the Lord will let us get together again. More than that, I pray *every day* that you will open your heart to Jesus and be saved. I love you, and I want you in heaven with me when this life is over. I can never give up on that. Please write to me again. In the meantime, I will look in on Meggie every week or so.
>
> Your loving friend,
> Hennie

Kathleen slipped the letter back in the envelope and mumbled,

"Hennie, I love you too, but you might as well give up. I'm just not interested in your beliefs, nor Pastor Humbert's."

When she arrived home, her first inclination was to burn the letter, as she had done with the previous one. But as she held it in her hand, it struck her that the letter was her only physical contact with Meggie. It came from Chicago. Instead of burning it, she placed it in a shoe box in her bedroom closet. Tom never opened her shoe boxes.

20

ONE DAY IN EARLY JULY, Kathleen Harned was watering her flower garden at the side of the house while Caleb and two boys from down the street played cowboys and Indians in the front yard.

She chuckled to herself as she watched the boys at play. Caleb's friends were both dark-headed, but it was Caleb who was the Indian.

Suddenly there was a sound of galloping hooves and the rattle of a wagon. The boys stopped their "gunfight" to watch the wagon as it raced down the street and stopped in front of the Harned house. The two horses that pulled the wagon were snorting, and their coats had a sheen of sweat.

Kathleen recognized Jack Wilmot, one of Tom's miners, as he leaped from the wagon seat. The look on his face made her heart skip a beat.

"Mrs. Harned!" he gasped. "There's been a cave-in at the mine!"

"Oh, no! Is—"

"Tom and four other men are trapped!" said Wilmot as he drew up, panting. "Hank Mitchell told me to come and bring you back with me! The other four wives are being picked up in another wagon."

Kathleen's face drained of color as she asked, "Is Tom—are the men alive?"

"We don't know, ma'am."

Sheer terror lanced her heart as she called to Caleb. When he reached her side she said, "Son, we have to go with Mr. Wilmot. Dad's trapped in the mine."

Caleb sat between his mother and Jack Wilmot while the wagon bounded and fishtailed on the dusty road as it headed due north.

"Jack," Kathleen said above the thunder of hooves and rattle of wagon, "how deep are Tom and the other men trapped?"

"About two hundred feet, ma'am, as best we can tell. Most of the men had come out of the mine to eat lunch. Tom and the other four had stayed in for a few minutes to shore up a large wooden beam that was slipping. Apparently that beam gave way and came down."

Kathleen felt sick all over and began praying silently, *O dear God…don't let Tom be dead! I lost Peter suddenly…please don't let it happen to Tom!*

"The rest of our men, along with about forty from other mines, are working as fast as they can to dig them out, Mrs. Harned."

Caleb began to cry. "Mommy, I want Dad to be all right. He will, won't he?"

Kathleen closed her eyes for the barest instant to get a grip on her own fear. Opening her eyes, she pulled Caleb onto her lap and said in a slightly unsteady voice, "Your father will be all right, Caleb. He's probably already been rescued by now. You heard Mr. Wilmot say there are lots of men working to rescue him and the other men."

The boy's body was trembling, but he seemed to grow calmer as he laid his head on her shoulder.

Kathleen wished she could believe what she'd just told Caleb.

Inside the mine, Tom Harned lay on his back with the fallen beam across his pelvis. The darkness was so thick he could feel it. He moved his arms and found dirt and rocks piled on both sides of him. He'd tried to move the beam, but it wouldn't budge.

After the cave-in, Tom called out to the other men who were in the mine with him but got no response. Dale Roy, Ed Harris, Stedman Stewart, and Darrold Manley all were young men with wives and small children. He hoped they were still alive.

One thing he knew: he was trapped in a small enclosure, and there was no air getting in.

He was sweating profusely, and hot pain wrenched at his muscles.

Inability to move his body was bad enough, but the stygian darkness was almost unbearable. And then there was the silence—the eerie dead silence that hung in the black hole like a pall.

Tom strained to push away panic and suppress his ragged breathing to conserve oxygen.

He wondered if someone had gone after Kathleen and Caleb. Or did they even know yet about the cave-in? And what about the wives and children of the other four men?

Time seemed to drag, yet there was no way to know how much time had passed. *Maybe it's night already. Maybe—*

It was getting harder to breathe.

He listened for any sound of voices or scraping of shovels.

Nothing but silence except for the sound of his own labored breathing.

Tom wished he could tell Kathleen and Caleb just one more time that he loved them.

It was getting harder to fill his lungs with air. He strained against the weight that held him to the tunnel floor, but the huge beam was not about to budge.

His thoughts flashed to Pastor Bruce Humbert's sermon the day they had visited the church, and the times Hank Mitchell had tried to get him to open his heart to Jesus. He had not listened to Hank, either.

And now Thomas Harned was about to die. He would go into eternity to face the God who had sent His Son to die for sinners. Tom had foolishly and stubbornly rejected Jesus Christ, thinking that to become a born-again Christian was to become a wild-eyed fanatic.

Even Caleb's questions at supper one night floated to the forefront of his mind. "What's hell?" *Hell is where I'm going!* Tom thought, his throat going dry. How wild-eyed would he be when he dropped into that awful place?

He clenched his fists in helpless terror and rolled his head back and forth on the floor of the tunnel. "O God! O God!" he gasped. "Don't let me die and go to hell!"

Suddenly he thought of the passage that both Hank and Pastor Humbert had shown him in the Bible:

That if thou shalt confess with thy mouth the Lord Jesus, and shalt believe in thine heart that God hath raised him from the dead, thou shalt be saved. For with the heart man believeth unto righteousness; and with the mouth confession is made unto salvation. *For whosoever shall call upon the name of the Lord shall be saved.*

With his fists still clenched, Tom Harned laid claim to the Scripture promises and called on the Lord Jesus to save him. He asked to be forgiven all his sins. Admitting that he was a sinner, he threw himself on the mercy of the One who had said, "Him that cometh to me I will in no wise cast out."

On the other side of the heap of rock and dirt—some thirty to forty feet thick—the miners labored frantically, calling out to the trapped men as they shoveled their way deeper into the mountain.

At the mouth of the mine, Kathleen was trying for all she was worth to put on a brave front for Caleb and for the other wives and children.

While they huddled with their children, the wives of Ed Harris and Stedman Stewart were audibly praying to God for the lives of the trapped men.

In his hopeless position inside the mine, Tom Harned sucked hard for air and said, "Thank You, Lord Jesus, that Your Word is true. I know I've been forgiven. I know You have saved me. Death is close, but I know You will take me to heaven when I take my last breath. Thank You! Please…please take care of Kathleen and Caleb. Work on Kathleen's heart and bring her to You…and Caleb, too. He understands more than I've given him credit for, Lord. Please keep Your hand on them, and—"

Suddenly Tom heard faint thumping sounds. Then the sounds grew slightly louder.

Picks and shovels! The rescuers were working their way toward him!

"Thank You, Lord!" he gasped.

Tom breathed as shallowly as he could. After several minutes, he could make out the sound of voices, and abruptly a tiny ray of light appeared above him in the direction of the mine's mouth.

Air! He was getting air!

The digging sounds, mixed with the sound of voices, quickly grew louder. After a few more minutes, Tom recognized Hank Mitchell's voice calling, "Hey! Can anybody hear me! Tom? Dale? Sted—"

"Hank!" came a loud reply. "It's Darrold! Dale, Stedman, and Ed are here with me! We're right in front of you, and we're okay! I don't know about Tom. He's farther back!"

"Hold on!" called Hank. "We'll get you out!"

Tom drew a deep breath and shouted, "Hey, can you hear me?"

"It's Tom!" cried Ed Harris. "Yeah, boss, we can hear you! Hank, Tom's alive! We just heard him!"

Tom could hear muffled cheers. "Hey, Hank!" he yelled. "Can you hear me?"

"Just barely!" came the reply.

Tom took another deep breath and shouted, "If Kathleen's out there, tell her I'm all right! I'm pinned beneath a beam, but I'm all right!"

The wives and children of the trapped men were collected at one spot outside the mine. Kathleen was doing her best to keep the others optimistic while fighting her own inward fears.

Suddenly Jack Wilmot ran toward them, waving his arms and shouting, "They're all right, ladies! All five of them! Tom's trapped a little deeper than the others, but we heard every one of them, including Tom! We'll have them out shortly!"

The women broke down and wept with relief, thanking God that their husbands were alive. They had to wait nearly a half hour before the rescuers came out with four of the men.

Jack Wilmot came back to assure Kathleen and Caleb that they would have Tom out in a few more minutes.

The reunion of the Roys, Harrises, Stewarts, and Manleys was a sweet one, and Kathleen and Caleb rejoiced with them. Shortly thereafter, Tom appeared with Hank at his side.

She and Caleb rushed to Tom, and the three of them wept with relief and joy as they clung to each other. Miraculously, the heavy beam that had fallen on Tom had broken neither bone nor skin. He was a bit shaky but assured his family and the rescuers that he was fine.

Hank, who had ridden to the mine that day with another employee, volunteered to drive the Harned wagon back to Virginia City so Tom wouldn't have to drive. All three Harneds crowded onto the wagon seat with Hank, Kathleen between Hank and Tom, and Caleb on Tom's lap.

Kathleen kept telling Tom how much she loved him and thanking God that he was alive.

"Honey," Tom said, giving Kathleen's shoulder a squeeze, "something big happened to me when I was trapped in the darkness and thought I was going to die."

"What do you mean?"

"I got saved."

Caleb looked up at his father and blinked. Kathleen stared at him blankly, and Hank shouted, "Praise God! Hallelujah! Tell us all about it, Tom."

Tom told his story in detail. When he finished, Hank started his shouting all over again.

Kathleen was quiet for a few minutes, then said, "Hank…"

"Yes'm?"

"Will Jesus save a man who waits to turn to Him till he's at the edge of death?"

"He sure will. Have you read the story of the repentant thief who was nailed to a cross beside Jesus at Calvary?"

"Well, I've heard about it."

"That thief was like all of us, Kathleen—a wicked sinner all his life. When he was dying, he turned to Jesus and asked Him to save him. Jesus saved him right then and there, and promised him they would be together in paradise that very day."

Kathleen nodded. She was quiet another moment, then turned to Tom and said, "I love you, darling. I'm so thankful you're alive."

The next Sunday the Harneds went to church, and Tom went forward at the altar call to present himself for baptism. Many tears of joy were shed as he gave his testimony before the people, and Pastor Bruce Humbert baptized him.

After church as the Harneds walked home, Tom put an arm around Kathleen and said, "Kathleen, I love you now more than I ever did. Somehow having Jesus in my heart and life has made that possible."

Kathleen smiled at him and said, "I'm very glad that you love me more. And having come close to losing you, I love you more, too."

"Do both of you love *me* more?" Caleb asked.

Happy laughter filled the air as both parents assured the seven-year-old that they loved him more than ever.

In the days that followed, the mine was repaired and continued to produce well. Tom gave his men a substantial raise in pay, especially Hank Mitchell, whose salary doubled. This let Donna quit her job at the hotel and be a housewife, which had long been her desire.

One evening a week, Pastor Humbert came to the Harned home to teach Tom from the Bible about his new life in Christ. Each time

Kathleen excused herself and went to another part of the house.

When the preacher talked to Tom in private about Kathleen, Tom told him she was carrying some kind of secret that she had refused to share with him—something she needed a great deal of money for. Humbert said he would make it a matter of prayer.

When each Sunday came, the Harneds were in church both morning and evening, though Kathleen would rather have stayed home. As she sat under the preaching, she hardly heard what was said. Her mind was consumed with getting Meggie back and having her revenge on the Stallworths.

Although the love between Tom and Kathleen grew deeper and stronger each day, there was a new friction between them. Tom wanted them to go to church even for the midweek services, and he established a daily Bible reading and prayer time in the home.

Kathleen found things to do at family altar time, so Tom read the Bible to Caleb and prayed with him.

One evening after the pastor had been at the house to teach Tom from Scripture, Caleb approached his dad and said, "Could I talk to you?"

"Sure, son. What about?"

"Could we go talk in my room?"

Kathleen was in the kitchen—where she usually busied herself when the preacher was there—and heard her men move down the hall and enter Caleb's room. A few minutes later, she headed toward the master bedroom.

As she drew near Caleb's open door, she heard Tom and the boy discussing salvation. She stopped at the edge of the door and listened. Tom was asking Caleb questions about sin and was getting honest answers from the child. Caleb admitted that he was a sinner and said he wanted to be saved.

Kathleen listened to Tom lead his son to Jesus.

After Caleb had called on the Lord to save him, Tom prayed, asking the Lord to help Caleb to grow up serving the Lord.

Kathleen hurried to the master bedroom. She was busy at the closet when she heard small feet pounding down the hall.

Caleb plunged into the room, smiling happily, and said, "Mommy! Guess what? I just asked Jesus to come into my heart! I'm saved and I'm going to heaven!"

Tom stood at the door and watched Kathleen feign happiness about Caleb's decision.

September came with cooler weather. At midafternoon one day, Kathleen was on the porch watching for Caleb to come home from school. When he appeared with his friends and left them to turn into the yard, she noticed he was carrying his lunch pail under one arm and held something small in both hands.

She rose from the rocking chair and stepped to the edge of the porch.

Caleb was holding a robin that was breathing rapidly and blinking its little eyes. He held the bird so Kathleen could look. "See, Mommy," he said, "I found him under a tree down at the end of the block. He's injured. I think his leg is broke. Would you look at him and see? I hope he doesn't die."

Kathleen took the robin into her hands and sat down in the rocking chair. She laid the bird on her lap and carefully rolled it from side to side.

"You're right, honey. His leg's broken. I'll splint it up, wrap it good, and we'll take good care of him. I think we can keep him from dying. We'll nurse him back to health."

"Oh, thank you, Mommy! I don't want him to die!"

Kathleen carried the injured robin into the kitchen. She left Caleb to watch over it and went out to the backyard, returning with a twig.

Caleb watched intently as Kathleen used the twig as a splint and wrapped it with white cloth. As she finished the job, Caleb said, "He needs something for a bed, Mommy."

There was a knock at the front door. Kathleen laid the robin on the tabletop and said, "Watch him while I go see who it is."

Donna Mitchell had come by for a visit.

"Well, just come right in, Donna!" Kathleen said. "I'm so glad to see you."

As Donna stepped into the parlor, Caleb's voice came from the kitchen. "Mommy, is that Mrs. Mitchell?"

"Yes, it is."

"Would you bring her back here so she can see my robin?"

"His robin?" Donna said, cocking her head.

"Mm-hmm. He found it on the ground on the way home from school. I just put a splint on its broken leg. So now we have a robin living in our house. At least until his leg is healed."

Donna made over the bird and bragged on Caleb for being so sensitive about God's wonderful little creatures.

Then the women left the kitchen to sit in the parlor and visit.

Caleb stayed in the kitchen, gently petting the robin's little head. "I've got to find something to use for your bed, Mr. Robin," he said. Suddenly he remembered there were some shoe boxes in his mother's closet. Certainly Mommy could spare one.

Kathleen and Donna were wrapped up in their conversation when Caleb appeared at the parlor door and said, "Mommy, could I have one of your shoe boxes to make a bed for Mr. Robin?"

"Sure, honey. Take good care of your bird." With that, she went back to her story.

Caleb hurried to the master bedroom.

He opened the closet and picked out a shoe box. He took out the high-button shoes and placed them on the closet floor next to the wall. Carrying the lid in one hand and the box in the other, he moved toward the bedroom door. His attention was drawn to an envelope in the bottom of the shoe box. It was addressed to Kathleen Harned from a Hennie O'Banion in Chicago.

Caleb laid the letter on the dresser and returned to his bird in the kitchen.

Tom arrived home from the mine with his usual coating of dust. These days he and Hank were switching off driving their wagons. Since Hank had driven that day, Tom came through the front door and made a beeline for the kitchen to find his family. The aroma of hot food made him smile.

Kathleen was at the stove. She left the pot she was stirring to kiss him—dust and all—and said, "How'd it go today?"

"Real good. It's like the Lord stuffed all that gold in the mountain just for us, way back when He created the earth."

Kathleen nodded. "Donna came by for a visit today."

"Good! Anything special?"

"No. Just wanted to spend some time with me. She's such a sweet person. She was here till about twenty minutes ago. We had a good time talking. When she realized how late it was she left in a hurry so she'd be home before Hank arrived."

Tom chuckled. He was happy that Kathleen and Donna were becoming good friends.

"Get washed up, sweetheart," she said. "Supper will be ready in just a few minutes."

"Okay." Tom looked around. "Where's Caleb?"

"Out on the back porch. He found an injured robin on the way home from school today. Picked it up and brought it home. It's got a broken leg. I splinted the leg and bound it up. Caleb's giving it plenty of attention."

"I'm proud of both of you. Well, see you in a few minutes. I'll wash up and change into something that doesn't smell like dust."

Tom walked into the bedroom, unbuttoning his shirt. His eyes immediately picked out the white envelope against the dark wood of the dresser. He stopped, glanced at it, then looked closer. He noted the postmark was a relatively recent date and then looked at the name in the corner. *Who is Hennie O'Banion?* Kathleen had not mentioned getting a letter from someone in Chicago.

Knowing that he shouldn't, but unable to resist, Tom slipped the letter from the envelope and began to read.

21

ON THE SAME AFTERNOON CALEB found the injured robin, Meggie Stallworth and her nanny were in the backyard of the mansion in Chicago.

Meggie pumped her legs as Alice Downing pushed her in the rope swing.

"Make me swing higher, Miss Alice! I want to go higher!"

"Meggie, you're too little to go higher. When you get bigger, I'll push you higher."

"I'm big enough. I'm five years old. Please! Push me higher."

"Well, maybe just a little," said the nanny as Meggie's momentum brought her back from a forward swing. She gave a little stronger shove, and as Meggie reached the peak of the arc, something caught her attention just outside the back fence.

A woman was moving away from the fence. As the swing went backward and carried her down, Meggie said in a low tone, "Mommy!"

"What did you say, honey?" asked Alice, giving her another forward shove.

Meggie didn't answer. Her attention was on the fence as she swung forward and reached the peak again. This time she saw the woman hurrying along the street, but her back was still toward her, and she couldn't tell the color of the woman's hair. The woman was about her mother's size, and Meggie had lived every day longing for her mother to come for her. In her mind, the woman was her mother.

"Mommy!" she cried as she went backward and down again.

Alice frowned and grabbed the seat, pulling Meggie to a stop.

"Honey, why are you calling for your mommy?"

"I saw her!"

Meggie slipped out of the swing and ran across the yard toward the back fence. "Mommy! Mommy!"

"Meggie! Come back here!"

By the time Alice reached her, Meggie was peering between the slats, repeatedly crying for her mother.

"Honey, come on now," Alice said, taking hold of her. "That couldn't have been your mommy. She's gone away and lives a long way from here. Your grandparents found out she moved way out west. Come on. It's time to go in now."

"No! Mommy wouldn't go away! She loves me, and that was her! She was looking at me through the fence! I saw her!"

Meggie struggled to free herself from the nanny's grasp, but Alice forced her back toward the house.

Maria Stallworth had heard the commotion and appeared on the back porch, frowning. As nanny and child drew near, she said, "What's she crying about, Alice?"

"She said she saw her mother, ma'am...when I was pushing her in the swing. But of course it wasn't Kathleen."

"It was too!" Meggie cried. "I saw her out there by the fence when the swing took me high! It was my mommy! I know she was looking at me through the fence because she loves me and misses me!"

"Bring Meggie in the house," Maria said. "Take her upstairs to her room, then come see me. I'll be in the library."

Moments later, Alice entered the library to find Maria pacing the floor.

When Maria saw the nanny, she stopped and said, "Did you get a look at this woman?"

"No, ma'am."

Maria's age-lined face was like stone. Her eyes were coals of fire as she hissed, "I've had a feeling down deep inside me that Kathleen was scheming to get Meggie back. I told John about it months ago. And now she's back!" She drew in a deep breath and wrung her shaking hands. "If she tries it, she'll be sorry!"

Tom Harned returned to the kitchen after washing up and changing clothes. "Sure smells good, sweetheart," he told Kathleen.

"I hope it tastes as good as it smells. Would you go tell Mommy's big angel boy to leave the bird on the porch and come in for supper, please? He needs to wash his hands."

Tom looked at her askance. "Don't you mean 'Mommy's *little* angel boy'?"

Kathleen shrugged. "No more. He told me the other day that since he's going on eight years old he's too big to be my *little* angel boy. He still wants to be my angel boy, but now he's my *big* angel boy."

Tom laughed and headed out the door. He found Caleb kneeling beside the shoe box.

"Hi, Dad! Did Mommy tell you about Mr. Robin?"

"She sure did, son." Tom dropped to one knee and looked at the little bird. "Look's like Mommy's got his leg bandaged up good."

"Mm-hmm. Mr. Robin's gonna get well. He's not gonna die."

Tom stroked the robin's head with the tip of his forefinger. "Between you and Mommy, I'm sure he'll get well. Caleb…"

"Yes, sir?"

"Does Mommy know you have her shoe box?"

"Mm-hmm. I asked her when Mrs. Mitchell was here if I could have one of the shoe boxes to make a bed for Mr. Robin. She said I could."

"Did you…ah…find the letter that's on the dresser in this shoe box?"

"Uh-huh. I put the letter on the dresser 'cause I knew Mommy would want it."

"That's a good boy, son. Well, it's time to eat. Mommy said I should tell you to leave Mr. Robin out here on the porch and get your hands washed."

"Okay, Dad." Caleb rose to his feet. Bending low over the box, he said, "You rest, now, Mr. Robin. Mommy and I will feed you after we have supper. Then you can come and sleep in my room." The boy looked up at his father. "It *will* be all right for Mr. Robin to sleep in my room, won't it?"

Tom smiled. "Unless your mother objects. And I don't think she will."

Moments later, when the Harneds sat down to supper, Tom reached across the corner for Kathleen's hand. Caleb took her other hand and bowed his head. Tom prayed, asking the Lord to bless the food to their strength and nourishment, and thanked Him for His bounties.

When the amen was said, Caleb looked at his mother. "Mommy, is it all right if Mr. Robin sleeps in my room tonight?"

"Sure, honey. That's fine."

"I've been talking to Mr. Robin about asking Jesus into his heart." Caleb frowned. "How can Mr. Robin get saved? He can't talk."

"Mr. Robin can't get saved, son," Tom said. "Birds don't sin, so they don't have to be saved."

"Oh. Okay."

As the meal progressed, Tom grew quiet, pensive even.

Caleb talked about his bird, wanting to know what his mother was going to feed it. When that was answered, he asked how long it would be until Mr. Robin would be well and could fly again. He went on about how he would miss the bird when it flew away.

When Caleb finally wound down and stopped talking, Kathleen looked at Tom and said, "Honey, is something troubling you?"

"Hmm?" he said, raising his eyebrows.

"You're unusually quiet. Is something bothering you? Does something at the mine have you concerned?"

Tom forced a smile. "Everything's going well at the mine. In fact, I meant to tell you when I first got home that we hit a new vein today on the north side of the mountain. It appears to be even better than the one we've been working all this time. If it proves out like that, people will be calling you 'that rich lady.'"

"That'll be something! But I want to know why you're so quiet this evening. It isn't like you to let Caleb and me do all the talking."

Tom pressed another smile on his lips. "I have something to discuss with you later on this evening."

"All right. It's a date."

When supper was over, Tom and Caleb helped Kathleen wash the dishes and clean up the kitchen. As she was putting the finishing touches on the stove and cupboard, Tom said, "Caleb, go out and get Mr. Robin and take him to your room. I need to talk to Mommy alone."

"When are you gonna feed him, Mommy?" Caleb asked.

"I'll do that after your father and I have our talk, honey. You go on now."

The boy went outside and quickly returned with the bird in its box.

When Kathleen saw the shoe box in Caleb's hands, her heart seemed to stop, and her throat went dry. She started to ask him what he was doing with it when she had a vague recollection of him asking to use a shoe box that afternoon during Donna's visit.

Why did the shoe box have to be *that* one?

Caleb left the kitchen, and Kathleen stood like a statue, looking at her husband.

Tom moved close to her and said, "Sweetheart, why have you kept Meggie a secret from me?"

Kathleen flinched as if she had been struck. Her hands trembled as she put them to her mouth.

Tom gently took her in his arms and said, "Is Meggie the reason you need the thirty thousand dollars?"

Kathleen's whole body began to shake.

Tom held her close for a few seconds, then eased back and looked into her tear-dimmed eyes.

"Who are these Stallworths, Kathleen? And why do they have your daughter?"

"I need to sit down." Kathleen barely choked out the words.

Tom pulled out a chair at the kitchen table and held on to her as she sat down. Then he grabbed another chair, sat in front of her, and took both of her hands in his.

"Kathleen, I love you with everything that's in me. Please don't be afraid. Just tell me about it."

Tears trickled down her pale cheeks. "Thank you for being so kind to me," she said shakily. "You have every right to be angry."

"Honey, I know I shouldn't have read the letter, since it's your private property. But…but I've been so concerned about your secret preoccupation that I had to see if the letter had anything to do with it."

Kathleen took a shuddering breath. "It's all right, darling. I wish I'd told you earlier."

Tom looked deep into her eyes and said, "Kathleen, I love you more than life itself. I know you had a good reason for keeping the secret, or you wouldn't have done it."

She broke into convulsive sobs, and Tom took her in his arms again, holding her until she brought her emotions under control. When she pulled back, he took her hands in his once more and said, "First, tell me how old Meggie is."

"She's…five. Her name is Megan Kathleen."

"And these Stallworths?"

"They're Peter's parents. I…I never told you his last name, and you never asked."

Tom frowned. "Stallworth…Chicago…wait a minute! Are you talking about *John* Stallworth, the guy who owns the Great Lakes Railroad Company?"

Kathleen nodded.

"You were married to John Stallworth's son?"

"Yes."

"And you came here with a mere five hundred dollars in your purse?"

"When Peter died, his parents manipulated the finances and kept every penny. I didn't get a thing. Three of the five hundred was what Peter and I had in our joint checking account. The other two hundred is money I managed to put aside from my washing and ironing jobs."

"And Meggie? They have her against your will?"

"Please, darling, could I have some water?"

Tom jumped up and poured a cup of water from the water bucket.

"Thank you," she whispered, and drank until the cup was empty. "More?"

"No, thank you."

Tom took the cup from her hand, set it on the table, and said, "I want to hear the whole story."

So Kathleen finally told the story, giving Tom every sordid detail of the Stallworths' heartless deeds against her from the time she and Peter got married. She explained how they used their great wealth and social power to take Meggie away from her through the court, even resorting to bribing the judge.

"I was afraid if I told you about Meggie, you wouldn't want me to be your mail order bride. You know…you wouldn't want to get entangled in such a mess. And after we were married, I didn't want to tell you because I feared that you might fly off the handle and go take on John Stallworth with what little money you had, and lose. Or you would tell me to forget ever trying to get Meggie back. I had to know I had enough money to go and take him on through the best attorneys available. Do you understand?"

Tom nodded. "Yes, I understand."

"I'm so glad. Oh, Tom, I love you so much!"

They held each other in a tight embrace.

"Sweetheart," Tom said in her ear, "as bad as this thing is, I'm actually relieved."

"Really?"

"My imagination had run wild as I tried to guess what your secret might be. All kinds of things went through my mind. I was afraid it might be something that could ultimately take you away from me."

Kathleen drew back and looked into his eyes. "Only death could do that, and I plan on living to be a hundred and ten."

Their lips came together in a tender kiss, then Kathleen said, "I'm relieved, myself, just to have this thing out in the open between us."

"We've got a task in front of us, Kathleen, but we'll face it together. I don't know how you've stood it being away from your little girl and not knowing how things were going for her. This Hennie O'Banion…she seems like a pretty nice person."

"She is, Tom. Hennie has been looking in on Meggie, peeking through the back fence of the Stallworth estate. At least I've known that she's alive and well."

"And Hennie is a Christian?"

There was a second or two of silence, then Kathleen nodded. "Yes."

"I hope I get to meet her someday."

Kathleen met his gaze, and tears misted her eyes again. "Oh, Tom, I hated hiding this from you. I wouldn't blame you if you threw me out and told me never to come back."

Tom brushed the tears from her cheeks and kissed her again. Looking into her dark blue eyes he said, "I understand and I'm relieved that it wasn't a whole lot worse. And you know what? We're going to Chicago right away. We'll hire the best lawyers and get Meggie away from her conniving grandparents. When we come home, Meggie will be with us."

"Oh, Tom, it sounds so wonderful. But it's going to be expensive. I mean, *really* expensive. The Stallworths have the money to buy anything they want—even a judge."

"I don't care what it costs. What those people and that judge did was wrong! Dead wrong! You and Meggie deserve to have your life together, and I'm going to see that you get it."

266

"Tom…I've been going to tell you that I was going to need at least forty thousand dollars for my secret problem. It could very well cost that much or more."

"Okay, so it does."

"But can we afford it?"

Tom smiled. "Sweetheart, I…ah…I've been sort of keeping a little secret myself."

Studying his eyes, Kathleen said, "What do you mean?"

Tom gave her a lopsided grin and cleared his throat. "Well, the mine has been doing better than I've let on. A whole lot better."

Grinning, she said, "Go on."

"Well…I've taken a big step on something that ordinarily a man's business partner and wife would be in on. What it is, Mrs. Harned…well, you see, what I've done is taken a chunk of the profits and bought some land."

Her eyebrows arched. "Bought some land?"

"Mm-hmm. Twenty acres. Choice land. It's on a country lane outside of Virginia City to the southeast, about four miles…with a brook running through it."

Kathleen's heart picked up its pace. "A brook running through it?"

"Yes."

An impish grin curled her lips. "And the brook is how deep and how wide?"

"About ten feet wide. The 'deep' depends on what time of year it is. In the spring and summer it's about three feet deep. In the winter it gets down to about eighteen inches. And there's lots of trees, brush, and grass."

"Lots of trees, brush, and grass, you say. Twenty acres of trees, brush, and grass?"

"Right. And a brook. Ten feet wide. Thirty-six inches deep in the summer, and—"

"Eighteen inches deep in the winter." Kathleen started to giggle. "Is that it? Brook, trees, brush, and grass?"

"There is one more item. Well, actually two."

"And they are?"

"A barn. Well, there isn't one yet, but there will be."

"Oh, I see. And what's the other item?"

"A two-story house. Well, it's not finished yet, but it's there!"

Kathleen blinked in disbelief. "A two-story house…"

"Mm-hmm. And it'll knock your eyes out. I hired the best architect and the best building contractor in Reno. Remember our conversations about what we'd like in a house whenever the time comes that we could build one…and you brought up things about the house that you wanted?"

"Yes, but I—"

"Well, I'm having all those things done in this house. The wraparound front porch. The extra-large kitchen with lots and lots of cupboard space, and an extra-large pantry. And wait'll you see the tapestries…and our huge bedroom…and a sewing room for you that's on the south, so you'll have lots of sunshine when you work in there…and four more bedrooms for our children, in case we have more. There'll be fireplaces in each bedroom, and in the parlor, dining room, sewing room, and library. And remember you said you like *big* windows, and lots of them?"

"Yes."

"Well, wait'll you see all the windows, and how big they are! You're going to love them!"

"Tom, I don't know what to say. I had no idea—"

"Would you like to see it tomorrow?"

Her eyes widened. "Oh, yes!"

"All right. I'll take the day off. We'll go out and see the house in the morning, then we'll drive to Reno and buy the train tickets for our Chicago trip."

Kathleen flung her arms around Tom and said, "Oh, darling, thank you, thank you, thank you! The land and the house…what a wonderful surprise!"

"You're not angry that I've been keeping a secret, too?"

"You wonderful man, how could I be angry?"

Tom kissed her tenderly.

Kathleen's face took on a sheepish look and she stepped backwards. "Tom?"

"What, honey?"

"The house must be costing us a bundle. Will we have the money to hire expensive attorneys?"

Tom gave her his lopsided grin again. "Sweetheart, I assure you we can handle it. I…ah…I've been holding out on you about our profits. I knew you needed at least thirty thousand, and you could have had it at any time in the last several months. But I was waiting for you to ask. I had no idea about Meggie. I didn't know how desperately you needed it."

"It's my fault, Tom. I should have told you."

"That's water under the bridge. But you do have the right to know that we are now millionaires, Mrs. Harned."

Kathleen's face went sheet white. "We've done that well?"

"Mm-hmm. And with the new, richer vein on the back side of the mountain, we'll do better yet."

Kathleen put the tips of her fingers to her forehead. "I had no idea!"

"I know. You're not angry with me for keeping it a secret, are you?"

"After what I kept from *you?* How could I be?"

She wrapped her arms around his neck, kissed him, and said, "What a wonderful husband you are, Tom Harned! Thank you for being so kind and understanding about Meggie."

"Honey, I might have reacted differently in all of this if I hadn't come to the Lord. Jesus has made such a difference in my life."

"I'm glad about that," she said sincerely. "Tom…will we take Caleb with us to Chicago?"

"I don't know. Do you think it would be wise? The battle could get ugly before it's won."

She pondered it a moment. "You're right. I don't think Caleb should have to go through it."

"Tell you what. We can ask Donna to keep him while we're gone, since she isn't working outside the home anymore."

"All right. She loves Caleb. I'm sure she'll do it."

"I'll go on over there right now," he said. "I have to let Hank know that I won't be in tomorrow. I'll ask Donna while I'm there."

Moments later, Kathleen stood at the front door and watched her husband fade into the darkness as he headed down the street on foot. The Mitchells only lived a couple of blocks away.

She closed the door and leaned her back against it, smiling to herself. "Tom, what a marvelous and wonderful man you are!" she whispered. The smile faded, and her eyes sharpened into dark pinpoints as she said, "And *you,* John and Maria Stallworth, when we take Meggie away from you, I hope it tears your hearts out! You deserve to suffer for what you've done to Meggie and me!"

MAIL ORDER BRIDE SERIES
NO. 1
1871
USA
AL & JOANNA LACY

CALEB AWAKENED TO THE SOUND of his parents' happy chatter down the hall. He yawned, stretched his arms wide, then threw back the covers and got out of bed. He went to the window where the shoe box rested on the sill, bathed in sunshine.

"Good morning, Mr. Robin. Mommy will feed you breakfast pretty soon. You feeling better today?"

Caleb turned his head when he heard the door open.

"Good morning, son," Tom said. "Sorry I didn't get to read the Bible and pray with you at bedtime last night. I was over at the Mitchells' house."

"That's what Mommy told me. Dad…how come Mommy doesn't want to pray with me and read the Bible to me? I asked her, and she said she had other things to do."

"Well, your mommy's got a lot on her mind these days, Caleb. I believe the time's coming when she will, but not just yet."

"I hope so."

Tom leaned over to look into Caleb's eyes. "Listen, son. Mommy and I have a surprise for you. You'll have to be a little late for school today in order to see it. Would that be all right?"

"Sure! What is it, Dad?"

"You have to wait till we get there. It's a little ways outside of town. Actually, Mommy hasn't seen it either. I didn't tell her about it until last night, so it's really a surprise for both of you. I told her about it when we had our private talk last night."

"Oh."

"And when I came home, she told me she hadn't mentioned it to you. She wanted *me* to tell you about it."

"Are we going to see it right now?"

"As soon as we eat breakfast and Mommy feeds Mr. Robin."

The Harned family buggy bounced along the road, heading east out of town. A flood of golden sunlight streamed across the rugged land. A fragrant breeze carried the scent of pine from off the surrounding hills. There was a fluttering of leaves in the nearby trees, the happy twitter of birds, and the gurgle of the very brook that eventually bisected the tract of land Tom had purchased for their new home.

Sunlight danced on Caleb's hair as he sat between his parents. Kathleen ruffled it and said, "You're Mommy's big angel boy."

Caleb grinned up at her. "Mommy, do you know what the surprise is?"

"I sure do."

"What?"

"Dad doesn't want you to know till we get there."

Soon they left the main road and turned south onto a narrower road that wound its way through heavy brush and tall trees, never straying too far from the general course of the brook. They passed several places where houses and barns dotted the land, many of them surrounded by cattle and horses in the fields.

A few more minutes brought them to a curve in the road, where Kathleen's line of sight focused on a large two-story house under construction about two hundred yards from the road. Tom turned onto the lane that led down to the house.

"Oh, Tom! Is this it? Look at this! It's beautiful! Trees, brush, grass in abundance, just like you told me! And look over there—the brook! It runs right by the house!"

He grinned. "I assume you like it."

"I *love* it!"

"Wow!" Caleb said. "Is this the surprise?"

"It sure is," Tom said.

"This is our place? That's our new house?"

"Yes!"

"Hey, look! The house has an *upstairs!* Will I get to sleep upstairs, Dad?"

"You sure will. I'll show you where the bedrooms are up there, and which one I think you'll like best."

"Oh, boy!"

The large house was about three-quarters finished. The roof was on, the windows were in, and the walls were ready for paper, paint, or tapestries. Tom led Kathleen and Caleb on a tour of every room while carpenters banged away with hammers and the sound of saws ripping into wood filled the air.

Kathleen was thrilled with the space she would have in her kitchen and amazed at the size of the master bedroom, which offered a view of the distant Sierra Nevada Range. She could see that with so many windows the entire house would be bright and cheery.

Caleb was overjoyed when Tom showed him the room that would be his. It was at the opposite end of the second floor from the master bedroom. This made him feel grown-up. Kathleen mentally chose a bedroom for Meggie and one adjacent to the master bedroom for a nursery, should a baby come along.

Tom took them outside to the site where the barn and corral would stand, and while Caleb ran across the open fields, Tom told Kathleen they would go to Reno and buy all new furniture for the house when they returned from Chicago with Meggie. She could pick out her wallpaper and tapestries, as well as curtains and drapes and carpets.

As Kathleen looked around at the beautiful country surroundings and the choice location of their property, she slid her hand into the crook of Tom's arm and said, "I don't know when I've been so happy. Thank you for all of this, and for being willing to stand by me as I fight for the custody of my daughter."

"*Our* daughter," he said, smiling. "Like Caleb is *our* son."

Tears filled Kathleen's eyes. "Yes. Oh, Tom, it sounds so wonderful!" Standing there, holding on to Tom, she silently marveled at the tremendous change that had come into her life. Once a scrub woman living in a Chicago slum…now, according to Tom, a millionaire.

As the Harneds drove back toward town, Tom said, "We'll take you to school now, son. And Mrs. Mitchell will come there to walk you to their house when school's out this afternoon. Mommy and I have to go to Reno today."

"How come?"

"We have to buy some railroad tickets. You see, we have to go back east to Chicago, where Mommy came from. We'll be going in a day or two, and we'll be gone several days. Mr. and Mrs. Mitchell are going to keep you at their house."

"Why can't I go to Chicago with you and Mommy?"

"You can't miss that much school. It would be too hard for you to catch up when we got back."

"Oh, all right."

Kathleen ran her fingers through Caleb's mop of blond hair. "You're such a good boy, honey."

"You'll only be gone a little while, right?"

"Mm-hmm. Probably not more than a couple of weeks or so."

"Can I take Mr. Robin to the Mitchells' house?"

"You can," said Tom. "I asked them about that. They're expecting Mr. Robin to stay with them, too."

Caleb smiled. "That's good." The boy was quiet for a few minutes, then said, "Dad, how come you and Mommy have to go back to where she used to live?"

Tom looked at Kathleen questioningly, and she made a slight shrug of her shoulders.

"Should we go ahead and tell him?" Tom asked.

"He has to know sooner or later. I think sooner is better."

"I agree," said Tom. "Be best if you tell him."

Caleb's small face was alive with curiosity. "Tell me what?"

The buggy rounded a curve, pressing Kathleen close to the boy. She took hold of his hand and said, "Caleb, you noticed that our new house has five bedrooms."

"Uh-huh. I sure like mine!"

"That's good. When your dad and I come back from Chicago, we're going to have someone with us who will be living in our house and will occupy one of those other bedrooms."

Caleb's eyes widened. "Are you gonna have a baby, Mommy?"

A grin spread across Tom's face. "That'd be good news!" he said under his breath.

Kathleen glanced at him and grinned, then turned back to Caleb. "Would you be happy if you had a little sister?"

"I had a little sister, but she…she died when she was born."

"I know, honey, and I'm sorry. You'd have been happy with a little sister, though, wouldn't you? I mean…it wouldn't have to be a brother, would it?"

"I'd like to have a brother who could play cowboys and Indians with me, but a sister would be all right. I like girls."

"Well, I'm glad to hear you like girls, since I'm a girl."

Caleb laughed. "Mommy, you're not a girl. You're a lady!"

"Oh, that's right. So anyway, Caleb, when your father and I come back from Chicago, we're going to have a little girl with us who is five years old. Her name is Meggie."

Caleb's eyes widened. "Really? She's gonna live with us?"

"Yes. You see, she's my daughter."

The boy looked confused. "Your *daughter? Your* little girl?"

"Yes."

"I didn't know you had a little girl."

"Neither did I, son," Tom said. "Not until Mommy told me last night. She was keeping it a secret because she had to. We'll explain that to you when you get older."

"Okay. Mommy…"

"Yes?"

"Does this mean Meggie is gonna be my sister?"

"That's right."

"And she's five years old?"

"She'll be six next June. But by that time, you'll be eight."

"Yeah. I'm two years older'n her, huh?"

"That's right."

"Then I can take care of her and that kind of stuff, huh. And if some ol' bully like Frankie Johnson slugs her, I'll slug him back!"

Tom and Kathleen exchanged smiles.

"You can take care of her, son," Tom said. "That's what big brothers do for little sisters."

The Harneds arrived in Chicago on a sunny September afternoon. Like Nevada, the leaves were beginning to turn gold and orange, and the grass was fading to a tawny color.

They rented a horse and buggy from a stable near the railroad station.

"Honey, which way is our hotel?" Tom asked.

"Take a left. It's only three blocks that way."

Tom pulled into the street after a break in traffic. "After we check in, I'd like to take a drive past the Stallworth mansion, just to get a look at it. Would that bother you?"

"Of course not."

"Even if you should get a glimpse of Meggie?"

Kathleen thought on it. "No, because I know I'll have her back soon. If she should happen to be in the front of the house, I'll turn away so she won't recognize me."

"How long will it take us to drive from the hotel to that neighborhood?"

"About a half hour. Since we're going that direction, I'd like to stop and see Hennie."

"Just guide me there."

"Thank you, Tom. And after we leave Hennie, we'll be close to the neighborhood where I lived after Peter died. I'd like you to see what you took me out of."

"I'd like that. We'll get our sightseeing done this afternoon. In the morning we'll go downtown and hire the best attorney in Chicago."

When she opened the door in response to the knock, it took Hennie O'Banion a couple of seconds to recognize the lovely, well-dressed, self-assured woman standing before her.

"Kathleen!" she squealed then lunged through the door and grasped Kathleen in a warm embrace. "I'm so surprised to see you back in Chicago!"

Hennie looked over Kathleen's shoulder at the tall, handsome man who stood behind her. There was a gleam in his eye as he observed the reunion of the two friends.

When the young women released each other, Kathleen introduced Hennie to Tom.

Hennie invited the Harneds in, and the sound of children playing somewhere in the rear of the house met their ears as Hennie took them into the parlor and sat them down.

"So what brings you to Chicago?" she asked.

"Meggie," said Kathleen. "We're here to take the Stallworths to court and gain custody."

Hennie's face lost some of its liveliness as she said, "I guess you know you're up against a mighty powerful pair."

"Yes, but we've got the law on our side. We just have to hire the right attorney to get it made right. You don't happen to know who's real good in this town, do you? You know, someone who's won big cases for people."

Hennie shrugged. "Couldn't tell you. I never read a newspaper anymore. I'm too busy being a mother, housewife, and Sunday school teacher."

Kathleen nodded. "That's enough to keep you hopping, all right. Are you still going to the same church?"

"Yes, we are. If you're going to be in town over Sunday, I'd love for you and Tom to come. Our pastor is a great preacher. You never heard him, Kathleen. It was Dwight Moody who preached the time you went to church with us."

"Yes," Kathleen said quietly, looking down at her hands. "Dwight Moody. I remember him well."

Hennie took a quick breath and said, "I saw Meggie just three days ago, Kathleen. She looked fine, but like I told you in my letter, she just doesn't seem happy. I've drifted by the Stallworth mansion several times since I wrote you. I would've told you if I'd seen anything that looked out of line."

"I appreciate that, Hennie. You'll never know how much it means to me that you'd go out of your way to do that."

"Well, I have a nice neighbor who's always glad to watch my children. So this gives me time to peek in on Meggie. Would you let me know how this court thing goes?"

"I sure will. Tom, we'd better be going."

"A little different than our new house in the country, wouldn't you say?" Kathleen said with a laugh. They were looking at the neighborhood and apartment building where Kathleen had lived after Peter died.

"Yeah…just a little. Thank God I was able to get you out of such squalor."

"Yes, it is rather bad, isn't it? Just think, I'd still be living here if it wasn't for you. How can I ever thank you enough, Tom?"

"Thank me enough? I'm the one who's been blessed, Kathleen."

The next morning, Tom and Kathleen drove downtown, left the horse and buggy at a stable, and headed for the First Bank of Chicago, where they would begin seeking referrals to the best law firms.

Before they entered the bank, Tom said, "Honey, do you know what law firm John Stallworth uses? We sure wouldn't want to walk into their offices!"

Kathleen nodded. "He always used the Zachary Hagen law firm. They're big in this city."

By noon, the Harneds had inquired of bankers, merchants, and accounting firms for their recommendations. As it turned out, the names of two law firms were mentioned most often—the J. H. Bledsoe law firm and the Zachary Hagen law firm.

When they reached the impressive office building where the Bledsoe offices were housed, Kathleen began to feel shaky. They stepped inside and eyed the register of offices.

"Fourth floor," said Tom. "Rooms 400 to 406."

Kathleen took hold of his arm and gave a gentle tug. "Before we go up there, I need to sit down for a few minutes."

"Sure," Tom said. He spotted a small bench near the stairs and guided her there. When they were seated, he took her trembling hands in his and said, "It's going to be all right, Kathleen. The Lord wants you to have Meggie. You're her mother, and it's only right. God gave Meggie to you, and she belongs with you."

Kathleen took several deep breaths and squared her shoulders, took another deep breath, and said, "All right, darling. I'm so thankful I have you. I'm ready to talk to the lawyers and to face whatever may come."

A middle-aged woman with her hair pulled back into a bun sat at the desk in the outer office of the J. H. Bledsoe law firm. She looked up as the Harneds came in.

"Hello," she said with a smile. "May I help you folks?"

"Yes, ma'am. I'm Thomas Harned from Virginia City, Nevada. This is my wife, Kathleen. We've come to seek help concerning a situation that took place here in Chicago some time ago. Your firm has been highly recommended to us."

"All right. Please be seated over there in the waiting area, and I'll see which one of our attorneys can see you."

"Ah...ma'am?"

"Yes?"

"If it's at all possible, we would like to see Mr. Bledsoe himself."

"Oh. Well, it is possible, of course, but it may be an hour or more before he could see you."

"We don't mind the wait. Our problem is very serious and involves the life of a five-year-old child. May we wait?"

"Certainly."

It was exactly an hour and twenty minutes later when the secretary ushered Tom and Kathleen into the office of J. H. Bledsoe, a distinguished-looking, silver-haired man in his sixties.

Bledsoe seated them in padded leather chairs facing his desk, then eased into his own chair. "All right, Mr. and Mrs. Harned," he said with a smile, "I understand you have a problem that involves a young child."

"That's right, sir," said Tom. "I'll explain it as best I can, and Kathleen can fill in where I leave gaps."

When Bledsoe had heard the entire story, he nodded, looking thoughtful for a moment, then said, "This case rings a bell, Mrs. Harned. I recall reading about it in the papers, and it struck me then that an injustice had been done."

"You're exactly right, sir," Tom said. "We want to hire you to get Meggie back for us. She belongs with her mother. I don't care what it costs us, I just want justice done. And that means Kathleen and Meggie must be together."

Bledsoe leaned forward and placed his elbows on the desktop, then ran his gaze between husband and wife. "I'm not sure you need me."

"What do you mean?"

"The Stallworths couldn't fight you in court if they wanted to."

Tom and Kathleen exchanged quizzical glances, then Tom said, "We don't understand, Mr. Bledsoe."

A smile curved the attorney's mouth. "It's simple. The Great Lakes Railroad Company went bankrupt last week. It was in all the newspapers. John and Maria Stallworth are dead broke, folks. They've lost their fortune. They're personally bankrupt as a result of the company going under. I understand that they've been given notice that the mansion will be taken from them shortly."

"So what caused the company to go under, Mr. Bledsoe?" Kathleen asked, a note of elation in her voice.

"A trusted officer of the company embezzled millions. He was using the money to pay off gambling debts. By the time he was caught, it was too late. The money's gone, the railroad company has been shut down, and soon it will be sold to the highest bidder."

Tom took Kathleen's hand in his and looked at the lawyer. "So the Stallworths have no way to fight us in court, you say."

"That's right. Unless—"

"Unless what?"

"Unless some rich friend would come to their aid if you took them to court."

"So what do we do to make sure we win if that should happen?"

"Well, I've been told enough by your wife to know there was manipulation of the law to take Meggie from her. If you want to officially hire me as your attorney, I can go to the Cook County courthouse and examine the court records of this case. If I feel I have the goods on the Stallworths and their attorneys, I'll take it from there. But even at this point, I have no question that a thorough investigation will prove that John Stallworth paid enough money in the right direction to bend the law his way. With proof in hand, I can go to the Stallworths on your behalf and tell them they're about to go to court over Meggie's custody versus her mother, who is going to fight them to get her back. I'll see, then, what their reaction is."

Tom looked at Kathleen. As their eyes met, she slowly nodded her head.

"Mr. Bledsoe," Tom said, "you are officially hired."

"All right. I'll get my evidence and put their feet to the fire. We'll see what they do. I have papers for you to sign right here in my desk."

"No matter what those people do, they're going to lose, Mr. Bledsoe!" Kathleen said. "They stole over a year of my daughter's time with me, and I hope they suffer to the utmost for it!"

Tom was embarrassed by Kathleen's outburst and saw the surprise in Bledsoe's eyes.

"I'll need both of you to sign right here," Bledsoe said as he shoved the papers across the desk and handed Tom a pen and ink bottle.

When it was done, Bledsoe said, "You folks come back to this office at this time tomorrow. I'll have news for you."

The sun was slanting westward in a partly cloudy sky as the Harneds drove away from the attorney's office. Kathleen had said little since they left the law offices, but suddenly she closed both hands into fists, pounded her knees, and said, "Yes! Yes! Oh, Tom, it's so wonderful! Those vile people are paupers! They're about to lose their fancy mansion! It feels so good to know they're penniless…on the verge of poverty! They looked down on this 'poor girl from the slums' and took my daughter from me. It'll be good for them to have to live in the *real* slums, just like I had to after Peter died. Now they'll get a dose of their own medicine!"

Tom remained silent.

When they entered their hotel room, Kathleen flopped on the bed and said, "Oh, I'm so happy, Tom! Revenge is so sweet!"

"Kathleen, this kind of hatred and bitterness will not hurt the Stallworths. It will serve only to dry you up on the inside. I'm glad we're going to get Meggie back, apparently without a fight. But seeing you like this, it—"

Kathleen sat up. "It what?"

"It's just not like you. I've never seen this in you before. You've always had such a sweetness to you. I don't like what I see."

Kathleen's lips quivered as she said, "I…I have a right to be angry at those people, don't I?"

"Of course you do. But don't let yourself become heartless and without compassion."

Kathleen stared at the floor, then said, "I…I don't know what to do, Tom. I don't know how to be different."

He knelt in front of her and took hold of her hands. "I can tell you what to do and how to be different. You need to be saved, Kathleen. If you'll open your heart to Jesus, not only will He save your soul, He'll take that bitterness and hatred you feel toward the Stallworths out of you."

Kathleen could think of nothing to say.

"I want you to think a moment about Jesus Christ, Kathleen. Look what this world full of wretched sinners has done to Him. If anybody had the right to be bitter, it was He. But was He? Did He act vindictively over what we caused Him to suffer on the cross in our place? No. He took the untold, unfathomable pain and agony because He loves us so much. He took it for *you*, Kathleen, as well as for me and for the rest of the world. But you've gone on rejecting Him."

Her blue Irish eyes blinked rapidly as she felt the familiar pricking of unshed tears.

"You need to ask Jesus to forgive your sins and to save you, Kathleen." Where Tom had previously felt restraint, he now felt great freedom as he saw that his words were sinking in.

"I want to show you a verse of Scripture Pastor Humbert read to me during one of our sessions." As Tom spoke, he went to the small table on his side of the bed where he had laid his Bible. Returning to sit beside her, Tom thumbed his way to the Psalms. "Here, honey. Psalm 44:21…'Shall not God search this out? for he knoweth the secrets of the heart.'

"Did you hear that? 'He knoweth the secrets of the heart.' Even though you kept Meggie's existence from me and held this bitter hatred toward the Stallworths, all the time God knew those secrets. You will one day face Him for it all. And unless you let Jesus save you, you will one day die in your sins and meet God without Jesus and without forgiveness."

Tears spilled from Kathleen's eyes as the Spirit of God ran

Scripture after Scripture through her mind. She was hearing Moody's sermons and Ira Sankey's singing and Hennie's pleading for her to be saved. Suddenly she pictured God's Son hanging on the cross for her.

> What Thou, my Lord, hath suffered
> Was all for sinners' gain:
> Mine, mine was the transgression,
> But Thine the deadly pain.

The floodgates broke, and she reached for her husband, sobbing, "Oh, Tom! I want to be saved! I want Jesus to save me!"

Tom Harned had the joy of leading his mail order bride to Jesus.

23

A HUMBLED AND BROKEN JOHN AND MARIA Stallworth sat side by side in their parlor as attorney J. H. Bledsoe opened his briefcase and took out some official-looking papers.

Bledsoe set his gaze on the dark-haired little girl with the big blue eyes and said, "Folks, before I tell you why I'm here, it might be best if Meggie doesn't witness this."

"We have no one to watch over her, Mr. Bledsoe," John said. "We had to let her nanny go."

Maria caressed Meggie's head and said, "I think she can play out in the backyard by herself for a while, John. Would you do that, Meggie?"

"Sure, Grandma. I'll take some of my dollies and play on the back porch."

Maria sent Meggie upstairs to fetch a couple of dolls, then left the men in the parlor for a moment while she took Meggie out on the back porch.

When she returned, she said, "Mr. Bledsoe, though John and I haven't had a moment to speak to each other since you arrived, I believe we both know that you are here because Kathleen wants to take Meggie away from us. Isn't that right?"

"Yes, ma'am, it is," the attorney said flatly.

Maria's deeply lined face looked at John and she said, "Didn't I tell you that Kathleen was working on a scheme to take Meggie away from us? Somehow, way out in Nevada, she learned of our misfortune and has decided to take advantage of it."

"That's not the way it is, Mrs. Stallworth," Bledsoe said. "Mrs. Harned and her husband arrived in Chicago day before yesterday, not knowing a thing about your bankruptcy. They came ready to fight you in court for legal custody of Mrs. Harned's daughter."

John and Maria stared at each other. Then Maria said, "Are you kidding? Fight us with what?"

"You must not be aware that the Harneds are very wealthy people. They own gold mines that are producing heavily."

Maria's mouth fell open. "No…we weren't aware of this."

"We've lost Meggie, Maria," John said.

The lawyer looked at the Stallworths dispassionately. "These papers I hold in my hand are court records, folks. Records of what you did to take Meggie from Kathleen shortly after she was widowed. I have proof that your attorneys used underhanded methods to steal Meggie from her mother and put her in your custody. And, with a little more effort, I believe I can prove that you bribed Judge Clarence Waymore."

When neither Stallworth commented, Bledsoe said, "Are you going to tell me it didn't happen?"

Their dead silence was answer enough.

J. H. Bledsoe placed the papers back in his briefcase, rose to his feet, and said, "That's it, folks. Thanks for letting me talk to you."

"What now, Mr. Bledsoe?" John asked with tears in his eyes.

"You'll hear from me soon," the attorney replied. "I'll let myself out."

As Bledsoe opened the front door to leave, he heard Maria break into sobs, and John—weeping, himself—trying to comfort her.

"Come in, come in, Mr. and Mrs. Harned."

As the secretary ushered them through his office door, Mr. Bledsoe showed them a triumphant smile.

When they were comfortably seated, the attorney said, "I've

examined the court records, and I can nail the hides of John and Maria Stallworth to the wall."

Tom and Kathleen nodded solemnly.

"I was at the Stallworth mansion two hours ago," Bledsoe said. "I saw that beautiful little Meggie. She's a doll if I ever saw one."

Tom smiled. "I can't wait to see her," he said, squeezing Kathleen's hand.

"Does she look healthy, Mr. Bledsoe?" Kathleen asked.

"Oh, yes. They've taken good care of her, that's evident." He leaned forward on his elbows. "But let me tell you, those two people are broken. They were both in tears when I left them. I let them see the court records in my hand, and they looked real sick when I said I could prove their attorneys had used underhanded methods to steal Meggie from her mother."

Bledsoe expected this to bring a smile to Kathleen's face. When it didn't, he went on. "And when I told them I believed I could also prove they had bribed Judge Waymore, they didn't say a word. We've got them. They have nothing to fight back with, even if they thought they had a chance.

"While Mrs. Stallworth was taking Meggie out on the back porch so she wouldn't hear any of this, John told me they must move out of their mansion within a month. They have to sell the furniture and all their fancy china and silverware. They've lost everything."

Both Harneds nodded without comment.

"So…" said the silver-haired lawyer, "I already have enough evidence to get a court order for Meggie's release from their custody. I can take law officers with me to enforce it if you think I should. One thing's for sure, you're going to have your pretty little daughter back by tomorrow, Mrs. Harned."

Kathleen leaned forward and said, "Tom and I very much appreciate your excellent work in this, Mr. Bledsoe, but you won't need the court order, nor the law officers. We're going to handle this situation in another way."

Bledsoe's eyes widened. "What do you mean?"

"We'll pay you for what you've done up to this point, sir," Tom said. "But we'll go to the Stallworth home and peacefully get Meggie on our own."

Bledsoe set his bewildered gaze on Kathleen and said, "Yesterday, Mrs. Harned, you displayed bitterness toward those people like I've seldom ever seen. You were ready to see them suffer. And now you seem so docile. May I ask what caused this change of heart?"

Kathleen smiled. "You used the right words, Mr. Bledsoe. Indeed it *was* a change of heart. I've been resisting the call of God for a long time. He's been working on me lovingly and patiently, but I was so full of hate and bitterness I didn't want Him interfering in my life. Well, last night I stopped fighting Him. I repented of my sin and opened my heart to the Lord Jesus Christ. He saved me and forgave me of all my sins. He made me a new creature in Christ and took all the hatred and bitterness out of me.

"I no longer hate the Stallworths, and though they did Meggie and me wrong, I'm ready to forgive them. I have absolute peace in my heart that I will have Meggie back for good very shortly. Thank you for laying the groundwork. It'll be all right now."

J. H. Bledsoe looked stunned. "I have to say, ma'am, that I've never seen anything quite like this. Ah…God bless you."

Tom pulled out his checkbook. "What's the charge for your services, Mr. Bledsoe?"

"Why…ah…let's make it three hundred dollars."

"Fair enough."

Tom borrowed pen and ink and wrote out a check. He laid it on the desk before the attorney and said, "There's the three hundred, sir, plus a little bonus for a job well done."

Bledsoe eyed the check. *"Five* hundred? Mr. Harned, really…you didn't need to—"

"Like I said, a job well done. Thank you, Mr. Bledsoe."

As Tom and Kathleen rode toward the lakeshore area, Kathleen could hardly contain herself. She had waited what seemed like a lifetime for this day. Over and over she'd visualized the first moment when she and Meggie would be reunited.

She'd dreamed of touching her little girl, holding her, drying her little-girl tears, calming her fears, watching her grow, and teaching her about life. She'd longed to be with her daily, and to be there to care for her every need.

Tom looked over at Kathleen and smiled. "It's going to be all right, sweetheart," he said. "The Lord has His mighty hand on this situation."

Kathleen blinked at the tears filming her eyes and took hold of Tom's callused hand. He lifted her hand to his lips and kissed it tenderly.

"Oh, Tom, I'm going to get to touch my sweet Meggie and hold her again. I know I can't make up for the time we've been apart, but I can make sure her future is secure and filled with love. And together, you and I can raise both of our children in church and teach them of God's love. I never gave up, darling. I came close a few times, but I never gave up. And now I'm going to have my Meggie back!"

"Yes, and all the praise goes to our Lord. How wonderful He is!"

Soon they were in the Stallworths' neighborhood. Many memories raced through Kathleen's mind as she let her gaze roam over the streets she used to walk.

"Turn left up here at the next street," Kathleen said. "Go one block, then turn right. We're almost there."

Tom guided the buggy up the circle drive and drew rein at a post at the edge of the porch, then went around to Kathleen's side of the vehicle to help her down.

When Kathleen looked at the stately mansion, for just an instant she relived the pain the Stallworths had put her through. The old bitterness came to life inside her, and she clenched her teeth as tears rushed to her eyes.

Tom sent a silent plea heavenward, asking the Lord to comfort and strengthen his wife, then spoke in a low tone: "Sweetheart, Jesus is here to help you. Lean on Him."

Kathleen bit down hard on her lower lip and nodded. At the same time, a quiet peace stole over her like a warm ocean wave. The hard lines vanished from her face, and a radiant glow appeared as she looked down at Tom with one foot on the buggy step.

He smiled up at her, arms open, and she smiled back, knowing that the Lord was also there with open arms to help her overcome the fresh rise of old bitterness and create in her a clean heart and a right spirit.

As Kathleen leaned into Tom's arms, she caught a glimpse of a small face in the parlor window. Big blue eyes popped, and even though Meggie was inside, her voice came through the window: "Mommy!"

Tom heard it, and as he helped Kathleen touch ground, he whirled around. By that time, Meggie had vanished.

"She's going to the door," Kathleen said, hurrying toward the porch.

Tom took Kathleen's hand and guided her up the steps. The door flew open, and the beautiful little brunette bolted for her mother, yelling, "Mommy!"

As Meggie threw herself at her mother, Kathleen went down on her knees and clasped the child to her breast as though she would never let go.

Happy tears coursed down both of their cheeks as Meggie cried, "Mommy, you came back! I knew you would! I missed you! I love you, Mommy!"

"Oh, and I've missed you too, my sweet Meggie. I've waited so long to hold you. I don't ever want to let you go."

Tom kept glancing at the open door, expecting to see the Stallworths, but as yet they hadn't appeared.

After several minutes of clinging to each other and weeping, mother and daughter finally broke apart. Kathleen kept her hands on

Meggie's shoulders as she gazed into her little girl's eyes. She studied them, then took in the rest of Meggie's face as if to make sure everything was there as it should be and as she remembered it.

It was at that moment that Tom saw two people come into view at the door. Both looked worn and downcast. They glanced at him, then set tired eyes on the scene before them.

"Mommy," said Meggie, "you won't go away again, will you?"

"Not without taking you with me, sweetheart. You're going to Mommy's new home in a nice place far away from here."

Suddenly Meggie spotted her grandparents at the door. "Grandma! Grandpa!" she cried. "Mommy's back, and she's going to take me to her new home with her!"

Kathleen stood up but kept a firm hold on Meggie's hand. It was going to be a long time before she was comfortable enough to let Meggie out of her sight. Slowly, she turned around to face the Stallworths.

She almost gasped when she saw them. They looked so different—wan, careworn, defeated. They watched her with hollow eyes.

John Stallworth took a step ahead of Maria and said, "Kathleen—" then choked up.

Maria's trembling hands touched her mouth.

Kathleen waited as she held John's gaze.

His face was deeply lined and haggard, the color of weathered stone. His shoulders slumped inside a gray suit that looked too big for him. He drew a ragged breath, glanced at Tom, then set tear-dimmed eyes on his daughter-in-law. "Kathleen," he said hoarsely, "Maria and I…we did you wrong. We—"

He broke into sobs, his chest heaving as he attempted to control himself.

Maria moved up beside him and touched his arm. "Kathleen," she said, "what John is trying to say is…we're so sorry for what we did. We were wrong. *Very* wrong. We should have accepted you, no matter what side of town you came from. And we were wrong to take Meggie from you. We should have bought you and Meggie a house to live in, and given you the funds to have your lives together without financial worries."

At this point, Maria's streaming tears were dripping off her chin. She sucked in a breath and held it, trying to control her emotions.

"Kathleen," John said, "Maria and I know that God has punished us for what we did to you and Meggie. We didn't see that until your attorney was here and left, but all that has happened to us of late is God's judgment on us. We've lost everything, and it's our own fault. Whatever punishment you want your attorney to mete out, we deserve."

Maria brushed tears from her cheeks. "What John and I need and want more than anything right now, Kathleen, is your forgiveness."

"Mr. and Mrs. Stallworth," Kathleen said, "this is my husband, Tom Harned. May we come inside and talk to you?"

"Of course," said John. "Please...come in."

When they entered the parlor, Meggie clung to her mother and sat between her and Tom. While the Stallworths sat facing them, Kathleen said to Meggie, "Honey, this wonderful man next to you is Mommy's husband. He's wanted to meet you for a long time."

"Hello, Meggie," Tom said. "Your mommy has told me so much about you, I feel like I already know you. I love your mommy very much, and I already love you very much, too."

Meggie, awed by the tall handsome man, managed a smile. "I am happy to meet you, sir."

Tom patted her hand. "We'll get better acquainted later."

Meggie smiled again and snuggled closer to her mother.

"Mr. and Mrs. Stallworth," Tom said, "Kathleen and I don't want you punished for what you did. All we want is to take Meggie home to Nevada with us. Kathleen is her mother, and they have a right to a life together."

"We know that," Maria said. "John and I wish we could reverse the calendar and give Kathleen and Meggie back lost time. We'll miss our little granddaughter, but her place is with her mother. What we want to know, Kathleen, is...can you find it in your heart to forgive us? If not, we certainly won't blame you."

Kathleen patted Meggie's arm and said, "You stay here, honey." Then she stepped to the shaken couple and said, "Mr. and Mrs. Stallworth, if we had met like this yesterday, I would not be saying what I'm about to say. But last night, a transformation happened in my life. You mentioned God's punishment a moment ago, Mr. Stallworth…as a guilty sinner, I had eternal punishment in store for me. But after years of fighting God and rejecting the Lord Jesus Christ, last night I opened my heart to Him. My husband became a Christian a short time ago, and he led me to the Lord. Jesus' blood washed my sins away. Because of this, God forgave me of all the wrong I had ever done Him.

"I held a great hatred toward you people for what you did to Meggie and me, and my husband knows I was full of bitterness toward you. Yesterday afternoon I was rejoicing that you've lost everything. It made me feel good. Revenge was sweet. But I don't feel that way anymore. Jesus changed me—He made me a new creature with a new heart. I no longer rejoice in what has happened to you, and I no longer want you to suffer for what you did."

Tears welled up in Kathleen's eyes. "Mr. and Mrs. Stallworth, the Lord forgave me for how I wronged Him; therefore I can forgive you for the way you wronged Meggie and me. And I *do* forgive you."

Maria wrapped her arms around Kathleen and held her close as she sobbed the words, "Thank you! Oh, thank you!"

John put his arms around both women and wept.

When their tears had subsided somewhat, Tom said, "There's something else Kathleen and I wish to discuss with you. And please be assured it is something good. Why don't you sit down again?"

Everyone took their places, and Meggie snuggled close to her mother again.

Kathleen put a hand on Tom's arm. "Before you get started, honey, you ought to tell John and Maria…and Meggie…about Caleb."

"Oh, yes! I have a seven-year-old son named Caleb. My first wife died giving birth to a baby girl, who was stillborn. Caleb and Kathleen have become very close, and he's looking forward to meeting his new little sister."

"Me?" Meggie said.

Tom smiled at her. "Yes, you!"

"Caleb is my brother?"

"We'll explain that to you later," Tom said. "You'll like him; Caleb is a very nice boy."

Tom leaned forward and put his elbows on his knees. "John…Maria, did Mr. Bledsoe tell you about our business out in Nevada?"

"He said you're into gold mining."

"Right. God has blessed us marvelously. We own the Harned Lode, which is situated about twenty miles north of Virginia City. We've done exceptionally well with our first mine, and now we've opened a second one with a richer vein than the first.

"Kathleen and I talked it over last night, and we agreed that if your attitude was right today, we would write you a check for whatever amount it takes to salvage this mansion. And if we have the funds to put the Great Lakes Railroad Company back in business, we'll write the company a check to do that."

The Stallworths looked at each other as if they had been in separate dreams and ended up in the same one.

"Are you serious, Tom?"

"We are, John."

"I…I can't let you do this. There's no way I'm going to accept money from you."

"You can't stop us," Tom said. "Let's work on the house first. What's it going to take to keep you from losing it?"

John looked at Maria. "Can you believe what we're hearing?"

"Only if I'm dreaming," she replied.

"Well, you're not dreaming," Tom said, "but you'll have to believe it anyhow."

John covered his face with his hands. "I can't let you do this."

"Would it help you, John, if you and I went to some private place and talked figures?"

"Well, yes, it would."

While the men were in the library, Maria asked Kathleen about her new life in the West. Kathleen was glad to give her every detail, especially about her new house in the country. Meggie listened intently, eager to hear about her new home.

After almost half an hour, the two men returned to the parlor. Kathleen looked up expectantly, and Tom smiled at her as he said, "All taken care of."

"By all, do you mean their personal property and the company?"

"Yes'm."

"Wonderful!" Kathleen said.

"Wonderful!" Meggie echoed.

Maria shed new tears. "What can we do for you people?" she asked.

"Nothing," Kathleen said. "Just go on and have a happy life."

John put his arm around his wife's shoulders. "Maria," he said, "I told Tom that once the company is on its feet financially and making a profit again, we'll pay him and Kathleen back."

"Of course," she said.

"But Tom said he'd like it better if we'd just pay it back in company stock. Tom doesn't want anyone to know that it was him and Kathleen who bailed the company out of trouble. He wants them to be silent partners as far as the public is concerned."

"I'm in full agreement," Kathleen said.

Tom grinned. "Then it's done. The Harneds are now considered potential stockholders in the Great Lakes Railroad Company."

"Oh, this is the happiest day of my life!" Maria exclaimed.

"Now, one other thing," Tom said.

The Stallworths looked at him attentively.

"Kathleen gave you her testimony of being saved, John and Maria. I would like to ask you one favor."

"Name it," John said.

"Would you two allow me a few minutes to show you from the Bible how to have your sins forgiven and know that you're going to heaven?"

"Why, yes," John said.

Maria nodded her agreement.

Tom hurried out to the buggy and brought in his Bible. Maria had an old one in a trunk upstairs, which John brought down.

The Harneds sat at the dining room table with the Stallworths, and with a Bible open in front of both of them, showed them the way of salvation.

Afterwards, Tom asked if they understood the gospel. Both said they did but that they needed to give it more thought.

Tom wrote down the chapters and verses they had discussed, closed his Bible, and said, "Tell you what, folks. Kathleen and I will be praying for you as you read these Scriptures again. But there's something else that will help you."

"What's that?" John asked.

"Kathleen has a dear friend who lives no more than twenty minutes from you. Her name is Hennie O'Banion, and her husband's name is Seth. They're fine Christians, and they go to a good Bible preaching church. If we asked them to come by, or if their pastor comes by to see you, would you go to the services and listen to the preaching?"

"Yes, we will," John said.

"Gladly," Maria said, nodding.

"Good." Tom turned to his wife and new daughter. "Well, Kathleen and Meggie, we need to be going." To the Stallworths he said, "We'll be catching a train tomorrow to head back home. We sure want you to come to Nevada and visit us."

John nodded. "When I can get the company rolling again, we'll do it."

Maria spoke up. "I assume you're staying in a hotel?"

"Yes. Near the railroad station," Kathleen replied.

"How about I fix supper for all of us this evening, and you can stay overnight here with us? We had to let our cook go, but I can still whip up a mean meal."

"Fine with me," Tom said, laughing.

"I'd love it," said Kathleen. "We need to pack Meggie's clothes anyhow."

Hennie O'Banion looked at Kathleen, her eyes brimming with tears, and cried, "Oh, praise the Lord!" The two friends held each other, weeping joyfully for several minutes while Tom and Seth looked on.

When the emotion of the moment had subsided, Tom and Kathleen told the O'Banions about witnessing to the Stallworths, and that even though they had not opened their hearts to the Lord, they were open to the gospel.

"We'll talk to the pastor and handle it in whatever way he suggests," Seth said. "From what you're telling us, with the Stallworths sitting under our pastor's preaching, it won't be long till they'll be saved."

"I believe it!" Kathleen said.

Tom rose to his feet. "Well, we have to keep moving."

Hennie looked longingly at Kathleen and said, "Let's keep in touch."

"Yes, letters. Lots of letters."

"We'll be coming back to Chicago on business periodically," Tom advised them.

"Oh! That'll be good," Hennie said.

As they headed toward the door, Hennie held Kathleen's hand, saying, "All these years of praying and witnessing to you has paid off, Kathleen. Praise the Lord."

Kathleen turned and took hold of her friend's hands. "Hennie, I can never thank you enough for witnessing to me so faithfully, and for praying that I would be saved. If you have other friends you're witnessing to and praying for, never give up, Hennie. Let me be your example. Never give up!"

24

THE SUN WAS GOING DOWN UNDER A PURPLE and orange butter-milk sky as Tom and Kathleen Harned drove away from the hotel and headed for the lakeshore section of Chicago.

Kathleen sat close to Tom with a hand in the crook of his arm. "So tell me, darling, what do you think of my little Meggie?"

Tom smiled, shaking his head. "Some little gal, that one. It's not going to take long for her to wrap me around her pinkie!"

"Captured your heart, didn't she?"

"That's putting it mildly."

"Poor little thing. Her life has been a rough one the last year and a half. First she lost her daddy. Then her mother disappeared, and all of a sudden she was living with her grandparents. Now her mother is back and has a new husband."

"Has to be confusing for her," Tom said. "We really should try to explain to her why you've been away so long and have finally returned. At least in terms a five-year-old could understand—so she'll know you weren't staying away because you wanted to."

"Yes, but we have to be very careful not to put John and Maria in a bad light in Meggie's mind. I want her to love and respect them."

After dinner and chatting around the table for a while, Kathleen explained to John and Maria that she and Tom needed some time alone with Meggie before her bedtime. They took Meggie to the guest room where they would spend the night and sat the child down.

Tom let Kathleen do most of the talking. She explained to Meggie in as simple terms as possible why she had gone away, and that her marriage to Tom had made it possible for her to come back.

Meggie's innocent little-girl heart took it all in, and when Kathleen said, "So you see, honey, you've got a new daddy and big brother in your life," the child looked at Tom and said, "I'm your little girl, then?"

"That's right, Meggie. Do you know what adoption means?"

"Huh-uh."

"Well, that means that when I adopt you, you'll really be my little girl because you'll have my last name like my boy Caleb does."

"Hmm?"

"Let me say it like this. Your daddy's name was Peter, wasn't it?"

"Uh-huh."

"What was his last name?"

"Stallworth."

"Okay. My last name is Harned. And your mommy's last name is Harned because we got married. Do you understand?"

"She's Mrs. Harned?"

"Right. Now, what's your last name?"

"Stallworth."

"And that's because your daddy's name was Stallworth. Understand?"

"Yes, sir."

"All right. Now, what's my last name?"

"Harned."

"Very good. If I adopt you, I'll be your new daddy. So what will your last name be then?"

Meggie pursed her lips, looked at the floor, then said, "Harned!"

"Right!" Tom picked her up and held her close. "Is it all right with you if I adopt you?"

"Yes!" Meggie said, giving him a sunny smile.

"Good! And the best way for me to know that you mean it is you'll give me a big hug and a kiss!"

Kathleen was elated when she watched her daughter hug Tom's neck hard and plant a kiss on his cheek.

When Tom put her down, she looked up at him and said, "Should I call you Daddy yet?"

"You can do that starting right now, sweetheart."

"Okay. Daddy?"

"What, honey?"

"Will my new brother like me?"

"Oh, yes! He'll like you, all right. I'm sure he'll love you, too."

"Will he play with me?"

"He sure will."

"That's good! I never have any children to play with."

When Kathleen took Meggie to her own room and put her in bed, she told her all about the long train ride to her new home.

Before Meggie fell asleep in her mother's arms, her last words were to thank her mommy for coming back.

At Chicago's railroad station the next morning, John and Maria said a tearful good-bye to Meggie, taking turns picking her up and holding her close.

After embracing Kathleen for the final time, John said, "Maria and I couldn't have lived with ourselves if you hadn't forgiven us."

Kathleen kissed his cheek. "Just keep in mind that even more importantly, Jesus wants to forgive you of all your sins."

"I will," he said, wiping moisture from his eyes.

"I love you, dear," said Maria, folding Kathleen in her arms.

"And I love you."

A tone of regret laced Maria's voice as she said, "This is the way it should have been all along."

"That's all past now," Kathleen said. "No more living in the past. No more regrets. Only a bright future ahead."

John and Maria hugged Tom and thanked him for his generosity.

"Kathleen and I will be back for the stockholders' meetings," he said with a smile. "Four times a year, right?"

"Right," said John.

"Then you'll get to see Kathleen and Meggie often, as well as Caleb and me. The whole family will come!"

"We'll look forward to it," John said, a broad smile on his face.

"Me, too!" Maria said, planting a kiss on Tom's cheek.

The Stallworths watched Tom, Kathleen, and Meggie board the train and take a seat next to a window on the platform side. They continued to gaze after the departing passenger car, tears of joy and humility coursing down their cheeks, until the train chugged down the track and disappeared around the bend.

Tom and Kathleen smiled at each other over the top of Meggie's head as the train rolled westward out of the windy city.

Kathleen held on to her little girl's hand and put her head back and closed her eyes. She remembered Tom's words spoken only moments before to John and Maria:

"You'll get to see Kathleen and Meggie often, as well as Caleb and me. The whole family!"

Kathleen smiled to herself and placed her hand over her abdomen, thinking, Time enough to get back to Virginia City before I tell Tom and the children the new secret I'm hiding in my heart!

Frontier Doctor Trilogy

ONE MORE SUNRISE
Frontier Doctor trilogy, book one
Countless perils menaced the early settlers of the Wild West—and not the least of them was the lack of medical care. Dr. Dane Logan, a former street waif puts his lifelong dream to work filling this need. His renown as a surgeon spreads throughout the frontier, even while his love grows for the beautiful Tharyn, an orphan he lost contact with when he left New York City as a child. Will happiness in love ever come to Dane—or will the roving Tag Moran gang bring his hopes to a dark end?

ISBN 1-59052-308-3

BELOVED PHYSICIAN
Frontier Doctor trilogy, book two
Dane and Tharyn Logan, back from their honeymoon, take over a medical practice in Central City and join the church there. It's not long before Dane establishes a name for himself. After he risks his life to rescue the mayor, the townspeople officially dub Dane the "beloved physician of Central City." Nurse Tharyn faces a challenge of her own when her dear friend Melinda is captured by the local band of renegade Utes. Melinda's friends and fiancé don't know any better than to give her up for dead…

ISBN 1-59052-313-X

Orphan Trains Trilogy

The Little Sparrows
#1 The Orphan Trains Trilogy

Follow the orphan train out West as children's hearts are mended and God's hand restores laughter to grieving families...in a marvelous story of His perfect providence.

ISBN 1-59052-063-7

All My Tomorrows
#2 The Orphan Trains Trilogy

Sixty-two abandoned children leave New York on a train headed west, oblivious of what's in store. But their paths are being watched by someone who carefully plans all t h e i r tomorrows.

ISBN 1-59052-130-7

Whispers in the Wind
#3 The Orphan Trains Trilogy

Dane Weston's dream is to become a doctor. Then his family is murdered and he ends up in a colony of street waifs begging for food...

ISBN 1-57673-880-9

Mail Order Bride Series

Desperate men who settled the West resorted to unconventional measures in their quest for companionship, advertising for and marrying women they'd never even met! Read about a unique and adventurous period in the history of romance.